GRAUSTARK

"Good Bye, My American."

—Frontispiece.

GRAUSTARK

George Barr McCutcheon

WILDSIDE PRESS

Published by
Wildside Press, LLC
P.O. Box 301
Holicong, PA 18928-0301 USA
www.wildsidepress.com

Wildside Press Edition: MMIII

GRAUSTARK.

I

MR. GRENFALL LORRY SEEKS ADVENTURE

Mr. Grenfall Lorry boarded the east-bound express at Denver with all the air of a martyr. He had traveled pretty much all over the world, and he was not without resources, but the prospect of a twenty-five hundred mile journey alone filled him with dismay. The country he knew; the scenery had long since lost its attractions for him; countless newsboys had failed to tempt him with the literature they thrust in his face, and as for his fellow-passengers—well, he preferred to be alone. And so it was that he gloomily motioned the porter to his boxes and mounted the steps with weariness.

As it happened, Mr. Grenfall Lorry did not have a dull moment after the train started. He stumbled on a figure that leaned toward the window in the dark passageway. With reluctant civility he apologized; a lady stood up to let him pass, and for an instant in the half light their eyes met, and that is why the miles rushed by with incredible speed.

Mr. Lorry had been dawdling away the months in Mexico and California. For years he had felt, together with many other people, that a sea-voyage was the essential beginning of every journey; he had started round the world soon after leaving Cambridge; he had fished through Norway and hunted in India, and shot everything from grouse on the Scottish moors to the rapids above Assouan. He had run in and out of countless towns and countries on the coast of South America; he had done Russia and the Rhone valley and Brittany and Damascus; he had seen them all—but not until then did it occur to him that there might be something of interest nearer home. True he had thought of joining some Englishmen on a hunting tour in the Rockies, but that had fallen through. When the idea of Mexico did occur to him he gave orders to pack his things, purchased interminable green tickets, dined unusually well at his club, and was off in no time to the unknown West.

There was a theory in his family that it would have been a decenter thing for him to stop running about and settle down to work. But his thoughtful father had given him a wealthy mother, and as earning a living was not a necessity, he failed to see why it was a duty. "Work is becoming to some men," he once declared, "like whiskers or red ties, but it

does not follow that all men can stand it." After
that the family found him "hopeless," and the argument dropped.

He was just under thirty years, as good-looking
as most men, with no one dependent upon him and
an income that had withstood both the Maison
Dorée and a dahabeah on the Nile. He never tired
of seeing things and peoples and places. "There's
game to be found anywhere," he said, "only it's
sometimes out of. season. If I had my way—and
millions—I should run a newspaper. Then all the
excitements would come to me. As it is—I'm poor,
and so I have to go all over the world after them."

This agreeable theory of life had worked well;
he was a little bored at times—not because he had
seen too much, but because there were not more
things left to see. He had managed somehow to keep
his enthusiasms through everything—and they made
life worth living. He felt, too, a certain elation—
like a spirited horse—at turning toward home, but
Washington had not much to offer him, and the
thrill did not last. His big bag and his hat-box—
pasted over with foolish labels from continental
hotels—were piled in the corner of his compartment, and he settled back in his seat with a pleasur-
able sense of expectancy. The presence in the next
room of a very smart appearing young woman was
prominent in his consciousness. It gave him an uneasiness which was the beginning of delight. He

had seen her for only a second in the passage-way, but that second had made him hold himself a little straighter. "Why is it," he wondered, "that some girls make you stand like a footman the moment you see them?" Grenfall had been in love too many times to think of marriage; his habit of mind was still general, and he classified women broadly. At the same time he had a feeling that in this case generalities did not apply well; there was something about the girl that made him hesitate at labelling her "Class A, or B, or Z." What it was he did not know, but—unaccountably—she filled him with an affected formality. He felt like bowing to her with a grand air and much dignity. And yet he realized that his successes had come from confidence.

At luncheon he saw her in the dining-car. Her companions were elderly persons—presumably her parents. They talked mostly in French—occasionally using a German word or phrase. The old gentleman was stately and austere—with an air of deference to the young woman which Grenfall did not understand. His appearance was very striking; his face pale and heavily lined; moustache and imperial gray; the eyebrows large and bushy, and the jaw and chin square and firm. The white-haired lady carried her head high with unmistakable gentility. They were all dressed in traveling suits which suggested something foreign, but not Vienna nor Paris; smart, but far from American tastes.

Lorry watched the trio with great interest. Twice during luncheon the young woman glanced toward him carelessly and left an annoying impression that she had not seen him. As they left the table and passed into the observation car, he stared at her with some defiance. But she was smiling, and her dimples showed, and Grenfall was ashamed. For some moments he sat gazing from the car window—forgetting his luncheon—dreaming.

When he got back to his compartment he rang vigorously for the porter. A coin was carelessly displayed in his fingers. "Do you suppose you could find out who has the next compartment, porter?"

"I don't know their name, suh, but they's goin' to New York jis as fas' as they can git thuh. I ain' ax um no questions, 'cause thuh's somethin' 'bout um makes me feel's if I ain' got no right to look at um even."

The porter thought a moment.

"I don' believe it'll do yuh any good, suh, to try to shine up to tha' young lady. She ain' the sawt, I can tell yuh that. I done see too many guhls in ma time——"

"What are you talking about? I am not trying to shine up to her. I only want to know who she is—just out of curiosity." Grenfall's face was a trifle red.

"Beg pahdon, suh; but I kind o' thought you was like oth' gent'men when they see a han'some woman.

Allus wants to fin' out somethin' 'bout huh, suh, yuh know. 'Scuse me foh misjedgin' yuh, suh. Th' lady in question is a foh'ner—she lives across th' ocean, 's fuh as I can fin' out. They's in a hurry to git home foh some reason, 'cause they ain' goin' to stop this side o' New York, 'cept to change cahs."

"Where do they change cars?"

"St. Louis—goin' by way of Cincinnati an' Washin'ton."

Grenfall's ticket carried him by way of Chicago. He caught himself wondering if he could exchange his ticket in St. Louis.

"Traveling with her father and mother, I suppose?"

"No, suh; they's huh uncle and aunt. I heah huh call 'em uncle an' aunt. Th' ole gent'man is Uncle Caspar. I don' know what they talk 'bout. It's mostly some foh'en language. Th' young lady allus speaks Amehican to me, but th' old folks cain't talk it ver' well. They all been to 'Frisco, an' the hired he'p they's got with 'em say they been to Mexico, too. Th' young lady's got good Amehican dollahs, don' care wha' she's been. She allus smiles when she ask me to do anythin', an' I wouldn' care if she nevah tipped me, 's long as she smiles thataway."

"Servants with them, you say?"

"Yas, suh; man an' woman, nex' section t'other side of ole folks. Can't say mor'n fifteen words in

Amehican. Th' woman is huh maid, an' the man he's the gen'ral hustler for th' hull pahty."

"And you don't know her name?"

"No, suh, an' I cain't ver' well fin' out."

"In what part of Europe does she live?"

"Australia, I think, suh."

"You mean Austria."

"Do I? 'Scuse ma ig'nance. I was jis' guessin' at it anyhow; one place's as good as 'nother ovah thuh, I reckon."

"Have you one of those dollars she gave you?"

"Yes, suh. Heh's a coin that ain' Amehican, but she says it's wuth seventy cents in our money. It's a foh'en piece. She tell me to keep it till I went ovah to huh country; then I could have a high time with it—that's what she says—'a high time'—an' smiled kind o' knowin' like."

"Let me see that coin," said Lorry eagerly taking the silver piece from the porter's hand. "I never saw one like it before. Greek, it looks to me, but I can't make a thing out of these letters. She gave it to you?"

"Yas, suh—las' evenin'. A high time on seventy cents. That's reediculous, ain' it?" demanded the porter scornfully.

"I'll give you a dollar for it. You can have a higher time on that."

The odd little coin changed owners immediately. and the new possessor dropped it into his pocket with the inward conviction that he was the silliest fool in existence. After the porter's departure he took the coin from his pocket, and with his back to the door, his face to the window, studied its lettering.

During the afternoon he strolled about the train, his hand constantly jingling the coins. He passed her compartment several times, yet refrained from looking in. But he wondered if she saw him pass.

At one little station a group of Indian bear hunters created considerable interest among the passengers. Grenfall was down at the station platform at once, looking over a great stack of game. As he left the car he met Uncle Caspar, who was hurrying toward his niece's section. A few moments later she came down the steps, followed by the dignified old gentleman. Grenfall tingled with a strange delight as she moved quite close to his side in her desire to see. Once he glanced at her face; there was a pretty look of fear in her eyes as she surveyed the massive bears and the stark, stiff antelopes. But she laughed as she turned away with her uncle.

Grenfall was smoking his cigarette and vigorously jingling the coins in his pocket when the train pulled out. Then he swung on the car steps and found himself at her feet. She was standing at the top, where she had lingered a moment. There was an expression of anxiety in her eyes as he looked up into them, followed instantly by one of relief. Then she passed into the car. She had seen him swing upon the moving steps and had feared for his safety—had shown in her glorious face that she was glad he did not fall beneath the wheels. Doubtless she would have been as solicitous had he been the porter or the brakeman, he reasoned, but that she had noticed him at all pleased him.

At Abilene he bought the Kansas City newspapers. After breakfast he found a seat in the observation car and settled himself to read. Presently some one took a seat behind him. He did not look back, but unconcernedly cast his eyes upon the broad mirror in the opposite car wall. Instantly he forgot his paper. She was sitting within five feet of him, a book in her lap, her gaze bent briefly on the flitting buildings outside. He studied the reflection furtively until she took up the book and began to read. Up to this time he had wondered why some nonsensical idiot had wasted looking-glasses on the walls of a railway coach; now he was thinking of him as a far-sighted man.

The first page of his paper was fairly alive with fresh and important dispatches, chiefly foreign. At length, after allowing himself to become really interested in a Paris dispatch of some international consequence, he turned his eyes again to the mirror. She was leaning slightly forward, holding the open book in her lap, but reading, with straining eyes, an article in the paper he held.

He calmly turned to the next page and looked leisurely ovei it. Another glance, quickly taken, showed to him a disappointed frown on the pretty face and a reluctant resumption of novel reading. A few moments later he turned back to the first page, holding the paper in such a position that she could not see, and, full of curiosity, read every line of the foreign news, wondering what had interested her.

Under ordinary circumstances Lorry would have offered her the paper, and thought nothing more of it. With her, however, there was an air that made him hesitate. He felt strangely awkward and inexperienced beside her; precedents did not seem to count. He arose, tossed the paper over the back of the chair as if casting it aside forever, and strolled to the opposite window and looked out for a few moments, jingling his coins carelessly. The jingle of the pieces suggested something else to him. His paper still hung invitingly, upside down, as he had left it, on the chair, and the lady was pouring over her novel. As he passed her he drew his right hand from his pocket and a piece of money dropped to the floor at her feet. Then began an embarrassed search for the coin—in the wrong direction, of course. He knew precisely where it had rolled, but purposely looked under the seats on the other side of the car. She drew her skirts aside and assisted

in the search. Four different times he saw the little
piece of money, but did not pick it up. Finally,
laughing awkwardly, he began to search on her side
of the car. Whereupon she rose and gave him more
room. She became interested in the search and bent
over to scan the dark corners with eager eyes. Their
heads were very close together more than once. At
last she uttered an exclamation, and her hand went
to the floor in triumph. They arose together, flushed
and smiling. She had the coin in her hand.

"I have it," she said, gaily, a delicious foreign
tinge to the words.

"I thank you——" he began, holding out his hand
as if in a dream of ecstacy, but her eyes had fallen
momentarily on the object of their search.

"Oh!" she exclaimed, the prettiest surprise in the
world coming into her face. It was a coin from
her faraway homeland, and she was betrayed into
the involuntary exclamation. Instantly, however,
she regained her composure and dropped the piece
into his outstretched hand, a proud flush mounting
to her cheek, a look of cold reserve to her eyes. He
had hoped she would offer some comment on what
she must have considered a strange coincidence, but
he was disappointed. He wondered if she even
heard him say:

"I am sorry to have troubled you."

She had resumed her seat, and, to him, there
seemed a thousand miles between them. Feeling de-

cidedly uncomfortable and not a little abashed, he left her and strode to the door. Again a mirror gave him a thrill. This time it was the glass in the car's end. He had taken but half a dozen steps when the brown head was turned slyly and a pair of interested eyes looked after him. She did not know that he could see her, so he had the satisfaction of observing that pretty, puzzled face plainly until he passed through the door.

Grenfall had formed many chance acquaintances during his travels, sometimes taking risks and liberties that were refreshingly bold. He had seldom been repulsed, strange to say, and as he went to his section dizzily, he thought of the good fortune that had been his in other attempts, and asked himself why it had not occurred to him to make the same advances in the present instance. Somehow she was different. There was that strange dignity, that pure beauty, that imperial manner, all combining to forbid the faintest thought of familiarity.

He was more than astonished at himself for having tricked her a few moments before into a perfectly natural departure from indifference. She had been so reserved and so natural that he looked back and asked himself what had happened to flatter his vanity except a passing show of interest. With this, he smiled and recalled similar opportunities in days gone by, all of which had been turned to advantage and had resulted in amusing pastimes. And here was a pretty girl with an air of mystery about her, worthy of his best efforts, but toward whom he had not dared to turn a frivolous eye.

He took out the coin and leaned back in his chair, wondering where it came from. "In any case," he thought, "it'll make a good pocket-piece and some day I'll find some idiot who knows more about geography than I do." Mr. Lorry's own ideas of geography were jumbled and vague—as if he had got them by studying the labels on his hat-box. He knew the places he had been to, and he recognized a new country by the annoyances of the customs house, but beyond this his ignorance was complete. The coin, so far as he knew, might have come from any one of a hundred small principalities scattered about the continent. Yet it bothered him a little that he could not tell which one. He was more than curious about a very beautiful young woman—in fact, he was undeniably interested in her. He pleasantly called himself an "ass" to have his head turned by a pretty face, a foreign accent and an insignificant coin, and yet he was fascinated.

Before the train reached St. Louis he made up his mind to change cars there and go to Washington with her. It also occurred to him that he might go on to New York if the spell lasted. During the day he telegraphed ahead for accommodations; and when the flyer arrived in St. Louis that evening he hurriedly attended to the transferring and rechecking of his baggage, bought a new ticket, and dined. At eight he was in the station, and at 8:15 he passed her in the aisle. She was standing in her stateroom door, directing her maid. He saw a look of surprise flit across her face as he passed. He slept soundly that night, and dreamed that he was crossing the ocean with her.

At breakfast he saw her, but if she saw him it was when he was not looking at her. Once he caught Uncle Caspar staring at him through his monocle, which dropped instantly from his eye in the manner that is always self-explanatory. She had evidently called the uncle's attention to him, but was herself looking sedately from the window when Lorry unfortunately spoiled the scrutiny. His spirits took a furious bound with the realization that she had deigned to honor him by recognition, if only to call attention to him because he possessed a certain coin.

Once the old gentleman asked him the time of day and set his watch according to the reply. In Ohio the man-servant scowled at him because he involuntarily stared after his mistress as she paced the platform while the train waited at a station. Again, in Ohio, they met in the vestibule, and he was compelled to step aside to allow her to pass. He did not feel particularly jubilant over this meeting; she did not even glance at him.

Lorry realized that his opportunities were fast

disappearing, and that he did not seem to be any
nearer meeting her than when they started. He had
hoped to get Uncle Caspar into a conversation and
then use him, but Uncle Caspar was as distant as an
iceberg. "If there should be a wreck," Grenfall
caught himself thinking, "then my chance would
come; but I don't see how Providence is going to
help me in any other way."

Near the close of the day, after they left St. Louis,
the train began to wind through the foothills of the
Alleghenies. Bellaire, Grafton and other towns were
left behind, and they were soon whirling up the steep
mountain, higher and higher, through tunnel after
tunnel, nearer and nearer to Washington every minute. As they were pulling out of a little mining
town built on the mountain side, a sudden jar
stopped the train. There was some little excitement
and a scramble for information. Some part of the
engine was disabled, and it would be necessary to
replace it before the "run" could proceed.

Lorry strolled up to the crowd of passengers who
were watching the engineer and fireman at work. A'
clear, musical voice, almost in his ear, startled him,
for he knew to whom it belonged. She addressed
the conductor, who, impatient and annoyed, stood
immediately behind him.

"How long are we to be delayed?" she asked.
Just two minutes before this same conductor had
responded most ungraciously to a simple question

Lorry had asked and had gone so far as to instruct another inquisitive traveler to go to a warmer climate because he persisted in asking for information which could not be given except by a clairvoyant. But now he answered in most affable tones:

"We'll be here for thirty minutes at least, Miss—perhaps longer."

She walked away, after thanking him, and Grenfall looked at his watch.

Off the main street of the town ran little lanes leading to the mines below. They all ended at the edge of a steep declivity. There was a drop of almost four hundred feet straight into the valley below. Along the sides of this valley were the entrances to the mines. Above, on the ledge, was the machinery for lifting the ore to the high ground on which stood the town and railroad yards.

Down one of these streets walked a young lady, curiously interested in all about her. She seemed glad to escape from the train and its people, and she hurried along, the fresh spring wind blowing her hair from beneath her cap, the ends of her long coat fluttering.

Lorry stood on the platform watching her; then he lighted a cigarette and followed. He had a vague feeling that she ought not to be alone with all the workmen. She started to come back before he reached her, however, and he turned again toward the station. Then he heard a sudden whistle, and a minute later from the end of the street he saw the train pulling out. Lorry had rather distinguished himself in college as a runner, and instinctively he dashed up the street, reaching the tracks just in time to catch the railing of the last coach. But there he stopped and stood with thumping heart while the coaches slid smoothly up the track, leaving him behind. He remembered that he was not the only one left, and he panted and smiled. It occurred to him—when it was too late—that he might have got on the train and pulled the rope or called the conductor, but that was out of the question now. After all, it might not be such a merry game to stay in that filthy little town; it did not follow that she would prove friendly.

A few moments later she appeared—wholly unconscious of what had happened. A glance down the track and her face was the picture of despair.

Then she saw him coming toward her with long strides, flushed and excited. Regardless of appearances, conditions or consequences, she hurried to meet him.

"Where is the train?" she gasped, as the distance between them grew short, her blue eyes seeking his beseechingly, her hands clasped.

"It has gone."

"Gone? And we—we are left?"

He nodded, delighted by the word "we."

"The conductor said thirty minutes; it has been

but twenty," she cried, half tearfully, half angrily, looking at her watch. Oh, what shall I do?" she went on, distractedly. He had enjoyed the sweet, despairing tones, but this last wail called for manly and instant action.

"Can we catch the train? We must! I will give one thousand dollars. I must catch it." She had placed her gloved hand against a telegraph pole to steady her trembling, but her face was resolute, imperious, commanding. She was ordering him to obey as she would have commanded a slave. In her voice there was authority, in her eye there was fear. She could control the one but not the other.

"We cannot catch the flyer. I want to catch it as much as you and"—here he straightened himself—"I would add a thousand to yours." He hesitated a moment—thinking. "There is but one way, and no time to lose."

With this he turned and ran rapidly toward the little depot and telegraph office.

TWO STRANGERS IN A COACH

Lorry wasted very little time. He dashed into the depot and up to the operator's window.

"What's the nearest station east of here?"

"P——," leisurely answered the agent, in some surprise.

"How far is it?"

"Four miles."

"Telegraph ahead and hold the train that just left here."

"The train don't stop there."

"It's got to stop there—or there'll be more trouble than this road has had since it began business. The conductor pulled out and left two of his passengers —gave out wrong information, and he'll have to hold his train there or bring her back here. If you don't send that order I'll report you as well as the conductor." Grenfall's manner was commanding. The agent's impression was that he was important— that he had a right to give orders. But he hesitated.

"There's no way for you to get to P—— anyway," he said, while turning the matter over in his mind.

"You stop that train! I'll get there inside of twenty minutes. Now, be quick! Wire them to hold her—or there'll be an order from headquarters for some ninety-day lay-offs." The agent stared at him; then turned to his instrument, and the message went forward. Lorry rushed out. On the platform he nearly ran over the hurrying figure in the tan coat.

"Pardon me. I'll explain things in a minute," he gasped and dashed away. Her troubled eyes blinked with astonishment.

At the end of the platform stood a mountain coach, along the sides of which was printed in yellow letters: "Happy Springs." The driver was climbing up to his seat and the cumbersome trap was empty.

"Want to make ten dollars?" cried Grenfall.

"What say?" demanded the driver, half falling to the ground.

"Get me to P—— inside of twenty minutes, and I'll give you ten dollars. Hurry up! Answer!"

"Yes, but, you see, I'm hired to——"

"Oh, that's all right! You'll never make money easier. Can you get us there in twenty minutes?"

"It's four mile, pardner, and not very good road, either. Pile in, and we'll make it er kill old Hip and Jim. Miss the train?"

"Get yourself ready for a race with an express train and don't ask questions. Kill 'em both if you have to. I'll be back in a second!"

Back to the station he tore. She was standing near the door, looking up the track miserably. Already night was falling. Men were lighting the switch lanterns and the mountains were turning into great dark shadows.

"Come quickly; I have a wagon out here."

Resistlessly she was hurried along and fairly shoved through the open door of the odd-looking coach. He was beside her on the seat in an instant, and her bewildered ears heard him say:

"Drive like the very deuce!" Then the door slammed, the driver clattered up to his seat, and the horses were off with a rush.

"Where are we going?" she demanded, sitting very straight and defiant.

"After that train. I'll tell you all about it when I get my breath. This is to be the quickest escape from a dilemma on record—providing it is an escape." By this time they were bumping along the flinty road at a lively rate, jolting about on the seat in a most disconcerting manner. After a few long, deep breaths he told her how the ride in the Springs hack had been conceived and of the arrangement he had made with the despatcher. He furthermore acquainted her with the cause of his being left when he might have caught the train.

"Just as I reached the track, out of breath but rejoicing, I remembered having seen you on that side street, and knew that you would be left. It would have been heartless to leave you here without protection, so I felt it my duty to let the train go and help you out of a very ugly predicament."

"How can I ever repay you?" she murmured. "It was so good and so thoughtful of you. Oh, I should have died had I been left alone. Do you not think my uncle will miss me and have the train sent back?" she went on, sagely.

"That's so!" he exclaimed, somewhat disconcerted. "But I don't know, either. He may not miss you for a long time, thinking you are in some other car, you know. That could easily happen," triumphantly.

"Can this man get us to the next station in time?" she questioned, looking at the black mountains and the dense foliage. It was now quite dark.

"If he doesn't bump us to death before we get half way there. He's driving like the wind."

"You must let me pay half his bill," she said, decidedly, from the dark corner in which she was huddling.

He could find no response to this peremptory request.

"The road is growing rougher. If you will allow me to make a suggestion, I think you will see its wisdom. You can escape a great deal of ugly jost-

ling if you will take hold of my arm and cling to it
tightly. I will brace myself with this strap. I am
sure it will save you many hard bumps."

Without a word she moved to his side and wound
her strong little arm about his big one.

"I had thought of that," she said, simply. "Thank
you." Then, after a moment, while his heart
thumped madly: "Had it occurred to you that after
you ran so hard you might have climbed aboard the
train and ordered the conductor to stop it for me?"

"I—I never thought of that!" he cried confusedly.

"Please do not think me ungrateful. You have
been very good to me, a stranger. One often thinks
afterward of things one might have done, don't you
know? You did the noblest when you inconveni-
enced yourself for me. What trouble I have made
for you." She said this so prettily that he came
gaily from the despondency into which her shrewd-
ness, bordering on criticism, had thrown him. He
knew perfectly well that she was questioning his
judgment and presence of mind, and, the more he
thought of it, the more transparent became the ab-
surdity of his action.

"It has been no trouble," he floundered. "An adventure like this is worth no end of—er—inconveni-
ence, as you call it. I'm sure I must have lost my
head completely, and I am ashamed of myself. How
much anxiety I could have saved you had I been possessed of an ounce of brains!"

"Hush! I will not allow you to say that. You would have me appear ungrateful when I certainly am not. Ach, how he is driving! Do you think it dangerous?" she cried, as the hack gave two or three wild lurches, throwing him into the corner, and the girl half upon him.

"Not in the least," he gasped, the breath knocked out of his body. Just the same, he was very much alarmed. It was as dark as pitch outside and in, and he could not help wondering how near the edge of the mountain side they were running. A false move of the flying horses and they might go rolling to the bottom of the ravine, hundreds of feet below. Still, he must not let her see his apprehension. "This fellow is considered the best driver in the mountains," he prevaricated. Just then he remembered having detected liquor on the man's breath as he closed the door behind him. Perhaps he was intoxicated!

"Do you know him?" questioned the clear voice, her lips close to his ear, her warm body pressing against his.

"Perfectly. He is no other than Light-horse Jerry, the king of stage drivers." In the darkness he smiled to himself maliciously.

"Oh, then we need fear no alarm," she said, reassured, not knowing that Jerry existed only in the yellow-backed novel her informant had read when a boy.

There was such a roaring and clattering that con-

versation became almost impossible. When either
spoke it was with the mouth close to the ear of the
other. At such times Grenfall could feel her breath
on his cheek. Her sweet voice went tingling to his
toes with every word she uttered. He was in a daze,
out of which sung the mad wish that he might clasp
her in his arms, kiss her, and then go tumbling down
the mountain. She trembled in the next fierce lurches,
but gave forth no complaint. He knew that she was
in terror but too brave to murmur.

Unable to resist, he released the strap to which he
had clung so grimly, and placed his strong, firm
hand encouragingly over the little one that gripped
his arm with the clutch of death. It was very dark
and very lonely, too.

"Oh!" she cried, as his hand clasped hers. "You
must hold to the strap."

"It is broken!" he lied, gladly. "There is no danger. See! My hand does not tremble, does it? Be
calm! It cannot be much farther."

"Will it not be dreadful if the conductor refuses
to stop?" she cried, her hand resting calmly beneath
its protector. He detected a tone of security in her
voice.

"But he will stop! Your uncle will see to that,
even if the operator fails."

"My uncle will kill him if he does not stop or
come back for me," she said, complacently.

"I was not wrong," thought Grenfall; "he looks

like a duelist. Who the devil are they, anyhow?"
Then aloud: "At this rate we'd be able to beat the
train to Washington in a straight-away race. Isn't
it a delightfully wild ride?"

"I have acquired a great deal of knowledge in
America, but this is the first time I have heard your
definition of delight. I agree that it is wild."

For some moments there was silence in the noisy
conveyance. Outside, the crack of the driver's whip,
his hoarse cries, and the nerve-destroying crash of
the wheels produced impressions of a mighty storm
rather than of peace and pleasure.

"I am curious to know where you obtained the
coin you lost in the car yesterday," she said at last,
as if relieving her mind of a question that had been
long subdued.

"The one you so kindly found for me?" he asked,
procrastinatingly.

"Yes. They are certainly rare in this country."

"I never saw a coin like it until after I had seen
you," he confessed. He felt her arm press his a
little tighter, and there was a quick movement of her
head which told him, dark as it was, that she was
trying to see his face and that her blue eyes were
wide with something more than terror.

"I do not understand," she exclaimed.

"I obtained the coin from a sleeping-car porter
who said some one gave it to him and told him to

have a 'high time' with it," he explained in her
ear.

"He evidently did not care for the 'high time,' "
she said, after a moment. He would have given a
fortune for one glimpse of her face at that instant.

"I think he said it would be necessary to go to
Europe in order to follow the injunction of the
donor. As I am more likely to go to Europe than
he, I relieved him of the necessity and bought his
right to a 'high time.' "

There was a long pause, during which she attempted to withdraw herself from his side, her little
fingers struggling timidly beneath the big ones.

"Are you a collector of coins?" she asked at
length, a perceptible coldness in her voice.

"No. I am considered a dispenser of coins. Still,
I rather like the idea of possessing this queer bit of
money as a pocket-piece. I intend to keep it forever, and let it descend as an heirloom to the generations that follow me," he said, laughingly. "Why
are you so curious about it?"

"Because it comes from the city and country in
which I live," she responded. "If you were in a
land far from your own would you not be interested in anything—even a coin—that reminded you
of home?"

"Especially if I had not seen one of its kind since
leaving home," he replied, insinuatingly.

"Oh, but I have seen many like it. In my purse there are several at this minute."

"Isn't it strange that this particular coin should have reminded you of home?"

"You have no right to question me, sir," she said, coldly, drawing away, only to be lurched back again. In spite of herself she laughed audibly.

"I beg your pardon," he said, tantalizingly.

"When did he give it to you?"

"Who?"

"The porter, sir."

"You have no right to question me," he said.

"Oh!" she gasped. "I did not mean to be inquisitive."

"But I grant the right. He gave it me inside of two hours after I first entered the car."

"At Denver?"

"How do you know I got on at Denver?"

"Why, you passed me in the aisle with your luggage. Don't you remember?"

Did he remember! His heart almost turned over with the joy of knowing that she had really noticed and remembered him. Involuntarily his glad fingers closed down upon the gloved hand that lay beneath them.

"I believe I do remember, now that you speak of it," he said, in a stifled voice. "You were standing at a window?"

"Yes; and I saw you kissing those ladies good-bye, too. Was one of them your wife, or were they all your sisters? I have wondered."

"They—they were—cousins," he informed her, confusedly, recalling an incident that had been forgotten. He *had* kissed Mary Lyons and Edna Burrage—but their brothers were present. "A foolish habit, isn't it?"

"I do not know. I have no grown cousins," she replied, demurely. "You Americans have such funny customs, though. Where I live, no gentleman would think of pressing a lady's hand until it pained her. Is it necessary?" In the question there was a quiet dignity, half submerged in scorn, so pointed, so unmistakable that he flushed, turned cold with mortification, and hastily removed the amorous fingers.

"I crave your pardon. It is such a strain to hold myself and you against the rolling of this wagon that I unconsciously gripped your hand harder than I knew. You—you will not misunderstand my motive?" he begged, fearful lest he had offended her by his ruthlessness.

"I could not misunderstand something that does not exist," she said, simply, proudly.

"By Jove, she's beyond comparison!" he thought. "You have explained, and I am sorry I spoke as I did. I shall not again forget how much I owe you."

"Your indebtedness, if there be one, does not deprive you of the liberty to speak to me as you will.

You could not say anything unjust without asking my forgiveness, and when you do that you more than pay the debt. It is worth a great deal to me to hear you say that you owe something to me, for I am only too glad to be your creditor. If there *is* a debt, you shall never pay it; it is too pleasant an account to be settled with 'you're welcome.' If you insist that you owe much to me, I shall refuse to cancel the debt, and allow it to draw interest forever."

"What a financier!" she cried. "That jest was worthy of a courtier's deepest flattery. Let me say that I am proud to owe my gratitude to you. You will not permit it to grow less."

"That was either irony or the prettiest speech a woman ever uttered," he said, warmly. "I also am curious about something. You were reading over my shoulder in the observation car——"

"I was not!" she exclaimed, indignantly. "How did you know that?" she inconsistently went on.

"You forget the mirror on the opposite side of the car."

"Ach, now I *am* offended."

"With a poor old mirror? For shame! Yet, in the name of our American glass industry, I ask your forgiveness. It shall not happen again. You will admit that you were trying to read over my shoulder. Thanks for that immutable nod. Well, I am curious to know what you were so eager to read."

"Since you presume to believe the mirror instead of me, I will tell you. There was a despatch on the first page that interested me deeply."

"I believe I thought as much at the time. Oh, confound this road!" For half a mile or more the road had been fairly level, but, as the ejaculation indicates, a rough place had been reached. He was flung back in the corner violently, his head coming in contact with a sharp projection of some kind. The pain was almost unbearable, but it was eased by the fact that she had involuntarily thrown ·her arm across his chest, her hand grasping his shoulder spasmodically.

"Oh, we shall be killed!" she half shrieked. "Can you not stop him? This is madness—madness!"

"Pray be calm! I was to blame, for I had become careless. He is earning his money, that's all. It was not stipulated in the contract that he was to consider the comfort of his passengers." Grenfall could feel himself turn pale as something warm began to trickle down his neck. "Now tell me which despatch it was. I read all of them."

"You did? Of what interest could they have been?"

"Curiosity does not recognize reason."

"You read every one of them?"

"Assuredly."

"Then I shall grant you the right to guess which

interested me the most.   You Americans delight in
puzzles, I am told."

"Now, that is unfair."

"So it is.   Did you read the despatch from Constantinople?" Her arm fell to her side suddenly as if
she had just realized its position.

"The one that told of the French ambassador's
visit to the Sultan?"

"Concerning the small matter of a loan of some
millions—Yes.   Well, that was of interest to me, in-
asmuch as the loan, if made, will affect my country."

"Will you tell me what country you are from?"

"I am from Graustark."

"Yes; but I don't remember where that is."

"Is it possible that your American schools do not
teach geography?   Ours tell us where the United
States are located."

"I confess ignorance," he admitted.

"Then I shall insist that you study a map.   Graustark is small, but I am as proud of it as you are of
this great broad country that reaches from ocean to
ocean.   I can scarcely wait until I again see our dear
crags and valleys, our rivers and ever-blue skies, our
plains and our towns.   I wonder if you worship your
country as I love mine."

"From the tenor of your remarks, I judge that
you have been away from home for a long time," he
volunteered.

"We have seen something of Asia, Australia,

Mexico and the United States since we left Edelweiss, six months ago. Now we are going home—
home!" She uttered the words so lovingly, so long-
ingly, so tenderly, that he envied the homeland.

There was a long break in the conversation, both
evidently wrapped in thought which could not be
disturbed by the whirl of the coach. He was wondering how he could give her up, now that she had
been tossed into his keeping so strangely. She was
asking herself over and over again how so thrilling
an adventure would end.

They were sore and fatigued with the strain on
nerve and flesh. It was an experience never to be
forgotten, this romantic race over the wild mountain road, the result still in doubt. Ten minutes
ago—strangers; now—friends at least, neither
knowing the other. She was admiring him for his
generalship, his wonderful energy; he was blessing
the fate that had come to his rescue when hope was
almost dead. He could scarcely realize that he was
awake. Could it be anything but a vivid fancy from
which he was to awaken and find himself alone in
his berth, the buzzing, clacking car-wheels piercing
his ears with sounds so unlike those that had been
whispered into them by a voice, sweet and maddening, from out of the darkness of a dreamland cab?

"Surely we must be almost at the end of this
awful ride," she moaned, yielding completely to the
long suppressed alarm. "Every bone in my body

aches. What shall we do if they have not held the train?"

"Send for an undertaker," he replied grimly, seeing policy in jest. They were now ascending an incline, bumping over boulders, hurtling through treacherous ruts and water-washed holes, rolling, swinging, jerking, crashing. "You have been brave all along; don't give up now. It is almost over. You'll soon be with your friends."

"How can I thank you?" she cried, gripping his arm once more. Again his hand dropped upon hers and closed gently.

"I wish that I could do a thousand times as much for you," he said, thrillingly, her disheveled hair touching his face, so close were his lips. "Ah, the lights of the town!" he cried an instant later. "Look!"

He held her so that she could peer through the rattling glass window. Close at hand, higher up the steep, many lights were twinkling against the blackness.

Almost before they realized how near they were to the lights, the horses began to slacken their speed, a moment later coming to a standstill. The awful ride was over.

"The train! the train!" she cried, in ecstacy. "Here, on the other side. Thank heaven!"

He could not speak for the joyful pride that distended his heart almost to bursting. The coach door flew open, and Light-horse Jerry yelled:

"Here y'are! I made her!"

"I should say you did!" exclaimed Grenfall, climbing out and drawing her after him gently. "Here's your ten."

"I must send you something, too, my good fellow," cried the lady. "What is your address— quick?"

"William Perkins, O——, West Virginny, ma'am."

Lorry was dragging her toward the cars as the driver completed the sentence. Several persons were running down the platform, dimly lighted from the string of car windows. She found time to pant as they sped along:

"He was not Light-horse Jerry, at all!"

III

MISS GUGGENSLOCKER

He laughed, looking down into her serious upturned face. A brief smile of understanding flitted
across her lips as she broke away from him and
threw herself into the arms of tall, excited Uncle
Caspar. The conductor, several trainmen and a few
eager passengers came up, the former crusty and
snappish.

"Well, get aboard!" he growled. "We can't wait
all night."

The young lady looked up quickly, her sensitive
face cringing beneath the rough command. Lorry
stepped instantly to the conductor's side, shook his
finger vigorously under his nose, and exclaimed in
no uncertain tones:

"Now, that's enough from you! If I hear another word out of you, I'll make you sweat blood
before to-morrow morning. Understand, my
friend."

"Aw, who are you?" demanded the conductor,
belligerently.

"You'll learn that soon enough. After this you'll

have sense enough to find out whom you are talking
to before you open that mouth of yours. Not another word!" Mr. Grenfall Lorry was not president
of the road, nor was he in any way connected with
it, but his well-assumed air of authority caused the
trainman's ire to dissolve at once.

"Excuse me, sir. I've been worried to death on
this run. I meant no offence. That old gentleman
has threatened to kill me. Just now he took out his
watch and said if I did not run back for his niece in
two minutes he'd call me out and run me through.
I've been nearly crazy here. For the life of me, I
don't see how you happened to be——"

"Oh, that's all right. Let's be off," cried Lorry,
who had fallen some distance behind his late companion and her uncle. Hurrying after them, he
reached her side in time to assist her in mounting
the car steps.

"Thank you," smiling down upon him bewitch-
ingly. At the top of the steps she was met by her
aunt, behind whom stood the anxious man-servant
and the maid. Into the coach she was drawn by the
relieved old lady, who was critically inspecting her
personal appearance when Lorry and the foreigner
entered.

"Ach, it was so wild and exhilarating, Aunt
Yvonne," the girl was saying, her eyes sparkling.
She stood straight and firm, her chin in the air, her
hands in those of her aunt. The little traveling cap

was on the side of her head, her hair was loose and very much awry, strands straying here, curls blowing there in utter confusion. Lorry fairly gasped with admiration for the loveliness that would not be vanquished.

"We came like the wind! I shall never, never forget it!" she said.

"But how could you have remained there, child? Tell me how it happened. We have been frantic," said her aunt, half in English, half in German.

"Not now, dear Aunt Yvonne. See my hair! What a fright I must be! Fortunate man, your hair cannot be so unruly as mine. Oh!" The exclamation was one of alarm. In an instant she was at his side, peering with terrified eyes at the bloodstains on his neck and face. "It is blood! You are hurt! Uncle Caspar, Hedrick—quick! Attend him! Come to my room at once. You are suffering. Minna, find bandages!"

She dragged him to the door of her section before he could interpose a remonstrance.

"It is nothing—a mere scratch. Bumped my head against the side of the coach. Please don't worry about it; I can care for myself. Really, it doesn't——"

"But it does! It has bled terribly. Sit there! Now, Hedrick, some water."

Hedrick rushed off and was back in a moment with a basin of water, a sponge and a towel, and before Grenfall fully knew what was happening, the man-servant was bathing his head, the others looking on anxiously, the young lady apprehensively, her hands clasped before her as she bent over to inspect the wound above his ear.

"It is quite an ugly cut," said Uncle Caspar, critically. "Does it pain you, sir?"

"Oh, not a great deal," answered Lorry, closing his eyes comfortably. It was all very pleasant, he thought.

"Should it not have stitches, Uncle Caspar?" asked the sweet, eager voice.

"I think not. The flow is staunched. If the gentleman will allow Hedrick to trim the hair away for a plaster and then bandage it I think the wound will give him no trouble." The old man spoke slowly and in very good English.

"Really, Uncle, is it not serious?"

"No, no," interposed Grenfall Lorry. "I knew it was a trifle. You cannot break an American's head. Let me go to my own section and I'll be ready to present myself as good as new, in ten minutes."

"You must let Hedrick bandage your head," she insisted. "Go with him, Hedrick."

Grenfall arose and started toward his section, followed by Hedrick.

"I trust you were not hurt during that reckless ride," he said, more as a question, stopping in the aisle to look back at her.

"I should have been a mass of bruises, gashes and lumps had it not been for one thing," she said, a faint flush coming to her cheek, although her eyes looked unfaltering into his. "Will you join us in the dining car? I will have a place prepared for you at our table."

"Thank you. You are very good. I shall join you as soon as I am presentable."

"We are to be honored, sir," said the old gentleman, but in such a way that Grenfall had a distinct feeling that it was he who was to be honored. Aunt Yvonne smiled graciously, and he took his departure. While Hedrick was dressing the jagged little cut, Grenfall complacently surveyed the patient in the mirror opposite, and said to himself a hundred times: "You lucky dog! It was worth forty gashes like this. By Jove, she's divine!"

In a fever of eager haste he bathed and attired himself for dinner, the imperturbable Hedrick assisting. One query filled the American's mind: "I wonder if I am to sit beside her." And then: "I have sat beside her! There can never again be such delight!"

It was seven o'clock before his rather unusual toilet was completed. "See if they have gone to dinner, Hedrick," he said to the man-servant, who departed ceremoniously.

"I don't know why he should be so damned polite," observed Lorry, gazing wonderingly after him.

"I'm not a king. That reminds me. I must introduce myself. She doesn't know me from Adam."

Hedrick returned and announced that they had just gone to the dining car and were awaiting him there. He hurried to the dinner and made his way to their table. Uncle Caspar and his niece were facing him as he came up between the tables, and he saw, with no little regret, that he was to sit beside the aunt—directly opposite the girl, however. She smiled up at him as he stood before them, bowing. He saw the expression of injury in those deep, liquid eyes of violet as their gaze wandered over his hair.

"Your head? I see no bandage," she said, reproachfully.

"There is a small plaster and that is all. Only heroes may have dangerous wounds," he said, laughingly.

"Is heroism in America measured by the number of stitches or the size of the plaster?" she asked. pointedly. "In my country it is a joy, and not a calamity. Wounds are the misfortune of valor. Pray, be seated, Mr. Lorry—is it not?" she said, pronouncing it quaintly.

He sat down rather suddenly on hearing her utter his name. How had she learned it? Not a soul on the train knew it, he was sure.

"I am Caspar Guggenslocker. Permit me, Mr. Lorry, to present my wife and my niece, Miss Guggenslocker," said the uncle, more gracefully than he had ever heard such a thing uttered before.

In a daze, stunned by the name,—Guggenslocker, —mystified over their acquaintance with his own when he had been foiled at every fair attempt to learn theirs, Lorry could only mumble his acknowledgments. In all his life he had never lost command of himself as at this moment. Guggenslocker! He could feel the dank sweat of disappointment starting on his brow. A butcher,—a beer maker,— a cobbler,—a gardener,—all synonyms of Guggenslocker. A sausage manufacturer's niece—Miss Guggenslocker! He tried to glance unconcernedly at her as he took up his napkin, but his eyes wavered helplessly. She was looking serenely at him, yet he fancied he saw a shadow of mockery in her blue eyes.

"If you were a novel writer, Mr. Lorry, what manner of heroine would you choose?" she asked, with a smile so tantalizing that he understood instinctively why she was reviving a topic once abandoned. His confusion was increased. Her uncle and aunt were regarding him calmly,—expectantly, he imagined.

"I—I have no ambition to be a novel writer," he said, "so I have not made a study of heroines."

"But you would have an ideal," she persisted.

"I'm sure I—I don't—that is, she would not necessarily be a heroine. Unless, of course, it would require heroism to pose as an ideal for such a prosaic fellow as I."

"To begin with, you would call her Clarabel Montrose or something equally as impossible. You know the name of a heroine in a novel must be euphonious. That is an exacting rule." It was an open taunt, and he could see that she was enjoying his discomfiture. It aroused his indignation and his wits.

"I would first give my hero a distinguished name. No matter what the heroine's name might be—pretty or otherwise—I could easily change it to his in the last chapter." She flushed beneath his now bright, keen eyes and the ready, though unexpected retort. Uncle Caspar placed his napkin to his lips and coughed. Aunt Vvonne studiously inspected her bill of fare. "No matter what you call a rose, it is always sweet," he added, meaningly.

At this she laughed good-naturedly. He marveled at her white teeth and red lips. A rose, after all. Guggenslocker, rose; rose, not Guggenslocker. No, no! A rose only! He fancied he caught a sly look of triumph in her uncle's swift glance toward her. But Uncle Caspar was not a rose—he was Guggenslocker. Guggenslocker—butcher! Still, he did not look the part—no, indeed. That extraordinary man a butcher, a gardener, a—and Aunt Yvonne? Yet they were Guggenslockers.

"Here is the waiter," the girl observed, to his relief. "I am famished after my pleasant drive. It was so bracing, was it not, Mr. Grenfall Lorry?"

"Give me a mountain ride always as an appetizer," he said, obligingly, and so ended the jest about a name.

The orders for the dinner were given and the quartette sat back in their chairs to await the coming of the soup. Grenfall was still wondering how she had learned his name, and was on the point of asking several times during the conventional discussion of the weather, the train and the mountains. He considerately refrained, however, unwilling to embarrass her.

"Aunt Yvonne tells me she never expected to see me alive after the station agent telegraphed that we were coming overland in that awful old carriage. The agent at P—— says it is a dangerous road, at the very edge of the mountain. He also increased the composure of my uncle and aunt by telling them that a wagon rolled off yesterday, killing a man, two women and two horses. Dear Aunt Yvonne, how troubled you must have been."

"I'll confess there were times when I thought we were rolling down the mountain," said Lorry, with a relieved shake of the head.

"Sometimes I thought we were soaring through space, whether upward or downward, I could not tell. We never failed to come to earth, though, did we?" she laughingly asked.

"Emphatically! Earth and a little grief," he said, putting his hand to his head.

"Does it pain you?" she asked, quickly.

"Not in the least. I was merely feeling to see if the cut were still there. Mr.—Mr. Guggenslocker, did the conductor object to holding the train?" he asked, remembering what the conductor had told him of the old gentleman's actions.

"At first, but I soon convinced him that it should be held," said the other, quietly.

"My husband spoke very harshly to the poor man," added Aunt Yvonne. "But I am afraid, Caspar, he did not understand a word you said. You were very much excited." The sweet old lady's attempts at English were much more laborious than her husband's.

"If he did not understand my English, he was very good at guessing," said her husband, grimly.

"He told me you had threatened to call him out," ventured the young man.

"Call him out? Ach, a railroad conductor!" exclaimed Uncle Caspar, in fine scorn.

"Caspar, I heard you say that you would call him out," interposed his wife, with reproving eyes.

"Ach, God! I have made a mistake! I see it all! It was the other word I meant—*down* not *out*. I intended to call him down, as you Americans say. I hope he will not think I challenged him." He was very much perturbed.

"I think he was *afraid* you would," said Lorry.

"He should never fear. I could not meet a rail-road conductor. Will you please tell him I could not so condescend? Besides, dueling is murder in your country, I am told."

"It usually is, sir. Much more so than in Europe." The others looked at him inquiringly. "I mean that in America when two men pull their revolvers and go to shooting at each other, some one is killed—frequently both. In Europe, as I understand it, a scratch with the sword ends the combat."

"You have been misinformed," exclaimed Uncle Caspar, his eyebrows elevated.

"Why, Uncle Caspar has fought more duels than he can count," cried the girl, proudly.

"And has he slain his man every time?" asked Grenfall, smilingly, glancing from one to the other. Aunt Vvonne shot a reproving look at the girl, whose face paled instantly, her eyes going quickly in affright to the face of her uncle.

"God!" Lorry heard the old gentleman mutter. He was looking at his bill of fare, but his eyes were fixed and staring. The card was crumpling between the long, bony fingers. The American realized that a forbidden topic had been touched upon.

"He has fought and he has slain," he thought as quick as a flash. "He is no butcher, no gardener, no cobbler. That's certain!"

"Tell us, Uncle Caspar, what you said to the conductor," cried the young lady, nervously.

"Tell them, Caspar, how alarmed we were," added soft-voiced Aunt Yvonne. Grenfall was a silent, interested spectator. He somehow felt as if a scene from some tragedy had been reproduced in that briefest of moments. Calmly and composedly, a half-smile now on his face, the soldierly Caspar narrated the story of the train's run from one station to the other.

"We did not miss you until we had almost reached the other station. Then your Aunt Yvonne asked me where you had gone. I told her I had not seen you, but went into the coach ahead to search. You were not there. Then I went on to the dining car. Ach, you were not there. In alarm I returned to our car. Your aunt and I looked everywhere. You were not anywhere. I shall never forget your aunt's face when she sank into a chair, nor shall I feel again so near like dying as when she suggested that you might have fallen from the train. I sent Hedrick ahead to summon the conductor, but he had hardly left us when the engine whistled sharply and the train began to slow up in a jerky fashion. We were very pale as we looked at each other, for something told us that the stop was unusual. I rushed to the platform, meeting Hedrick, who was as much alarmed as I. He said the train had been flagged, and that there must be something wrong. Your aunt came out and told me that she had made a strange discovery."

Grenfall observed that he was addressing himself exclusively to the young lady.

"She had found that the gentleman in the next section was also missing. While we were standing there in doubt and perplexity, the train came to a standstill, and soon there was shouting on the outside. I climbed down from the car and saw that we were at a little station. The conductor came running toward me excitedly.

" 'Is the young lady in the car?' he asked.

" 'No. For Heaven's sake, what have you heard?' I cried.

" 'Then she has been left at O——,' he exclaimed, and used some very extraordinary American words.

"I then informed him that he should run back for you, first learning that you were alive and well. He said he would be damned if he would—pardon the word, ladies. He was very angry, and said he would give orders to go ahead, but I told him I would demand restitution of his government. He laughed in my face, and then I became shamelessly angry. I said to him:

" 'Sir, I shall call you down—not out, as you have said—and I shall run you through the mill.'

"That was good American talk, sir, was it not, Mr. Lorry? I wanted him to understand me, so I tried to use your very best language. Some gentle-

men who are traveling on this train and some very
excellent ladies also joined in the demand that the
train be held. His despatch from O—— said that
you, Mr. Lorry, insisted on having it held for
twenty minutes. The conductor insulted you, sir,
by saying that you had more—ah, what is it?—gall
than any idiot he had ever seen. When he said
that, although I did not fully understand that it was
a reflection on you, so ignorant am I of your language, I took occasion to tell him that you were a
gentleman and a friend of mine. He asked me your
name, but, as I did not know it, I could only tell
him that he would learn it soon enough. Then he
said something which has puzzled me ever since.
He told me to close my face. What did he mean
by that, Mr. Lorry?"

"Well, Mr. Guggenslocker, that means in refined American, 'stop talking,'" said Lorry, con-
trolling a desire to shout.

"Ach, that accounts for his surprise when I
talked louder and faster than ever. I did not know
what he meant. He said positively he would not
wait, but just then a second message came from the
other station. I did not know what it was then,
but a gentleman told me that it instructed him to
hold the train if he wanted to hold his job. Job is
situation, is it not? Well, when he read that message he said he would wait just twenty minutes. I
asked him to tell me how you were coming to us,

but he refused to answer. Your aunt and I went at once to the telegraph man and implored him to tell us the truth, and he said you were coming in a carriage over a very dangerous road. Imagine our feelings when he said some people had been killed yesterday on that very road. He said you would have to drive like the—the very devil if you got here in twenty minutes."

"We did, Uncle Caspar," interrupted Miss Guggenslocker, naïvely. "Our driver followed Mr. Lorry's instructions."

Mr. Grenfall Lorry blushed and laughed awkwardly. He had been admiring her eager face and expressive eyes during Uncle Caspar's recital. How sweet her voice when it pronounced his name, how charming the foreign flavor to the words.

"He would not have understood if I had said other things," he explained, hastily.

"When your aunt and I returned to the train we saw the conductor holding his watch. He said to me: 'In just three minutes we pull out. If they are not here by that time they can get on the best they know how. I've done all I can.' I did not say a word, but went to my section and had Hedrick get out my pistols. If the train had left before you arrived it would be without its conductor. In the meantime, your Aunt Yvonne was pleading with the wretch. I hastened back to his side with my pistols in my pocket. It was then that I told him to start the train if he dared. That man will never

know how close he was to death. One minute
passed, and he coolly announced that but one minute
was left. I had made up my mind to give him one
of my pistols when the time was up, and to tell him
to defend himself. It was not to be a duel, for
there was nothing regular about it. It was only a
question as to whether the train should move. Then
came the sound of carriage wheels and galloping horses. Almost before we knew it you were
with us. I am so happy that you were not a minute
later."

There was something so cool and grim in the
quiet voice, something so determined in those bril-
liant eyes, that Grenfall felt like looking up the
conductor to congratulate him. The dinner was
served, and while it was being discussed his fair
companion of the drive graphically described the
experience of twenty strange minutes in a shackle-
down mountain coach. He was surprised to find
that she omitted no part, not even the hand clasp or
the manner in which she clung to him. His ears
burned as he listened to this frank confession, for
he expected to hear words of disapproval from the
uncle and aunt. His astonishment was increased
by their utter disregard of these rather peculiar details. It was then that he realized how trusting she
had been, how serenely unconscious of his tender
and sudden passion. And had she told her relatives
that she had kissed him, he firmly believed they
would have smiled approvingly. Somehow the real

flavor of romance was stricken from the ride by her candid admissions. What he had considered a romantic treasure was being calmly robbed of its glitter, leaving for his memory the blurr of an adventure in which he had played the part of a gallant gentleman and she a grateful lady. He was beginning to feel ashamed of the conceit that had misled him. Down in his heart he was saying: "I might have known it. I did know it. She is not like other women." The perfect confidence that dwelt in the rapt faces of the others forced into his wondering mind the impression that this girl could do no wrong.

"And, Aunt Yvonne," she said, in conclusion, "the luck which you say is mine as birthright asserted itself. I escaped unhurt, while Mr. Lorry alone possesses the pain and unpleasantness of our ride."

"I possess neither," he objected. "The pain that you refer to is a pleasure."

"The pain that a man endures for a woman should always be a pleasure," said Uncle Caspar, smilingly.

"But it could not be a pleasure to him unless the woman considered it a pain," reasoned Miss Guggenslocker. "He could not feel happy if she did not respect the pain."

"And encourage it," supplemented Lorry, dryly. "If you do not remind me occasionally that I am hurt, Miss Guggenslocker, I am liable to forget it."

To himself he added: "I'll never learn how to say it in one breath."

"If I were not so soon to part from you I should be your physician, and, like all physicians, prolong your ailment interminably," she said, prettily.

"To my deepest satisfaction," he said, warmly, not lightly. There was nothing further from his mind than servile flattery, as his rejoinder might imply. "Alas!" he went on, "we no sooner meet than we part. May I ask when you are to sail?"

"On Thursday," replied Mr. Guggenslocker.

"On the Kaiser Wilhelm der Grosse," added his niece, a faraway look coming into her eyes.

"We are to stop off one day, to-morrow, in Washington," said Aunt Yvonne, and the jump that Lorry's heart gave was so mighty that he was afraid they could see it in his face.

"My uncle has some business to transact in your city, Mr. Lorry. We are to spend to-morrow there and Wednesday in New York. Then we sail. Ach, how I long for Thursday!" His heart sank like lead to the depths from which it had sprung. It required no effort on his part to see that he was alone in his infatuation. Thursday was more to her than his existence; she could forget him and think of Thursday, and when she thought of Thursday, the future, he was but a thing of the past, not even of the present.

"Have you always lived in Washington, Mr. Lorry?" asked Mrs. Guggenslocker.

"All my life," he replied, wishing at that moment that he was homeless and free to choose for himself.

"You Americans live in one city and then in another," she said. "Now, in our country generation after generation lives and dies in one town. We are not migratory."

"Mr. Lorry has offended us by not knowing where Graustark is located on the map," cried the young lady, and he could see the flash of resentment in her eyes.

"Why, my dear sir, Graustark is in——" began Uncle Caspar, but she checked him instantly.

"Uncle Caspar, you are not to tell him. I have recommended that he study geography and discover us for himself. He should be ashamed of his ignorance."

He was not ashamed, but he mentally vowed that before he was a day older he would find Graustark on the map and would stock his negligent brain with all that history and the encyclopedia had to say of the unknown land. Her uncle laughed, and, to Lorry's disappointment, obeyed the young lady's command.

"Shall I study the map of Europe, Asia or Africa?" asked he, and they laughed

"Study the map of the world," said Miss Guggenslocker, proudly.

"Edelweiss is the capital?"

"Yes, our home city,—the queen of the crags,"

cried she. "You should see Edelweiss, Mr. Lorry.
It is of the mountain, the plain and the sky. There
are homes in the valley, homes on the mountain side
and homes in the clouds."

"And yours? From what you say it must be
above the clouds—in heaven."

"We are farthest from the clouds, for we live in
the green valley, shaded by the white topped mountains. We may, in Edelweiss, have what climate we
will. Doctors do not send us on long journeys for our
health. They tell us to move up or down the mountain. We have balmy spring, glorious summer, refreshing autumn and chilly winter, just as we like."

"Ideal! I think you must be pretty well toward
the south. You could not have July and January if
you were far north."

"True; yet we have January in July. Study your
map. We are discernible to the naked eye," she
said, half ironically.

"I care not if there are but three inhabitants of
Graustark, all told, it is certainly worthy of a position on any map," said Lorry, gallantly; and his listeners applauded with patriotic appreciation. "By
the way, Mr. Gug—Guggenslocker, you say the conductor asked you for my name and you did not
know it. May I ask you how you learned it later
on?" His curiosity got the better of him, and his
courage was increased by the champagne the old
gentleman had ordered.

"I did not know your name until my niece told it

to me after your arrival in the carriage," said Uncle Caspar.

"I don't remember giving it to Miss Guggenslocker at any time," said Lorry.

"You were not my informant," she said, demurely.

"Surely you did not guess it."

"Oh, no, indeed. I am no mind reader."

"My own name was the last thing you could have read in my mind, in that event, for I have not thought of it in three days."

She was sitting with her elbows on the table, her chin in her hands, a dreamy look in her blue eyes.

"You say you obtained that coin from the porter on the Denver train?"

"Within two hours after I got aboard."

"Well that coin purchased your name for me," she said, calmly, candidly. He gasped.

"You—you don't mean that you——" he stammered.

"You see, Mr. Lorry, I wanted to know the name of a man who came nearest my ideal of what an American should be. As soon as I saw you I knew that you were *the* American as I had grown to know him through the books,—big, strong, bold and comely. That is why I bought your name of the porter. I shall always say that I know the name of an ideal American,—Grenfall Lorry."

The ideal American was not unmoved. He was

in a fever of fear and happiness,—fear because he thought she was jesting, happiness because he hoped she was not. He laughed awkwardly, absolutely unable to express himself in words. Her frank statement staggered him almost beyond the power of recovery. There was joy in the knowledge that she had been attracted to him at first sight, but there was bitterness in the thought that he had come to her notice as a sort of specimen, the name of which she had sought as a botanist would look for the name of an unknown flower.

"I—I am honored," he at last managed to say, his eyes gleaming with embarrassment. "I trust you have not found your first judgment a faulty one." He felt very foolish after this flat remark.

"I have remembered your name," she said, graciously. His heart swelled.

"There are a great many better Americans than I," he said. "You forget our President and our statesmen."

"I thought they were mere politicians."

Grenfall Lorry, idealized, retired to his berth that night, his head whirling with the emotions inspired by this strange, beautiful woman. How lovely, how charming, how naïve, how queenly, how indifferent, how warm, how cold—how everything that puzzled him was she. His last waking thought was:

"Guggenslocker! An angel with a name like that!"

IV

They were called by the porter early the next morning. The train was pulling into Washington, five hours late. Grenfall wondered, as he dressed, whether fortune would permit him to see much of her during her brief day in the capital. He dreamed of a drive over the avenues, a trip to the monument. a visit to the halls of congress, an inspection of public buildings, a dinner at his mother's home, luncheon at the Ebbitt, and other attentions which might give to him every moment of her day in Washington. But even as he dreamed, he was certain that his hopes could not be gratified.

After the train had come to a standstill he could hear the rustle of her garments in the next compartment. Then he heard her sweep into the passage, greet her uncle and aunt, utter a few commands to the maid, and, while he was adjusting his collar and necktie, pass from the car. No man ever made quicker time in dressing than did Lorry. She could hardly have believed him ideal had she seen his scowling face or heard the words that hissed through his impatient teeth.

"She'll get away, and that'll be the end of it," he

growled, seizing his traps and rushing from the
train two minutes after her departure. The porter
attempted to relieve him of his bags on the platform,
but he brushed him aside and was off toward the
station.

"Nice time for you to call a man, you idiot," was
his parting shot for the porter, forgetting, of course,
that the foreigners had been called at the same time.
With eyes intent on the crowd ahead, he plunged
along, seeing nobody in his disappointed flight. "I'll
never forgive myself if I miss her," he was wailing
to himself. She was not to be seen in the waiting-
rooms, so he rushed to the sidewalk.

"Baggage transferred?"

"Cab, sir?"

"Go to the devil—yes, here! Take these traps
and these checks and rush my stuff to No. ———,
W——— Avenue. Trunks just in on B. & O.," he
cried, tossing his burdens to a transfer man and
giving him the checks so quickly that the fellow's
sleepy eyes opened wider than they had been for a
month. Relieved of his impedimenta, he returned
to the station.

"Good morning, Mr. Lorry. Are you in too
much of a hurry to see your friends?" cried a clear,
musical voice, and he stopped as if shot. The
anxious frown flew from his brow and was succeeded instantaneously by a glad smile. He wheeled
and beheld her, with Aunt Yvonne, standing near
the main entrance to the station. "Why, good morn-

ing," he exclaimed, extending his hand gladly. To his amazement she drew herself up haughtily and ignored the proffered hand. Only for a brief second did this strange and uncalled-for hauteur obtain. A bright smile swept over her face, and her repentant fingers sought his timidly, even awkwardly. Something told him that she was not accustomed to handshaking; that same something impelled him to bend low and touch the gloved fingers with his lips. He straightened, with face flushed, half fearful lest his act had been observed by curious loungers, and he had taken the liberty in a public place which could not be condoned. But she smiled serenely, approvingly. There was not the faintest sign of embarrassment or confusion in the lovely face. Any other girl in the world, he thought, would have jerked her hand away and giggled furiously. Aunt Yvonne inclined her head slightly, but did not proffer her hand. He wisely refrained from extending his own. "I thought you had left the station," he said.

"We are waiting for Uncle Caspar, who is giving Hedrick instructions. Hedrick, you know, is to go on to New York with our boxes. He will have them aboard ship when we arrive there. All that we have with us is hand luggage. We leave Washington to-night."

"I had hoped you might stay over a few days."

"It is urgent business that compels us to leave so hastily, Mr. Lorry. Of all the cities in the world,

I have most desired to see the capital of your country. Perhaps I may return some day. But do not let us detain you, if you are in a hurry."

He started, looked guilty, stammered something about baggage, said he would return in a moment, and rushed aimlessly away, his ears fiery.

"I'm all kinds of a fool," he muttered, as he raced around the baggage-room and then back to where he had left the two ladies. Mr. Guggenslocker had joined them and they were preparing to depart. Miss Guggenslocker's face expressed pleasure at seeing him.

"We thought you would never return, so long were you gone," she cried, gaily. He had been gone just two minutes by the watch! The old gentleman greeted him warmly, and Lorry asked them to what hotel they were going. On being informed that they expected to spend the day at the Ebbitt, he volunteered to accompany them, saying that he intended to breakfast there. Quicker than a flash a glance, unfathomable as it was brief, passed between the three, not quickly enough, however, to escape his keen, watchful eyes, on the alert since the beginning of his acquaintance with them, in conjunction with his ears, to catch something that might satisfy, in a measure, his burning curiosity. What was the meaning of that glance? It half angered him, for in it he thought he could distinguish annoyance, apprehension, dismay or something equally disquieting. Before he could stiffen his long frame and

give vent to the dignified reconsideration that flew
to his mind, the young lady dispelled all pain and
displeasure, sending him into raptures, by saying:

"How good of you! We shall be so delighted to
have you breakfast with us, Mr. Lorry, if it is con-
venient for you. You can talk to us of your wonderful city. Now, say that you will be good to us;
stay your hunger and neglect your personal affairs
long enough to give us these early morning hours.
I am sure we cannot trouble you much longer."

He expostulated gallantly and delightedly, and
then hurried forth to call a cab. At eight o'clock he
breakfasted with them, his infatuation growing
deeper and stronger as he sat for the hour beneath
the spell of those eyes, the glorious face, the sweet,
imperial air that was a part of her, strange and un-
affected. As they were leaving the dining-room, he
asked her if she would not drive with him.

His ardent gallantry met with a surprising rebuke.
The conversation up to that moment had been
bright and cheery, her face had been the constant
reflector of his own good spirits, and he had every
reason in the world to feel that his suggestion would
be received with pleasure. It was a shock to him,
therefore, to see the friendly smile fade from her
eyes and a disdainful gleam succeed it. Her voice,
a moment ago sweet and affable, changed its tone
instantly to one so proud and arrogant that he could
scarcely believe his ears.

"I shall be engaged during the entire day, Mr.

Lorry," she said, slowly, looking him fairly in the eyes with cruel positiveness. Those eyes of his were wide with surprise and the glowing gleam of injured pride. His lips closed tightly; little red spots flew to his cheeks and then disappeared, leaving his face white and cold; his heart throbbed painfully with mingled emotions of shame and anger. For a moment he dared not speak.

"I have reason to feel thankful that you are to be engaged," he said at last, calmly, without taking his eyes from hers. "I am forced to believe, much to my regret, that I have offended when I intended to please. You will pardon my temerity."

There was no mistaking the resentment in his voice or the glitter in his eyes. Impulsively her little hand was stretched forth, falling upon his arm, while into her eyes came again the soft glow and to her lips the most pathetic, appealing smile, the forerunner of a pretty plea for forgiveness. The change startled and puzzled him more than ever. In one moment she was unreasonably rude and imperious, in the next gracious and imploring.

"Forgive me," she cried, the blue eyes battling bravely against the steel in the grey ones above. "I was so uncivil! Perhaps I cannot make you understand why I spoke as I did, but, let me say, I richly deserved the rebuke. Pray forgive me and forget that I have been disagreeable. Do not ask me to tell you why I was so rude to you just now, but overlook my unkind treatment of your invitation.

Please, Mr. Lorry, I beg of you—I beg for the first time in my life. You have been so good to me; be good to me still."

His wrath melted away like snow before the sunshine. How could he resist such an appeal? "I beg for the first time in my life," whirled in his brain. What did she mean by that?

"I absolve the penitent," he said, gravely.

"I thank you. You are still my ideal American—courteous, bold and gentle. I do not wonder that Americans can be masterful men. And now I thank you for your invitation, and ask you to let me withdraw my implied refusal. If you will take me for the drive, I shall be delighted and more than grateful."

"You make me happy again," he said, softly, as they drew near the elder members of the party, who had paused to wait for them. "I shall ask your uncle and aunt to accompany us."

"Uncle Caspar will be busy all day, but I am sure my aunt will be charmed. Aunt Yvonne, Mr. Lorry has asked us to drive with him over the city, and I have accepted for you. When are we to start, Mr. Lorry?"

Mr. and Mrs. Guggenslocker stared in a bewildered sort of manner at their niece. Then Aunt Yvonne turned questioning eyes toward her husband, who promptly bowed low before the tall American, and said:

"Your kind offices shall never be forgotten, sir. When are the ladies to be ready?"

Lorry was weighing in his mind the advisability of asking them to dine in the evening with his mother, but two objections presented themselves readily. First, he was afraid of this perverse maid; second, he had not seen his mother. In fact, he did not know that she was in town.

"At two o'clock, I fancy. That will give us the afternoon. You leave at nine to-night, do you not?"

"Yes. And will you dine with us this evening?" Her invitation was so unexpected, in view of all that had happened, that he looked askance. "Ach, you must not treat my invitation as I did yours!" she cried, merrily, although he could detect the blush that returns with the recollection of a reprimand. "You should profit by what I have been taught." The girl abruptly threw her arm about her aunt and cried, as she drew away in the direction of her room: "At two, then, and at dinner this evening. I bid you good morning, Mr. Lorry."

The young man, delighted with the turn of affairs, but dismayed by what seemed a summary dismissal, bowed low. He waited until the strange trio entered the elevator and then sauntered downstairs, his hands in his pockets, his heart as light as air. Unconsciously he jingled the coins. A broad smile came over his face as he drew forth a certain piece.

Holding it between his thumb and forefinger, he said:

"You are what it cost her to learn my name, are you? Well, my good fellow, you may be very small, but you bought something that looks better than Guggenslocker on a hotel register. Your mistress is an odd bit of humanity, a most whimsical bit, I must say. First, she's no and then she's yes. You're lucky, my coin, to have fallen into the custody of one who will not give you over to the mercy of strangers for the sake of a whim. You are now retired on a pension, well deserved after valiant service in the cause of a most capricious queen."

In an hour he was at home and relating to his mother the story of his wanderings, neglecting, for reasons best known to himself, the events which occurred after Denver had been left behind, except for casual allusion to "a party of foreigners." At one o'clock, faultlessly attired, he descended to the brougham, telling Mrs. Lorry that he had invited some strangers to see the city. On the way downtown he remembered that he was in business—the law business—and that it would be well to drop in and let his uncle know he was in the city. On second thought, however, he concluded it was too near two o'clock to waste any time on business, so the office did not know that he was in town until the next day, and then to no great extent.

For several hours he reveled in her society, sitting beside her in the roomy brougham, Aunt

Yvonne opposite, explaining to her the many places of interest as they passed. They entered the Capitol; they saw the White House, and, as they were driving back to the hotel, passed the President of the United States.

Miss Guggenslocker, when informed that the President's carriage was approaching, relaxed gracefully from the stately reserve that had been puzzling him, and revealed an eager curiosity. Her eyes fastened themselves upon the President, Lorry finding entertainment in the changes that came over her unconscious face. Instead of noting the veneration he had expected, he was astonished and somewhat provoked to see a slight curl of disgust at the corners of her mouth, a pronounced disappointment in her eyes. Her face expressed ridicule, pure and simple, and, he was shocked to observe, the exposure was unconscious, therefore sincere.

"You do not like our ruler?" he said, as the carriage whirled by. He was returning his hat to his head as he spoke.

"I cannot say. I do not know him," she replied, a tinge of sarcasm in her voice. "You Americans have one consolation; when you tire of a ruler you can put another in his place. Is it not wise to do so quite often?"

"I don't think wise is the word. Expedient is better. I am to infer that you have no politics."

"One house has ruled our land for centuries. Since I came to your land I have not once seen a

man wave his hat with mad adulation and cry from
his heart: 'Long live the President!' For centuries, in my country, every child has been born with
the words: 'Long live the Prince!' in his heart, and
he learns to say them next after the dear parental
words are mastered. 'Long live the Prince!' 'Long
live the Princess!' are tributes of love and honor
that greet our rulers from birth to death. We are
not fickle, and we have no politics."

"Do your rulers hear tin horns, brass bands, campaign yells, firecrackers and stump speeches every
four years? Do they know what it means to be
the voluntary choice of a whole nation? Do they
know what it is to rule because they have won the
right and not because they were born to it?
Has there ever been a homage-surfeited ruler in
your land who has known the joy that comes with
the knowledge that he has earned the right to be
cheered from one end of the country to the other?
Is there not a difference between your hereditary
'Long live the Prince' and our wild, enthusiastic,
spontaneous 'Hurrah for Cleveland!' Miss Guggenslocker? All men are equal at the beginning in our
land. The man who wins the highest gift that can
be bestowed by seventy millions of people is the man
who had brains and not title as a birthright." He
was a bit exasperated.

"There! I have displeased you again. You must
pardon my antiquated ideas. We, as true and loyal
subjects of a good sovereign, cannot forget that our

rulers are born, not made. Perhaps we are afflicted at times with brainless monarchs and are to be pitied. You are generous in your selection of potentates, be generous, then, with me, a benighted royalist, who craves leniency of one who may some day be President of the United States."

"Granted, without discussion. As possible, though not probable, President of the United States. I am magnanimous to an unfortunate who can never hope to be princess, no matter how well she might grace the gilded throne."

She greeted this glowing remark with a smile so intoxicating that he felt himself the most favored of men. He saw that smile in his mind's eye for months afterward, that maddening sparkle of joy, which flashed from her eyes to the very bottom of his heart, there to snuggle forever with Memory's most priceless treasures.

Their dinner was but one more phase of this fascinating dream. More than once he feared that he was about to awake to find bleak unhappiness where exquisite joy had reigned so gloriously. As it drew to an end a sense of depression came over him. An hour at most was all that he could have with her. Nine o'clock was drawing nigh with its regrets, its longings, its desolation. He determined to retain the pleasures of the present until, amid the clanging of bells and the roll of car wheels, the dismal future began. His intention to accompany them to the station was expressed as they were leaving the table.

She had begun to say good-bye to him when he interrupted, self-consciousness forcing the words hurriedly and disjointedly from his lips:

"You will let me go to the station with you. I shall—er—deem it a pleasure."

She raised her eyebrows slightly, but thanked him and said she would consider it an honor. His face grew hot and his heart cold with the fancy that there was in her eyes a gleam which said: "I pity you, poor fellow."

Notwithstanding his strange misgiving and the fact that his pride had sustained quite a perceptible shock, he drove with them to the station. They went to the sleeping car a few minutes before the time set for the train's departure, and stood at the bottom of the steps, uttering the good-byes, the God speeds and the sincere hope that they might meet again. Then came the sharp activity of the trainmen, the hurry of belated passengers. He glanced soberly at his watch.

"It is nine o'clock. Perhaps you would better get aboard," he said, and proceeded to assist Aunt Yvonne up the steps. She turned and pressed his hand gently before passing into the car.

"Adieu, good friend. You have made it so very pleasant for us," she said, earnestly.

The tall, soldierly old gentleman was waiting to assist his niece into the coach.

"Go first, Uncle Caspar," the girl made Lorry happy by saying. "I can easily come up unaided."

"Or I can assist her," Lorry hastened to add, giving her a grateful look which she could not misunderstand. The uncle shook hands warmly with the young man and passed up the steps. She was following when Lorry cried:

"Will you not allow me?"

She laughingly turned to him from the steps and stretched forth her hand.

"And now it is good-bye forever. I am so sorry that I have not seen more of you," she said. He took her hand and held it tightly for a moment.

"I shall never forget the past few days," he said, a thrill in his voice. "You have put something into my life that can never be taken away. You will forget me before you are out of Washington, but I—I shall always see you as you are now."

She drew her hand away gently, but did not take her eyes from his upturned face.

"You are mistaken. Why should I forget you— ever? Are you not the ideal American whose name I bought? I shall always remember you as I saw you—at Denver."

"Not as I have been since?" he cried.

"Have you changed since first I saw you?" she asked, quaintly.

"I have, indeed, for you saw me before I saw you. I am glad I have not changed for the worse in your eyes."

"As I first knew you with my eyes I will say that they are trustworthy," she said, tantalizingly.

"I do not mean that I have changed externally."

"In any other case my eyes would not serve," she cried, with mock disappointment. "Still," she added, sweepingly, "you are my ideal American. Good-bye! The man has called 'All aboard!'"

"Good-bye!" he cried, swinging up on the narrow step beside her. Again he clasped her hand, as she drew back in surprise. "You are going out of my land, but not out of my mind. If you wish your eyes to see the change in me, you have only to look at them in a mirror. *They* are the change—they themselves! Good-bye! I hope that I may see you again."

She hesitated an instant, her eyes wavering beneath his. The train was moving slowly now.

"I pray that we may meet," she said, softly, at last,—so softly that he barely heard the words. Had she uttered no sound he could have been sure of her response, for it was in her telltale eyes. His blood leaped madly. "You will be hurt if you wait till the train is running at full speed," she cried, suddenly returning to the abandoned merry mood. She pushed him gently in her excitement. "Don't you see how rapidly we are moving? Please go!" There was a terror in her eyes that pleased him.

"Good-bye, then," he cried.

"Adieu, my American," she cried, quickly.

As he swung out, ready to drop to the ground, she said, her eyes sparkling with something that suggested mischief, her face more bewitching than ever under the flicker of the great arc lights:

"You must come to Edelweiss to see me. I shall expect you!" He thought there was a challenge in the tones. Or was it mockery?

"I will, by heaven, I will!" he exclaimed.

A startled expression flashed across her face, and her lips parted as if in protestation. As she leaned forward, holding stoutly to the hand-rail, there was no smile on her countenance.

A white hand fluttered before his eyes, and she was gone. He stood, hat in hand, watching the two red lights at the end of the train until they were lost in the night.

V

SENTIMENTAL EXCHANGE

If Lorry slept that night he was not aware of it. The next morning, after he had breakfasted with his mother, he tried in vain to recall a minute of the time between midnight and eight a. m. in which he did not think of the young woman who had flown away with his tranquility. All night long he tossed and thought. He counted ten thousand black sheep jumping over a pasture fence, but, after the task was done and the sheep had scattered, he was as far from sleep as ever. Her face was everywhere. Her voice filled his ear with music never-ceasing, but it was not the lulling music that invites drowsiness. He heard the clock strike the hours from one to eight, when he arose, thoroughly disgusted with himself. Everything seemed to taste bitter or to look blue. That breakfast was a great strain on his natural politeness. He worshipped his mother, but in several instances that morning he caught himself just in time to prevent the utterance of some sharp rejoinder to her pleasant, motherly queries. Twice she was compelled to repeat questions, his mind being so far away that he heard nothing save words that another woman had uttered, say twenty-four hours before. His eyes were red, and there was a heavy droop to the lids; his tones were drawling and his voice strangely without warmth; his face was white and tired.

"You are not well, Grenfall," his mother said, peering anxiously into his eyes. "The trip has done you up. Now, you must take a good, long rest and recover from your vacation."

He smiled grimly.

"A man never needs a rest so much as he does at the end of his vacation, eh, mother? Well, work will be restful. I shall go to the office this morning and do three days' work before night. That will prove to you that I am perfectly well."

He made a pretense of reading the morning paper. There was nothing to interest him on those cold, commonplace pages, not one thing—but wait! A thought struck him suddenly, and for ten minutes he searched the columns assiduously, even nervously. Then he threw down the paper with a sigh of relief.

There was nothing to indicate that her train had been wrecked. She had undoubtedly reached New York in safety. He looked at his watch. She was probably enjoying her breakfast at that very moment. Perhaps she was thinking of him and—perhaps not. The memory of the last tender hand clasp and the soft glow in her eyes stood like a wall between the fear that she had forgotten and the certainty that she remembered. Had not this memory kept him awake? That and the final, mysterious emotion which had shown itself in her face as he had last looked upon it? A thousand times had he pondered over the startled look and the signs of agitation. Was it fear? Was it dismay? Was it renunciation? Whatever it was, it sorely disturbed him; it had partly undone the charm of the moment before—the charm that could not and would not be gainsaid.

True to his intention, he went to the office early, virtuously inclined to work. His uncle greeted him warmly and a long conference over business affairs followed. To Lorry's annoyance and discomfiture, he found himself frequently inattentive. Several important cases were pending, and in a day or two they were to go into court with a damage suit of more than ordinary consequence. Lorry, senior, could not repress his gratification over the return of his clever, active nephew at such an opportune time. He had felt himself unable to handle the case alone; the endurance of a young and vigorous mind was required for the coming battle in chancery.

They lunched together, the elder eager and confidential, the other respectful and—absent-minded. In the afternoon the junior went over the case, and renewed search for authorities and opinions, fully determined to be constant in spite of his inclination to be fickle. Late in the day he petulantly threw aside the books, curtly informed his astonished uncle that he was not feeling well, and left the office. Until dinner time he played billiards atrociously at his club; at dinner his mother sharply reproved him for flagrant inattentions; after dinner he smoked and wondered despondently. To-morrow she was to sail! If he could but see her once more!

At 7:30 his mother found him in the library, searching diligently through the volume of the encyclopedia that contained the G's. When she asked what he was looking for he laughed idiotically, and, in confusion, informed her that he was trying to find the name of the most important city in Indiana. She was glancing at the books in the case when she was startled by hearing him utter an exclamation and then leap to his feet.

"Half-past seven! I can make it!"

"What is the matter, Gren, dear?"

"Oh!" he ejaculated, bringing himself up with a start. "I forgot—er—yes, mother, I'll just have time to catch the train, you know. Will you kindly have Mary clean up this muss of books and so forth? I'm off, you see, to New York—for a day only, mother,—back to-morrow! Important business—just remembered it, you know,—ahem! Good-bye, mother! Good-bye!" He had kissed her and was in the hall before she fairly understood what he was talking about. Then she ran after him, gaining the hallway in time to see him pass

through the street door, his hat on the side of his
head, his overcoat fluttering furiously as he shoved
his arms into the sleeves. The door slammed, and
he was off to New York.

The train was ready to pull out when he reached
the station, and it was only by a hard run that he
caught the last platform, panting but happy. Just
twenty-four hours before she had left Washington,
and it was right here that she had smiled and said
she would expect him to come to Edelweiss. He had
had no time to secure a berth in the sleeper, but was
fortunately able to get one after taking the train.
Grenfall went to sleep, feeling both disappointed and
disgusted. Disappointed because of his submission
to sentiment; disgusted because of the man who occupied the next section. A man who is in love and
in doubt has no patience with the prosaic wretch who
can sleep so audibly.

After a hasty breakfast in New York he tele-
phoned to the steamship company's pier and asked
the time of sailing for the Kaiser Wilhelm. On being informed that the ship was to cast off at her
usual hour, he straightway called a cab and was
soon bowling along toward the busy waterway. Directly he sat bolt upright, rigid and startled to find
himself more awakened to the realization of his
absurd action. Again it entered his infatuated head
that he was performing the veriest schoolboy trick
in rushing to a steamship pier in the hope of catch-

ing a final, and at best, unsatisfactory glimpse of a young woman who had appealed to his sensitive admiration. A love-sick boy could be excused for such a display of imbecility, but a man—a man of the world! Never!

"The idea of chasing down to the water's edge to see that girl is enough to make you ashamed of yourself for life, Grenfall Lorry," he apostrophized. "It's worse than any love-sick fool ever dreamed of doing. I am blushing, I'll be bound. The idiocy, the rank idiocy of the thing! And suppose she should see me staring at her out there on the pier? What would she think of me? I'll not go another foot! I won't be a fool!"

He was excited and self-conscious and thoroughly ashamed of the trip into which his impetuous adoration had driven him. Just as he was tugging at the door in the effort to open it that he might order the driver to take him back to the hotel, a sly tempter whispered something in his ear; his fancy was caught, and he listened:

"Why not go down to the pier and look over the passenger list, just to see if she has been booked safely? That would be perfectly proper and sensible, and besides it will be a satisfaction to know that she gets off all right. Certainly! There's nothing foolish in that. . . . Especially as I am right on the way there. . . . And as I have come so far . . . there's no sense in going back without seeing whether she has secured passage. . . . I can find out in a minute and then go home. . . . There won't be anything wrong in that. And then I may have a glimpse of her before the ship leaves the pier. She must not see me, of course. Never! She'd laugh at me! How I'd hate to see her laughing at me!" Then, sinking back again with a smile of justification on his face, he muttered: "We won't turn back; we'll go right ahead. We'll be a kind of a fool, but not so foolish as to allow her to see us and recognize us as one."

Before long they arrived at the wharf, and he hurried to the office near by. The clerk permitted him to look over the list. First he ran through the first-class passengers, and was surprised to find that there was no such name as Guggenslocker in the list. Then he went over the second-class, but still no Guggenslocker.

"Hasn't Mr. Guggenslocker taken passage?" he demanded, unwilling to believe his eyes.

"Not on the Kaiser Wilhelm, sir."

"Then, by George, they'll miss the boat!" Lorry exclaimed. "Maybe they'll be here in a few minutes."

"They can't get anything but steerage now, sir. Everything else is gone."

"Are you sure they haven't taken passage?" asked the bewildered Lorry, weakly.

"You can see for yourself," answered the young man, curtly.

Lorry was again in a perspiration, this time the result of a vague, growing suspicion that had forced itself into his mind. He wandered aimlessly away, his brain a chaos of speculation. The suspicion to which he had given countenance grew, and as it enlarged he suffered torment untold. Gradually he came to the conclusion that she had fooled him, had lied to him. She did not intend to sail on the Wilhelm, at all. It was all very clear to him now, that strangeness in her manner, those odd occasional smiles. What was she? An adventuress! That sweet-faced girl a little ordinary coquette, a liar? He turned cold with the thought. Nor was she alone in her duplicity. Had not her uncle and aunt been as ready to deceive him? Were they trying to throw him off their track for some subtle purpose? Had they done something for which they were compelled to fly the country as quickly as possible? No! Not that! They certainly were not fleeing from justice. But why were they not on board the Kaiser Wilhelm?

Suddenly he started as if he had been struck, and an involuntary exclamation of pain and horror escaped his lips. Perhaps something unforeseen had happened—an accident—illness—even death!

The clanging of bells broke upon his ears and he knew that the great ship was about to depart. Me-

chanically, disconsolately, he walked out and paced
the broad, crowded wharf. All was excitement.
There was the rush of people, the shouts, the cheers,
the puffing of tugs, the churning of water, and the
Kaiser Wilhelm was off on its long voyage. Half-
heartedly, miserably, and in a dazed condition, he
found a place in the front row along the rail. There
were tears in his eyes, tears of anger, shame and
mortification. She had played with him!

Moodily he watched the crowd of voyagers hanging over the rails of the moving leviathan of the
deep. A faint smile of irony came to his lips. This
was the boat on which his heart was to have been
freighted from native shores. The craft was sailing, but it was not carrying the cargo that he had,
in very good faith, consigned to Graustark. His
heart was certainly not on board the Kaiser Wilhelm der Grosse.

Gloomily his disappointed eyes swept along the
rail of the big steamer, half interested in spite of
themselves. Twice they passed a certain point on
the forward deck, unconscious of a force that was
attracting them in that direction. The third time
he allowed them to settle for an instant on the group
of faces and figures and then stray off to other parts
of the ship. Some strange power drew them again
to the forward deck, and this time he was startled
into an intent stare. Could he believe those eyes?
Surely that was her figure at the rail—there between

the two young women who were waving their handkerchiefs so frantically. His heart began to jump up and down, wildly, doubting, impatiently. Why could not that face be turned toward the wharf as the others were? There was the blue coat but not the blue cap. A jaunty sailor hat sat where the never-to-be-forgotten cap had perched. The change was slight, but it was sufficient to throw him into the most feverish state of uncertainty. An insane desire to shout a command to this strange young woman came over him.

The ship was slowly opening a gap between herself and the wharf, and he knew that in a few moments recognition would be impossible. Just as he was losing hope and was ready to groan with despair, the face beneath the sailor hat was turned squarely in his direction. A glaze obscured his eyes, a numbness attacked his brain. It was Miss Guggenslocker!

Why was her name omitted from the passenger list? That question was the first to whirl through his addled brain. He forgot the questionings, forgot everything a moment later, for, to his amazement and delight and discomfiture, he saw that she was peering intently at him. A pair of big glasses was leveled at him for a second and then lowered. He plainly saw the smile on her face, and the fluttering cambric in her hand. She had seen him, after all,—had caught him in a silly exhibition of weakness. Her last impression of him, then, was to be one of which he could not feel proud. While his heart burned with shame, it could not have been suspected from the appearance of his face. His eyes were dancing, his mouth was wide open with joy, his lips were quivering with a suppressed shout, his cheeks were flushed and his whole aspect bespoke ecstacy. He waved his hat and then his handkerchief, obtaining from her vigorous and unrestrained signs of approbation. Her face was wreathed in smiles as she leaned far over the rail, the picture of animated pleasure.

Making sure that her uncle and aunt were not visible, he boldly placed his fingers to his lips and wafted a kiss out over the water!

"Now she'll crush me," he cried to himself, regretting the rash act and praying that she had not observed it.

Her handkerchief ceased fluttering in an instant, and, with sinking heart, he realized that she had observed. There was a moment of indecision on the part of the fair one going out to sea, and then the little finger tips of both hands went to her lips and his kiss came back to him!

The people near him were surprised to hear a wild yell from his lips and then to see him wave his hat so madly that there was some danger of it being knocked to pieces against the railing or upon the persons of those who stood too close to escape the

whirling consequences. So unexpected had been
her reception of what he considered a calamitous
indiscretion that he was to be pardoned for the ebul-
lition of relief and joy that followed. Had she
drawn a revolver and fired angrily at him he could
not have been more astounded. But to actually
throw a kiss to him—to meet his imprudence in the
same spirit that had inspired it! Too much to believe! In the midst of his elation, however, there
came a reminder that she did not expect to see him
again, that she was playing with him, that it was a
merry jest and not a heartache that filled her bosom
at the parting.

While he was still waving his handkerchief, de-
bating savagely and joyously the wisdom of the act,
she became a part of the distant color scheme; the
blue figure faded and blended into the general tone
and could no longer be distinguished. She was
gone, but she had tossed him a kiss from lips that
he should always see. As he turned away from
the water, he found himself wondering if there had
been tears in her eyes, but the probability was so
remote that he laughed foolishly and aloud. A
couple of girls heard the laugh and giggled in sympathy, but he turned a scowling face upon them and
disappeared in the throng.

Uppermost in his bewildered mind was the question: Why is she not in the passenger list? Act-
ing on a sudden impulse, he again sought out the

clerk in charge and made a most thorough inspection. There was no Guggenslocker among the names. As a last resort, he asked:

"They could not have sailed under an assumed name, could they?"

"I can't say as to that. Where are they going?"

"Graustark."

But the young man shook his head slowly, Lorry's shaking in unconscious accord.

"Are you sure that you saw the young lady on board?"

"Well, rather!" exclaimed Lorry, emphatically.

"I was going to say there are a lot of Italian and German singers on the ship, and you might have been mistaken. But since you are so positive, it seems very strange that your friends are not on the list."

So Lorry went away discouraged and with a vague fear that she might have been a prima donna whose real name was Guggenslocker but whose stage name was something more euphonious. He instantly put away the thought and the fear. She was certainly not an opera singer—impossible! He drove back to his hotel, and made preparations for his return to Washington. Glancing casually over the register, he came to the name that had been haunting him—Guggenslocker. There were the names, "Caspar Guggenslocker and four, Graustark. Without hesitation, he began to question the clerk.

"They sailed on the Kaiser Wilhelm to-day," said that worthy. "That's all I know about them. They came yesterday and left to-day."

Mr. Grenfall Lorry returned to Washington as in a dream—a fairy dream. The air of mystery that had grown from the first was now an impenetrable wall, the top of which his curiosity could not scale. Even his fancy, his imagination, served him not. There was but one point on which he was satisfied: he was in love. His own condition was no mystery.

Several weeks later he went to New York to question the Captain of the Wilhelm, hoping to clear away the clouds satisfactorily. To his amazement, the captain said there had been no Guggenslockers on board nor had there been persons answering the description, so far as he could tell.

Through the long hot summer he worked, and worried, and wondered. In the first, he did little that was satisfactory to himself or to his uncle; in the second, he did so much that he was advised by his physician to take a rest; in the last, he indulged himself so extensively that it had become unbearable. He must know all about her! But how?

The early months of autumn found him pale and tired and indifferent alike to work and play. He found no pleasure in the society that had known

him as a lion. Women bored him; men annoyed
him; the play suffocated him; the tiresome club was
ruining his temper; the whole world was going
wrong. The doctor told him he was approaching
nervous prostration; his mother's anxious eyes
could no longer be denied, so he realized grimly that
there was but one course left open to him. He suggested it to the doctor, to his mother and to his
uncle, and they agreed with him. It involved
Europe.

Having fully decided again to cross the sea, his
spirits revived. He became more cheerful, took an
interest in things that were going on, and, by the
time the Kaiser Wilhelm sailed in September, was
the picture of health and life.

He was off for Edelweiss—to the strange Miss
Guggenslocker who had thrown him a kiss from
the deck that sailing-day.

VI

GRAUSTARK

Two weeks later Grenfall Lorry was landed and enjoying the sensations, the delights of that wonderful world called by the name of Paris. The second day after his arrival he met a Harvard man of his time on the street. Harry Anguish had been a pseudo art student for two years. When at college he was a hail-fellow-well-met, a leader in athletics and in matters upon which faculties frown. He and Lorry were warm friends, although utterly unlike in temperament; to know either of these men was to like him; between the two one found all that was admirable and interesting in man. The faults and virtues of each were along such different lines that they balanced perfectly when lumped upon the scale of personal estimation. Their unexpected meeting in Paris was an exhilarating pleasure to both, and for the next week or so they were inseparable. Together they sipped absinthe at the cafés and strolled into the theatres, the opera, the dance halls and the homes of some of Anguish's friends, French and American.

Lorry did not speak to his friend of Graustark

until nearly two weeks after his arrival in the city. He had discussed with himself the advisability of revealing his plans to Anguish, fearing the latter's ridicule with all the cowardice of a man who knows that scoffing is, in a large measure, justifiable. Growing impatient to begin the search for the unheard-of country, its capital and at least one of its inhabitants, he was at last compelled to inform Anguish, to a certain extent, of his plans for the future. He began by telling him of his intention to take a run over toward Vienna, Buda-Pesth and some of the Eastern cities, expecting to be gone a couple of months. To his surprise and consternation, Anguish enthusiastically volunteered to take the trip with him, having the same project in view for nearly a year.

There was nothing left for Lorry but to make a clear breast of it, which he did shamefacedly, expecting the laughter and raillery of his light-hearted friend as payment for his confidence. Instead, however, Anguish, who possessed a lively and romantic nature, was charmed by the story and proclaimed it to be the most delightful adventure that had ever happened outside of a story-book.

"Tell me all about her," he urged, his eyes sparkling with boyish enthusiasm. And Lorry proceeded to give him a personal description of the mysterious beauty, introducing him, in the same manner, to the distinguished uncle and aunt, adding all those details which had confounded and upset him during his own investigations.

"This is rich!" exclaimed Anguish. "Beats any novel written, I declare. Begad, old man, I don't blame you for hunting down this wonderful bit of femininity. With a curiosity and an admiration that had been sharpened so keenly as yours, I'd go to the end of the world myself to have them satis-fied."

"I may be able to satisfy but one—curiosity. And maybe not that. But who knows of Graustark?"

"Don't give up before you've tried. If these people live in such a place, why, it is to be found, of course. Any railroad guide-book can locate this land of mystery. There are so many infernal little kingdoms and principalities over here that it would take a lifetime to get 'em all straightened out in one's head. To-morrow morning we will go to one of the big railway stations and make inquiries. We'll locate Graustark and then we'll go over and pluck the flower that grows there. All you need, my boy, is a manager. I'll do the arranging, and your little act will be the plucking."

"Easier said than done."

"She threw a kiss to you, didn't she?"

"Certainly, but, confound it, that was because she never expected to see me again."

"Same reason why you threw a kiss to her, I sup-pose?"

"I know why; I wasn't accountable."

"Well, if she did it any more wittingly than you did, she is accountable, and I'd hunt her up and demand an explanation."

Lorry laughed at his apparent fervor, but was glad that he had confided in his energetic countryman. Two heads were better than one, and he was forced to admit to himself that he rather liked the idea of company in the undertaking. Not that he expected to encounter any particular difficulty, but that he saw a strange loneliness ahead. Therefore he welcomed his friend's avowed intention to accompany him to Edelweiss as a relief instead of an annoyance. Until late in the night they discussed the coming trip, Anguish finally startling him with a question, just as he was stretching himself preparatory to the walk to his hotel.

"What are you going to do with her after you find her, Gren, old man?"

Grenfall's brow puckered and he brought himself up with a jerk, puzzled uncertainty expressing itself in his posture as well as in his face.

"I'll think about that after I have found her," he replied.

"Think you'll marry her?" persisted the other.

"How do I know?" exclaimed the woman hunter, savagely.

"Oh, of course you don't know—how could you?" apologized Anguish. "Maybe she won't have

GRENFALL LORRY MEETS "MISS GUGGENSLOCKER."

you—maybe she is married—all sorts of contingencies, you know. But, if you'll pardon my inquisitiveness, I'd like to ask why you are making this wild-goose chase half around the world? Just to have another look at her?"

"You asked me if I thought——" Here he stopped.

"I take it for granted, then, that you'd like to. Well, I'm glad I've got something definite on which to base operations. The one object of our endeavors, from now on, is to exchange Guggenslocker for Lorry—certainly no robbery. A charity, I should say. Good-night! See you in the morning."

The next morning the two friends took a cab to several railway stations and inquired about Graustark and Edelweiss.

"She was stringing you, old man," said Anguish, after they had turned away from the third station. He spoke commiseratingly, as he really felt sorry.

"No!" exclaimed Lorry. "She told me the truth. There is a Graustark, and she lives there. I'll stake my life on those eyes of hers."

"Are you sure she said it was in Europe?" asked Harry, looking up and down the street as if he would not have been surprised to see her in Paris. In his heart he believed that she and her precious relatives had deceived old Gren. Perhaps their home was in Paris, and nowhere else. But for

Lorry's positiveness he would have laughed heartily, at the other's simple credulity, or branded him a dolt, the victim of some merry actress's whim. Still, he was forced to admit, he was not in a position to see matters as they appeared, and was charitable enough to bide his time and to humor the faith that was leading them from place to place in the effort to find a land that they knew nothing about. Lorry seemed so sure, so positive, that he was loath to see his dream dispelled, his ideal shattered. There was certainly no Graustark; neither had the Guggenslockers sailed on the Wilhelm, all apparent evidence to the contrary notwithstanding. Lorry had been in a delirium and had imagined he saw her on the ship. If there, why was not her name in the list? But that problem tortured the sanguine searcher himself.

At last, in despair, after a fruitless search of two days, Lorry was willing to submit. With the perverseness common to half-defeated fighters, Anguish at once protested, forgetting that he had sought to dissuade his friend the day before.

"We'll go to the library of Paris and take a look through the books and maps," he said. "Or, better still, let us go to the post-office. There! Why have we not thought of that? What there is of a Graustark they'll know in the postal service."

Together they visited the chief post-office, where, after being directed to various deputies and clerks, they at length found the department in which the information was obtainable. Inside of five minutes they were in possession of facts that vindicated Miss Guggenslocker, lifted Lorry to the seventh heaven, and put Mr. Anguish into an agony of impatience. Graustark was a small principality away off to the east, and Edelweiss was a city of some seventy-five thousand inhabitants, according to the postal guide-book.

The Americans could learn no more there, so they went to Baedecker's office. Here they found a great map, and, after diligent and almost micro-scopic search, succeeded in discovering the princi-pality of Graustark. Then they looked at each other in dismay.

"It's a devil of a distance to that little red blot on the map," mused Lorry, pulling his nose reflectively. "What an outlandish place for a girl like her to live in," he continued. "And that sweet-faced old lady and noble Uncle Caspar! Ye gods! one would think barbarians existed there and not such people as the Guggenslockers, refined, cultivated, smart, rich. I'm more interested than ever in the place."

"So am I! I'm willing and ready to make the trip, old man, if you are still of a mind. It's a lark, and, besides, she may not be the only pretty and gracious girl there. We've had hard work to find it on the map, let's not stop till we see Edelweiss on the earth itself."

They made hasty preparations for the journey. Anguish, romantic and full of adventure, advised the purchase of a pair of pistols and a knife apiece, maintaining that, as they were going into an unknown and mountainous region, they should be prepared for brigands and other elements of danger. Lorry pooh-poohed the suggestion of brigands, but indulged his mood by buying some ugly-looking revolvers and inviting the prospect of something really thrilling in the way of an adventure. With their traps they were soon whirling through France, bound for a certain great city, on the road to Edelweiss, one filled with excitement, eagerness and boyish zeal, the other harassed by the sombre fear that a grave disappointment was in store for him. Through the glamour and the picturesqueness of the adventure there always crept the unconquerable feeling that he was on a fool's errand, that he was committing a deed so weak and brainless that it was sure to make him a veritable laughing-stock when it became known. After all, who was Miss Guggenslocker—brewer, baker, gardener or sausage-maker?

Traveling, of course, was pleasant at this time of the year, and the two Americans saw much that interested them along the way. Their French, especially Anguish's, was of great value to them, for they found occasion to use it at all times and in all places. Both spoke German fairly well, and took every opportunity to brush up in that language,

Lorry remembering that the Guggenslockers used many expressions that showed a preference for the Teutonic. The blithe Anguish, confident and in high feather, was heart and soul in the odd expedition of love, and talked incessantly of their reception by the far-away hostess, their impressions and the final result. His camera and sketching materials were packed away with his traps. It was his avowed intention to immortalize the trip by means of plate, palate and brush.

At the end of two days they reached a certain large city,—the first change, and then seven hundred miles to another. The distance from this point to the capital of Graustark was two hundred miles or more, chiefly through the mountainous lands. Somewhat elated by the cheerful information there received, they resumed the journey to Edelweiss, the city of vale, slope and park—summer, fall and winter. Changing cars at the end of the second day out, they sat back in the dusty seats of their carriage and sighed with relief.

"Unless we jump the track, this train will land us in the city we are looking for," said Anguish, stretching out his legs comfortably. "I'll admit it has been a tiresome journey, and I'll be glad when we can step into a decent hotel, have a rub, and feel like white men once more. I am beginning to feel like those dirty Slavs and Huns we saw 'way back there."

"There's one thing certain," said Lorry, looking out of the window. "The people and the habitations are different and the whole world seems changed since we left that station. Look at those fellows on horseback over there."

"What did I tell you about brigands and robbers!" exclaimed Anguish. "If those fellows are not bandits I'll lose faith in every novel I ever read."

The train rolled slowly past three mounted men whose steeds stood like statues upon a little knoll to the right of the track, men and beasts engaged in silent contemplation of the cars. The men, picturesquely attired and looking fierce, carrying long rifles, certainly bore an aspect that suggested the brigand. When the guard entered the carriage Anguish asked in German for some information concerning the riders.

"Dey're frontier police-guards," responded the man in English, smiling at their astonishment. Both Americans arose and shook hands with him.

"By George, it's good to hear a man talk white man's language," cried Anguish.

"How do you come to be holding a job on this road? An Englishman?" demanded Lorry. He looked anything but English.

"I'm not an Englishman," said the guard, flushing slightly. "My name's Sitzky, and I'm an American, sir."

"An American!" exclaimed Lorry. Sitzky grew loquacious.

"Sure! I used to be a sailor on a United States man-o'-war. A couple of years ago I got into trouble down at Constantinople and had to get out of the service. After dat I drifted up dis way and went to railroadin'." He hadn't exactly the manner of a man-o'-warsman.

"How long have you been on this road?" asked Grenfall.

" 'Bout a year, I should t'ink. Been on this branch only two months, dough."

"Are you pretty well acquainted in Edelweiss?"

"Oh, I run in dere every other day—in an' out ag'in. It's a fine place,—purtiest you ever saw in your life. The town runs right up the mountain to the tip-top where the monks are—clear up in d' clouds. Dey say it snows up dere almost all d' time."

Later on, from the loquacious guard, the two Americans learned quite a good bit about the country and city to which they were going. His knowledge was somewhat limited along certain lines, but quite clear as to others.

"Dis Graustark, 's fer as I know, is eeder a sort o' State or somet'ing belongin' to de Umpire, governed by its own rulers. Edelweiss is de capital, d' big guns of d' land lives dere. I've walked out and saw d' castle where d' Princess and d' royalty hangs out. D' people speak a language of deir own, and I can't get next to a t'ing dey say. But once in a while you find some guy dat talks French or German. Dey've got a little standin' army of two, t'ree t'ousand men an' dey've got de hottest uniforms you ever did see—red an' black an' gold. I don't see why d' United States can't get up somethin' foxy fer her soldiers to wear. Had a war over here not long ago, I understand—somethin' like ten or fifteen years ago. Dere's another little country up north of Graustark, and dey got in a wrangle 'bout somethin', and dey tell me in Edelweiss dat for 'bout a year dey fought like Sam Patch."

"Which was victorious?" demanded Lorry, deeply interested.

"I'm not sure. To hear d' Edelweiss people talk you'd t'ink dey licked d' daylights out of d' other slobs, but somehow I got next to d' fact dat dem other fellows captured de city an' went after a slashin' big war indemnity. I don't know much 'bout it, an' maybe I'm clear off, but I t'ink d' Graustark army was t'rashed. Everyt'ing is prosperous now, dough, an' you'd never know dere'd been a war. It's d' most peaceable town I ever saw."

"Did you ever hear of the Guggenslockers?" asked the irrepressible Anguish, and Lorry felt like kicking him.

"In Edelweiss? Never did. Friends of yours?"

"Acquaintances," interposed Lorry, hastily, frowning at Anguish.

"You won't have any trouble findin' 'em if dere anybody at all," said Sitzky, easily. "D' hotel people ought to be able to tell you all 'bout 'em."

"By the way, what is the best hotel there?" asked Anguish.

"Dere's the Burnowentz, one block north of d' depot." The travelers looked at one another and smiled, Sitzky observing the action. "Oh," he said, pleasantly, "dere's a swell joint uptown called d' Regengetz. It's too steep fer me, but maybe you gents can stand it. If you'll hang around d' depot fer a little while after we get in I'll steer you up 'dere."

"We'll make it worth your while, Sitzky," said Lorry.

"Never mind dat, now. Americans ought to stick together, no matter where dey are. We'll have a drink an' 'at's all, just to show we're fellow-countrymen."

"We'll have several drinks, and we'll eat and 'drink to-night at the 'swell joint' you talk about," said Anguish.

"We may drink dere, but I'll not eat dere. Dey wouldn't let a railroad guard inside de feedin' pen. Why, nothin' but royal guys eat dere when dey're 'downtown shoppin' or exposin' demselves to public gaze."

True to his word, when they reached Edelweiss late that afternoon Sitzky, their friend of uncertain origin, hurriedly finished his work and joined the travelers in the station. Lorry and Anguish were deeply interested in all they saw, the strange people, the queer buildings, the odd costumes and the air of antiquity that prevailed. Once upon the narrow, clean street they saw that Edelweiss was truly a city of the mountain-side. They had expected something wonderful, but were not prepared for what they found. The city actually ran up into the clouds. There was something so grand, so improbable, so unusual in the spectacle confronting them that they stared like children, aghast and stupefied. Each had the startling impression that a great human-dotted mountain was falling over upon his head; it was impossible to subdue the sensation of dizziness that the toppling town inspired.

"I know how you feel," observed Sitzky, laughing. "I was just d' same at first. To-morrow you walk a little way up d' side of d' mountain an' you'll see how much of d' city dere is on level ground down here. Dem buildings up dere ain't more'n one-fiftieth part of d' town. Dey're mostly summer homes. It gets hot as blazes down here in d' valley in d' middle of d' summer and d' rich ones move up d' mountain."

"How in thunder do people get up to those houses?" demanded Anguish.

"Mules," answered Sitzky, specifically. "Say! See dat little old feller comin' on horseback—wid 'd' white uniform? Well, dat's de chief of police, an' d' fellers behind him are police guards. 'At's old Dangloss himself. He's a peach, dey say."

A short, grizzly faced man, attired in a white uniform with red trimmings, followed by three men similarly garbed, rode by, going in the direction of the passenger station. Dangloss, as Sitzky had called him, was quite small in stature, rather stout, gray-bearded and eagle-nosed. His face was keen and red, and not at all the kind to invite familiarity. As he passed them the railroad guard of American citizenship touched his cap and the two travelers bowed, whereupon the chief of police gave them a most profound salutation, fairly sweeping his saddleskirts with his white cap.

"Polite old codger," observed Anguish.

"His company manners. Just let him get you in d' sweat-box, if you t'ink he's polite."

"Ever been there?"

"Well," a little confusedly, "I pasted a Graustark baggage-smasher down in d' yards two weeks ago, an' dey had me up. I proved d' feller insulted a lady, an' old Dangloss let me off, sayin' I'd ought to have a medal. Dese guys are great on gallantry when ladies is concerned. It it hadn't been fer dat, I'd be in d' lock-up now. An' say, you ought to see d' lock-up! It's a tower, wid dungeons an' all dat

sort of t'ing. A man couldn't no more get out 'n'
he could fly up to d' monastery. Dey're great on
law an' order here, too. D' Princess has issued
strictest kind of rules an' everybody has to live up
to 'em like as if dey was real Gospel. I t'ought I'd
put you next, gents, so's you wouldn't be doin' any-
t'ing crooked here."

"Thanks," said Lorry, dryly. "We shall try to
conduct ourselves discreetly in the city."

Probably a quarter mile farther down the narrow,
level street they came to the bazaars, the gaudy
stores, and then the hotel. It was truly a hostelry
to inspire respect and admiration in the mind of
such as Sitzky, for it was huge and well equipped
with the modern appointments. As soon as the two
Americans had been given their rooms, they sent for
their luggage. Then they went out to the broad
piazza, with its columns and marble balustrades, and
looked for Sitzky, remembering their invitation to
drink. The guard had refused to enter the hotel
with them, urging them to allow him to remain on
the piazza. He was not there when they returned,
but they soon saw him. On the sidewalk he was
arguing with a white-uniformed police guard, and
they realized that he had been ejected from sacred
precincts.

They promptly rescued him from the officer, who
bowed and strode away as soon as they interceded.

"Dese fellers are slick enough to see you are

swells and I'm not," said Sitzky, not a bit annoyed by his encounter. "I'll bet my head 'at inside ten minutes old Dangloss will know who you are, where you come from an' what you're doin' here."

"I'll bet fifty heads he won't find out what we're doing here," grinned Anguish, looking at Lorry. "Well, let's hunt up the thirst department."

They found the little apartment in which drinks were served at tables, and before they said good-bye to Sitzky in front of the hotel, a half hour later, that worthy was in exceedingly good humor and very much flushed in the face. He said he would be back in two days, and if they needed him for any purpose whatever, they could reach him by a note at the railway station.

"Funny how you run across an American in every nook and corner of the world," mused Lorry, as they watched the stocky ex-man-o'-warsman stroll off towards his hotel.

"If we can run across the Guggenslockers as easily, we'll be in luck. When shall we begin the hunt? To-night?"

"We can make a few inquiries concerning them. They certainly are people of importance here."

"I don't see the name on any of the brewery signs around town," observed Anguish, consolingly. "There's evidently no Guggenslocker here."

They strolled through the streets near the hotel until after six o'clock, wondering at the quaint archi-

tecture, the pretty gardens and the pastoral atmosphere that enveloped the city. Everybody was busy,
contented, quiet and happy. There was no bustle
or strife, no rush, no beggars. At six they saw
hundreds of workingmen on the streets, going to
their homes; shops were closed and there came to
their ears the distant boom of cannon, evidently
fired from different points of the compass and from
the highland as well as the lowland.

"The toy army is shooting off the good-night
guns," speculated Anguish. "I suppose everybody
goes to bed now."

"Or to dinner," substituted Lorry, and they returned to the Regengetz. The dining hall was
spacious and beautiful, a mixture of the Oriental
and the mediæval. It rapidly filled.

"Who the dickens can all these people be? They
look well," Anguish whispered, as if he feared their
nearest neighbors might understand his English.

"They are unquestionably of the class in which
we must expect to find the Guggenslockers."

Before the meal was over the two strangers saw
that they were attracting a great deal of attention
from the other guests of the house. The women,
as well as the men, were eyeing them and comment-
ing quite freely, it was easy to see. These two handsome, smooth-faced young Americans were as men
from another world, so utterly unlike their companions were they in personal appearance. They

were taller, broader and more powerfully built than the swarthy-faced men about them, and it was no wonder that the women allowed admiration to show in their eyes. Toward the end of the dinner several officers came in, and the Americans took particular pains to study them. They were cleanly-built fellows, about medium height, wiry and active. As a class, the men appeared to average five feet seven inches in height, some a little taller, some a little shorter. The two strangers were over six feet tall, broad-shouldered and athletic. They looked like giants among these Graustark men.

"They're not very big, but they look as if they'd be nasty in a scrap," observed Anguish, unconsciously throwing out his chest.

"Strong as wildcats, I'll wager. The women are perfect, though. Have you ever seen a smarter set of women, Harry?"

"Never, never! A paradise of pretty women. I believe I'll take out naturalization papers."

When the two strangers left the dining-room they were conscious that every eye in the place was upon them. They drew themselves to their full height and strode between the tables toward the door, feeling that as they were on exhibition they ought to appear to the best advantage. During the evening they heard frequent allusions to "The Americans," but could not understand what was said. The hotel men were more than obsequious; the military men and citizens were exceedingly deferential; the women who strolled on the piazza or in the great garden back of the hotel were discreetly curious.

"We seem to be the whole show here, Gren," said Anguish, as they sat down at one of the tables in the garden.

"I guess Americans are rare."

"I've found one fellow who can speak German and French, and not one, except our guard, who can talk English. That clerk talks German fairly well. I never heard such a language as these other people use. Say, old man, we'd better make inquiry about our friends to-night. That clerk probably won't be on duty to-morrow."

"We'll ask him before we go to bed," agreed Lorry, and upon leaving the brilliantly lighted garden they sought the landlord and asked if he could tell them where Caspar Guggenslocker lived. He looked politely incredulous and thoughtful, and then, with profound regret, assured them he had never heard the name. He said he had lived in Edelweiss all his life, and knew everybody of consequence in the town.

"Surely there must be such people here," cried Lorry, almost appealingly. He felt disheartened and cheated. Anguish was biting his lips.

"Oh, possibly among the poorer classes. If I were you, sir, I should call on Captain Dangloss, the Chief of Police. He knows every soul in Edelweiss. I am positive I have never heard the name. You will find the Captain at the Tower to-morrow morning."

The two Americans went to bed, one so dismayed by his disappointment that he could not sleep for hours.

VII

They slept rather late in the morning, first because they were very much fatigued after their long journey, second for the reason that they had been unable to woo slumber until long past midnight. Anguish stretched himself lazily in bed when he heard Lorry's voice from the adjoining room.

"I suppose we are to consult the police in order to get a clue to your charmer," he yawned. "Nice friends you pick up on railway journeys. I'd be ashamed."

"Well, Harry, I'll confess I'm disgusted. This has been the most idiotic thing I've ever done, and if you say the word we'll get out of here on the first train—freight or passenger. The Guggenslockers—pigs——" Mr. Lorry was savage.

"Not a bit of it, my boy, not a bit of it. We'll make a house-to-house canvass if the police fail us. Cheer up, cheer up!"

"You go to thunder!"

"Hold on! Don't talk like that, or I'll go back on you in a minute. I'm here because I choose to be, and I've more heart in the chase at this minute than you have. I've not lost hope. We'll find the Guggenslockers if we have to hire detectives to trace 'em from the United States to their very doorstep. We're going to see the police after breakfast."

After breakfast they did go to see the Baron Dangloss. After some inquiry they found the gloomy, foreboding prison, and Mr. Anguish boldly pounded on the huge gates. A little shutter flew open, and a man's face appeared. Evidently he asked what was wanted, but he might as well have demanded their lives, so far were they from understanding his query.

"Baron Dangloss?" asked Anguish, promptly. The man asked something else, but as the Americans shook their heads deprecatingly, he withdrew his face and presently swung open the gates. They entered and he closed the doors behind them, locking them in. Then he directed them across the court to an open door in the aged mass of gray stone. As they strode away from the guard Lorry created consternation by demanding:

"How are we to talk to the Chief if he doesn't understand us or we him? We should have brought an interpreter."

"I forgot about the confounded language. But if he's real he can talk Irish." Lorry told him he wasn't funny.

"Is this His Excellency, Baron Dangloss?" asked Anguish, stepping into a small room and stopping suddenly in the presence of the short, fierce man they had seen the day before. The American spoke in French.

"It is, gentlemen. Of what service can I be to Messieurs Lorry and Anguish?" responded the grim little Chief, politely rising from beside his desk. The visitors looked at one another in surprise.

"If he knows our names on such short notice, he'll certainly know the Guggenslockers," said Anguish to his friend in English.

"Ah, you are looking for some one named Guggenslocker?" asked the Chief, smiling broadly and speaking excellent English. "You must not be surprised, gentlemen. I speak many languages. I heard last night that you were inquiring about one Caspar Guggenslocker, and I have racked my brain, searched my books, questioned my officers, and I am sorry to inform you that there is no such person in Edelweiss."

"I was so well assured of it, Baron Dangloss," Lorry said.

"The name is totally unknown to me, sir. May I ask why you are searching for him?"

"Certainly. I met Mr. Guggenslocker, his wife and his niece last spring in the United States. They invited me to come and see them if I ever happened to be in this part of the world. As my friend and I were near here I undertook to avail myself of their invitation."

"And they said they lived in Edelweiss, Graustark?"

"They did, and I'll humbly confess I did not know much of the principality of Graustark."

"That is certainly complimentary, but, then, we are a little out of the beaten path, so it is pardonable. I was at first under the impression that you were American detectives with extradition papers for criminals bearing the name you mention."

"Oh!" gasped Anguish. "We couldn't find ourselves if we should be separated, Captain."

The grizzly-bearded Captain laughed lightly with them, and then asked Lorry if he would object to giving him the full story of his acquaintanceship with the alleged Graustarkians. The bewildered and disheartened American promptly told all he knew about them, omitting certain tender details, of course. As he proceeded the Chief grew more and more interested, and, when at last Lorry came to the description of the strange trio, he gave a sudden start, exposed a queer little smile for a second or so, and then was as sphynxlike as before. The ever-vigilant Anguish observed the involuntary start and smile, quick as the Chief had been to recover himself, and felt a thrill of triumph. To his anger and impatience, however, the old officer calmly shook his head at the end of the narrative, and announced that he was as much in the dark as ever.

"Well, we'll search awhile for ourselves," declared Anguish, stubbornly, not at all satisfied.

"You will be wasting your time," said the Chief, meaningly.

"We've plenty to waste," retorted the other.

After a few moments they departed, Baron Dangloss accompanying them to the gate and assuring them that he and his men always would be at their command. His nation admired the American people, he warmly declared.

"That old codger knows our people, and I'll bet a thousand on it," said Harry, angrily, when they had gone some little distance down the street. Then he told of the queer exposure Dangloss had unwittingly made. Lorry, more excited than he cared to show, agreed that there was something very suspicious about this new discovery.

They walked about the quaint town for an hour or two, examining the buildings, the people and the soldiery with deep interest. From the head of the main street,—Castle Avenue,—they could plainly see the royal palace, nearly a mile away. Its towers and turrets, gray and gaunt, ran up among the green tree-tops and were outlined plainly against the yellow hills. Countless houses studded the steep mountain slope, and many people were discerned walking and riding along the narrow, ledge-like streets which wound toward the summit, far up in the clouds. Clearly and distinctly could be seen the grim monastery, perched at the very pinnacle of the mountain, several miles away. Up there it looked bleak and cold and uninviting, in great contrast to the loveliness and warmth of the valley. Down below the grass was moist and soft, trees were approaching the stage where yellow and red tints mingle with the rich green, flowers were blooming, the land was redolent of the sweet fragrance of autumn, the atmosphere warm, clear and invigorating. It was paradise surmounted by desolation, drear and deadening.

Wherever the tall, distinguished Americans walked they formed the center of observation, and were the cause of comment that bore unmistakable signs of admiration. They bowed pleasantly to many of those who passed them, and received in return gracious and profound recognition. Military men saluted courteously; the women stared modestly and prettily—perhaps covetously; the merchants and citizens in general bowed and smiled a welcome that could not have been heartier. The strangers remarked the absence of vehicles on the main streets. There were pack mules and horses, human carriers—both male and female—but during the entire morning they saw not more than six or eight carriages. Vehicles were used solely by the quality and as a means of transportation for their persons only. Everybody, with the few exceptions mentioned, walked or rode horseback. The two friends were delighted with the place, and Anguish advocated a sojourn of several weeks, even though they did not find the Guggenslockers, his object being to secure photographs and sketches of the picturesque people and the strange scenery, and to idle away some hours upon the glittering boulevards. Grenfall, since he was in the project so deeply, was so nearly reconciled as to be exhilarated by the plan. They decided to visit the royal grounds in the afternoon, providing there was no prohibition, reserving a ride up the hill for the next day. A gendarme who spoke German fairly well told them that they could enter the palace park if they obtained a signed order from the chief steward, who might be found at any time in his home near the gates.

They were strolling leisurely toward the hotel, for the moment forgetting their quest in this strange, sunny land, when they espied a carriage, the most conspicuous of any they had seen. The white horses were gaily caparisoned, the driver and the footman beside him wore rich uniforms, the vehicle itself gleamed and glistened with gold and silver trimmings. A short distance behind rode two young soldiers, swords to their shoulders, scabbards clanking against their stirrups. Each was attired in the tight red trousers, shiny boots, close-fitting black coat with gilt trimmings, and the red cap which the Americans had noted before because of its brilliancy. People along the street were bowing deeply to the occupants, two ladies.

"Harry! Look!" exclaimed Lorry, clutching his friend's arm like a vise. "There in the carriage—on this side!" His voice was hoarse and trembling.

"Miss Gug—Guggenslocker?" cried Anguish.

"Yes! Yes!" They had stopped and Lorry was grasping a garden wall with one hand.

"Then it's funny nobody knows the name here. She seems to be someone of consequence. Good heaven, I don't blame you! She's the most beautiful——"

By this time the carriage was almost opposite and within forty feet of where they stood. The ladies, Miss Guggenslocker's companion as young and almost as beautiful as herself, had not observed the agitated two, but Lorry's face was beaming, his hat was off, and he was ready to spring to the carriage side at a moment's warning. Then the young girl at the side of the woman whose beauty had drawn a man half around the world saw the tall strangers, and called her companion's attention to them. Once more Grenfall Lorry and Miss Guggenslocker were looking into each other's eyes.

The lady started violently, her eyes grew wide, her lips parted, and her body was bent forward eagerly, a little gloved hand grasping the side of the open carriage. Her "ideal American" was bowing low, as was the tall fellow at his side. When he looked up again his eyes were glowing, his handsome face was flushed, and he saw her smile, blush furiously and incline her head gravely. The carriage had swept past, but she turned her head, and he detected an appealing glance in her eyes, a perplexed wrinkle across her brow, both of which were swept away an instant later by the most bewitching of smiles. Again her head was inclined, this time a trifle more energetically, and then the maddening face was turned from him. The equipage rolled onward, and there was no effort on her part to check its progress. The men were left standing alone and disappointed on the streets of Edelweiss, the object of their search slipping away as soon as she had been found. Her companion was amazed by the little scene, it was evident, judging by the eager look on her face as she turned with a question in her eyes.

"Turned down!" exclaimed the irrepressible Anguish, dolefully. "That's pretty shabby treatment, old man. But she's quite worth the journey."

"I'll not go back to America without her. Do you hear that, Harry Anguish?" He was excited and trembling. "But why didn't she stop?" he went on, dismally.

"Oh, you dear old fool!" said Anguish.

The two stood looking after the carriage until it turned into a side street, half way down the shady stretch toward the castle. They saw her companion glance back, but could not tell whether she did or not. Lorry looked uneasily at Anguish, and the latter read his thought.

"You are wondering about the Guggenslocker name, eh? I'll tell you what I've worked out during the past two minutes. Her name is no more Guggenslocker than mine is. She and the uncle used that name as a blind. Mark my words, she's quality over here; that's all there is about it. Now, we must find out just who she really is. Here comes a smart-looking soldier chap. Let's ask him, providing we can make him understand."

A young soldier approached, leisurely twirling a cane, for he was without his side arms. Anguish accosted him in French and then in German. He understood the latter and was very polite.

"Who was the young lady in the carriage that just passed?" asked Lorry, eagerly.

The face of the soldier flushed and then grew pale with anger.

"Hold on! I beg pardon, but we are strangers and don't quite understand your ways. I can't see anything improper in asking such a question," said Anguish, attempting to detain him. The young man struck his hand from his arm and his eyes fairly blazed.

"You must learn our ways. We never pass comment on a lady. If you do so in your land, I am sorry for your ladies. I refuse to be questioned by you. Stand aside, fellow!"

Anguish stood aside in astonishment, and they watched the wrathful gallant strut down the street, his back stiff as a board.

"Damned touchy!" growled Anguish.

"You remember what Sitzky said about their respect for the weaker sex. I guess we'd better keep off that track or we'll hatch up a duel or two. They seem to be fire-eaters. We must content ourselves with searching out her home and without assistance, too. I've cooled off a bit, Harry, and, now that I've seen her, I'm willing to go slowly and deliberately. Let's take our time and be perfectly cool. I am beginning to agree with your incog. proposition. It's all clearing up in my mind now. We'll go back to the hotel and get ready for the visit to the palace grounds."

"Don't you intend to hunt her up? 'Gad, I wouldn't miss a minute if I had a chance to be with a girl like that! And the other was no scarecrow. She is rather a beauty, too. Greatest town for pretty women I ever struck. Vienna is out of it entirely."

They strolled on to the hotel, discussing the encounter in all its exhilarating details. Scarcely had they seated themselves on the piazza, after partaking of a light luncheon, when a man came galloping up to the walk in front of the hotel. Throwing his bridle rein to a guard, he hastened to the piazza. His attire was that of a groom, and something about him reminded them of the footman who sat beside the driver of the carriage they had seen a short time before. He came straight to where the Americans sat smoking, and, bowing low, held before them an envelope. The address was "Grenfall Lorry, Esqre," but the man was in doubt as to which was he.

Lorry grasped the envelope, tore it open, and drew forth a daintily written note. It read:

"My Dear Mr. Lorry:

"I was very much surprised to see you this morning—I may add that I was delighted. If you will accompany this messenger when he calls for you at three o'clock to-morrow afternoon, he will conduct you to my home, where I shall truly be charmed to see you again. Will you bring your friend?
                    "SOPHIA GUGGENSLOCKER."

Lorry could have embraced the messenger. There was a suspicion of breathlessness in his voice when he tried to say calmly to Harry:

"An invitation for to-morrow."

"I knew it would come that way."

"Also wants you to come."

"Sha'n't I be in the way?"

"Not at all, my boy. I'll accept for you. After this fellow goes, I'll let you read the note. Wait until I write an answer."

Motioning for the man to remain, he hastened to his room, pulled out some stationery, and feverishly wrote:

"My Dear Miss Guggenslocker:

"I shall be delighted to accompany your messenger to-morrow, and my friend, Mr. Harry Anguish, will be with me. I have come half way across the continent to see you, and I shall be repaid if I am with you but for a moment. You will pardon me if I say that your name has caused me despair. No one seems to have heard it here, and I was beginning to lose hope. You may expect me at three, and I thank you for the pleasure you bestow.

"Yours sincerely,

"GRENFALL LORRY."

This note, part of which had been written with misgiving, he gave to the messenger, who rode away quickly.

"She didn't wait long to write to you, I notice. Is it possible she is suffering from the effects of those three days on the other side of the Atlantic? Come to think of it, she blushed when she saw you this morning," said Anguish. Lorry handed him her note, which he read, and then solemnly shook hands with its recipient. "Congratulations. I am a very far-sighted young man, having lived in Paris."

VIII

That afternoon they went to the palace grounds and inquired for the chief steward. After a few moments they were shown to his office in a small dwelling house just inside the gates. The steward was a red-faced little man, pleasant and accommodating. He could speak German—in fact, he was a German by birth—and they had no difficulty in presenting their request. Mr. Fraasch—Jacob Fraasch—was at first dubious, but their frank, eager faces soon gained for them his consent to see that part of the great park open to the public. Beyond certain lines they were not to trespass. Anguish asked how they could be expected to distinguish these lines, being unacquainted, and the steward grimly informed them that the members of the royal guard would establish the lines so plainly that it would be quite clear.

He then wrote for them a pass to the grounds of the royal palace of Graustark, affixing his seal. In giving this pass to them, he found occasion to say that the princess had instructed him to extend every courtesy possible to an American citizen. It was then that Anguish asked if he might be permitted to use his camera. There was an instant and emphatic refusal, and they were told that the pass would be rescinded if they did not leave the camera outside the gates. Reluctantly, Anguish deposited his luckless box in the steward's office, and they passed into the broad avenue which led toward the palace.

A guard, who served also as a guide, stepped to their side before they had taken ten paces. Where he came from they never knew, so instantaneous was his appearance. He remained with them during the two hours spent in the wonderful park.

The palace stood in the northwestern part of the grounds, possibly a half mile from the base of the mountain. Its front faced the mountain side. The visitors were not permitted to go closer than a quarter of a mile from the structure, but attained a position from which it could be seen in all its massive, ancient splendor. Anguish, who had studied churches and old structures, painted the castles on the Rhine, and was something of a connoisseur in architecture, was of the opinion that it had been standing for more than five hundred years. It was a vast, mediæval mass of stone, covered with moss and ivy, with towers, turrets and battlements. There had been a moat in bygone days, but modern ideas had transformed the waterway into solid, level ground. This they learned afterwards. Broad avenues approached in several directions, the castle

standing at the far side of a wide circle or parade
ground. The open space before the balconies was
fully three hundred yards square, and was paved.
From each side stretched the velvety green with its
fountains, its trees, its arbors, its flowers, its grottos
and its red-legged soldiers.

The park was probably a mile square, and was
surrounded by a high wall, on the top of which were
little guard-houses and several masked cannon. In
all their travels the Americans had not seen a more
delightful bit of artifice, and they wandered about
with a serene content that would have appealed to
anyone but their voiceless guide. He led them about
the place, allowing them to form their own conclusions, draw their own inferences and make their
own calculations. His only acts were to salute the
guards who passed and to present arms when he
had conducted his charges to the edge of forbidden
territory. When they had completed their tour of
inspection their guide rapidly led the way to the
wall that encircled the grounds, reaching it at a
point not far from the castle itself. Here was situated another large gate, through which they did
not pass. Instead, they ascended some steps and
came out upon the high wall. The top of this wall
was several feet wide, and walking was compara-
tively safe. They soon understood the guide's de-
sign. The object was to walk along this wall until
they reached the main gate. Why this peculiar

course was to be taken they could not imagine at first. Anguish's fertile brain came to the rescue. He saw a number of women in a distant part of the grounds, and, remembering their guide's haste in conducting them to the wall, rightly conjectured that it was against custom for visitors to meet and gaze upon members of the royal household. The men and women, none of whom could be plainly distinguished from the far-away wall, were undoubtedly a part of the castle's family, and were not to be subjected to the curious gaze of sightseers. Perhaps Her Royal Highness, the Princess of Graustark, was among them.

They reached the main gate and descended, Anguish securing his camera, after which they thanked the steward and turned to fee the guide. But he had disappeared as if the ground had swallowed him.

"Well, it's a fair Versailles," observed Anguish, as they walked down the street, glancing back at the frowning wall.

"It all goes to make me wonder why in the name of heaven we have never heard of this land of Graustark," said Lorry, still thinking of the castle's grandeur.

"My boy, there are lots of things we don't know. We're too busy. Don't you remember that but one-half the world knows how the other half lives? I'll wager there are not twenty-five people in the United

States who know there is such a country as Graustark."

"I don't believe that a single soul over there has heard of the place," vouchsafed Lorry, very truthfully.

"I'll accept the amendment," said Anguish. Then he proceeded to take a snap-shot of the castle from the middle of the street. He also secured a number of views of the mountain side, of some odd little dwelling houses, and two or three interesting exposures of red-robed children. Everybody, from the children up, wore loose robes, some red, some black, some blue, but all in solid colors. Beneath these robes were baggy trousers and blouses among the men, short skirts among the women. All wore low boots and a sort of turban. These costumes, of course, were confined to the native civilians. At the hotel the garb of the aristocrats was vastly different. The women were gowned after the latest Viennese patterns, and the men, except those of the army, wore clothes almost as smart as those which covered the Americans. Miss Guggenslocker—or whatever her name might be—and her carriage companion were as exquisitely gowned as any women to be seen on the boulevards or in Hyde Park of an afternoon.

It was late in the afternoon when they returned to the hotel. After dinner, during which they were again objects of interest, they strolled off towards the castle, smoking their cigars and enjoying the glorious air. Being a stranger in a strange land, Lorry acted on the romantic painter's advice and also stuck a revolver in his pocket. He laughed at the suggestion that there might be use for the weapon in such a quiet, model, well-regulated town, but Anguish insisted:

"I've seen a lot of these fellows around town who look like genuine brigands and cut-throats, and I think it just as well that we be prepared," asserted he, positively, and his friend gratified what he called a whim.

At ten o'clock the slender moon dropped behind the mountain, and the valley, which had been touched with its tender light, gradually took on the sombreness and stillness of a star-lit night. The town slumbered at eleven, and there were few lights to be seen in the streets or in the houses. Here and there strolled the white-uniformed police guards; occasionally soldiers hurried barracks-ward; now and then belated citizens moved through the dense shadows on the sidewalks, but the Americans saw still life in its reality. Returning from their stroll beside the castle-walls, far to the west of where they had entered the grounds that afternoon, they paused in the middle of Castle Avenue, near the main gate, and looked down the dark, deserted street. Far away could be seen the faint glare from their hotel; one or two street-lamps burned in the

business part of the city; aside from these evidences
of life there was nothing but darkness, silence,
peacefulness about them everywhere.

"Think of Paris or New York at eleven o'clock,"
said Lorry, a trifle awed by the solitude of the sleeping city.

"It's as dead as a piece of prairie-land," said his
friend. " 'Gad, it makes me sleepy to look down
that street. It's a mile to the hotel, too, Lorry.
We'd better move along."

"Let's lie down near the hedge, smoke another
cigar and wait till midnight. It is too glorious a
night to be lost in sleep," urged Lorry, whose heart
was light over the joys of the day to come. "I can
dream just as well here, looking at the dark old
castle with its one little tower-light, as I could if I
tried to sleep in a hard bed down at the hotel."

Anguish, who was more or less of a dreamer himself, consented, and, after lighting fresh cigars, they
threw themselves on the soft, dry grass near the tall
hedge that fenced the avenue as it neared the castle
grounds. For half an hour they talked by fits and
starts; long silences were common, broken only by
brief phrases which seemed so to disturb the one to
whom they were addressed that he answered gruffly
and not at all politely. Their cigars, burnt to mere
stubs, were thrown away, and still the waking
dreamers stretched themselves in the almost impenetrable shade of the hedge, one thinking of the face

he had seen, the other picturing in his artist eye the painting he had vowed to create from the moon-lit castle of an hour ago.

"Some one coming," murmured the painter, half rising to his elbow attentively.

"Soldiers," said the other briefly. "They'll not disturb us."

"They'll not even see us, I should say. It's as dark as Egypt under this hedge. They'll pass if we keep quiet."

The figures of two men could be seen approaching from the city, dim and ghostly in the semi-blackness of the night. Like two thieves, the Americans waited for them to pass. To their exceeding discomfiture, however, the pedestrians halted directly in front of their resting place and seated themselves leisurely upon a broad, flat stone at the roadside. It was too dark to see if they were soldiers, notwithstanding the fact that they were less than fifteen feet away.

"He should be here at twelve," said one of the newcomers in a low voice and in fairly good English. The other merely grunted. There was a silence of some duration, broken by the first speaker.

"If this job fails and you are caught it will mean years of servitude."

"But in that case we are to have ten thousand gavvos apiece for each year we lie in prison. It's fair pay—not only for our failure, but for our silence," said the other, whose English was more difficult to understand.

Anguish's fingers gripped Lorry's leg, but there was no sound from either of the thoroughly aroused dreamers. "A plot, as I live," thought each, with a thrill.

"We must be careful to speak only in English. There are not twenty people in Edelweiss who understand it, but the night has ears. It is the only safe tongue. Geddos speaks it well. He should be here." It was the first speaker who uttered these words, little knowing that he had listeners other than the man to whom he spoke.

A dark figure shot across the roadway, and, almost before the Americans were aware of it, the party numbered three.

"Ah, Geddos, you are punctual."

"I' have found it ever a virtue," responded the newcomer.

"Have you secured your men?"

"I have your——"

"Sh! Call me Michael, on your life! They are ready and willing to undertake the venture?"

"Yes, but they do not understand the true conditions. I have told them that we are to rob the castle and carry the booty to Ganlook before morning."

"They do not know the real object of the raid,

then. That is as I desired. Are they trusty and experienced men?"

"The best—or the worst—that I could find in Vienna. Not one understands our language, and they are so ignorant of our town that they are entirely dependent on me. They know nothing whatever of the Princess, Michael, and will do only as they are told, realizing that if caught they will be guillotined. I have told them it is the royal palace we are to rifle. Ostrom, here, and I, are the only ones, except yourself and the men who will aid us inside the castle, who know the truth, sir."

"It cannot fail, unless those inside prove false or unworthy," said the hoarse-voiced Ostrom. Anguish's fingers were gripping Lorry's leg so fiercely that the blood was ready to burst out, but he did not feel the pain. Here, then, was some gigantic plot in which the person of the Princess herself was to be considered. Was it an assassination?

"You have five of these Viennese?"

"Yes. Two to stand beneath the window to receive the booty as we lower it to the ground, one to stand guard at the west gate and two to attend the carriage and horses in the ravine beyond the castle."

"When did these men arrive?"

"This morning. I kept them in my sister's home until an hour ago. They are now in the ravine, awaiting Ostrom and myself. Are you sure,

Michael, that the guards and the cook have been made to understand every detail? The faintest slip will mean ruin."

"They are to be trusted fully. Their pay is to be high enough to make it an object to be infallible. The guard, Dushan, will leave the gate unwatched, and you will chloroform him—with his consent, of course. You will enter, as I have explained before, crawl along the dark shadow of the wall until you reach the arbor that leads to the kitchen and scullery. Here another guard, Rabbo—known to Ostrom as a comrade in Her Royal Highness's service not more than a year ago—will be encountered. He will be bound and gagged without the least noise or struggle. Just as the clock strikes two the cook will walk past the scullery window, in the basement, thrice, carrying a lighted candle. You will see this light through the window, and will know that all is well inside the castle. Ostrom, you will then lead the two Viennese to a place directly beneath the third window in the Princess's sleeping apartment. There are several clumps of shrubbery there, and under these they will hide, protected from the gaze of any watchman who is not with us. You and Geddos will be admitted to the scullery by the cook, who will conduct you to the hall leading to Her Highness's bedroom. The man who guards her door is called Dannox. He will not be at his post, but will accompany you when you leave the castle.

You will understand how carefully you must enter her room and how deeply she must be chloroformed. In the adjoining room her lady-in-waiting, the Countess Dagmar, sleeps. If her door is ajar, you are to creep in and chloroform her, leaving her undisturbed. Then the Princess is to be wrapped in the cloth you take with you and lowered from the window to the men below. They are to remain in hiding until you have left the castle and have reached their side. It will not be difficult, if caution is observed, for you to get outside of the wall and to the carriage in the ravine. I have given you this plan of action before, I know, but I desire to impress it firmly upon your minds. There must not be the slightest deviation. The precision of clockwork is necessary."

The man named Michael hissed the foregoing into the ears of his companions, the palsied Americans hearing every word distinctly. They scarcely breathed, so tremendous was the restraint imposed upon their nerves. A crime so huge, so daring, as the abduction of a Princess, the actual invasion of a castle to commit the theft of a human being just as an ordinary burglar would steal in and make way with the contents of a silver chest, was beyond their power of comprehension.

"We understand fully how it is to be done, and we shall get her to Ganlook on time," said Geddos, confidently.

"Not a hair of her head must be harmed," cautioned the arch-conspirator. "In four days I shall meet you at Ganlook. You will keep her in close confinement until you hear from me. Have you the guards' uniforms that you are to wear to-night?"

"They are with the carriage in the ravine; Ostrom and I will don them before going to the castle. In case we are seen, they will throw observers off the track long enough for us to secure a good start in our flight."

"Remember, there is to be no failure. This may mean death to you; certainly a long prison term if you are apprehended. I know it is a daring deed, but it is just the kind that succeeds. Who would dream that mortal man could find the courage to steal a Princess of the realm from her bed and spirit her away from under the very noses of her vaunted guardsmen? It is the bold, the impossible plan that wins."

"We cannot fail if your men on the inside do their work well," said Geddos, repeating what Ostrom had said. "All depends on their faithfulness."

"They will not be found wanting. Your cutthroats must be sent on to Caias with the empty carriage after you have reached Ganlook in safety. You will need them no more. Ostrom will pay them, and they are to leave the country as quickly

as possible. At Caias they will be able to join a
pack-train that will carry them to the Great Northern Railroad. From there they will have no trouble
in reaching Vienna. You will explain to them,
Geddos. All we need them for, as you know, is to
prove by their mere presence in case of capture that
the attempt was no more than a case of burglary
conceived by a band of Viennese robbers. There
will be no danger of capture if you once get her
outside the walls. You can be half way to Ganlook
before she is missed from the castle. Nor can she
be found at Ganlook if you follow the instructions
I gave last night. It is now nearly one o'clock, and
in half an hour the night will be as dark as Erebus.
Go, men; you have no more time to lose, for this
must be accomplished slowly, carefully, deliberately.
There must be no haste until you are ready for the
race to Ganlook. Go, but for God's sake, do not
harm her! *And do not fail!*"

"Failure means more to us than to you, Michael,"
half whispered the hoarse Ostrom.

"Failure means everything to me! I must have
her!"

Already the two hirelings were moving off toward the road that ran west of the castle grounds.
Michael watched them for a moment and then
started swiftly in the direction of the city. The
watchers had not been able to distinguish the faces
of the conspirators, but they could never forget the

calm, cold voice of Michael, with its quaint, jerky
English.

"What shall we do?" whispered Anguish, when
the men were out of hearing.

"God knows!" answered Lorry. "This is the
most damnable thing I ever heard of. Are we
dreaming? Did we really see and hear those men?"
He had risen to his feet, his companion sitting
weakly before him.

"There's no question about it! It's a case of abduction, and we have it in our power to spoil the
whole job. By Gad, but this is luck, Gren!" Anguish was quivering with excitement as he rose to
his feet. "Shall we notify old Dangloss or alarm
the steward? There's no time to be lost if we want
to trap these fellows. The chief devil is bound to
escape, for we can't get him and the others, too,
and they won't peach on him. Come, we must be
lively! What are you standing there for? Damn
it, the trap must be set!"

"Wait! Why not do the whole job ourselves?"

"How—what do you mean?"

"Why should we alarm anybody? We know the
plans as well as these scoundrels themselves. Why
not follow them right into the castle, capture them
red-handed, and then do the alarming? I'm in for
saving the Princess of Graustark with our own
hands and right under the noses of her vaunted
guardsmen, as Michael says." Lorry was thrilled

by the spirit of adventure. His hand gripped his friend's arm and his face was close to his ear. "It is the grandest opportunity two human beings ever had to distinguish themselves!"

"Great heaven, man! We can't do such a thing!" gasped Anguish.

"It's the easiest thing in the world. Besides, if we fail, we have nothing to lose. If we succeed, see what we've done! Don't hesitate, old man! Come on! Come on! We'll take 'em ourselves, as sure as fate. Have you no nerve? What kind of an American are you? This chance won't come in ten lifetimes! Good God, man, are we not equal to those two scoundrels?"

"Two? There are at least ten of them!"

"You fool! The three guards are disposed of in advance, two of the Viennese are left with the horses, two are chucked off under the Princess's window, and one stands at the gate. We can slug the man at the gate, the fellows under the window are harmless, and that leaves but our two friends and the cook. We have every advantage in the world. Can't you see?"

"You are right! Come on! I'll risk it with you. We will save the Princess of Graustark!"

"Don't you see it will be just as easy for us to enter the castle as for these robbers? The way will be clear, and will be kept clear. Jove, man, we need not be more than thirty seconds behind them. Is your pistol all right?"

By this time the two men were speeding along the grassy stretch toward the road that ran beside the wall. They looked at their pistols, and placed them carefully in outside coat pockets.

"We must throw away these heavy canes," whispered the painter to his friend, who was a pace or so ahead.

"Keep it! We'll need one of them to crack that fellow's head at the gate. 'Gad, it's dark along here!"

"How the devil are we to know where to go?"

"We'll stop when we come to the gate where we climbed up the wall to-day. That is the only entrance I saw along the west wall, and it is near the castle. Just as soon as the gang enters that gate we'll crawl up and get rid of the fellow who stands watch."

It was so dark that they could barely see the roadway, and they found it necessary to cease talking as they slunk along beside the wall. Occasionally they paused to listen, fearing that they might draw too close upon the men who had gone before. At last they came to a big gate and halted.

"Is this the gate?" whispered Anguish.

"Sh! Yes, I'm quite sure. We are undoubtedly near the castle, judging by the distance we have

come. Let us cross the road and lie directly opposite. Be careful!"

Like panthers, they stole across the road and
down a short, grassy embankment. At Anguish's
suggestion, Lorry wrapped his handkerchief tightly
about the heavy end of his cane, preparing in that
way to deaden the sound of the blow that was to
fall upon the Vienna man's head. Then they threw
aside their hats, buttoned their coats tightly, and
sank down to wait, with bounding hearts and tingling nerves, the arrival of the abductors, mutely
praying that they were at the right gate.

IX

During the half hour spent in the grassy ditch
or gutter, they spoke not more than half a dozen
times, and in the faintest of whispers. They could
hear the guard pacing the driveway inside the pon-
derous gate, but aside from his footsteps no sound
was distinguishable. A sense of oppression came
over the two watchers as the minutes grew longer
and more deathlike in their stillness. Each found
himself wondering why the leaves did not stir in
the trees, why there were no nightbirds, no crickets,
no croaking frogs, no sign of life save that
steady, clocklike tread inside the wall. So dark was
it that the wall itself was but a deeper shadow
against the almost opaque blackness beyond. No
night, it seemed to them, had ever been so dark, so
still. After the oppression came the strange feeling
of dread, the result of an enforced contemplation
of the affair in which they were to take a hand,
ignorant of everything except the general plan.

They knew nothing of the surroundings. If they
failed, there was the danger of being shot by the
guards before an explanation could be made. If they

141

succeeded, it must be through sheer good fortune and
not through prowess of mind or muscle. Once inside the castle, how could they hope to follow the
abductors at a safe distance and still avoid the danger of being lost or running into trusty guards?
The longer they lay there the more hazardous became the part they had so recklessly ventured to
play. In the heart of each there surged a growing
desire to abandon the plan, yet neither could bring
himself to the point of proposing the retreat from
the inspired undertaking. Both knew the sensible,
judicious act would be to alarm the guards and thus
avoid all possible chance of a fiasco. With misgiv-
ings and doubts in their hearts the two self-ap-
pointed guardians of the Princess lay there upon
the grass, afraid to give up the project, yet fearing
the outcome.

"The dickens will be to pay, Lorry, if they dis-
pose of this guard *on the inside* and lock the gate.
Then how are we to follow?" whispered Anguish.

Lorry was thoughtful for a while. He felt the
chill of discouragement in his heart.

"In that case we must lie outside and wait till
they come out with the Princess. Then make a
sudden assault and rescue her. In the darkness we
can make them think there are a dozen rescuers," he
whispered at length. After a while Anguish asked
another appalling question, the outgrowth of brain-
racking study:

"Suppose these fellows who will be in guards' uniform, should turn about and capture us. What then? We are strangers, and our story would not be believed. They could slip away in the excitement and leave us in a very awkward position."

"Harry, if we are going to hatch up all sorts of possibilities, let's give up the thing right now. I have thought of a thousand contingencies, and I realize how desperate the job is to be. We must either cast discretion to the winds or we must retreat. Which shall we do?"

"Cast aside discretion and hang our fears," said the other, once more inspired. "We'll take chances and hope for the best. If we see we are going to fail we can then call for the guards. The grounds are doubtless full of soldiers. The only part I'm worried about is the groping through that strange, dark castle."

"We must do some calculating and we must stick close together. By watching where they station the two Viennese we can figure about what direction we must take to get to the princess's room. Sh! Isn't that some one approaching?"

They strained their ears for a moment and then involuntarily, spasmodically shook hands, each heaving the deep breath of excitement. The stealthy rustle of moving bodies was heard, faint, but positive. It was a moment of suspense that would have strained the nerve of a stone image. Where were the abductors? On which side of the road and from what direction did they come? Oh, for the eyes of a cat?

There was a slight shuffling of feet near the gate, a suppressed "Sh!" and then deathly silence. The gate opened, a faint creaking attesting the fact, followed by the heavy breathing of men, the noise of subdued activity, the scent of chloroform. Some whispering, and then the creaking of the gate.

"They've gone," whispered Anguish. Lorry's form arose to a crouching posture and a moment later he was crossing the road with the tread of a cat, his cane gripped firmly in his hand. Anguish followed with drawn revolver. So still was their approach that they were upon the figure of a man before they were aware of the fact. In the darkness the foremost American saw the outline of a human figure bending over a long object on the ground. He could smell chloroform strongly, and grasped the situation. The Viennese was administering the drug, his companions having left that duty for him to perform. No doubt the treacherous guardsman was lying calmly on his back, bound and gagged, welcoming unconsciousness with a smile of security.

As soon as Lorry gained his bearings fully he prepared to fell the wretch who was to stand watch. Anguish heard his friend's figure suddenly shoot to an erect position. A whirring sound as of disturbed air and then a dull thud. Something rolled over on

the ground, and all was still. He was at Lorry's
side in an instant.

"I hope I haven't killed him," whispered Lorry.
"Quick! Here is his bottle of ether. Hold it beneath his nose. I am going to pile the body of this
guard crosswise on top of him. He will not be
able to arise if he should recover consciousness."

All this was done in a moment's time, and the
two trackers were headed for the entrance. The
gate was ajar two or three feet. With turbulent
hearts, they stole through.

"Keep along the wall," whispered Lorry, "and
trust to luck. The castle is to the left."

Without hesitation they crept over the noiseless
grass, close beside the wall. Directly they heard
sounds near at hand. The abductors were binding
and chloroforming the guard at the arbor. After
waiting for some moments they heard the party
glide away in the darkness, and followed. The
body of the guard was lying just outside the mouth
of the arbor, and the odor of chloroform was almost
overpowering. Once inside the long arbor, the
Americans moved slowly and with greater caution.
There was a dim light in a basement window ahead.
Toward the front of the castle and in the second
story a faint glow came from another window.
They guessed it to be from the Princess's room or
from that of the Countess.

At last they saw four figures steal past the dim

basement light. One of them halted near the window, and three crept away in the darkness. Presently one of them returned, and all activity was at an end for the time being. How near it was to two o'clock the watchers could not tell. They only knew that they were within twenty-five feet of Geddos and Ostrom, and that they would not have long to wait.

Soon a bright little blaze of light crossed the basement opening. Then it returned, crossing a second time, and a third. All was still again. The soft shuffle of a foot, the rustle of arbor vines, and the form of a man crawled up to the window. With inconceivable stealth and carefulness it glided through the aperture, followed by a companion.

Lorry and Anguish were at the opening a second or two later, lying flat on their stomachs and listening for sounds from within. The dim light was still there, the window was open, and there was a sound of whispering. Lorry raised his head and peered through, taking calculations while the light made it possible. He saw an open door on the opposite side of the low room, with steps beyond, leading upward. Between the window and the door there were no obstacles. Up those steps he saw three men creep, the leader carrying the dim light. The door was left open, doubtless to afford unimpeded exit from the building in case of emergency. Harry Anguish touched Lorry's arm.

"I took the two pistols from that Vienna man out there. We may need them. Here is one for yourself. Go first, Lorry," he whispered.

Lorry stuck the revolver in his coat pocket and gently slid through the window to the floor below. His friend followed, and they paused to listen. Taking Anguish by the hand, the other led the way straight to the spot where he remembered seeing the door.

Boldly the two men began the breathless ascent of the stone steps. The top was reached, and far ahead, down a narrow hall, they saw the three men and the dim light moving. Two of them wore uniforms of guards. Keeping close to the wall, their followers crept after them. Up another flight of steps they went, and then through a spacious hall. The Americans had no time and no desire to inspect their surroundings. The wide doors at the far side of the room opened softly, and here the trio paused. Down a great marble hallway a dim red light shed its soft glow. It came from the lamp at the foot of the broad staircase.

The cook pointed to the steps, and then gave his thumb a jerk toward the left. Without the least sign of fear, Geddos and Ostrom glided into the hall and made for the staircase. The watchers could not but feel a thrill of admiration for these daring wretches. But now a new danger confronted them. The cook remained standing in the doorway, watch-

ing his fellows in crime! How were they to pass
him?

There was no time to be lost. The abductors were
creeping up the steps already, and the cook must be
disposed of. He had blown out the light which he
carried, and was now a very dim shadow. Lorry
glided forward and in an instant stood before the
amazed fellow, jamming a pistol into his face.

"A sound and you die!" he hissed.

"Don't move!" came another whisper, and a second revolver touched his ear. The cook, perhaps,
did not know their language, but he certainly understood its meaning. He trembled, and would have
fallen to the floor had not the strong hand of Lorry
pinned him to the wall. The hand was on his throat,
too.

"Chloroform him, Harry, and don't let him make
a sound!" whispered the owner of the hand. Anguish's twitching fingers succeeded those of his
friend on the cook's throat, his pistol was returned
to his pocket, and the little bottle came again into
use.

"I'll go ahead. Follow me as soon as you have
finished this fellow. Be careful, and turn to the left
when you come to the top."

Lorry was off across the marble floor, headed for
the stairway, and Anguish was left in charge of the
cook, of whom he was to make short work. Now
came the desperate, uncertain part of the transac-

tion. Suppose he were to meet the two conspirators at the head of the stairs, or in the hall, or that the other traitor, Dannox, should appear to frustrate all. It was the most trying moment in the whole life of the reckless Lorry.

When near the top of the steps he hugged the light balustrade and cautiously peered ahead. He found himself looking down a long hall, at the far end of which, to his right, a dim light was burning. There was no sound and there was no sign of the two men, either to the right or to the left. His heart felt like lead! They evidently had entered the Princess's room! How was he to find that room? Slowly he wriggled across the broad, dark hall, straightening up in the shadow of a great post. From this point he edged along the wall for a distance of ten or twelve feet to the left. A sound came from farther down the hall, and he imagined he heard some one approaching.

His hand came in contact with a heavy hanging or tapestry, and he quickly squirmed behind its folds, finding himself against a door which moved as his body touched it. He felt it swing open slightly and drew back, intending to return to the hall, uncertain and very much undecided as to the course to pursue. His revolver was in his hand. Just as he was about to pull aside the curtain a man glided past, quickly followed by another. Providence had kept him from running squarely into them. They

were going toward the left, and he realized that they
were now approaching the Princess's room. How
he came to be ahead of them he could not imagine.
Strange trembling seized his legs, so great was the
relief after the narrow escape. Again he felt the
door move slightly as he pressed against it. The
necessity for a partial recovery of his composure before the next and most important step impelled
him softly to enter the room for an instant's breath.

Holding to the door, he stood inside and drew
himself to his full height, taking a long and tremu-
lous breath. There was no light in the room, but
through the door crack to his left came a dim, broad
streak. He now knew where he was. This room
was next to that in which the Princess slept, for had
he not seen the light from her window? Perhaps
he was now in the room of the Countess Dagmar.
Next door! Next door! Even now the daring
Geddos and Ostrom were crawling towards the bed
of the ruler of Graustark, not twenty feet away.
His first impulse was to cross and open the door
leading to the next room, surmising that it would be
unlocked, but he remembered Anguish, who was
doubtless, by this time, stealing up the stairs. They
must not be separated, for it would require two
steady, cool heads to deal with the villains. It was
not one man's work. As he turned to leave the
room, he thought how wonderfully well they had
succeeded in the delicate enterprise so far.

His knees struck the door, and there was a dull thump, not loud in reality, but like the report of a gun to him. A sudden rustle in the darkness of the room and then a sleepy voice, soft and quick, as of a woman awakening with a start.

"Who is it?"

His heart ceased beating, his body grew stiff and immovable. Again the voice, a touch of alarm in it now:

"Is that you, Dannox?"

She spoke in German, and the voice came from somewhere in front and to his right. He could not answer, could not move. The paralysis of indecision was upon him.

"How is it that the outer door is open?"

This time there was something like a reprimand in the tones, still low. He almost could see the wide-open, searching eyes.

X

There could be no further hesitation. Something
must be done, and instantly. He gently closed the
door before answering the third question. In his
nervousness he spoke in English, advancing to the
middle of the room. Impossible to see the woman
to whom he hissed this alarming threat—he only
could speculate as to its effect:

"If you utter a sound, madam, I shall kill you.
Be calm, and allow me to explain my presence
here!"

He expected her to shriek, forgetting that she
might not understand his words. Instead there was
a deathly silence. Had she swooned? His heart
was leaping with hope. But she spoke softly again,
tremulously, and in English:

"You will find my jewels on the dressing-table.
Take them and go. You will not hurt me?"

"I am not here to do you injury, but to serve your
Princess," whispered the man. "For God's sake,
do not make an outcry. You will ruin everything.
Will you let me explain?"

"Go! Go! Take anything! I can be calm no
longer. Oh, how can I expect mercy at your
hands!" Her tones were rising to a wail of terror.

"Sh! Do you want to die?" he hissed, striding to the canopy bed, discernible as his eyes grew accustomed to the darkness. "I will kill you if you utter a sound, so help me God!"

"Oh!" she moaned.

"Listen! You must aid me! Do you hear?"

Another heart-breaking moan. "I am here to save the Princess. There is a plot to abduct her to-night. Already there are men in the castle, perhaps in her room. You must tell me where she sleeps. There is no time to be lost. I am no thief, before God! I am telling you the truth. Do not be alarmed, I implore you. Trust me, madam, and you will not regret it. Where does the Princess sleep?" He jerked out these eager, pleading words quickly, breathlessly.

"How am I to trust you?" came back a whisper from the bed.

"Here is a revolver! Take it and kill me if I attempt the slightest injury. Where are you?" He felt along the bed with his hand.

"Keep away! Please! Please!" she sobbed.

"Take the pistol! Be calm, and in heaven's name help me to save her. Those wretches may have killed her already!"

The revolver dropped upon the clothes. He was bending eagerly over, holding the curtains back.

"My friend is in the hall. We have traced the

men to the Princess's door, I think. My God, be quick! Do you wish to see her stolen from under your eyes?"

"You are now in the Princess's room," answered the voice from the bed, calmer and with some alacrity. "Is this true that you tell me?"

"As God is my witness! And you—you—are the Princess?" gasped the man, drawing back.

"I am. Where is Dannox?" She was sitting bolt upright in the bed, the pistol in her trembling fingers.

"He is one of the conspirators. One of the cooks and two other guards are in the plot. Can you trust me enough to leave your bed and hide in another part of the room? The scoundrels have mistaken the door, but they may be here at any moment. You must be quick! I will protect you—I swear it! Come, your Highness! Hide!"

"Something in the fierce, anxious whisper gave her confidence. The miracle had been wrought! He had composed this woman under the most trying circumstances that could have been imagined. She slipped from the bed and threw a long, loose silken gown about her.

"Who are you?" she asked, touching his arm.

"I am a foreigner—an American—Grenfall Lorry! Hurry!" he implored.

She did not move for a moment, but he distinctly heard her catch her breath.

"Am I dreaming?" she murmured, faintly. Her fingers now clutched his arm tightly.

"I should say not! I don't like to order you around, your Highness, but——"

"Come—come to the light!" she interrupted, excitedly. "Over here!"

Noiselessly she drew him across the room until the light fell across his face. It was not a bright light, but what she saw satisfied her. He could not see her face, for she stood outside the strip of dusky yellow.

"Two men lie beneath your window, and two are coming to this room. Where shall I go? Come, be quick, madam! Do you want to be carted off to Ganlook? Then don't stand there like a—like a—pardon me, I won't say it!"

"I trust you fully. Shall I alarm the guard?" she whispered, recovering her self-possession.

"By no means! I want to catch those devils myself. Afterwards we can alarm the guards!"

"An ideal American!" she surprised him by saying. "Follow me!"

She led him to the doorway. "Stand here, and I will call the Countess. At this side, where it is dark."

She opened the door gently and stood in the light for a second. He saw before him a graceful figure in trailing white, and then he saw her face. She was Miss Guggenslocker!

"My God!" he hoarsely gasped, staggering toward her. "You! You! The Princess?"

"Yes, I am the Princess," she whispered, smiling as she glided away from his side. His eyes went round in his head, his legs seemed to be anywhere but beneath him, he felt as though he were rushing toward the ceiling. For the moment he was actually unconscious. Then his senses rushed back, recalling his mission and his danger.

"She is sleeping so soundly that I fear to awaken her," whispered a soft voice at his back, and he turned. The Princess was standing in the doorway.

"Then pray stand back where you will be out of danger. They will be here in a moment, unless they have been frightened away."

"You shall not expose yourself," she said, positively. "Why should you risk your life *now?* You have accomplished your object. You have saved the Princess!"

"Ah—yes, the Princess!" he said. "And I am sorry you *are* the Princess," he added, in her ear.

"Sh!" she whispered, softly.

The door through which he had first come was softly opened, and they were conscious that some one was entering. Lorry and the Princess stood in the dark shadow of a curtain, she close behind his stalwart figure. He could hear his own heart and hers beating, could feel the warmth of her body,

"I'M SORRY YOU ARE THE PRINCESS."

although it did not touch his. His heart beat with the pride of possession, of power, with the knowledge that he had but to stretch out his hand and touch the one woman in all the world.

Across the dim belt of light from the open doorway in which they stood, crawled the dark figure of a man. Her hand unconsciously touched his back as if seeking reassurance. He shivered beneath its gentle weight. Another form followed the first, pausing in the light to look toward their doorway. The abductor was doubtless remembering the instructions to chloroform the Countess. Then came the odor of chloroform. Oh, if Anguish were only there!

The second figure was lost in the darkness and a faint glow of light came from the canopied bed in the corner. The chloroformer, holding the curtains, had turned his screen-lantern toward the pillow in order to apply the dampened cloth. Now was the time to act!

Pushing the Princess behind the curtain and in the shelter of the door-post, Lorry leaped toward the center of the room, a pistol in each hand. Before him crouched the astonished desperadoes.

"If you move you are dead men!" said he, in slow, decided tones. "Here, Harry!" he shouted. "Scoundrels, you are trapped! Throw up your hands!"

Suddenly the room was a blaze of light; flashing

candles, lamps, sprung into life from the walls, while a great chandelier above his head dazzled him with its unexpected glare.

"Hell!" he shouted, half throwing his hands to his eyes.

Something rushed upon him from behind; there was a scream and then a stinging blow across the head and neck. As he sank helplessly, angrily, to his knees he heard the Princess wail:

"Dannox! Do not strike again! You have killed him!"

As he rolled to the floor he saw the two forms near the bed moving about like shadows; two red objects that resembled dancing telegraph poles leaped past him from he knew not where, and then there was a shout, the report of a pistol, a horrid yell. Something heavy crashed down beside him and writhed. His eyes were closing, his senses were going, he was numb and sleepy. Away off in the distance he heard Harry Anguish crying:

"That settles you, damn you!"

Some one lifted his head from the carpet and a woman's voice was crying something unintelligible. He was conscious of an effort on his part to prevent the blood from streaming over her gown—a last bit of gallantry. The sound of rushing feet, shouts, firearms—oblivion!

．　　　．　　　．　　　　　．　　　．　　　．

When Lorry regained consciousness he blinked in

abject amazement. There was a dull, whirring sound in his ears, and his eyes had a glaze over them that was slow in wearing off. There were persons in the room. He could see them moving about and could hear them talking. As his eyes tried to take in the strange surroundings, a hand was lifted from his forehead and a soft, dream-like voice said:

"He is recovering, Mr. Anguish. See, his eyes are open! Do you know me, Mr. Lorry?"

The unsteady eyes wandered until they fell upon the face near his pillow. A brighter gleam came into them, and there was a ray of returning intelligence. He tried to speak, but could only move his lips. As he remembered her, she was in white, and he was puzzled now to see her in a garment of some dark material, suggestive of the night or the green of a shady hillside. There was the odor of roses and violets and carnations. Then he looked for the fatal, fearful, glaring chandelier. It was gone. The room was becoming lighter and lighter as his eyes grew stronger, but it was through a window near where he lay. So it was daylight! Where was he?

"How do you feel, old man?" asked a familiar voice. A man sat down beside him on the couch or bed, and a big hand grasped his own. Still he could not answer.

"Doctor," cried the voice near his head, "you really think it is not serious?"

"I am quite sure," answered the man's voice from somewhere out in the light. "It is a bad cut, and he is just recovering from the effect of the ether. Had the blow not been a glancing one his skull would have been crushed. He will be perfectly conscious in a short time. There is no concussion, Your Highness."

"I am so happy to hear you say that," said the soft voice. Lorry's eyes sought hers and thanked her. A lump came into his throat as he looked up into the tender, anxious blue eyes. A thrill came over him. Princess or not, he loved her—he loved her! "You were very brave—oh, *so* brave!" she whispered in his ear, her hand touching his hair caressingly. "My American!"

He tried to reach the hand before it faded, but he was too weak. She glided away, and he closed his eyes again as if in pain.

"Look up, old man; you're all right," said Anguish. "Smell this handkerchief. It will make you feel better." A moist cloth was held beneath his nose, and a strong, pungent odor darted through his nostrils. In a moment he tried to raise himself to his elbow. The world was clearing up.

"Lie still a bit, Lorry. Don't be too hasty. The doctor says you must not."

"Where am I, Harry?" asked the wounded man, weakly.

"In the castle. I'll tell you all about it presently."

"Am I in her room?"

"No, but she is in yours. You are across the hall in"—here he whispered—"Uncle Caspar's room. Caspar is a Count."

"And she is the Princess—truly?"

"What luck!"

"What misery—what misery!" half moaned the other.

"Bosh! Be a man! Don't talk so loud, either! There are a half-dozen in the room."

Lorry remained perfectly quiet for ten minutes, his staring eyes fixed on the ceiling. He was thinking of the abyss he had reached and could not cross.

"What time is it?" he asked at last, turning his eyes toward his friend.

"It's just seven o'clock. You have been unconscious or under the influence of ether for over four hours. That guard hit you a fearful crack."

"I heard a shot—a lot of them. Was any one killed? Did those fellows escape?"

"Killed! There have been eight executions besides the one I attended to. Lord, they don't wait long here before handing out justice."

"Tell me all that happened. Was she hurt?"

"I should say not! Say, Gren, I have killed a man. Dannox got my bullet right in the head and he never knew what hit him. Ghastly, isn't it? I feel beastly queer. It was he who turned on the

lights and went at you with a club. I heard you
call, and was in the door just as he hit you. His
finish came inside of a second. You and he spoiled
the handsomest rug I ever saw."

"Ruined it?"

"Not in her estimation. I'll wager she has it
framed, blood and all. The stains will always be
there as a reminder of your bravery, and that's what
she says she's bound to keep. She was very much
excited and alarmed about you until the room filled
with men and then she remembered how she was
attired. I never saw anything so pretty as her embarrassment when the Countess and her aunt led
her into the next room. These people are going out,
so I'll tell you what happened after you left me with
the cook. He was a long time falling under the influence, and I had barely reached the top of the
stairs when I saw Dannox rush down the hall. Then
you called, and I knew the jig was on in full blast.
The door was open, and I saw him strike you. I
shot him, but she was at your side before I could
get to you. The other fellows who were in the
room succeeded in escaping while I was bending
over you, but neither of them shot at me. They
were too badly frightened. I had sense enough left
to follow and shoot a couple of times as they tore
down the stairs. One of them stumbled and rolled
all the way to the bottom. He was unconscious and
bleeding when I reached his side. The other fel-

low flew toward the dining hall, where he was nabbed by two white-uniformed men and throttled. Other men in white—they were regular police officers—pounced upon me, and I was a prisoner. By George, I was knocked off my feet the next minute to see old Dangloss himself come puffing and blowing into the hall, redder and fiercer than ever. 'Now I know what you want in Edelweiss!' he shrieked, and it took me three minutes to convince him of his error. Then he and some of the men went up to the Princess's room, while I quickly led the way to the big gate and directed a half-dozen officers toward the ravine. By this time the grounds were alive with guards. They came up finally with the two fellows who had been stationed beneath the window and who were unable to find the gate. When I got back to where you were the room was full of terrified men and women, half dressed. I was still dazed over the sudden appearance of the police, but managed to tell my story in full to Dangloss and Count Halfont—that's Uncle Caspar—and then the chief told me how he and his men happened to be there. In the meantime, the castle physician was attending to you. Dannox had been carried away. I never talked to a more interested audience in my life! There was the Princess at my elbow and the Countess—pretty as a picture—back of her, all eyes, both of 'em; and there was the old gray-haired lady, the Countess Halfont, and a half-dozen shivering

maids, with men galore, Dangloss and the Count and
a lot of servants,—a great and increasing crowd.
The captain of the guards, a young fellow named
Quinnox, as I heard him called, came in, worried
and humiliated. I fancy he was afraid he'd lose his
job. You see, it was this way: Old Dangloss has
had a man watching us all day. Think of it! Shad-
owing us like a couple of thieves. This fellow traced
us to the castle gate and then ran back for reinforce-
ments, confident that we were there to rob. In twenty
minutes he had a squad of officers at the gate, the
chief trailing along behind. They found the pile
of tools we had left there, and later the other chap
in the arbor. A couple of guards came charging up
to learn the cause of the commotion, and the whole
crew sailed into the castle, arriving just in time.
Well, just as soon as I had told them the full story
of the plot, old Caspar, the chief and the captain
held a short consultation, the result of which I can
tell in mighty few words. At six o'clock they took
the whole gang of prisoners down in the ravine and
shot them. The mounted guards are still looking
for the two Viennese who were left with the carriage. They escaped. About an hour after you
were hurt you were carried over here and laid on
this couch. I want to tell you, Mr. Lorry, you are
the most interesting object that ever found its way
into a royal household. They have been hanging
over you as if you were a new-born baby, and

everybody's charmed because you are a boy and are going to live. As an adventure, this has been a record-breaker, my son! We are cocks of the walk!"

Lorry was smiling faintly over his enthusiasm.

"You are the real hero, Harry. You saved my life, and probably hers. I'll not allow you or anybody to give me the glory," he said, pressing the other's hand.

"Oh, that's nonsense! Anybody could have rushed in as I did. I was only capping the climax you had prepared—merely a timely arrival, as the novels say. There is a little of the credit due me, of course, and I'll take it gracefully, but I only come in as an accessory, a sort of bushwhacker who had only to do the shoot, slap-bang work and close the act. You did the hero's work. But what do you think of the way they hand out justice over here? All but two of 'em dead!"

"Whose plan was it to kill those men?" cried Lorry, suddenly sitting upright.

"Everybody's, I fancy. They didn't consult me, though, come to think of it. Ah, here is Her Royal Highness!"

The Princess and Aunt Yvonne were at his side again, while Count Caspar was coming rapidly toward them.

"You must not sit up, Mr. Lorry," began the Princess, but he was crying:

"Did they make a confession, Harry?"

"I don't know. Did they, Unc—Count Halfont? Did they confess? Great heavens, I never thought of that before."

"What was there to confess?" asked the Count, taking Lorry's hand, kindly. "They were caught in the act. My dear sir, they were not even tried."

"I thought your police chief was such a shrewd man," cried Lorry, angrily.

"What's that?" asked a gruff voice, and Baron Dangloss was a member of the party, red and panting.

"Don't you know you should not have killed those men?" demanded Lorry. They surveyed him in amazement, except Anguish, who had buried his face in his hands dejectedly.

"And, sir, I'd like to know why not?" blustered Dangloss.

"And sir, I'd like to know, since you have shot the only beings on earth who knew the man that hired them, how in the name of your alleged justice are you going to apprehend him?" said Lorry, sinking back on his pillow, exhausted.

No reserve could hide the consternation, embarrassment and shame that overwhelmed a very worthy but very impetuous nobleman, Baron Jasto Dangloss, chief of the police of Edelweiss. He could only sputter his excuses and withdraw, swearing to catch the arch-conspirator or die in the attempt. Not

a soul in the castle, not a being in all Graustark
could offer the faintest clew to the identity of the
man or explain his motive. No one knew a Michael,
who might have been inadvertently addressed as
"your" possible "Highness." The greatest wonder reigned; vexation, uneasiness and perplexity existed everywhere.

Standing there with her head on her aunt's shoulder, her face grave and troubled, the Princess asked:

"Why should they seek to abduct me? Was it
to imprison or to kill me? Oh, Aunt Yvonne, have
I not been good to my people? God knows I have
done all that I can. I could have done no more. Is
it a conspiracy to force me from the throne? Who
can be so cruel?"

And no one could answer. They could simply
offer words of comfort and promises of protection.
Later in the day gruff Dangloss marched in and
apologized to the Americans for his suspicions concerning them, imploring their assistance in running
down the chief villain. And as the hours went by
Count Halfont came in and, sitting beside Grenfall,
begged his pardon and asked him to forget the deception that had been practiced in the United States.
He explained the necessity for traveling incognito
at that time. After which the Count entered a plea
for Her Royal Highness, who had expressed contrition and wished to be absolved.

XI

As the day wore on Lorry grew irritable and rest-less. He could not bring himself into full touch with the situation, notwithstanding Harry's frequent and graphic recollections of incidents that had occurred and that had led to their present condition. Their luncheon was served in the Count's room, as it was inadvisable for the injured man to go to the dining hall until he was stronger. The court physician assured him that he would be incapacitated for several days, but that in a very short time his wound would lose the power to annoy him in the least. The Count and Countess Halfont, Anguish and others came to cheer him and to make his surroundings endurable. Still he was dissatisfied, even unhappy.

The cause of his uneasiness and depression was revealed only by the manner in which it was removed. He was lying stretched out on the couch, staring from the window, his head aching, his heart full of a longing that knows but one solace. Anguish had gone out in the grounds after assuring himself that his charge was asleep, so there was no one in the room when he awakened from a sickening dream to shudder alone over its memory. A cool breeze from an open window fanned his head kindly; a bright sun gleamed across the trees, turning them into gold and purple and red and green; a quiet repose was in all that touched him outwardly; inwardly there was burning turmoil. He turned on his side and curiously felt the bandages about his head. They were tight and smooth, and he knew they were perfectly white. How lonely those bandages made him feel, away off there in Graustark!

The door of his room opened softly, but he did not turn, thinking it was Anguish—always Anguish —and not the one he most desired to——

"Her Royal Highness," announced a maid, and then:

"May I come in?" asked a voice that went to his troubled soul like a cooling draught to the fevered throat. He turned toward her instantly, all the irritation, all the uneasiness, all the loneliness vanishing like mist before the sun. Behind her was a lady-in-waiting.

"I cannot deny the request of a Princess," he responded, smiling gaily. He held forth his hand toward her, half fearing she would not take it.

The Princess Yetive came straight to his couch and laid her hand in his. He drew it to his lips and then released it lingeringly. She stood before him, looking down with an anxiety in her eyes that would have repaid him had death been there to claim his next breath.

"Are you better?" she asked, with her pretty accent. "I have been so troubled about you."

"I thought you had forgotten me," he said, with childish petulance.

"Forgotten you!" she cried, quick to resent the imputation. "Let me tell you, then, what I have been doing while forgetting. I have sent to the Regengetz for your luggage and your friend's. You will find it much more comfortable here. You are to make this house your home as long as you are in Edelweiss. That is how I have been forgetting."

"Forgive me!" he cried, his eyes gleaming. "I have been so lonely that I imagined all sorts of things. But, Your Highness, you must not expect us to remain here after I am able to leave. That would be imposing——"

"I will not allow you to say it!" she objected, decisively. "You are the guest of honor in Graustark. Have you not preserved its ruler? Was it an imposition to risk your life to save one in whom you had but passing interest, even though she were a poor Princess? No, my American, this castle is yours, in all rejoicing, for had you not come within its doors to-day would have found it in mournful terror. Besides, Mr. Anguish has said he will stay a year if we insist."

"That's like Harry," laughed Lorry. "But I am afraid you are glorifying two rattle-brained chaps who should be in a home for imbeciles instead of in the castle their audacity might have blighted. Our rashness was only surpassed by our phenomenal good luck. By chance it turned out well; there were ten thousand chances of ignominious failure. Had we failed would we have been guests of honor? No! We would have been stoned from Graustark. You don't know how thin the thread was that held your fate. It makes me shudder to think of the crime our act might have been. Ah, had I but known you were the Princess, no chances should have been taken," he said, fervently.

"And a romance spoiled," she laughed.

"So you are a Princess,—a real Princess," he went on, as if he had not heard her. "I knew it. Something told me you were not an ordinary woman——"

"Oh, but I am a very ordinary woman," she remonstrated. "You do not know how easy it is to be a Princess and a mere woman at the same time. I have a heart, a head. I breathe and eat and drink and sleep and love. Is it not that way with other women?"

"You breathe and eat and drink and sleep and love in a different world, though, Your Highness."

"Ach! my little maid, Thérèsa, sleeps as soundly,

eats as heartily and loves as warmly as I, so a fig
for your argument."

"You may breathe the same air, but would you
love the same man that your maid might love?"

"Is a man the only excuse for love?" she asked.
"If so, then I must say that I breathe and eat and
drink and sleep—and that is all."

"Pardon me, but some day you will find that love
is a man, and"—here he laughed—"you will neither
breathe, nor eat, nor sleep except with him in your
heart. Even a Princess is not proof against a
man."

"Is a man proof against a Princess?" she asked,
as she leaned against the casement.

"It depends on the"—he paused—"the Princess,
I should say."

"Alas! There is one more fresh responsibility
acquired. It seems to me that everything depends
on the Princess," she said, merrily.

"Not entirely," he said, quickly. "A great deal—
a very great deal—depends on circumstances. For
instance, when you were Miss Guggenslocker it
wouldn't have been necessary for a man to be a
Prince, you know."

"But I was Miss Guggenslocker because a man
was unnecessary," she said, so gravely that he
smiled. "I was without a title because it was more
womanly than to be a 'freak,' as I should have been
had every man, woman and child looked upon me as

"IT IS MY WILL!"

a Princess. I did not travel through your land for the purpose of exhibiting myself, but to learn and unlearn."

"I remember it cost you a certain coin to learn one thing," he observed.

"It was money well spent, as subsequent events have proved. I shall never regret the spending of that half gavvo. Was it not the means of bringing you to Edelweiss?"

"Well, it was largely responsible, but I am inclined to believe that a certain desire on my part would have found a way without the assistance of the coin. You don't know how persistent an American can be."

"Would you have persisted had you known I was a Princess?" she asked.

"Well, I can hardly tell about that, but you must remember I didn't know who or what you were."

"Would you have come to Graustark had you known I was its Princess?"

"I'll admit I came because you were Miss Guggenslocker."

"A mere woman."

"I will not consent to the word 'mere.' What would you think of a man who came half-way across the earth for the sake of a *mere* woman?"

"I should say he had a great deal of curiosity," she responded, coolly.

"And not much sense. There is but one woman

a man would do so much for, and she could not be a *mere* woman in his eyes." Lorry's face was white and his eyes gleamed as he hurled this bold conclusion at her.

"Especially when he learns that she is a Princess!" said she, her voice so cold and repellent that his eyes closed involuntarily, as if an unexpected horror had come before them. "You must not tell me that you came to see me."

"But I did come to see *you* and not Her Royal Highness the Princess Yetive of Graustark. How was I to know?" he cried, impulsively.

"But you are no longer ignorant," she said, looking from the window.

"I thought you said you were a mere woman!"

"I am—and that is the trouble!" she said, slowly turning her eyes back to him. Then she abruptly sank to the window seat near his head. "That is the trouble, I say. A woman is a woman, although she be a Princess. Don't you understand why you must not say such things to me?"

"Because you *are* a Princess," he said, bitterly.

"No; because I am a woman. As a woman, I want to hear them, as a Princess I cannot. Now, have I made you understand? Have I been bold enough?" Her face was burning.

"You—you don't mean that you——" he half whispered, drawing himself toward her, his face glowing.

"Ach! What have I said?"

"You have said enough to drive me mad with desire for more," he cried, seizing her hand, which she withdrew instantly, rising to her feet.

"I have only said that I wanted to hear you say you had come to see me. Is not that something for a woman's vanity to value? I am sorry you have presumed to misunderstand me?" She was cold again, but he was not to be baffled.

"Then be a woman and forget that you are a Princess until I tell you why I came," he cried.

"I cannot. I mean, I will not listen to you," she said, glancing about helplessly, yet standing still within the danger circle.

"I came because I have thought of you and dreamed of you since the day you sailed from New York. God, can I ever forget that day!"

"Please do not recall——" she began, blushing and turning to the window.

"The kiss you threw to me? Were you a Princess then?" She did not answer, and he paused for a moment, a thought striking him which at first he did not dare to voice. Then he blurted out: "If you do not want to hear me say these things, why do you stand there?"

"Oh," she faltered.

"Don't leave me now. I want to say what I came over here to say, and then you can go back to your throne and your royal reserve, and I can go back

to the land from which you drew me. I came because I love you. Is not that enough to drag a man
to the end of the world? I came to marry you if I
could, for you were Miss Guggenslocker to me.
Then you were within my reach, but not now! I
can only *love* a Princess!" He stopped because she
had dropped to the couch beside him, her serious
face turned appealingly to his, her fingers clasping
his hands fiercely.

"I forbid you to continue—I forbid you! Do
you hear? I, too, have thought and dreamed of
you, and I have prayed that you might come. But
you must not tell me that you love me—you *shall*
not!"

"I only want to know that you love me," he whispered.

"Do you think I can tell you the truth?" she cried.
"I do *not* love you!"

Before he had fairly grasped the importance of
the contradictory sentences, she left his side and
stood in the window, her breast heaving and her
face flaming.

"Then I am to believe you do," he groaned, after
a moment. "I find a Princess and lose a woman!"

"I did not intend that you should have said what
you have, or that I should have told you what I
have. I knew you loved me or you would not have
come to me," she said, softly.

"You would have been selfish enough to enjoy

that knowledge without giving joy in return. I see. What else could you have done? A Princess! Oh, I would to God you were Miss Guggenslocker, the woman I sought!"

"Amen to that!" she said. "Can I trust you never to renew this subject? We have each learned what had better been left unknown. You understand my position. Surely you will be good enough to look upon me ever afterward as a Princess and forget that I have been a woman unwittingly. I ask you, for your sake and my own, to refrain from a renewal of this unhappy subject. You can see how hopeless it is for both of us. I have said much to you that I trust you will cherish as coming from a woman who could not have helped herself and who has given you the power to undo her with a single word. I know you will always be the brave, true man my heart has told me you are. You will let the beginning be the end?"

The appeal was so earnest, so noble that honor swelled in his heart and came from his lips in this promise:

"You may trust me, Your Highness. Your secret is worth a thousand-fold more than mine. It is sacred with me. The joy of my life has ended, but the happiness of knowing the truth will never die. I shall remember that you love me—yes, I know you do,—and I shall never forget to love you. I will not promise that I shall never speak of it again to you. As I lie here, there comes to me a courage I did not know I could feel."

"No, no!" she cried, vehemently.

"Forgive me! You can at least let me say that as long as I live I may cherish and encourage a little hope that all is not dead. Your Highness, let me say that my family never knows when it is defeated, either in love or in war."

"The walls which surround the heart of a Princess are black and grim, impenetrable when she defends it, my boasting American," she said, smiling sadly.

"Yet some Prince of the realm will batter down the wall and win at a single blow that which a *mere* man could not conquer in ten lifetimes. Such is the world."

"The Prince may batter down and seize, but he can never conquer. But enough of this! I am the Princess of Graustark; you are my friend, Grenfall Lorry, and there is only a dear friendship between us," she cried, resuming her merry humor so easily that he started with surprise and not a little displeasure.

"And a throne," he added, smiling, however.

"And a promise," she reminded him.

"From which I trust I may some day be released," said he, sinking back, afflicted with a discouragement and a determination of equal power. He could see hope and hopelessness ahead.

"By death!"

"No; by life! It may be sooner than you think!"

"You are forgetting your promise already."

"Your Highness's pardon," he begged.

They laughed, but their hearts were sad, this luckless American and hapless sovereign who would, if she could, be a woman.

"It is now three o'clock—the hour when you were to have called to see me," she said, again sitting unconcernedly before him in the window seat. She was not afraid of him. She was a Princess.

"I misunderstood you, Your Highness. I remembered the engagement, but it seems I was mistaken as to the time. I came at three in the morning!"

"And found me at home!"

"In an impregnable castle, with ogres all about."

XII

Lorry was removed to another room before dinner, as she had promised.

After they had dined the two strangers were left alone for several hours. Anguish regaled his friend with an enthusiastic dissertation on the charms of the Countess Dagmar, lady-in-waiting to the Princess. In conclusion he said glowingly, his cigar having been out for half an hour or more because his energy had been spent in another direction:

"You haven't seen much of her, Lorry, but I tell you she is rare. And she's not betrothed to any of these confounded Counts or Dukes either. They all adore her, but she's not committed."

"How do you know all this?" demanded Lorry, who but half heard through his dreams.

"Asked her, of course. How in thunder do you suppose?"

"And you've known her but a day? Well, you *are* progressive."

"Oh, perfectly natural conversation, you know," explained Anguish, composedly. "She began it by asking me if I were married, and I said I wasn't even engaged. Then I asked her if she were mar-

ried. You see, from the title, you can't tell whether
a Countess is married or single. She said she wasn't,
and I promptly and very properly expressed my
amazement. By Jove, she has a will and a mind of
her own, that young woman has. She's not going
to marry until she finds a man of the right sort—
which is refreshing. I like to hear a girl talk like
that, especially a pretty girl who can deal in Princes,
Counts and all kinds of nobility when it comes to
a matrimonial trade. By Jove, I'm sorry for the
Princess, though."

"Sorry for the Princess? Why?" asked the other,
alert at once.

"Oh, just because it's not in her power to be so
independent. The Countess says she cries every
night when she thinks of what the poor girl has to
contend with."

"Tell me about it."

"I don't know anything to tell. I'm not interested in the Princess, and I didn't have the nerve to
ask many questions. I do know, however, that she
is going to have an unpleasant matrimonial alliance
forced upon her in some way."

"That is usual."

"That's what I gather from the Countess. Maybe
you can pump the Countess and get all you want to
know in connection with the matter. It's a pretty
serious state of affairs, I should say, or she wouldn't
be weeping through sympathy."

Lorry recalled a part of the afternoon's sweetly dangerous conversation and the perspiration stood cold and damp on his brow.

"Well, old man, you've chased Miss Guggenslocker to earth only to find her an impossibility. Pretty hopeless for you, Lorry, but don't let it break you up completely. We can go back home after a while and you will forget her. A Countess, of course, is different."

"Harry, I know it is downright madness for me to act like this," said Lorry, his jaws set and his hands clinched as he raised himself to his elbow. "You don't know how much I love her."

"Your nerve is to be admired, but—well, I'm sorry for you."

"Thanks for your sympathy. I suppose I'll need it," and he sank back gloomily. Anguish was right —absurdly right.

There was a rap at the door and Anguish hastened to open it. A servant presented Count Halfont's compliments and begged leave to call.

"Shall we see the old boy?" asked Harry.

"Yes, yes," responded the other. The servant understood the sign made by Anguish and disappeared. "Diplomatic call, I suspect."

"He is the Prime Minister, I understand. Well, we'll diplome with him until bedtime, if he cares to stay. I'm getting rather accustomed to the nobility. They are not so bad, after all. Friendly and all

that—— Ah, good-evening, Your Excellency! We
are honored."

The Count had entered the room and was advancing toward the couch, tall, easy and the per-
sonification of cordiality.

"I could not retire until I had satisfied myself as
to Mr. Lorry's condition and his comfort," said he,
in his broken English. He seated himself near the
couch and bent sharp, anxious eyes on the recum-
bent figure.

"Oh, he's all right," volunteered Anguish, readily.
"Be able to go into a battle again to-morrow."

"That is the way with you aggressive Americans,
I am told. They never give up until they are dead,"
said the Count, courteously. "Your head is better?"

"It does not pain me as it did, and I'm sure I'll
be able to get out to-morrow. Thank you very
much for your interest," said Lorry. "May I inquire after the health of the Countess Halfont?
The excitement of last night has not had an unpleasant effect, I hope."

"She is with the Princess, and both are quite well.
Since our war, gentlemen, Graustark women have
nothing to acquire in the way of courage and endurance. You, of course, know nothing of the horrors of that war."

"But we would be thankful for the story of it,
Your Excellency. War is a hobby of mine. I read

every war scare that gets into print," said Anguish, eagerly.

"We, of Graustark, at present have every reason to recall the last war and bitterly to lament its ending. The war occurred just fifteen years ago—but will the recital tire you, Mr. Lorry? I came to spend a few moments socially and not to go into history. At any other time I shall be——"

"It will please and not tire me. I am deeply interested. Pray go on," Lorry hastened to say, for he was interested more than the Count suspected.

"Fifteen years ago Prince Ganlook, of this principality,—the father of our Princess,—became incensed over the depredations of the Axphain soldiers who patrolled our border on the north. He demanded restitution for the devastation they had created, but was refused. Graustark is a province comprising some eight hundred square miles of the best land in this part of the world. Our neighbor is smaller in area and population. Our army was better equipped but not so hardy. For several months the fighting in the north was in our favor, but the result was that our forces were finally driven back to Edelweiss, hacked and battered by the fierce thousands that came over the border. The nation was staggered by the shock, for such an outcome had not been considered possible. We had been too confident. Our soldiers were sick and worn by six months of hard fighting, and the men of Edelweiss

—the merchants, the laborers and the nobility it-self—flew to arms in defense of the city. For over a month we fought, hundreds of our best and bravest citizens going down to death. They at last began a bombardment of the city. To-day you can see the marks on nearly every house in Edelweiss. Hundreds of graves in the valley to the south attest the terrors of that siege. The castle was stormed, and Prince Ganlook, with many of the chief men of the land, met death. The Prince was killed in front of the castle gates, from which he had sallied in a last brave attempt to beat off the conquerors. A bronze statue now marks the spot on which he fell. The Princess, his wife, was my sister, and as I held the portfolio of finance, it was through me that the city surrendered, bringing the siege to an end. Fifteen years ago this autumn—the twentieth of November, to be explicit—the treaty of peace was signed in Sofia. We were compelled to cede a portion of territory in the far northwest, valuable for its mines. Indemnity was agreed upon by the peace commissioners, amounting to 20,000,000 gavvos, or nearly $30,000,000 in your money. In fifteen years this money was to be paid, with interest. On the twentieth of November, this year, the people of Graustark must pay 25,000,000 gavvos. The time is at hand, and that is why we recall the war so vividly. It means the bankruptcy of the nation, gentlemen."

Neither of his listeners spoke for some moments. Then Lorry broke the silence.

"You mean that the money cannot be raised?" he asked.

"It is not in our treasury. Our people have been taxed so sorely in rebuilding their homes and in recuperating from the effect of that dreadful invasion that they have been unable to pay the levies. You must remember that we are a small nation and of limited resources. Your nation could secure $30,-000,000 in one hour for the mere asking. To us it is like a death blow. I am not betraying a State secret in telling you of the sore straits in which we are placed, for every man in the nation has been made cognizant of the true conditions. We are all facing it together."

There was something so quietly heroic in his manner that both men felt pity. Anguish, looking at the military figure, asked:

"You fought through the war, Your Excellency?"

"I resigned as Minister, sir, to go to the front. I was in the first battle and I was in the last," he said, simply.

"And the Princess,—the present ruler, I mean,—was a mere child at that time. When did she succeed to the throne?" asked Lorry.

"Oh, the great world does not remember our little history! Within a year after the death of Prince

Ganlook, his wife, my sister, passed away, dying of a broken heart. Her daughter, their only child, was, according to our custom, crowned at once. She has reigned for fourteen years, and wisely since assuming full power. For three years she has been ruler de facto. She has been frugal, and has done all in her power to meet the shadow that is descending."

"And what is the alternative in case the indemnity is not paid?" asked Lorry, breathlessly, for he saw something bright in the approaching calamity.

"The cession of all that part of Graustark lying north of Edelweiss, including fourteen towns, all of our mines and our most productive farming and grazing lands. In that event Graustark will be no larger than one of the good-sized farms in your Western country. There will be nothing left for Her Royal Highness to rule save a tract so small that the word principality will be a travesty and a jest. This city and twenty-five miles to the south, a strip about one hundred and fifty miles long. Think of it! Twenty-five by one hundred and fifty miles, and yet called a principality! Once the proudest and most prosperous State in the East, considering its size, reduced to that! Ach, gentlemen—gentlemen! I cannot think of it without tearing out a heart-string and suffering such pains as mortal man has never endured. I lived in Graustark's days of wealth, power and supremacy; God has condemned me to live in the days of her dependency, weakness and poverty. Let us talk no more of this unpleasant subject."

His hearers pitied the frank, proud old man from the bottom of their hearts. He had told them the story with the candor and simplicity of a child, admitting weakness and despondency. Still he sat erect and defiant, his face white and drawn, his figure suggesting the famous picture of the stag at bay.

"Willingly, Your Excellency, since it is distasteful to you. I hope, however, you will permit me to ask how much you are short of the amount," said Lorry, considerately, yet curiously.

"Our Minister of Finance, Gaspon, will be able to produce fifteen million gavvos at the stated time —far from enough. This amount has been sucked from the people from excessive levy, and has been hoarded for the dreaded day. Try as we would, it has been impossible to raise the full amount. The people have been bled and have responded nobly, sacrificing everything to meet the treaty terms honorably, but the strain has been too great. Our army has cost us large sums. We have strengthened our defenses, and could, should we go to war, defeat Axphain. But we have our treaty to honor; we could not take up arms to save ourselves from that honest bond. Our levies have barely brought the amount necessary to maintain an army large enough

to inspire respect among those who are ready to
leap upon us the instant we show the least sign of
distress. There are about us powers that have held
aloof from war with us simply because we have
awed them with our show of force. It has been
our safeguard, and there is not a citizen of Graustark who objects to the manner in which State
affairs are conducted. They know that our army is
an economy at any price. Until last spring we were
confident that we could raise the full amount due
Axphain, but the people in the rural districts were
unable to meet the levies on account of the panic
that came at a most unfortunate time. That is why
we were hurrying home from your country, Mr.
Lorry. Gaspon had cabled the Princess that affairs
were in a hopeless condition, begging her to come
home and do what she could in a final appeal to the
people, knowing the love they had for her. She
came, and has seen these loyal subjects offer their
lives for her and for Graustark, but utterly unable
to give what they have not—money. She asked
them if she should disband the army, and there was
a negative wail from one end of the land to the
other. Then the army agreed to serve on half pay
until all was tided over. Public officers are giving
their services free, and many of our wealthy people
have advanced loans on bonds, worthless as they
may seen, and still we have not the required
amount."

"Cannot the loan be extended a few years?" asked Lorry, angry with the ruler in the North, taking the woes of Graustark as much to heart as if they were his own.

"Not one day! Not in London, Paris, nor Berlin."

Lorry lay back and allowed Anguish to lead the conversation into other channels. The Count remained for half an hour, saying as he left that the Princess and his wife had expressed a desire to be remembered to their guests.

"Her Royal Highness spent the evening with the Ministers of Finance and War, and her poor head, I doubt not, is racking from the effects of the consultation. These are weighty matters for a girl to have on her hands," solemnly stated the Count, pausing for an instant at the door of the apartment.

After he had closed it, the Americans looked long and thoughtfully at each other, each feeling a respect for the grim old gentleman that they had never felt for man before.

"So they are in a devil of a shape," mused Anguish. "I tell you, Gren, I never knew anything that made me feel so badly as does the trouble that hangs over that girl and her people. A week ago I wouldn't have cared a rap for Graustark, but tonight I feel like weeping for her."

"There seems to be no help for her, either," said Lorry, reflectively.

"Graustark, you mean?"

"No—I mean yes, of course,—who else?" demanded the other, who certainly had not meant Graustark.

"I believe, confound your selfish soul, you'd like to see the nation, the crown and everything else, taken away from this helpless, harassed child. Then you'd have a chance," exclaimed Anguish, pacing the floor, half angrily, half encouragingly.

"Don't say that, Harry, don't say that. Don't accuse me of it, for I'll confess I had in my heart that meanest of longings—the selfish, base, heartless hope that you have guessed. It hurts me to be accused of it though, so don't do it again, old man. I'll put away the miserable hope, if I can, and I'll pray God that she may find a way out of the difficulty."

They went to sleep that night, Anguish at once, Lorry not for hours, harboring a determination to learn more about the condition of affairs touching the people of Graustark and the heart of their Princess.

XIII

For two days Lorry lived through intermittent stages of delight and despondency. His recovery from the effects of the blow administered by Dannox was naturally rapid, his strong young constitution coming to the rescue bravely. He saw much of the Princess, more of the Countess Dagmar, and made the acquaintance of many lords and ladies for whom he cared but little except when they chose to talk of their girlish ruler. The atmosphere of the castle was laden with a depression that could not be overcome by an assimilated gaiety. There was the presence of a shadow that grew darker and nearer as the days went by, and there were anxious hearts under the brave, proud spirits of those who held the destiny of Graustark in their hands.

The Princess could not hide the trouble that had sprung up in her eyes. Her laugh, her gay conversation, her rare composure and gentle hauteur were powerless to drive away the haunted, worried gleam in those expressive eyes of blue. Lorry had it on his tongue's end a dozen times during the next day or so after the Count's narrative to question her

about the condition of affairs as they appeared to
her. He wondered whether she, little more than a
girl, could see and understand the enormity of the
situation that confronted her and her people. A
strange, tender fear prevented him from speaking
to her of the thing which was oppressing her life.
Not that he expected a rebuff from her, but that
he could not endure the thought of hearing her
brave, calm recital of the merciless story. He knew
that she could narrate it all to him more plainly than
had her uncle. Something told him that she was
fully aware of the real and underlying conditions.
He could see, in his imagination, the proud, resigned
face and manner of this perplexed Princess, as she
would have talked to him of her woes, and he could
also picture the telltale eyes and the troubled expression that would not be disguised.

The Countess Dagmar, when monopolized by the
very progressive, or aggressive, Anguish, unfolded
to Lorry certain pages in the personal history of the
Princess, and he, of course, encouraged her confidential humor, although there was nothing encour-
aging in it for him.

Down by the great fountain, while the soldiers
were on parade, the fair but volatile Countess unfolded to Lorry a story that wrenched his heart so
savagely that anger, resentment, helplessness and
love oozed forth and enveloped him in a multitude
of emotions that would not disperse. To have gone

to the Princess and laid down his life to save her
would have given him pleasure, but he had promised something to her that could not be forgotten in
a day. In his swelling heart he prayed for the time
to come when he could take her in his arms, cancel
his promise and defy the troubles that opposed
her.

"She will not mind my telling you, because she
considers you the very best of men, Mr. Lorry,"
said the Countess, who had learned her English
under the Princess Yetive's tutor. The demure,
sympathetic little Countess, her face glowing with
excitement and indignation, could not resist the desire to pour into the ears of this strong and resourceful man the secrets of the Princess, as if trusting to
him, the child of a powerful race, to provide relief.
It was the old story of the weak appealing to the
strong.

It seems, according to the very truthful account
given by the lady, that the Princess had it in her
power to save Graustark from disgrace and practi-
cal destruction. The Prince of Axphain's son,
Lorenz, was deeply enamoured of her, infatuated by
her marvelous beauty and accomplishments. He
had persuaded his father to consider a matrimonial
alliance with her to be one of great value to Axphain. The old Prince, therefore, some months before the arrival of the Americans in Graustark, sent
to the Princess a substitute ultimatum, couched in

terms so polite and conciliatory that there could be no mistaking his sincerity. He agreed to give Graustark a new lease of life, as it were, by extending the fifteen years, or, in other words, to grant the conquered an additional ten years in which to pay off the obligations imposed by the treaty. He furthermore offered a considerable reduction in the rate of interest for the next ten years. But he had a condition attached to this good and gracious proposition; the marriage of Graustark's sovereign. His Ambassador set forth the advantages of such an alliance, and departed with a message that the matter should have most serious consideration.

The old Prince's proposition was a blow to the Princess, who was placed in a trying position. By sacrificing herself she could save her country, but in so doing her life was to be plunged into interminable darkness. She did not love, nor did she respect Lorenz, who was not favorably supplied with civilized intelligence. The proposition was laid before the Cabinet and the nobility by the Princess herself, who said that she would be guided by any decision they might reach. The counsellors, to a man, refused to sacrifice their girlish ruler, and the people vociferously ratified the resolution. But the Princess would not allow them to send an answer to Axphain until she could see a way clear to save her people in some other manner. An embassy was sent to the Prince of Dawsbergen. His domain touched Graustark on the south, and he ruled a wild, turbulent class of mountaineers and herdsmen. The embassy sought to secure an endorsement of the loan from Prince Gabriel sufficient to meet the coming crisis. Gabriel, himself smitten by the charms of the Princess, at once offered himself in marriage, agreeing to advance, in case she accepted him, twenty million gavvos, at a rather high rate of interest, for fifteen years. His love for her was so great that he would pawn the entire principality for an answer that would make him the happiest man on earth. Now, the troubled Princess abhorred Gabriel. Of the two, Lorenz was much to be preferred. Gabriel flew into a rage upon the receipt of this rebuff, and openly avowed his intention to make her suffer. His infatuation became a mania, and, up to the very day on which the Countess told the story, he persisted in his appeals to the Princess. In person he had gone to her to plead his suit, on his knees, grovelling at her feet. He went so far as to exclaim madly in the presence of the alarmed but relentless object of his love that he would win her or turn the whole earth into everything unpleasant.

So it was that the Princess of Graustark, erstwhile Miss Guggenslocker, was being dragged through the most unhappy affairs that ever beset a sovereign. Within a month she was to sign away two-thirds of her domain, transforming multitudes

of her beloved and loving people into subjects of the
hated Axphain, or to sell herself, body and soul, to
a loathsome bidder in the guise of a suitor. And,
with all this confronting her, she had come to the
realization of a truth so sad and distracting that it
was breaking her tortured heart. She was in love—
but with no royal Prince! Of this, however, the
Countess knew nothing, so Lorry had one great secret to cherish alone.

"Has she chosen the course she will pursue?"
asked Lorry, as the Countess concluded her story.
His face was turned away.

"She cannot decide. We have wept together over
this dreadful, this horrible thing. You do not know
what it means to all of us, Mr. Lorry. We love her,
and there is not one in our land who would sacrifice
her to save this territory. As for Gabriel, Graustark would kill her before she should go to him.
Still, she cannot let herself sacrifice those Northern
subjects when by a single act she can save them.
You see, the Princess has not forgotten that her
father brought this war upon the people, and she
feels it her duty to pay the penalty of his error,
whatever the cost."

"Is there no other to whom she can turn—no
other course?" asked Lorry.

"There is none who would assist us, bankrupt as
we are. There is a question I want to ask, Mr.
Lorry. Please look at me—do not stare at the

fountain all the time. Why have you come to Edelweiss?" She asked the question so boldly that his startled embarrassment was an unspoken confession. He calmed himself and hesitated long before answering, weighing his reply. She sat close beside him, her clear gray eyes reading him like a book.

"I came to see a Miss Guggenslocker," he answered at last.

"For what purpose? There must have been an urgent cause to bring you so far. You are not an American banker?"

"I had intended to ask her to be my wife," he said, knowing that secrecy was useless and seeing a faint hope.

"You did not find Miss Guggenslocker."

"No. I have not found her."

"And are you going home disappointed, Mr. Lorry, because she is not here?"

"I leave the answer to your tender imagination." There was a long pause.

"May I ask when you expect to leave Graustark?" she asked, somewhat timidly.

"Why do you wish to know?" he asked in turn.

"Because I know how hopeless your quest has been. You have found Miss Guggenslocker, but she is held behind a wall so strong and impregnable that you cannot reach her with the question you came to ask. You have come to that wall, and now you must turn back. I have asked, how soon?"

"Not until your Princess bids me take up my load and go. You see, my lady, I love to sit beneath the shadow of the wall you describe. It will require a royal edict to compel me to abandon my position."

"You cannot expect the Princess to drive you from her country,—you who have done so much for her. You must go, Mr. Lorry, without her bidding."

"I must?"

"Yes, for your presence outside that wall may make the imprisonment all the more unendurable for the one your love cannot reach. Do you understand me?"

"Has the one behind the wall instructed you to say this to me?" he asked, miserably.

"She has not. I do not know her heart, but I am a woman and have a woman's foresight. If you wish to be kind and good to her, go!"

"I cannot!" he exclaimed, his pent feelings bursting forth. "I cannot go!"

"You will not be so selfish and so cruel as to increase the horror of the wreck that is sure to come," she said, drawing back.

"You know, Countess, of the life-saving crews who draw from the wrecks of ships lives that were hopelessly lost? There is to be a wreck here; is there to be a life-saver? When the night is darkest, the sea wildest, when hope is gone, is not that the time when rescue is most precious? Tell me, you know all there is of this approaching disaster?"

"I cannot command you to leave Edelweiss; I can only tell you that you will have something to answer for if you stay," said the Countess.

"Will you help me if I show you that I can reach the wreck and save the one who clings to it despairingly?" he asked, smiling, suddenly calm and confident.

"Willingly, for I love the one who is going down in the sea. I have spoken to you seriously, though, and I trust you will not misunderstand me. I like you and I like Mr. Anguish. You could stay here forever so far as I am concerned."

He thought long and intently over what she had said as he smoked his cigar on the great balcony that night. In his heart he knew he was adding horror, but that persistent hope of the life-saver came up fresh and strong to combat the argument. He saw, in one moment, the vast chasm between the man and the Princess; in the next, he laughed at the puny space.

Down on the promenade he could see the figures of men and women strolling in the moonlight. To his ears came the occasional laugh of a man, the silvery gurgle of a woman. The royal military band was playing in the stand near the edge of the great circle. There was gaiety, comfort, charm and security about everything that came to his eyes and ears. Was it possible that this peace, unruffled, was so near its end?

He smiled as he heard Harry Anguish laugh gaily

in his good old way, his ringing tones mingling with a woman's. There was no trouble in the hearts of the Countess and his blithe comrade. Behind him rose the grim castle walls, from the windows of which, here and there, gleamed the lights of the night. Where was she? He had seen her in the afternoon and had talked with her, had walked with her. Their conversation had been bright, but of the commonplace kind. She had said nothing to indicate that she remembered the hour spent beside his couch a day or so before; he had uttered none of the words that struggled to rush from his lips,— the questions, the pleadings, the vows. Where was she now? Not in that gay crowd below, for he had scanned every figure with the hawk's eye. Closeted again, no doubt, with her Ministers, wearying her tired brain, her brave heart into fatigue without rest.

Her court still trembled with the excitement of the daring attempt of the abductors and their swift punishment. Functionaries flocked to Edelweiss to inquire after the welfare of the Princess, and indignation was at the highest pitch. There were theories innumerable as to the identity of the arch-conspirator. Baron Dangloss was at sea completely. He cursed himself and everybody else for the hasty and ill-timed execution of the hirelings. It was quite evident that the buzzing wonder and intense feeling of the people had for the moment driven out all thought of the coming day of judgment and its bitter atonement for all Graustark. To-day the castle was full of the nobility, drawn to its walls by the news that had startled them beyond all expression. The police were at work, the military trembled with rage, the people clamored for the apprehension of the man who had been the instigator of this audacity. The general belief was that some brigand chief from the South had planned the great theft for the purpose of securing a fabulous ransom. Grenfall Lorry had an astonishing theory in his mind, and the more he thought it over the more firmly it was imbedded.

The warm, blue coils from the cigar wafted away into the night, carrying with them a myriad of tangled thoughts,—of her, of Axphain, of the abductor, of himself, of everything. A light step on the stone floor of the shadowy balcony attracted his attention. He turned his head—and saw the Princess Yetive. She was walking slowly toward the balustrade, not aware of his presence. There was no covering for the dark hair, no wrap about the white shoulders. She wore an exquisite gown of white, shimmering with reflections from the moon that scaled the mountain top. She stood at the balustrade, her hands clasping a bouquet of red roses, her chin lifted, her eyes gazing toward the mountain's crest, the prettiest picture he had ever seen. The strange dizziness of love overpowered him. His hungry eyes glanced upward towards the sky which she was blessing with her gaze, and beheld another picture, gloomy, grim, cheerless.

Against the moonlit screen of the universe clung the black tower of that far-away monastery in the clouds, the home of the monks of Saint Valentine. Out of the world, above the world, a part of the sky itself, it stood like the spectre of a sentinel whose ghostly guardianship appalled and yet soothed.

He could not, would not, move. To have done so meant the desecration of a picture so delicate that a breath upon its surface would have swept it forever from the vision. How long he revelled in the glory of the picture he knew not, for it was as if he looked from a dream. At last he saw her look down upon the roses, lift them slowly and drop them over the rail. They fell to the ground below. He thought he understood; the gift of a Prince despised.

They were not twenty feet apart. He advanced to her side, his hat in one hand, his stick—the one that felled the Viennese—trembling in the other.

"I did not know you were here," she exclaimed, in half frightened amazement. "I left my ladies inside."

He was standing beside her, looking down into the eyes.

"And I am richer because of your ignorance," he said, softly. "I have seen a picture that shall never leave my memory—never! Its beauty enthralled, enraptured. Then I saw the drama of the roses.

Ah, Your Highness, the crown is not always a mask."

"The roses were—were of no consequence," she faltered.

"I have heard how you stand between two suitors and that wretched treaty. My heart ached to tell you how I pity you."

"It is not pity I need, but courage. Pity will not aid me in my duty, Mr. Lorry. It stands plainly before me, this duty, but I have not the courage to take it up and place it about my neck forever."

"You do not, cannot love this Lorenz?" he asked.

"Love him!" she cried. "Ach, I forget! You do not know him. Yet I shall doubtless be his wife." There was an eternity of despair in that low, steady voice.

"You shall not! I swear you shall not!"

"Oh, he is a Prince! I must accept the offer that means salvation to Graustark. Why do you make it harder with torture which you think is kindness. Listen to me. Next week I am to give my answer. He will be here, in this castle. My father brought this calamity upon Graustark; I must lift it from the people. What has my happiness to do with it?"

Her sudden strength silenced him, crushed him with the real awakening of helplessness. He stood beside her, looking up at the cold monastery, strangely conscious that she was gazing toward the same dizzy height.

"It looks so peaceful up there," she said at last.

"But so cold and cheerless," he added, drearily. There was another long silence in which two hearts communed through the medium of that faraway sentinel. "They have not discovered a clue to the chief abductor, have they?" he asked, in an effort to return to his proper sphere.

"Baron Dangloss believes he has a clue—a meager and unsatisfactory one, he admits—and to-day sent officers to Ganlook to investigate the actions of a strange man who was there last week, a man who styled himself the Count of Arabazon, and who claimed to be of Vienna. Some Austrians had been hunting stags and bears in the North, however, and it is possible he is one of them." She spoke slowly, her eyes still bent on the home of the monks.

"Your Highness, I have a theory, a bold and perhaps a criminal theory, but you will allow me to tell you why I am possessed of it. I am aware that there is a Prince Gabriel. It is my opinion that no Viennese is guilty, nor are the brigands to be accused of this masterpiece in crime. Have you thought how far a man may go to obtain his heart's desire?"

She looked at him instantly, her eyes wide with growing comprehension, the solution to the mystery darting into her mind like a flash.

"You mean——" she began, stopping as if afraid to voice the suspicion.

"That Prince Gabriel is the man who bought your

guards and hired Geddos and Ostrom to carry you
to the place where he could own you, whether you
would or no," said Lorry.

"But he could never have forced me to marry him,
and I should, sooner or later, have exposed him,"
she whispered, argumentatively. "He could not expect me to be silent and submit to a marriage under
such circumstances. He knows that I would denounce him, even at the altar."

"You do not appreciate my estimate of that gentleman."

"What is to become of me!" she almost sobbed,
in an anguish of fear. "I see now—I see plainly!
It was Gabriel, and he would have done as you say."
A shudder ran through her figure, and he tenderly
whispered in her ear:

"The danger is past. He can do no more, Your
Highness. Were I positive that he is the man—and
I believe he is—I would hunt him down this night."

Her eyes closed happily under his gaze, her hand
dropped timidly from his arm and a sweet sense of
security filled her soul.

"I am not afraid," she murmured.

"Because I am here?" he asked, bending nearer.

"Because God can bless with the same hand that
punishes," she answered, enigmatically, lifting her
lashes again, and looking into his eyes with a love
at last unmasked. "He gives me a man to love and
denies me happiness. He makes of me a woman,

but He does not unmake me a Princess. Through you, He thwarts a villain; through you, He crushes the innocent. More than ever, I thank you for coming into my life. You and you alone, guided by the God who loves and despises me, saved me from Gabriel."

"I only ask——" he began, eagerly, but she interrupted.

"You should not ask anything, for I have said I cannot pay. I owe to you all I have, but cannot pay the debt."

"I shall not again forget," he murmured.

"To-morrow, if you like, I will take you over the castle and let you see the squalor in which I exist,— my throne room, my chapel, my banquet hall, my ball room, my conservatory, my sepulchre. You may say it is wealth, but I shall call it poverty," she said, after they had watched the black monastery cut a square corner from the moon's circle.

"To-morrow, if you will be so kind."

"Perhaps I may be poorer after I have saved Graustark," she said.

"I would to God I could save you from that!" he said.

"I would to God you could," she said. Her manner changed suddenly. She laughed gaily, turning a light face to his. "I hear your friend's laugh out there in the darkness. It is delightfully infectious."

XIV

"This is the throne room. Allode!"

The Princess Yetive paused before two massive doors. It was the next afternoon, and she had already shown him the palace of a Queen—the hovel of a pauper!

Through the afternoon not one word other than those which might have passed between good friends escaped the lips of either. He was all interest, she all graciousness. Allode, the sturdy guard, swung open the doors, drew the curtain, and stood aside for them to pass. Into the quiet hall she led him, a Princess in a gown of gray, a courtier in tweeds. Inside the doors he paused.

"And I thought you were Miss Guggenslocker," he said. She laughed with the glee of a child who had charmed and delighted through surprise.

"Am I not a feeble mite to sit on that throne and rule all that comes within its reach?" She directed his attention to the throne at the opposite end of the hall. "From its seat I calmly instruct gray-haired statesmen, weigh their wisdom and pass upon it as if I were Demosthenes, challenge the evils that may drive monarchs mad, and wonder if my crown is on straight."

"Let me be Ambassador from the United States and kneel at the throne, Your Highness."

"I could not engage in a jest with the crown my ancestors wore, Mr. Lorry. It is sacred, thou thoughtless American. Come, we will draw nearer, that you may see the beauty of the workmanship in that great old chair."

They stood at the base of the low, velveted stage on which stood the chair, with its high back, its massive arms and legs ashimmer in the light from the lofty windows. It was of gold, inlaid with precious stones—diamonds, rubies, emeralds, sapphires and other wondrous jewels—a relic of ancient Graustark.

"I never sit in the center. Always at one side or the other, usually leaning my elbow on the arm. You see, the discussions are generally so long and dreary that I become fatigued. One time,—I am ashamed to confess it,—I went to sleep on the throne. That was long ago. I manage to keep awake very well of late. Do you like my throne room?"

"And to think that it is yours!"

"It is this room that gives me the right to be hailed with 'Long live the Princess!' Not with campaign yells and 'Hurrah for Yetive!' How does that sound? 'Hurrah for Yetive!'" She was laughing merrily.

"Don't say it! It sounds sacrilegious—revolting!"

"For over three years—since I was eighteen—I have been supreme in that chair. During the years of my reign prior to that time I sat there with my Uncle Caspar standing beside me. How often I begged him to sit down with me! There was so much room and he certainly must have grown tired of standing. One time I cried because he frowned at me when I persisted in the presence of a great assemblage of nobles from Dawsbergen. It seems that it was a most important audience that I was granting, but I thought more of my uncle's tired old legs. I remember saying, through my sobs of mortification, that I would have him beheaded. You are to guess whether that startling threat created consternation or mirth."

"What a whimsical little Princess you must have been, weeping and pouting and going to sleep," he laughed. "And how sedate and wise you have become."

"Thank you. How very nice you are. I have felt all along that some one would discern my effort to be dignified and sedate. They say I am wise and good and gracious, but that is to be expected. They said that of sovereigns as far back as the deluge, I've heard. Would you really like to see me in that old chair?" she asked.

"Ah, you are still a woman," he said, smiling at

her pretty vanity. "Nothing could impress me more pleasantly."

She stepped carelessly and impulsively upon the royal platform, leaned against the arm of the throne, and with the charming blush of consciousness turned to him with the quickness of a guilty conscience, eager to hear his praise but fearful lest he secretly condemned her conceit. His eyes were burning with the admiration that knows no defining, and his breath came quick and sharp through parted lips. He involuntarily placed a foot upon the bottom step as if to spring to her side.

"You must not come up here!" she cried, shrinking back, her hands extended in fluttering remonstrance. "I cannot permit that, at all!"

"I beg your pardon," he cried. "That is all the humble plebeian can say. That I may be more completely under this fairy spell, pray cast about yourself the robe of rank and take up the sceptre. Perhaps I may fall upon my face."

"And hurt your head all over again," she said, laughing nervously. She hesitated for a moment, a perplexed frown crossing her brow. Then she jerked a rich robe from the back of the throne and placed it about her shoulders as only a woman can. Taking up the sceptre, she stood before the great chair, and, with a smile on her lips, held it above his head, saying softly:

"Graustark welcomes the American Prince."

He sank to his knees before the real Princess, kissed the hem of her robe and arose with face pallid. The chasm was now endless in its immensity. The Princess gingerly seated herself on the throne, placed her elbow on the broad arm, her white chin in her hand, and tranquilly surveyed the voiceless American Prince.

"You have not said, 'Thank you,'" she said, finally, her eyes wavering beneath his steady gaze.

"I am only thinking how easy it would be to cross the gulf that lies between us. With two movements of my body I can place it before you, with a third I can be sitting at your side. It is not so difficult, after all," he said hungrily eyeing the broad chair.

"No man, unless a Prince, ever sat upon this throne," she said.

"You have called me a Prince."

"Oh, I jested," she cried quickly, comprehending his intention. "I forbid you!"

Her command came too late, for he was beside her on the throne of Graustark! She sat perfectly rigid for a moment, intense fear in her eyes.

"Do you know what you have done?" she whispered, miserably.

"Usurped the throne," he replied, assuming an ease and complacence he did not feel. Truly he was guilty of unprecedented presumption.

"You have desecrated—desecrated! Do you

"Graustark Welcomes the American Prince."

hear?" she went on, paying no attention to his remark.

"Peccavi. Ah, Your Highness, I delight in my sin. For once I am a power; I speak from the throne. You will not have me abdicate in the zenith of my glory? Be kind, most gracious one. Besides, did you not once cry because your uncle refused to sit with you? Had he been the possessor of a dangerous wound, as I am, and had he found himself so weak that he could stand no longer, I am sure he would have done as I have—sat down in preference to falling limp at your feet. You do not know how badly I am wounded," he pleaded, with the subtlest double meaning.

"Why should you wound me?" she asked, plaintively. "You have no right to treat the throne I occupy as a subject for pranks and indignities. I did not believe you could be so—forgetful." There was a proud and pitiful resentment in her voice that brought him to his senses at once. He had defiled her throne. In shame and humiliation, he cried:

"I am a fool—an ingrate. You have been too gentle with me. For this despicable act of mine I cannot ask pardon, and it would be beneath you to grant it. I have hurt you, and I can never atone. I forgot how sacred is your throne. Let me depart in disgrace." He stood erect, as if to forsake the throne he had stained, but she, swayed by a com-

plete reversal of feeling, timidly, pleadingly, touched
his arm.

"Stay! It is my throne, after all. I shall divide
it, as well as the sin, with you. Sit down again, I
beg of you. For a brief spell I would rule beside
a man who is fit to be a King, but who is a desecra-
tor. There can be no harm, and no one shall be the
wiser for this sentimental departure from royal custom. We are children, anyhow—mere children."

With an exclamation of delight, he resumed his
position beside her. His hand trembled as he took
up hers to carry it to his lips. "We are children—
playing with fire," he murmured, this ingrate, this
fool!

She allowed her hand to lie limply in his, her head
sinking to the back of the chair. When her hand
was near his feverish lips, cool and white and trusting, he checked the upward progress. Slowly he
raised his eyes to study her face, finding that hers
were closed, the semblance of a smile touching her
lips, as if they were in a happy dream.

The lips! The lips! The lips! The madness of
love rushed into his heart; the expectant hand was
forgotten; his every hope and every desire measured themselves against his discretion as he looked
upon the tempting face. Could he kiss those lips but
once his life would be complete.

With a start, she opened her eyes, doubtless at the
command of the masterful ones above. The eyes

of blue met the eyes of gray in a short, sharp struggle, and the blue went down in surrender. His lips triumphed slowly, drawing closer and closer, as if restrained and impelled by the same emotion—arrogant love.

"Open your eyes, darling," he whispered, and she obeyed. Then their lips met—her first kiss of love!

She trembled from head to foot, perfectly powerless beneath the spell. Again he kissed a Princess on her throne. At this second kiss her eyes grew wide with terror, and she sprang from his side, standing before him like one bereft of reason.

"Oh, my God! What have you done?" she wailed. He staggered to his feet, dizzy with joy.

"Ha!" cried a gruff voice from the doorway, and the guilty ones whirled to look upon the witness to their blissful crime. Inside the curtains, with carbine leveled at the head of the American, stood Allode, the guard, his face distorted by rage. The Princess screamed and leaped between Lorry and the threatening carbine.

"Allode!" she cried, in frantic terror.

He angrily cried out something in his native tongue and she breathlessly, imploringly replied. Lorry did not understand their words, but he knew that she had saved him from death at the hand of her loyal, erring guard. Allode lowered his gun, bowed low and turned his back upon the throne.

"He—he would have killed you," she said, tremulously, her face the picture of combined agony and relief. She remembered the blighting kisses and the averted disaster.

"You—what did you say to him?" he asked.

"I—I—oh, I will not tell you," she cried.

"I beg of you!"

"I told him that he was to—was to put down his gun."

"I know that, but why?" he persisted.

"I—Ach, to save you, stupid!"

"How did you explain the—the——" He hesitated, generously.

"I told him that I had not been—that I had not been——"

"Say it!"

"That I had not been—offended!" she gasped, standing stiff and straight, with eyes glued upon the obedient guard.

"You were not?" he rapturously cried.

"I said it only to save your life!" she cried, turning fiercely upon him. "I shall never forgive you! Never! You must go—you must leave here at once! Do you hear? I cannot have you near me now—I cannot see you again. Ach, God! What have I given you the right to say of me?"

"Stop! It is as sacred as——"

"Yes, yes—I understand! I trust you, but you must go! Find some excuse to give your friend and go to-day! Go now!" she cried, intensely, first putting her hands to her temples, then to her eyes.

Without waiting to hear his remonstrance, if indeed he had the power to utter one, she glided swiftly toward the curtains, allowing him to follow at his will. Dazed and crushed at the sudden end to everything, he dragged his footsteps after. At the door she spoke in low, imperative tones to the motionless Allode, who dropped to his knees and muttered a reverential response. As Lorry passed beneath the hand that held the curtain aside, he glanced at the face of the man who had been witness to their weakness. He was looking straight ahead, and, from his expression, it could not have been detected that he knew there was a man on earth save himself. In the hall, she turned to him, her face cold and pale.

"I have faithful guards about me now. Allode has said he did not see you in the throne room. He will die before he will say otherwise," she said, her lips trembling with shame.

"By your command?"

"By my request. I do not command my men to lie."

Side by side they passed down the quiet hall, silent, thoughtful, the strain of death upon their hearts.

"I shall obey the only command you have given, then. This day I leave the castle. You will let me come again—to see you? There can be no harm——"

"No! You must leave Graustark at once!" she interrupted, the tones low.

"I refuse to go! I shall remain in Edelweiss, near you, just so long as I feel that I may be of service to you."

"I cannot drive you out as I would a thief," she said, pointedly.

At the top of the broad staircase he held out his hand and murmured:

"Good-bye, Your Highness!"

"Good-bye," she said, simply, placing her hand in his after a moment's hesitation. Then she left him.

An hour later the two Americans, one strangely subdued, the other curious, excited and impatient, stood before the castle waiting for the carriage. Count Halfont was with them, begging them to remain, as he could see no reason for the sudden leave-taking. Lorry assured him that they had trespassed long enough on the court's hospitality, and that he would feel much more comfortable at the hotel. Anguish looked narrowly at his friend's face, but said nothing. He was beginning to understand.

"Let us walk to the gates. The Count will oblige us by instructing the coachman to follow," said Lorry, eager to be off.

"Allow me to join you in the walk, gentlemen,"

said Count Caspar, immediately instructing a lackey to send the carriage after them. He and Lorry walked on together, Anguish lingering behind, having caught sight of the Countess Dagmar. That charming and unconventional piece of nobility promptly followed the Prime Minister's example and escorted the remaining guest to the gate.

Far down on the walk Lorry turned for a last glance at the castle from which love had banished him. Yetive was standing on the balcony, looking not at the monastery but at the exile.

She remained there long after the carriage had passed her gates, bearing the Americans swiftly over the white Castle Avenue, and there were tears in her eyes.

XV

Harry Anguish was a discreet, forbearing fellow. He did not demand a full explanation of his friend. There was enough natural wit in his merry head to see that in connection with their departure there was something that would not admit of discussion, even by confidential friends. He shrewdly formed his own conclusions and held his peace. Nor did he betray surprise when Lorry informed him, in answer to a question, that he intended to remain in Edelweiss for some time, adding that he could not expect him to do likewise if he preferred to return to Paris. But Mr. Anguish preferred to remain in Edelweiss. Had not the Countess Dagmar told him she would always be happy to see him at the castle, and had he any reason to renounce its walls? And so it was that they tarried together.

Lorry loitered aimlessly, moodily about the town, spending gloomy days and wretched nights. He reasoned that it were wisdom to fly, but a force stronger than reason held him in Edelweiss. He ventured several times to the castle wall, but turned back resolutely. There was hope in his breast that she might send for him; there was, at least, the possibility of seeing her should she ride through the streets. Anguish, on the other hand, visited the castle daily. He spent hours with the pretty Countess, undismayed by the noble moths that fluttered about her flame, and he was ever persistent, light-hearted and gay. He brought to Lorry's ears all that he could learn of the Princess. Several times he had seen her and had spoken with her. She inquired casually after the health of his friend, but nothing more. From the Countess he ascertained that Her Highness was sleeping soundly, eating heartily and apparently enjoying the best of spirits—information decidedly irritating to the one who received it second-hand.

They had been at the hotel for over a week when one afternoon Anguish rushed into the room, out of breath and scarcely able to control his excitement.

"What's up?" cried Lorry. "Has the Countess sacked you?"

"Not on your coin! But something is up, and I am its discoverer. You remember what you said about suspecting Prince Gabriel of being the chief rascal in the abduction job? Well, my boy, I am now willing to stake my life that he is the man." The news-bearer sat down on the edge of the bed and drew the first long breath he had had in a long time.

"Why do you think so?" demanded the other, all interest.

"Heard him talking just now. I didn't know who the fellow was at first, but he was talking to some strange-looking soldiers as I passed. As soon as I heard his voice I knew he was Michael. There isn't any question about it, Lorry. I am positive. He didn't observe me, but I suppose by this time he has learned that his little job was frustrated by two Americans who heard the plot near the castle gates. He has nerve to come here, hasn't he?"

"If he is guilty, yes. Still, he may feel secure because he is a powerful Prince and able to resent any accusation with a show of force. Where is he now?"

"I left him there. Come on! We'll go down and you can see for yourself."

They hurried to the corridor, which was swarming with men in strange uniforms. There were a few Graustark officers, but the majority of the buzzing conversationalists were dressed in a rich gray uniform.

"Who are these strangers?" asked Lorry.

"Oh, I forgot to tell you. Prince Lorenz is also here, and these gray fellows are a part of his retinue. Lorenz has gone on to the castle. What's the matter?" Lorry had turned pale and was reaching for the wall with unsteady hand.

"He has come for his answer," he said, slowly, painfully.

"That's right! I hadn't thought of that. I hope

she turns him down. But there's Gabriel over yonder. See those three fellows in blue? The middle one is the Prince."

Near the door leading to the piazza stood several men, gray and blue. The man designated as Gabriel was in the center, talking gaily and somewhat loudly, puffing at a cigarette between sentences. He was not tall, but he was strongly and compactly built. His hair and cropped beard were as black as coal, his eyes wide, black and lined. It was a pleasure-worn face, and Lorry shuddered as he thought of the Princess in the power of this evil-looking wretch. They leisurely made their way to a spot near the talkers. There was no mistaking the voice. Prince Gabriel and Michael were one and the same, beyond all doubt. But how to prove it to the satisfaction of others? Skepticism would follow any attempt to proclaim the Prince guilty because his voice sounded like that of the chief conspirator. In a matter where whole nations were concerned the gravest importance would be attached to the accusation of a ruler. Satisfying themselves as to the identity of that peculiar voice, the friends passed through to the piazza.

"What's to be done?" asked Anguish, boiling over with excitement.

"We must go to Baron Dangloss, tell him of our positive discovery, and then consult Count Halfont."

"And Her Royal Highness, of course."

"Yes, I suppose so," said Lorry, flicking the ashes from his cigar with a finger that was not steady. He was serving the Princess again.

They hurried to the Tower, and were soon in the presence of the fierce little Chief of Police. Lorry spent many hours with Dangloss of late, and they had become friends. His grim old face blanched perceptibly as he heard the assertions of the young men. He shook his head despairingly.

"It may be as you say, gentlemen, but I am afraid we can do nothing. To charge a Prince with such a crime on such evidence would be madness. I am of your belief, however. Prince Gabriel is the man I have suspected. Now I am convinced. Before we can do anything in such a grave matter it will be necessary to consult the Princess and her Ministers. In case we conclude to accuse the Prince of Dawsbergen, it must be after careful and judicious thought. There are many things to consider, gentlemen. For my part, I would be overjoyed to seize the villain and to serve him as we did his tools, but my hands are tied, you see. I would suggest that you go at once to the Princess and Count Halfont, tell them of your suspicions——"

"Not suspicions, my lord,—facts," interrupted Anguish.

"Well, then, facts, and ascertain how they feel about taking up a proposition that may mean war.

May I ask you to come at once to me with their an- swer. It is possible that they will call for a consultation with the Ministers, nobles and high officers. Still, I fear they will be unwilling to risk much on the rather flimsy proof you can give. Gabriel is powerful, and we do not seek war with him. There is another foe for whom we are quietly whetting our swords." The significant remark caused both listeners to prick up their ears. But he disappointed their curiosity, and they were left to speculate as to whom the other foe might be. Did he mean that Graustark was secretly, slyly making ready to resist, treaty or no treaty?

It required prolonged urging on the part of Anguish to persuade Lorry to accompany him to the castle, but, when once determined to go before the Princess with their tale, he was eager, impatient to cross the distance that lay between the hotel and the forbidden grounds. They walked rapidly down Castle Avenue and were soon at the gates. The guard knew them, and they were admitted without a word. As they hurried through the park, they saw many strange men in gray, gaudy uniforms, and it occurred to Lorry that their visit, no matter how great its importance, was ill-timed. Prince Lorenz was holding the center of the stage.

Anguish, with his customary impulsiveness, overruled Lorry's objections, and they proceeded toward the entrance. The guards of the Princess saluted profoundly, while the minions of Lorenz stared with ill-bred wonder upon these two tall men from another world. It could be seen that the castle was astir with excitement, subdued and pregnant with thriving hopes and fears. The nobility of Graustark was there; the visitors of Axphain were being entertained.

At the castle doors the two met their first obstacle, but they anticipated its presence. Two guards halted them peremptorily.

"We must see Her Royal Highness," said Anguish, but the men could not understand him. They stoically stood their ground, shaking their heads.

"Let us find some one who can understand us," advised Lorry, and in a few moments they presented themselves before the guards, accompanied by a young nobleman with whom they had acquaintance. He succeeded in advancing them to the reception hall inside the doors and found for them a servant who would carry a message to the Princess if it were possible to gain her presence. The nobleman doubted very much, however, if the missive hastily written by Lorry could find its way to her, as she had never been so occupied as now.

Lorry, in his brief note, prayed for a short audience for himself and Mr. Anguish, requesting that Count Halfont be present. He informed her that his mission was of the most imperative nature and that it related to a discovery made concerning the Prince who had tried to abduct her. In conclusion, he wrote that Baron Dangloss had required him to lay certain facts before her and that he had come with no intention to annoy her.

While they sat in the waiting-room they saw, through the glass doors, dozens of richly attired men and women in the hall beyond. They were conversing animatedly, Graustark men and women with dejected faces, Axphainians with exultation glowing in every glance. Lorry's heart sank within him. It seemed hours before the servant returned to bid them follow him. Then his blood leaped madly through veins that had been chilled and lifeless. He was to see her again!

Their guide conducted them to a small ante-room, where he left them. A few moments later the door opened and there swept quickly into the room—the Countess Dagmar, not the Princess. Her face was drawn with the trouble and sorrow she was trying so hard to conceal. Both men were on their feet in an instant, advancing to meet her.

"The Princess? Is she ill?" demanded Lorry.

"Not ill, but mad, I fear," answered she, giving a hand to each. "Mr. Lorry, she bids me say to you that she cannot see you. She appreciates the importance of your mission and thanks you for the interest you have taken. Also, she authorizes me to assure you that nothing can be done at present regarding the business on which you come."

"She refuses to see us," said he, slowly, his face whiter than ever.

"Nay; she *begs* that you will excuse her. Her Highness is sorely worn and distressed to-day, and I fear cannot endure all that is happening. She is apparently calm and composed, but I, who know her so well, can see the strain beneath."

"Surely she must see the urgency of quick action in this matter of ours," cried Anguish, half angrily. "We are not dogs to be kicked out of the castle. We have a right to be treated fairly——"

"We cannot censure the Princess, Harry," said Lorry, calmly. "We have come because we would befriend her, and she sees fit to reject our good offices. There is but one thing left for us to do— depart as we came."

"But I don't like it a little bit," growled the other.

"If you only knew, Mr. Anguish, you would not be so harsh and unjust," remonstrated the lady warmly. Turning to Lorry, she said: "She asked me to hand you this and bid you retain it as a token of her undying esteem."

She handed him a small, exquisite miniature of the Princess, framed in gold inlaid with rubies. He took it dumbly in his fingers, but dared not look at the portrait it contained. With what might have seemed disrespect, he dropped the treasure into his coat pocket.

"Tell her I shall always retain it as a token of her—esteem," he said. "And now may I ask whether she handed my note to her uncle, the Count?"

The Countess blushed in a most unaccountable manner.

"Not while I was with her," she said, recovering the presence of mind she apparently had lost.

"She destroyed it, I presume," said he, laughing harshly.

"I saw her place it in her bosom, sir, and with the right hand," cried the Countess, as if betraying a State secret.

"In her—you are telling me the truth?" cried he, his face lighting up.

"Now, see here, Lorry, don't begin to question the Countess's word. I won't stand for that," interposed Anguish, good-humoredly.

"I should be more than base to say falsely that she had done anything so absurd," said the Countess, indignantly.

"Where is she now?" asked Lorry.

"In her boudoir. The Prince Lorenz is with her—alone."

"What!" he cried, jealousy darting into his existence. He had never known jealousy before.

"They are betrothed," said she, with an effort.

There was a dead silence, broken by Lorry's deep groan as he turned and walked blindly to the opposite side of the room. He stopped in front of a huge painting and stared at it, but did not see a line or a tint.

"You don't mean to say she has accepted?" half whispered Anguish.

"Nothing less."

"Thank God, you are only a Countess," he said, tenderly.

"Why—why—what difference can it make—I mean, why do you say that?" she stammered, crimson to her hair.

"Because you won't have to sell yourself at a sacrifice," he said, foolishly. Lorry came back to them at this juncture, outwardly calm and deliberate.

"Tell us about it, pray. We had guessed as much."

"Out there are his people,—the wretches!" she cried, vindictively, her pretty face in a helpless frown. "To-day was the day, you know, on which he was to have his answer. He came and knelt in the audience chamber. All Graustark had implored her to refuse the hated offer, but she bade him rise, and there, before us all, promised to become his bride.

"The greatest sorrow Graustark has ever known grows out of that decision. She is determined to save for us what her father's folly lost. To do this, she becomes the bride of a vile wretch, a man who soils her pure nature when he thinks of her. Oh, we sought to dissuade her,—we begged, we entreated, but without avail. She will not sacrifice one foot of Graustark to save herself. See the triumphant smiles on their faces—the brutes!" She pointed maliciously to the chattering visitors in the hall. "Already they think the castle is theirs. The union of Graustark and Axphain! Just what they most desired, but we could not make her see it so."

"Is the day set?" asked Lorry, bravely, after a moment's silent inspection of the dark-browed victors.

"Yes, and there is to be no delay. The marriage contract has already been signed. The date is November 20th, the day on which we are to account to Bolaroz for our war debt. The old Prince's wedding gift to Graustark is to be a document favoring us with a ten years' extension," she said, scornfully.

"And where is she to live?"

"Here, of course. She is Graustark's ruler, and here she insists on abiding. Just contemplate our court! Over-run with those Axphain dogs! Ah, she has wounded Graustark more than she has helped her."

There was nothing more to be said or done, so, after a few moments, the Americans took their departure. The Countess bade them farewell, saying that she must return to the Princess.

"I'll see you to-morrow," said Anguish, with rare assurance and the air of an old and indispensable friend.

"And you, Mr. Lorry?" she said, curiously.

"I am very much occupied," he mumbled.

"You do wrong in seeking to deceive me," she whispered, as Anguish passed through the door ahead of them. "I know why you do not come."

"Has she told you?"

"I have guessed. Would that it could have been you and not the other."

"One cannot be a man and a Prince at the same time, I fancy," he said, bitterly.

"Nor can one be a Princess and a woman."

Lorry recalled the conversation in the sick-room two weeks before, and smiled ironically. The friendly girl left them at the door and they passed out of the castle.

"I shall leave Edelweiss to-morrow," said one, more to himself than to his companion, as they crossed the parade. The other gave a start and did not look pleased. Then he instinctively glanced toward the castle.

"The Princess is at her window," he cried, clutching Lorry's arm and pointing back. But the other refused to turn, walking on blindly.

"You ought not to have acted like that, Gren," said Anguish, a few moments later. "She saw me call your attention to her, and she saw you refuse to look back. I don't think that you should have hurt her." Lorry did not respond, and there was no word between them until they were outside the castle gates.

"You may leave to-morrow, Lorry, if you like, but I'm going to stay a while," said Harry, a trifle confusedly.

"Haven't you had enough of the place?"

"I don't care a whoop for the place. You see, it's this way: I'm just as hard hit as you, and it is not a Princess that I have to contend with."

"You mean that you are in love with the Countess?"

"Emphatically."

"I'm sorry for you."

"Think she'll turn me down?"

"Unless you buy a title from one of these miserable Counts or Dukes."

"Oh, I'm not so sure about that. These Counts and Dukes come over and marry our American girls. I don't see why I can't step in and pick out a nice little Countess if I want to."

"She is not as avaricious as the Counts and Dukes, I'll wager. She cares nothing for your money."

"Well, she's as poor as a church mouse," said the other, doggedly.

"The Countess poor? How do you know?"

"I asked her one day and she told me all about it," said Anguish.

XVI

A CLASH AND ITS RESULT

"I feel like spending the rest of my days in that monastery up there," said Lorry, after dinner that evening. They were strolling about the town. One was determined to leave the city, the other firm in his resolve to stay. The latter won the day when he shrewdly, if explosively, reminded the former that it was their duty as men to stay and protect the Princess from the machinations of Gabriel, that knave of purgatory. Lorry, at last recognizing the hopelessness of his suit, was ready to throw down his arms and abandon the field to superior odds. His presumption in aspiring for the hand of a Princess began to touch his sense of humor, and he laughed, not very merrily, it is true, but long and loudly, at his folly. At first he cursed the world and every one in it, giving up in despair, but later he cursed only himself. Yet, as he despaired and scoffed, he felt within himself the ever-present hope that luck might turn the tide of battle.

This puny ray grew perceptibly when Anguish brought him to feel that she needed his protection from the man who had once sought to despoil and who might reasonably be expected to persevere. He agreed to linger in Edelweiss, knowing that each day would add pain to the torture he was already suffering, his sole object being, he convinced himself, to frustrate Gabriel's evil plans.

Returning late in the evening from their stroll, they entered a café celebrated in Edelweiss. In all his life, Lorry had never known the loneliness that makes death welcome. To-night he felt that he could not live, so maddening was the certainty that he could never regain joy. His heart bled with the longing to be near her who dwelt inside those castle walls. He scoffed and grieved, but grieved the more.

The café was crowded with men and women. In a far corner sat a party of Axphain nobles, their Prince, a most democratic fellow, at the head of a long table. There were songs, jests and boisterous laughter. The celebration grew wilder, and Lorry and Anguish crossed the room, and, taking seats at a table, ordered wine and cigars, both eager for a closer view of the Prince. How Lorry loathed him!

Lorenz was a good-looking young fellow, little more than a boy. His smooth face was flushed, and there was about him an air of dissipation that suggested depravity in its advanced stage. The face that might have been handsome was the reflection of a *roué,* dashing, devilish. He was fair-haired and tall, taller than his companions by half a head. With reckless abandon, he drank and sang and jested, arrogant in his flighty merriment. His cohorts were not far behind him in riotous wit.

At length one of the revelers, speaking in German, called on Lorenz for a toast to the Princess Yetive, his promised bride. Without a moment's hesitation the Prince sprang to his feet, held his glass aloft, and cried:

"Here's to the fairest of the fair, sweet Yetive, so hard to win, too good to lose. She loves me, God bless her heart! And I love her, God bless my heart, too! For each kiss from her wondrous lips I shall credit myself with oue thousand gavvos. That is the price of a kiss."

"I'll give two thousand!" roared one of the nobles, and there was a laugh in which the Prince joined.

"Nay! I'll not sell them now. In after years, when she has grown old and her lips are parched and dry from the sippings I have had, I'll sell them all at a bargain. Alas, she has not yet kissed me!"

Lorry's heart bounded with joy, though his hands were clenched in rage.

"She will kiss me to-morrow. To-morrow I shall taste what no other man has touched, what all men have coveted. And I'll be generous, gentlemen. She is so fair that your foul mouths would blight with but one caress upon her tender lips, and yet you shall not be deprived of bliss. I shall kiss her thrice for each of you. Let me count: thrice eleven is thirty-

"Two's Company. Three's a Crowd."

three. Aye, thirty-three of my kisses shall be wasted for the sake of my friends, lucky dogs! Drink to my Princess!"

"Bravo!" cried the others, and the glasses were raised to lip.

A chair was overturned. The form of a man landed suddenly at the side of the Prince and a rough hand dashed the glass from his fingers, the contents flying over his immaculate English evening dress.

"Don't you dare drink to that toast!" cried a voice in his astonished ear, a voice speaking in excited German. He whirled and saw a scowling face beside his own, a pair of gray eyes that flashed fire.

"What do you mean?" he demanded, anger replacing amazement. The other members of his party stood as if spellbound.

"I mean that you speak of the Princess of Graustark. Do you understand that, you miserable cur?"

"Oh!" screamed the Prince, convulsed with rage, starting back and instinctively reaching for the sword he did not carry. "You shall pay for this! I will teach you to interfere——"

"I'll insult you more decidedly, just to avoid misapprehension," snarled Lorry, swinging his big fist squarely upon the mouth of the Prince. His Royal Highness landed under a table ten feet away.

Instantly the café was in an uproar. The stupefied Axphainians regained their senses and a general assault was made upon the hot-headed American. He knocked another down, Harry Anguish coming to his assistance with several savage blows, after which the Graustark spectators and the waiters interfered. It was all over in an instant, yet a sensation that would live in the gossip of generations had been created. A Prince of the realm had been brutally assaulted! Holding his jaw, Lorenz picked himself from the floor, several of his friends running to his aid. There was blood on his lips and chin; it trickled to his shirt front. For some moments he stood panting, glaring at Lorry's mocking face.

"I am Lorenz of Axphain, sir," he said at last, his voice quivering with suppressed anger.

"It shall be a pleasure to kill you, Lorenz," observed his adversary, displaying his ignorance of lese-majesté.

Anguish, pale and very much concerned, dragged him away, the Prince leaving the café ahead of them, followed by his chattering, cursing companions. Prince Gabriel was standing near the door as they passed out. He looked at the Americans sharply, and Anguish detected something like triumphant joy in his eyes.

"Good Lord, Lorry; this means a duel! Don't you know that?" cried he, as they started upstairs.

"Of course, I do. And I'm going to kill that

villain, too," exclaimed Lorry, loud enough to be heard from one end of the room to the other.

"This is horrible, horrible! Let me square it up some way if——" began the alarmed Anguish.

"Square it up! Look here, Harry Anguish, I am the one who will do the squaring. If he wants a duel he can have it any old time and in any style he desires."

"He may kill you!"

"Not while a just God rules over our destinies. I'll take my chances with pistols, and now let me tell you one thing, my boy; he'll never live to touch his lips to hers, nor will there be a royal wedding. She cannot marry a dead man." He was beside himself with excitement, and it was fully half an hour before Anguish could bring him to a sensible discussion of the affair. Gradually he became cool, and, the fever once gone, he did not lose his head again.

"Choose pistols at ten paces and at eight to-morrow," he said, nonchalantly, as a rap at the door of their apartment announced the arrival of the Prince's friend.

Anguish admitted two well-dressed, black-bearded men, both of whom had sat at the Prince's table in the café. They introduced themselves as the Duke of Mizrox and Colonel Attobawn. Their visit was brief, formal and conclusive.

"We understand that you are persons of rank in

your own America?" said the Duke of Mizrox, after a few moments.

"We are sons of business men," responded Mr. Anguish.

"Oh, well, I hardly know. But His Highness is very willing to waive his rank, and to grant you a meeting."

"I'm delighted by His Highness's condescension, which I perfectly understand," observed Mr. Anguish. "Now, what have we to settle, gentlemen?"

"The detail of weapons."

When Anguish announced that his principal chose pistols, a strange gleam crept into the eyes of the Axphainians, and they seemed satisfied. Colonel Attobawn acted as interpreter during this short but very important interview which was carried on in the Axphain language. Lorry sat on the window-sill, steadfastly gazing into the night. The visitors departed soon, and it was understood that Prince Lorenz would condescend to meet Mr. Lorry at eight o'clock on the next morning in the valley beyond the castle, two miles from town. There was no law prohibiting duels in Graustark.

"Well, you're in for it, old man," said Anguish, gloomily, his chin in his hands as he fastened melancholy eyes upon his friend.

"Don't worry about me, Harry. There's only one way for this thing to end. His Royal Highness is doomed." Lorry spoke with the earnestness and conviction of one who is permitted to see into the future.

Calmly, he prepared to write some letters, not to say farewell, but to explain to certain persons the cause of the duel and to say that he gloried in the good fortune which had presented itself. One of these letters was addressed to his mother, another to the father of Prince Lorenz, and the last to the Princess of Graustark. To the latter he wrote much that did not appear in the epistles directed to the others. Anguish had been in his room more than an hour, and had frequently called to his friend and begged him to secure what rest he could in order that their nerves might be steady in the morning. But it was not until after midnight that the duelist sealed the envelopes, directed them and knocked at his second's door to say:

"I shall entrust these letters to you, Harry. You must see that they start on their way to-morrow."

Then he went to bed and to sleep.

At six his second, who had slept but little, called him. They dressed hurriedly and prepared for the ride to the valley. Their own new English bulldog revolvers were to serve as weapons in the coming combat, and a carriage was to be in waiting for them in a side street at seven o'clock.

Before leaving their room they heard evidences of a commotion in the hotel, and were apprehensive lest the inmates had learned of the duel and were making ready to follow the fighters to the appointed spot. There was a confusion of voices, the sound of rushing feet, the banging of doors, the noise increasing as the two men stepped into the open hall. They were amazed to see half-dressed men and women standing or running about the halls, intense excitement in their faces and in their actions. White uniformed policemen were flocking into the corridors; soldiers, coatless and hatless, fresh from their beds, came dashing upon the scene. There were excited cries, angry shouts and, more mystifying than all, horrified looks and whispers.

"What has happened?" asked Lorry, stopping near the door.

"It can't be a fire. Look! The door to that room down there seems to be the center of attraction. Hold on! Don't go over there, Lorry. There may be something to unnerve you, and that must not happen now. Let us go down this stairway—it leads to a side entrance, I think." They were half way down the stairs when the thunder of rushing feet in the hall above came to their ears, causing them to hesitate between curiosity and good judgment. "They are coming this way."

"Hear them howl! What the devil can be the cause of all this rumpus?" cried the other.

At that instant half a dozen police guards appeared at the head of the stairs. Upon seeing the Americans, they stopped and turned as if to oppose a foe approaching from the opposite direction. Baron Dangloss separated himself from the white coats above and called to the men below. In alarm, they started for the street door. He was with them in an instant, his usually red face changing from white to purple, his anxious eyes darting first toward the group above and then toward the bewildered Americans.

"What's the matter?" demanded Lorry.

"There! See!" cried Dangloss, and even as he spoke a conflict began at the head of the stairs, the police, augmented by a few soldiers, struggling against a howling, enraged mass of Axphainians. Dangloss dragged his reluctant charges through a small door, and they found themselves in the baggage-room of the hotel. Despite their queries, he offered no explanation, but rushed them along, passing out of the opposite door, down a short stairway and into a side street. A half dozen police-guards were awaiting them, and before they could catch the faintest idea of what it all meant, they were running with the officers through an alley, as if pursued by demons.

"Now, what in thunder does this mean?" panted Lorry, attempting to slacken the pace. He and Anguish were just beginning to regain their senses.

"Do not stop! Do not stop!" wheezed Dangloss. "You must get to a place of safety. We cannot pre-

vent something dreadful happening if you are
caught!"

"If we are caught!" cried Anguish. "Why, what
have we done?"

"Unhand me, Baron Dangloss! This is an outrage!" shouted Lorry.

"For God's sake, be calm! We are befriending
you. When we reach the Tower, where you will be
safe, I shall explain," gasped the panting Chief of
Police. A few moments later they were inside the
prison gates, angry, impatient, fatigued.

"Is this a plan to prevent the duel?" demanded
Lorry, turning upon the chief, who had dropped
limply into a chair and was moping his brow. When
he could find his breath enough to answer, Dangloss
did so, and he might as well have thrown a bomb-
shell at their feet.

"There'll be no duel. Prince Lorenz is dead!"

"Dead!" gasped the others.

"Found dead in his bed, stabbed to the heart!"
exclaimed the chief. "We have saved you from his
friends, gentlemen, but I must say that you are still
in a tight place."

He then related to them the whole story. Just
before six o'clock Mizrox had gone to the Prince's
room to prepare him for the duel. The door was
closed but unlocked, as he found after repeated
knockings. Lorenz was lying on the bed, undressed
and covered with blood. The horrified Duke made

a hasty examination and found that he was dead. A dagger had been driven to his heart as he slept. The hotel was aroused, the police called, and the excitement was at its highest pitch when the two friends came from their room a few minutes after six.

"But what have we to do with this dreadful affair? Why are we rushed off here like criminals?" asked Lorry, a feeling of cruel gladness growing out of the knowledge that Lorenz was dead and that the Princess was freed from her compact.

"My friend," said Dangloss, slowly, "you are accused of the murder."

Lorry was too much stunned to be angry, too weak to protest. For some moments after the blow fell he and Anguish were speechless. Then came the protestations, the rage and the threats, through all of which Dangloss sat calmly. Finally he sought to quiet them, partially succeeding.

"Mr. Lorry, the evidence is very strong against you, but you shall not be unjustly treated. You are not a prisoner as yet. In Graustark a man who is accused of murder, and who was not seen by any one to commit the crime, cannot be legally arrested until an accuser shall go before the Princess, who is also High Priestess, and swear on his life that he knows the guilty man. The man who so accuses agrees to forfeit his own life in case the other is proved innocent. If you are to be charged with the

murder of the Prince, some one must go before the
Princess and take oath—his life against yours. I
am holding you here, sir, because it is the only place
in which you are safe. Lorenz's friends would have
torn you to pieces had we not found you first. You
are not prisoners, and you may depart if you think
it wise."

"But, my God, how can they accuse me? I knew
nothing of the murder until I reached this place,"
cried Lorry, stopping short in his restless walk before the little Baron.

"So you say, but——"

"If you accuse me, damn you, I'll kill you!" whispered Lorry, holding himself tense. Anguish caught
and held him.

"Be calm, sir," cautioned Dangloss. "I may have
my views, but I am not willing to take oath before
Her Royal Highness. Listen: You were heard to
say you would kill him; you began the fight; you
were the aggressor, and there is no one else on
earth, it is said, who could have wished to murder
him. The man who did the stabbing entered the
room through the hall door and left by the same.
There are drops of blood in the carpet, leading direct
to your door. On your knob are the prints of
bloody fingers where you—or some one else—placed
his hand in opening the door. It was this discovery,
made by me and my men, that fully convinced the
enraged friends of the dead Prince that you were

guilty. When we opened the door you were gone.
Then came the search, the fight at the head of the
stairs, and the race to the prison. The reason I
saved you from that mob should be plain to you. I
love my Princess, and I do not forget that you
risked your life—each of you—to protect her. I
have done all that I can, gentlemen, to protect you
in return. It means death to you if you fall into
the hands of his followers just now. A few hours
will cool them off, no doubt, but now—now it would
be madness to face them. I know not what they
have done to my men at the hotel!—perhaps butch-
ered them."

There was anxiety in Dangloss's voice and there
was honesty in his keen old eyes. His charges now
saw the situation clearly and apologized warmly for
the words they had uttered under the pressure of
somewhat extenuating circumstances. They expressed a willingness to remain in the prison until
the excitement abated or until some one swore his
life against the supposed murderer. They were
virtually prisoners, and they knew it well. Furthermore, they could see that Baron Dangloss believed
Lorry guilty of the murder; protestation of innocence had been politely received and politely dis-
regarded.

"Do you expect one of his friends to take the
oath?" asked Lorry.

"Yes; it is sure to come."

"But you will not do so yourself?"

"No."

"I thank you, captain, for I see that you believe me guilty."

"I do not say you are guilty, remember, but I will say that if you did murder Prince Lorenz you have made the people of Graustark rejoice from the bottoms of their hearts, and you will be eulogized from one end of the land to the other."

"Hanged and eulogized," said Lorry, grimly.

XVI

The two captives who were not prisoners were so dazed by the unexpected events of the morning that they did not realize the vast seriousness of the situation for hours. Then it dawned upon them that appearances were really against them, and that they were alone in a land far beyond the reach of help from home. One circumstance puzzled them with its damning mystery:—how came the blood stains upon the door-knob? Dangloss courteously discussed this strange and unfortunate feature with them, but with ill-concealed skepticism. It was evident that his mind was clear in regard to the whole affair.

Anguish was of the opinion that the real murderer had stained the knob intentionally, aiming to cast suspicion on the man who had been challenged. The assassin had an object in leaving those convicting finger-marks where they would do the most damage. He either desired the arrest and death of the American or hoped that his own guilt might escape attention through the misleading evidence. Lorry held, from his deductions, that the crime had been committed by a fanatic who loved his sovereign too devotedly to see her wedded to Lorenz. Then why should he wantonly cast guilt upon the man who had been her protector, objected Dangloss.

The police guards came in from the hotel about ten o'clock, bearing marks of an ugly conflict with the Axphainians. They reported that the avengers had been quelled for the time being, but that a deputation had already started for the castle to lay the matter before the Princess. Officers had searched the rooms of the Americans for blood stains, but had found no sign of them.

"Did you find bloody water in which hands had been washed?" asked Anguish.

"No," responded one of the guards. "There was nothing to be found in the bowls and jars except soapy water. There is not a blood stain in the room, Captain."

"That shakes your theory a little, eh?" cried Anguish, triumphantly. "Examine Mr. Lorry's hands and see if there is blood upon them." Lorry's hands were white and uncontaminated. Dangloss wore a pucker on his brow.

Shortly afterward a crowd of Axphain men came to the prison gates and demanded the person of Grenfall Lorry, departing after an ugly show of rage. Curious Edelweiss citizens stood afar off, watching the walls and windows eagerly.

"This may cost Edelweiss a great deal of trouble, gentlemen, but there is more happiness here this morning than the city has known in months. Everybody believes you killed him, Mr. Lorry, but they all love you for the deed," said Dangloss, returning at noon from a visit to the hotel and a ride through the streets. "The Prince's friends have been at the castle since nine o'clock, and I am of the opinion that they are having a hard time with the High Priestess."

"God bless her!" cried Lorry.

"The town is crazy with excitement. Messengers have been sent to old Prince Bolaroz to inform him of the murder and to urge him to hasten hither, where he may fully enjoy the vengeance that is to be wreaked upon his son's slayer. I have not seen a wilder time in Edelweiss since the close of the siege, fifteen years ago. By my soul, you are in a bad box, sir. They are lurking in every part of town to kill you if you attempt to leave the Tower before the Princess signs an order to restrain you legally. Your life, outside these walls, would not be worth a snap of the fingers."

Captain Quinnox, of the Princess's bodyguard, accompanied by half a dozen of his men, rode up to the prison gates about two o'clock and was promptly admitted. The young captain was in sore distress.

"The Duke of Mizrox has sworn that you are the murderer, Mr. Lorry, and stakes his life," said he, after greetings. "Her Highness has just placed in my hands an order for your arrest as the assassin of Prince Lorenz."

Lorry turned as pale as death. "You—you don't mean to say that she has signed a warrant—that she believes me guilty," he cried, aghast.

"She has signed the warrant, but very much against her inclination. Count Halfont informed me that she pleaded and argued with the Duke for hours, seeking to avert the act which is bound to give pain to all of us. He was obdurate, and threatened to carry complaint to Bolaroz, who would instantly demand satisfaction. As the Duke is willing to die if you are proved innocent, there was no other course left for her than to dictate and sign this royal decree. Captain Dangloss, I am instructed to give you these papers. One is the warrant for Mr. Lorry's arrest, the other orders you to assume charge of him and to place him in confinement until the day of trial."

While Quinnox was making this statement, the accused stood with bowed head and throbless heart. He did not see the captain's hand tremble as he passed the documents to Dangloss, nor did he hear the unhappy sigh that came from the latter's lips. Anguish, fiery and impulsive, was not to be subdued.

"Is there no warrant for my arrest?" he demanded.

"There is not. You are at liberty to go, sir," responded Quinnox.

"I'd like to know why there isn't. I'm just as guilty as Lorry."

"The Duke charges the crime to but one of you. Baron Dangloss, will you read the warrant?"

The old chief read the decree of the Princess slowly and impressively. It was as follows:

"Jacot, Duke of Mizrox, before his God and on his life, swears that Grenfall Lorry did foully, maliciously and designedly slay Lorenz, Prince of Axphain, on the 20th day of October, in the year of our Lord 189—, and in the city of Edelweiss, Graustark. It is therefore my decree that Grenfall Lorry be declared murderer of Lorenz, Prince of Axphain, until he be proved innocent, in which instance, his accuser, Jacot, Duke of Mizrox, shall forfeit his life, according to the law of this land providing penalty for false witness, and by which he, himself, has sworn to abide faithfully.

"Signed: Yetive."

There was silence for some moments, broken by the dreary tones of the accused.

"What chance have I to prove my innocence?" he asked, hopelessly.

"The same opportunity that he has to prove your guilt. The Duke must, according to our law, prove you guilty beyond all doubt," spoke the young captain.

"When am I to be tried?"

"Here is my order from the Princess," said Dangloss, glancing over the other paper. "It says that I am to confine you securely and to produce you before the tribunal on the 26th day of October."

"A week! That is a long time," said Lorry. "May I have permission to see the signature affixed to those papers?" Dangloss handed them to him. He glanced at the name he loved, written by the hand he had kissed, now signing away his life, perhaps. A mist came over his eyes and a strange joy filled his soul. The hand that signed the name had trembled in doing so, had trembled pitifully. The heart had not guided the fingers. "I am your prisoner, Captain Dangloss. Do with me as you will," he said, simply.

"I regret that I am obliged to place you in a cell, sir, and under guard. Believe me, I am sorry this happened. I am your friend," said the old man, gloomily.

"And I," cried Quinnox.

"But what is to become of me?" cried poor Anguish, half in tears. "I won't leave you, Gren. It's an infernal outrage!"

"Be cool, Harry, and it will come out right. He has no proof, you know," said the other, wringing his friend's hand.

"But I'll have to stay here, too. If I go outside these walls, I'll be killed like a dog," protested Harry.

"You are to have a guard of six men while you are in Edelweiss, Mr. Anguish. Those are the instructions of the Princess. I do not believe the scoundrels—I mean the Axphain nobles—will molest you if you do not cross them. When you are ready to go to your hotel, I will accompany you."

Half an hour later Lorry was in a cell from which there could be no escape, while Anguish was riding toward the hotel, surrounded by Graustark soldiers. He had sworn to his friend that he would unearth the murderer if it lay within the power of man. Captain Dangloss heard the oath and smiled sadly.

At the castle there was depression and relief, grief and joy. The royal family, the nobility, even the servants, soldiers and attendants, rejoiced in the stroke that had saved the Princess from a fate worse than death. Her preserver's misfortune was deplored deeply; expressions of sympathy were whispered among them all, high and low. The Axphainians were detested—the Prince most of all— and the crime had come as a joy instead of a shock. There were, of course, serious complications for the future, involving ugly conditions that were bound to force themselves upon the land. The dead man's father would demand the life of his murderer. If not Lorry, who? Graustark would certainly be asked to produce the man who killed the heir to the throne of Axphain, or to make reparation—bloody reparation, no doubt.

In the privacy of her room the stricken Princess collapsed from the effects of the ordeal. Her poor brain had striven in vain to invent means by which she might save the man she loved. She had surrendered to the inevitable because there was justice in the claims of the inexorable Duke and his vindictive friends. Against her will, she had issued the decree, but not, however, until she had learned that he was in prison and unable to fly the country. The hope that delay might aid him in escaping was rudely crushed when her uncle informed her of Lorry's whereabouts. She signed the decree as if in a dream, a nightmare, with trembling hand and broken heart. His death warrant! And yet, like all others, she believed him guilty. Guilty for her sake! And this was how she rewarded him.

Mizrox and his friends departed in triumph, revenge written on every face. She walked blindly, numbly, to her room, assisted by her uncle, the Count. Without observing her aunt or the Countess Dagmar, she staggered to the window and looked below. The Axphainians were crossing the parade ground jubilantly. Then came the clatter of a horse's hoof, and Captain Quinnox, with the fatal papers in his possession, galloped down the avenue.

She clutched the curtains distractedly, and, leaning far forward, cried from the open window:

"Quinnox! Quinnox! Come back! I forbid— I forbid! Destroy those papers! Quinnox!"

But Quinnox heard not the pitiful wail. He rode on, his dark face stamped with pity for the man whose arrest he was to make. Had he heard the cry from his sovereign, the papers would have been in her destroying grasp with the speed that comes only to the winged birds. Seeing him disappear down the avenue, she threw her hands to her head and sank back with a moan, fainting. Count Halfont caught her in his arms. It was nightfall before she was fully revived. The faithful young Countess clung to her caressingly, lovingly, uttering words of consolation until long after the shades of night had dropped. They were alone in the Princess's boudoir, seated together upon the divan, the tired head of the one resting wearily against the shoulder of the other. Gentle fingers toyed with the tawny tresses, and a soft voice lulled with its consoling promise of hope. Wide and dark and troubled were the eyes of the ruler of Graustark.

An attendant appeared and announced the arrival of one of the American gentlemen, who insisted on seeing Her Royal Highness. The card on the tray bore the name of Harry Anguish. At once the Princess was aflutter with eagerness and excitement.

"Anguish! Show him to this room quickly. Oh, Dagmar, he brings word from him! He comes from him! Why is he so slow? Ach, I cannot wait!"

Far from being slow, Anguish was exceedingly swift in approaching the room to which he feared admittance might be denied. He strode boldly, impetuously into the apartment, his feet muddy, his clothing splashed with rain, his appearance far from that of a gentleman.

"Tell me! What is it?" she cried, as he stopped in the center of the room and glared at her.

"I don't care whether you like it, and it doesn't matter if you are a Princess," he exploded, "there are a few things I'm going to say to you. First, I want to know what kind of a woman you are to throw into prison a man like—like—— Oh, it drives me crazy to think of it! I don't care if you are insulted. He's a friend of mine, and he is no more guilty than you are, and I want to know what you mean by ordering his arrest?"

Her lips parted as if to speak, her face grew deathly pale, her fingers clutched the edge of the divan. She stared at him piteously, unable to move, to speak. Then the blue eyes filled with tears, a sob came to her lips, and her tortured heart made a last, brave effort at defense.

"I—I—Mr. Anguish, you wrong me,—I—I——"
She tried to whisper through the closed throat and

stiffened lips. Words failed her, but she pleaded
with those wet, imploring eyes. His heart melted,
his anger was swept away in a twinkling. He saw
that he had wounded her most unjustly.

"You brute!" hissed the Countess, with flashing,
indignant eyes, throwing her arms about the Princess and drawing her head to her breast.

"Forgive me," he cried, sinking to his knee before
the Princess, shame and contrition in his face. "I
have been half mad this whole day, and I have
thought harshly of you. I now see that you are
suffering more intensely than I. I love Lorry, and
that is my only excuse. He is being foully wronged,
Your Highness, foully wronged."

"I deserve your contempt, after all. Whether he
be guilty or innocent, I should have refused to sign
the decree. It is too late now. I have signed away
something that is very dear to me,—his life. You
are his friend and mine. Can you tell me what he
thinks of me—what he says—how he feels?" She
asked the triple question breathlessly.

"He believes you were forced into the act, and
said as much to me. And how he feels, I can only
ask how you would feel if you were in his place,
innocent and yet almost sure of conviction. These
friends of Axphain will resort to any subterfuge,
now that one of their number has staked his life.
Mark my word, some one will deliberately swear
that he saw Grenfall Lorry strike the blow and that

will be as villainous a lie as man ever told. What I am here for, Your Highness, is to ask if that decree cannot be withdrawn."

"Alas, it cannot! I would gladly order his release if I could, but you can see what that would mean to us. A war, Mr. Anguish," she sighed, miserably.

"But you will not see an innocent man condemned?" cried he, again indignant.

"I have only your statement for that, sir, if you will pardon me. I hope, from the bottom of my heart, that he did not murder the Prince after being honorably challenged."

"He is no coward!" thundered Anguish, startling both women with his vehemence. "I say he did not kill the Prince, but I'll stake my life he would have done so had they met this morning. There's no use trying to have the decree rescinded, I see, so I'll take my departure. I don't blame you, Your Highness; it is your duty, of course. But it's pretty hard on Lorry, that's all."

"He may be able to clear himself," suggested the Countess, nervously.

"And he may not, so there you have it. What chance have two Americans over here with everybody against us?"

"Stop! You shall not say that! He shall have full justice, at any cost, and there is one here who is not against him," cried the Princess, with flashing eyes.

"I am aware that everybody admires him because he has done Graustark a service in ridding it of something obnoxious—a prospective husband. But that does not get him out of jail."

"You are unkind again," said the Princess, slowly. "I chose my husband, and you assume much when you intimate that I am glad because he was murdered."

"Do not be angry," cried the Countess, impatiently. "We all regret what has happened, and I, for one, hope that Mr. Lorry may escape from the Tower and laugh forevermore at his pursuers. If he could only dig his way out!"

The Princess shot a startled look toward the speaker as a new thought entered her weary brain; a short, involuntary gasp told that it had lodged and would grow. She laughed at the idea of an escape from the Tower, but as she laughed a tiny spot of red began to spread upon her cheek, and her eyes glistened strangely.

Anguish remained with them for half an hour. When he left the castle it was with a more hopeful feeling in his breast. In the Princess's bed-chamber late that night, two girls, in loose, silken gowns, sat before a low fire and talked of something that caused the Countess to tremble with excitement when first her pink-cheeked sovereign mentioned it in confidence.

XVIII

Lorry's cell was as comfortable as a cell could be made through the efforts of a kindly jailer and a sympathetic Chief of Police. It was not located in the dungeon, but high in the tower, a little rock-bound room, with a single barred window far above the floor. There was a bed of iron upon which had been placed a clean mattress, and there was a little chair. The next day after his arrest a comfortable arm chair replaced the latter; a table, a lamp, some books, flowers, a bottle of wine and some fruit found their way to his lonely apartment—whoever may have sent them. Harry Anguish was admitted to the cell during the afternoon. He promptly and truthfully denied all interest in the donations, but smiled wisely.

He reported that most of the Axphain contingent was still in town; a portion had hurried home, carrying the news to the old Prince, instructed by the aggressive Mizrox to fetch him forthwith to Edelweiss, where his august presence was necessary before the twenty-sixth. Those who remained in the Graustark capital were quiet but still in a threatening mood. The Princess, so Harry informed the prisoner, sent sincere expressions of sympathy and the hope that all would end well with him. Count Halfont, the Countess, Gaspon and many others had asked to be remembered. The prisoner smiled wearily and promised that they should not be forgotten in a week—which was as far as he expected his memory to extend.

Late in the evening, as he was lying on his bed, staring at the shadowy ceiling and puzzling his brain with most oppressive uncertainties, the rattle of keys in the lock announced the approach of visitors. The door swung open, and through the grate he saw Dangloss and Quinnox. The latter wore a long military rain coat and had just come in from a drenching downpour. Lorry's reverie had been so deep that he had not heard the thunder nor the howling of the winds. Springing to his feet, he advanced quickly to the grated door.

"Captain Quinnox brings a private message from the Princess," said the chief, the words scarcely more than whispered. It was plain that the message was important and of a secret nature. Quinnox looked up and down the corridor and stairway before thrusting the tiny note through the bars. It was grasped eagerly and trembling fingers broke the seal. Bending near the light, he read the lines, his vision blurred, his heart throbbing so fiercely that the blood seemed to be drowning out other sounds for all time to come. In the dim corridor stood the two men, watching him with bated breath and guilty, quaking nerves.

"Oh!" gasped Lorry, kissing the missive insanely, as his greedy eyes careened through the last line. There was no signature, but in every word he saw her face, felt the touch of her dear hand, heard her timid heart beating for him—for him alone. Rapture thrilled him from head to foot, the delirious rapture of love. He could not speak, so overpowering was the joy, the surprise, the awakening.

"Obey!" whispered Quinnox, his face aglow with pleasure, his finger quivering as he pointed commandingly toward the letter.

"Obey what?" asked Lorry, dully.

"The last line!"

He hastily re-read the last line and then deliberately held the precious missive over the lamp until it ignited. He would have given all he possessed to have preserved it. But the last line commanded: "Burn this at once, and in the presence of the bearer."

"There!" he said, regretfully, as he crumpled the charred remnants between his fingers and turned to the silent watchers.

"Her crime goes up in smoke," muttered Dangloss, sententiously.

"The Princess commits no crime," retorted Quinnox, angrily, "when she trusts four honest men."

"Where is she?" whispered the prisoner, with thrumming ears.

"Where all good women should be at nine o'clock —in bed," replied Dangloss, shortly. "But will you obey her command?"

"So she commands me to escape!" said Lorry, smiling. "I dare not disobey my sovereign, I suppose."

"We obey her because we love her," said the captain of the guard.

"And for that reason I also obey. But can this thing be accomplished without necessitating explanations and possible complications? I will not obey if it is likely to place her in an embarrassing position."

"She understands perfectly what she is doing, sir. In the first place, she has had my advice," said Dangloss, the good old betrayer of an official trust.

"You advised her to command you to allow me to escape?"

"She commanded first, and then I advised her how to command you. Axphain may declare a war a thousand times over, but you will be safe. That's all we—I mean, all she wants."

"But I cannot desert my friend. How is he to know where I've gone? Will not vengeance fall on him instead?"

"He shall know everything when the proper time comes. And now, will you be ready at the hour mentioned? You have but to follow the instructions—I should say, the commands of the writer."

"And be free! Tell her that I worship her for this. Tell her that every drop of blood in my body belongs to her. She offers me freedom, but makes me her slave for life. Yes, I shall be ready. If I do not see you again, good friends, remember that I love you because you love her and because she loves you enough to entrust a most dangerous secret to your keeping, the commission of an act that may mean the downfall of your nation." He shook hands with them fervently.

"It cannot be that, sir. It may cost the lives of three of her subjects, but no man save yourself can involve the Princess or the Crown. They may kill us, but they cannot force us to betray her. I trust you will be as loyal to the good girl who wears a crown, not upon her heart," said Dangloss, earnestly.

"I have said my life is hers, gentlemen," said Lorry, simply. "God, if I could but throw myself at her feet! I must see her before I go. I will not go without telling her what is in my heart!" he added, passionately.

"You must obey the commands implicitly, on your word of honor, or the transaction ends now," said Quinnox, firmly.

"This escape means, then, that I am not to see

her again," he said, his voice choking with emotion.

"Her instructions are that you are to go to-night, at once," said Dangloss, and the black-eyed soldier nodded confirmation.

The prisoner paced the floor of his cell, his mind a jumble of conflicting emotions. His clenched hands, twitching lips and half-closed eyes betrayed the battle that was inflicting him with its carnage. Suddenly he darted to the door, crying:

"Then I refuse to obey! Tell her that if she permits me to leave this hole I shall be at her feet before another night has passed. Say to her that I refuse to go from Graustark until I have seen her and talked with her. You, Quinnox, go to her now and tell her this, and say to her also that there is something she must hear from my own lips. Then I will leave Graustark and not till then, even though death be the alternative." The two men stared at him in amazement and consternation.

"You will not escape?" gasped Quinnox.

"I will not be dragged away without seeing her," he answered, resolutely, throwing himself on the bed.

"Damned young ass!" growled Dangloss. The soldier's teeth grated. A moment later the slab door closed softly, a key rattled, and his visitors were gone—messengers bearing to him the most positive proof of devotion that man could exact.

What had she offered to do for his sake? She had
planned his escape, had sanctioned the commission
of an unparalleled outrage against the laws of her
land—she, of all women, a Princess! But she also
had sought to banish him from the shrine at which
his very soul worshiped, a fate more cruel and unendurable than the one she would have saved him
from.

He looked at his hands and saw the black stains
from the charred letter, last evidence of the crime
against the State. A tender light came to his eyes,
a great lump struggled to his throat, and he kissed
the sooty spots, murmuring her name again and
again. How lonely he was! how cold and cheerless
his cage! For the first time he began to appreciate
the real seriousness of his position. Up to this time
he had regarded it optimistically, confident of vindi-
cation and acquittal. His only objection to imprisonment grew out of annoyance and the mere de-
privation of liberty. It had not entered his head
that he was actually facing death at close range. Of
course, it had been plain to him that the charges
were serious, and that he was awkwardly situated,
but the true enormity of his peril did not dawn upon
him until freedom was offered in such a remarkable
manner. He grew cold and shuddered instinctively
as he realized that his position was so critical that
the Princess had deemed it necessary to resort to
strategic measures in order to save him from im-

pending doom. Starting to his feet, he paced the
floor, nervousness turning to dread, dread to terror.
He pounded on the door and cried aloud. Oh, if
he could but bring back those kindly messengers!

Exhausted, torn by conflicting emotions, he at last
dropped to the bed and buried his face in his arms,
nearly mad with the sudden solitude of despair. He
recalled her dear letter—the tender, helping hand
that had been stretched out to lift him from the
depths into which he was sinking. She had written—he could see the words plainly—that his danger
was great; she could not endure life until she knew
him to be safely outside the bounds of Graustark.
His life was dear to her, and she would preserve it
by dishonoring her trust. Then she had unfolded
her plan of escape, disjointedly, guiltily, hopelessly.
In one place near the end, she wrote: "You have
done much more for me than you know, so I pray
that God may be good enough to let me repay you
so far as it lies within my power to do so." In another place she said: "You may trust my accom-
plices, for they love me, too." An admission unconsciously made, that word "too."

But she was offering him freedom only to send
him away without granting one moment of joy in
her presence. After all, with death staring him in
the face, the practically convicted murderer of a
Prince, he knew he could not have gone without seeing her. He had been ungrateful, perhaps, but the

message he had sent her was from his heart, and
something told him that it would give her pleasure.

A key turned suddenly in the lock, and his heart
bounded with the hope that it might be some one
with her surrender in response to his ultimatum.
He sat upright and rubbed his swollen eyes. The
door swung open, and a tall prison guard peered in
upon him, a sharp-eyed, low-browed fellow in rain
coat and helmet. His lantern's single unkind eye
was turned menacingly toward the bed.

"What do you want?" demanded the prisoner, ir-
ritably.

Instead of answering, the guard proceeded to un-
lock the second or grated door, stepping inside the
cell a moment later. Smothering an exclamation,
Lorry jerked out his watch and then sprang to his
feet, intensely excited. It was just twelve o'clock,
and he remembered now that she had said a guard
would come to him at that hour. Was this the
man? Was the plan to be carried out?

The two men stood staring at each other for a
moment or two, one in the agony of doubt and suspense, the other quizzically. A smile flitted over
the face of the guard; he calmly advanced to the
table, putting down his lantern. Then he drew off
his rain coat and helmet and placed in the other's
hand a gray envelope. Lorry reeled and would have
fallen but for the wall against which he staggered.
A note from her was in his hand. He tore open the

envelope and drew forth the letter. As he read he grew strangely calm and contented; a blissful repose rushed in to supplant the racking unrest of a moment before; the shadows fled and life's light was burning brightly once more. She had written:

"I entreat you to follow instructions and go to-night. You say you will not leave Graustark until you have seen me. How rash you are to refuse liberty and life for such a trifle. But why, I ask, am I offering you this chance to escape? Is it because I do not hope to see you again? Is it not enough that I am begging, imploring you to go? I can say no more."

He folded the brief note, written in agitation, and, after kissing it, proceeded to place it in his pocket, determined to keep it till the last hour of his life. Glancing up at a sound from the guard, he found himself looking into the muzzle of a revolver. A deep scowl overspread the face of the man as he pointed to the letter and then to the lamp. There was no mistaking his meaning. Lorry reluctantly held the note over the flame and saw it crumble away as had its predecessor. There was to be no proof of her complicity left behind. He knew it would be folly to offer a bribe to the loyal guard.

After this very significant act the guard's face cleared, and he deposited his big revolver on the table. Stepping to the cell's entrance, he listened intently, then softly closed the heavy iron doors.

Without a word, he began to strip off his uniform, Lorry watching him as if fascinated. The fellow looked up impatiently and motioned for him to be quick, taking it for granted that the prisoner understood his part of the transaction. Awakened by this sharp reminder, Lorry nervously began to remove his own clothes. In five minutes his garments were scattered over the floor and he was attired in the uniform of a guard. Not a word had been spoken. The prisoner was the guard, the guard a prisoner.

"Are you not afraid this will cost you your life?" asked Lorry, first in English, then in German. The guard merely shook his head, indicating that he could not understand.

He quickly turned to the bed, seized a sheet and tore it into strips, impatiently thrusting them into the other's hands. The first letter had foretold all this, and the prisoner knew what was expected of him. He therefore securely bound the guard's legs and arms. With a grim smile, the captive nodded his head toward the revolver, the lantern and the keys. His obliging prisoner secured them, as well as his own personal effects, and was ready to depart. According to instructions, he was to go forth, locking the doors behind him, leaving the man to be discovered the next morning by surprised keepers. It struck him that there was something absurd in this part of the plan. How was this guard to explain his position with absolutely no sign of a struggle to bear

him out? It was hardly plausible that a big, strong
fellow could be so easily overpowered single-handed;
there was something wretchedly incongruous about
the—but there came a startling and effective end to
all criticism.

The guard, bound as he was, suddenly turned and
lunged head-foremost against the sharp bedpost.
His head struck with a thud, and he rolled to the
floor as if dead. Uttering an exclamation of horror,
Lorry ran to his side. Blood was gushing from a
long gash across his head, and he was already unconscious. Sickened by the brave sacrifice, he
picked the man up and placed him on the bed. A
hasty examination proved that it was no more than
a scalp wound, and that death was too remote to be
feared. The guard had done his part nobly, and it
was now the prisoner's turn to act as resolutely and
as unflinchingly. Sorry to leave the poor fellow in
what seemed an inhuman manner, he strode into the
corridor, closed and locked the doors clumsily, and
began the descent of the stairs. He had been instructed to act unhesitatingly, as the slightest show
of nervousness would result in discovery.

With the helmet well down over his face and the
cape well up, he steadily, even noisily made his way
to the next floor below. There were prisoners on
this floor, while he had been the only occupant of
the floor above. Straight ahead he went, flashing
his lantern here and there, passing down another

stairway and into the main corridor. Here he met
a guard who had just come in from the outside. The
man addressed him in the language of the country,
and his heart almost stopped beating. How was he
to answer? Mumbling something almost inaudible,
he hurried on to the ground floor, trembling with
fear lest the man should call to him to halt. He
was relieved to find, in the end, that his progress was
not to be impeded. In another moment he was boldly
unlocking the door that led to the visitor's hall. Then
came the door to the warden's office. Here he found
three sleepy guards, none of whom paid any attention to him as he passed through and entered Captain Dangloss's private room. The gruff old captain sat at a desk, writing. The escaping man half
paused, as if to speak to him. A sharp cough from
the captain and a significant jerk of the head told
him that there must be no delay, no words. Opening
the door, he stepped out into a storm so fierce and
wild that he shuddered apprehensively.

"A fitting night!" he muttered, as he plunged into
the driving rain, forcing his way across the court-
yard toward the main gate. The little light in the
gate-keeper's window was his guide, so, blinded by
the torrents, blown by the winds, he soon found
himself before the final barrier. Peering through
the window, he saw the keeper dozing in his chair.
By the light from within, he selected from the bunch
of keys he carried one that had a white string

knotted in its ring. This was the key that was to open the big gate in case no one challenged him. In any other case, he was to give the countersign, "Dangloss," and trust fortune to pass him through without question.

Luck was with him, and, finding the great lock, he softly inserted and turned the key. The wind blew the heavy gate open violently, and it required all of his strength to keep it from banging against the wall beyond. The most difficult task that he had encountered grew from his efforts to close the gate against the blast. He was about to give up in despair, when a hand was laid on his shoulder, and some one hissed in his startled ear:

"Sh! Not a word!"

His legs almost went from under his body, so great was the shock and the fear. Two strong hands joined his own in the effort to pull the door into position, and he knew at once that they belonged to the man who was to meet him on the corner at the right of the prison wall. He undoubtedly had tired of the delay, and, feeling secure in the darkness of the storm, had come to meet his charge, the escaping prisoner. Their united efforts brought about the desired result, and together they left the prison behind, striking out against the storm in all its fury.

"You are late," called the prisoner in his ear.

"Not too late, am I?" he cried back, clutching the other's arm.

"No, but we must hasten."

"Captain Quinnox, is it you?"

"Have a care! The storm has ears and can hear names," cautioned the other. As rapidly as possible they made their way along the black streets, almost a river with its sheet of water. Lorry had lost his bearings, and knew not whither he went, trusting to the guidance of his struggling companion. There seemed to be no end to their journey, and he was growing weak beneath the exertion and the excitement.

"How far do we go?" he cried, at last.

"But a few rods. The carriage is at the next corner."

"Where is the carriage to take me?" he demanded.

"I am not at liberty to say."

"Am I to see her before I go?"

"That is something I cannot answer, sir. My instructions are to place you in the carriage and ride beside the driver until our destination is reached."

"Is it the castle?" cried the other, joyously.

"It is not the castle," was the disappointing answer.

At that moment they came upon a great dark hulk and heard the stamping of horses' hoofs close at hand. It was so dark they could scarcely discern the shape of the carriage, although they could touch its side with their hands.

A soldier stood in the shelter of the vehicle and opened the door for the American.

"Hurry! Get in!" exclaimed Quinnox.

"I wish to know if this is liable to get her into trouble," demanded Lorry, pausing with one foot on the steps.

"Get in!" commanded the soldier who was holding the door, pushing him forward uneasily. He floundered into the carriage, where all was dry and clean. In his hand he still carried the keys and the lantern, the slide of which he had closed before leaving the prison yard. He could not see, but he knew that the trappings of the vehicle were superior. Outside he heard the soldier, who was preparing to enter, say:

"This carriage travels on most urgent business for Her Royal Highness, captain. It is not to be stopped."

A moment later he was inside and the door slammed. The carriage rocked as Quinnox swung up beside the driver.

"You may as well be comfortable," said Lorry's companion, as he sat rigid and restless. "We have a long and rough ride before us."

XIX

Off went the carriage with a dash, the rumble of its wheels joining in the grewsome roar of the elements. For some time the two sat speechless, side by side. Outside the thunder rolled, the rain swirled and hissed, the wind howled and all the horrors of nature seemed crowded into the blackness of that thrilling night. Lorry wondered vaguely whither they were going, why he had seen no flashes of lightning, if he should ever see her again. His mind was busy with a thousand thoughts and queries.

"Where are we going?" he asked, after they had traveled half a mile or so.

"To a place of safety," came the reply from the darkness beside him.

"Thanks," he said, drily. "By the way, don't you have any lightning in this part of the world? I haven't seen a flash to-night."

"It is very rare," came the brief reply.

"Devilish uncommunicative," thought Lorry. After a moment he asked: "How far do we travel to-night?"

"A number of miles."

"Then I'm going to take off this wet coat. It weighs a ton. Won't you remove yours?" He jerked off the big rain coat and threw it across the opposite seat, with the keys and the lantern. There was a moment's hesitation on the part of his companion, and then a second wet coat followed the first. Their rain helmets were also tossed aside. "Makes a fellow feel more comfortable."

"This has been too easy to seem like an escape," went on Lorry, looking back reflectively over the surprises of the night. "Maybe I am dreaming. Pinch me."

A finger and a thumb came together on the fleshy part of his arm, causing him to start, first in amazement, then in pain. He had not expected his reserved guardian to obey the command literally.

"I am awake, thanks," he laughed, and the hand dropped from his arm.

After this there was a longer silence than at any time before. The soldier drew himself into the corner of the seat, an action which repelled further discussion, it seemed to Lorry, so he leaned back in the opposite corner and allowed his mind to wander far from the interior of that black, stuffy carriage. Where was he going? When was he to leave Graustark? Was he to see her soon?

Soon the carriage left the smooth streets of Edelweiss, and he could tell, by the jolting and careening, that they were in the country, racing over a

rough, rocky road. It reminded him of an overland trip he had taken in West Virginia some
months before, with the fairest girl in all the world
as his companion. Now he was riding in her carriage, but with a surly, untalkative soldier of the
guard. The more he allowed his thoughts to revel in
the American ride and its delights, the more uncontrollable became his desire to see the one who had
whirled with him in "Light-horse Jerry's" coach.

"I wish to know how soon I am to see your mistress," he exclaimed, impulsively, sitting up and
striking his companion's arm by way of emphasis.
To his surprise, the hand was dashed away, and he
distinctly heard the soldier gasp. "I beg your pardon!" he cried, fearing that he had given pain with
his eager strength.

"You startled me—I was half asleep," stammered
the other, apologetically. "Whom do you mean by
my mistress?"

"Her Royal Highness, of course," said Lorry, impatiently.

"I cannot say when you are to see the Princess,"
said his companion, after waiting so long that Lorry
felt like kicking him.

"Well, see here, my friend, do you know why I
agreed to leave that place back there? I said I
wouldn't go away from Graustark until I had seen
her. If you fellows are spiriting me away—kidnap-
ping me, as it were,—I want to tell you I won't have

it that way. I must know, right now, where we are going in this damnable storm."

"I have orders to tell you nothing," said the soldier, staunchly.

"Orders, eh! From whom?"

"That is my affair, sir!"

"I guess I'm about as much interested in this affair as anybody, and I insist on knowing our destination. I jumped into this thing blindly, but I'm going to see my way out of it before we go much farther. Where are we going?"

"You—you will learn that soon enough," insisted the other.

"Am I to see her soon? That's what I want to know."

"You must not insist," cried the soldier. "Why are you so anxious to see her?" he asked, suddenly.

"Don't be so blamed inquisitive," cried Grenfall, angrily, impatiently. "Tell me where we are going or I'll put a bullet into you!" Drawing his revolver, he leaned over, grasped the guard by the shoulder and placed the muzzle against his breast.

"For God's sake be calm! You would not kill me for obeying orders! I am serving one you love. Are you mad? I shall scream if you keep pressing that horrid thing against my side." Lorry felt him tremble, and was at once filled with compunction.

How could he expect a loyal fellow to disobey orders?

"I beg your pardon a thousand times," he cried, jamming the pistol into his pocket. "You are a brave gentleman and I am a fool. Take me where you will; I'll go like a lamb. You'll admit, however, that it is exasperating to be going in the dark like this."

"It is a very good thing that it is dark," said the soldier, quickly. "The darkness is very kind to us. No one can see us and we can see no one."

"I should say not. I haven't the faintest idea what you look like. Have I seen you at the castle?"

"Yes, frequently."

"Will you tell me your name?"

"You would not know me by name."

"Are you an officer?"

"No; I am new to the service."

"Then I'll see that you are promoted. I like your staunchness. How old are you?"

"I am—er—twenty-two."

"Of the nobility?"

"My father was of noble birth."

"Then you must be so, too. I hope you'll forgive my rudeness. I'm a bit nervous, you know."

"I forgive you gladly."

"Devilish rough road, this."

"Devilish. It is a mountain road."

"That's where we were, too."

"Where who were?"

"Oh, a young lady and I, some time ago. I just happened to think of it."

"It could not have been pleasant."

"You never made a bigger mistake in your life."

"Oh, she must have been pretty, then."

"You are right this time. She is glorious."

"Pardon me! They usually are in such adventures."

"By Jove, you're a clever one!"

"Does she live in America?"

"That's none of your affair."

"Oh!" And then there was silence between them.

"Inquisitive fool!" muttered Gren to himself.

For some time they bumped along over the rough road, jostling against each other frequently, both enduring stoically and silently. The rain was still falling, but the thunder storm had lost its fury. The crashing in the sky had abated, the winds were not so fierce, the night was being shorn of its terrors. Still the intense, almost suffocating darkness prevailed. But for the occasional touch neither could have told that there was another person on the seat. Suddenly Lorry remembered the lantern. It was still lit with the slide closed when he threw it on the seat. Perhaps it still burned and could relieve the oppressive darkness if but for a short time. He might, at least, satisfy his curiosity and look upon the face of his companion. Leaning forward, he fumbled among the traps on the opposite seat.

"I think I'll see if the lantern is lighted. Let's have it a little more cheerful in here," he said. There was a sharp exclamation, and two vigorous hands grasped him by the shoulder, jerking him back unceremoniously.

"No! No! You will ruin all! There must be no light," cried the soldier, his voice high and shrill.

"But we are out of the city."

"I know! I know! But I will not permit you to have a light. Against orders. We have not passed the outpost," expostulated the other, nervously.

"What's the matter with your voice?" demanded Lorry, struck by the change in it.

"My voice?" asked the other, the tones natural again. "It's changing. Didn't it embarrass you when your voice broke like that?" went on the questioner, breathlessly. Lorry was now leaning back in the seat, quite a little mystified.

"I don't believe mine ever broke like *that,*" he said, speculatively. There was no response, and he sat silent for some time, regretting more and more that it was so dark.

Gradually he became conscious of a strange, unaccountable presence in that dark cab. He could feel a change coming over him; he could not tell why, but he was sure that some one else was beside him, some one who was not the soldier. Something

soft and delicate and sweet came into existence, per-
meating the darkness with its undeniable presence.
A queer power seemed drawing him toward the
other end of the seat. The most delightful sensations took possession of him; his heart fluttered
oddly; his head began to reel under the spell.

"Who are you?" he cried in a sort of ecstacy.
There was no answer. He remembered his match-
safe, and, with trembling, eager fingers, drew it
from the pocket of the coat he was wearing. The
next instant he was scratching a match, but as it
flared the body of his companion was hurled against
his and a ruthless mouth blew out the feeble blaze.

"Oh, why do you persist?" was cried in his ears.

"I am determined to see your face," he answered,
sharply, and with a little cry of dismay the other
occupant of the carriage fell back in the corner.
The next match drove away the darkness and the
mystery. With blinking eyes, he saw the timid soldier huddling in the corner, one arm covering his
face, the other hand vainly striving to pull the skirt
of a military coat over a pair of red trouser-legs.
Below the arm that hid the eyes and nose he saw
parted lips and a beardless, dainty chin; above, long,
dark tresses strayed in condemning confusion. The
breast beneath the blue coat heaved convulsively.

The match dropped from his fingers, and, as darkness fell again, it hid the soldier in the strong arms
of the fugitive—not a soldier bold, but a gasping,

blushing, unresisting coward. The little form quivered and then became motionless in the fierce, straining embrace; the head dropped upon his shoulder, his hot lips caressing the burning face and pouring wild, incoherent words into the little ears.

"You! You!" he cried, mad with joy. "Oh, this is Heaven itself! My brave darling! Mine forever—mine forever! You shall never leave me now! Drive on! Drive on!" he shouted to the men outside, drunk with happiness. "We'll make this journey endless. I know you love me now—I know it! God, I shall die with joy!"

A hand stole gently into his hand, and her lips found his in a long, passionate kiss.

"I did not want you to know! Ach, I am so sorry! Why, why did I come to-night? I was so strong, so firm, I thought, but see how weak I am. You dominate,—you own me, body and soul, in spite of everything,—against my will. I love you— I love you—I love you!"

"I have won against the Princess and the potentates! I was losing hope, my Queen, losing hope. You were so far away, so unattainable. I would brave a thousand deaths rather than lose this single minute of my life. It makes me the richest man in all the world. How brave you are! This night you have given up everything for my sake. You are fleeing with me, away from all that has been dear to you."

"No, no. You must not be deluded. It is only for to-night, only till you are safe from pursuit. I shall go back. You must not hope for more than this hour of weakness, sweet as it is to me," she cried.

"You are going back, and not with me?" he cried, his heart chilling.

"You know I cannot. That is why I hoped you would never know how much I care for you. Alas, you have found me out! My love was made rash by fear. You could never have escaped the vengeance of Axphain. I could not have shielded you. This was the only course and I dared not hesitate. I should have died with terror had you gone to trial, knowing what I knew. You will not think me unwomanly for coming with you as I am. It was necessary—really it was! No one else could have——" But he smothered the wail in kisses.

"Unwomanly!" he exclaimed. "It was by divine inspiration. But you *will* come with me, away from Graustark, away from every one. Say that you will!"

"I cannot bear to hear you plead, and it breaks my heart to go back there. But I cannot leave Graustark—I cannot! It would be Heaven to go with you to the end of the world, but I have others besides myself to consider. You are my god, my idol. I can worship you from my unhappy throne, from my chamber, from the cell into which my heart

is to retreat. But I cannot, I will not, desert Graustark. Not even for you!"

He was silent, impressed by her nobility, her loy-
alty. Although the joy ebbed from his craving
heart, he saw the justice of her self-sacrifice.

"I would give my soul to see your face now,
Yetive. Your soul is in your eyes; I can feel it.
Why did you not let me stay in prison, meet death
and so end all? It would have been better for both
of us. I cannot live without you."

"We can live for each other, die for each other,—
apart. Distance will not lessen my love. You know
that it exists; it has been betrayed to you. Can you
not be satisfied—just a little bit—with that knowledge?" she pleaded.

"But I want you in reality, not in my dreams, my
imagination."

"Ach, we must not talk like this! There is no
alternative. You are to go, I am to stay. The future
is before us; God knows what it may bring to us.
Perhaps it may be good enough to give us happiness
—who knows? Do not plead with me. I cannot
endure it. Let me be strong again! You will not
be so cruel as to battle against me, now that I am
weak; it would only mean my destruction. You do
not seek that!"

His soul, his honor, the greatest reverence he
had ever known were in the kiss that touched her
brow.

"I shall love you as you command—without hope," he said, sadly.

"Without hope for either," she sobbed.

"My poor little soldier," he whispered, lovingly, as her body writhed under the storm of tears.

"I—I wish—I were a—soldier!" she wailed. He comforted her as best he could and soon she was quiet—oh, so very quiet. Her head was on his shoulder, her hands in his.

"How far do we drive?" he asked, at last.

"To the monastery. We are nearly there," she answered, in tones far away.

"The monastery? Why do we go there?" he cried.

"You are to stay there."

"What do you mean? I thought I was to leave Graustark."

"You are to leave—later on. Until the excitement is over the abbey is to be your hiding place. I have arranged everything, and it is the only safe place on earth for you at this time. No one will think of looking for you up there."

"I would to God I could stay there forever, living above you," he said, drearily.

"Your window looks down upon the castle; mine looks up to yours. The lights that burn in those two windows will send out beams of love and life for one of us at least."

"For both of us, my sweetheart," he corrected,

fondly. "You say I will be safe there. Can you trust these men who are aiding you?"

"With my life! Quinnox carried a message to the Abbot yesterday, and he grants you a temporary home there, secure and as secret as the tomb. He promises me this, and he is my best friend. Now, let me tell you why I am with you, masquerading so shamefully——"

"Adorably!" he protested.

"It is because the Abbot insisted that I bring you to him personally. He will not receive you except from my hands. There was nothing else for me to do, then, was there, Mr. Lorry? I was compelled to come and I could not come as the Princess —as a woman. Discovery would have meant degradation from which I could not have hoped to recover. The military garments were my only safeguard."

"And how many people know of your—deception?"

"Three—besides yourself. Dagmar, Quinnox and Captain Dangloss. The Abbot will know later on, and I shiver as I think of it. The driver and the man who went to your cell, Ogbot, know of the escape, but do not know I am here. Allode—you remember him—is our driver."

"Allode? He's the fellow who saw me—er—who was in the throne room."

"He is the man who saw nothing, sir."

"I remember his obedience," he said, laughing in spite of his unhappiness. "Am I to have no freedom up here—no liberty at all?"

"You are to act as the Abbot or the prior instructs. And, I must not forget, Quinnox will visit you occasionally. He will conduct you from the monastery and to the border line at the proper time."

"Alas! He will be my murderer, I fear. Yetive, you do not believe I killed Lorenz. I know that most of them do, but, I swear to you, I am no more the perpetrator of that cowardly crime than you. God bears testimony to my innocence. I want to hear you say that you do not believe I killed him."

"I feared so at first,—no, do not be angry—I feared you had killed him for my sake. But now I am sure that you are innocent."

The carriage stopped too soon, and Quinnox opened the door. It was still as dark as pitch, but the downpour had ceased except for a disagreeable, misty drizzle, cold and penetrating.

"We have reached the stopping place," he said.

"And we are to walk from here to the gate," said the Princess, resuming her hoarse, manly tones. While they were busy donning their rain coats, she whispered in Lorry's ear: "I beg of you, do not let him know that you have discovered who I am."

He promised, and lightly snatched a kiss, an act of indiscretion that almost brought fatal results. Forgetful of the darkness, she gave vent to a little protesting shriek, fearing that the eyes of the captain had witnessed the pretty transgression. Lorry laughed as he sprang to the road and turned to assist her in alighting. She promptly and thoughtfully averted the danger his gallantry presented by ignoring the outstretched hands, discernable as slender shadows protruding from an object a shade darker than the night, and leaped boldly to the ground. The driver was instructed to turn the carriage about and wait their return.

With Lorry in the center, the trio walked rapidly off in the darkness, the fugitive with the sense of fear that belongs only to a blind man. A little light far ahead told the position of the gate, and for this they bent their steps, Lorry and Quinnox conversing in low tones, the Princess striding along silently beside the former, her hand in his—a fact of which the real soldier was totally unaware. Reaching the gate, the captain pounded vigorously, and a sleepy monk soon peered from the little window through which shone the light.

"On important business with the Abbot, from Her Royal Highness, the Princess Yetive," said Quinnox, in response to a sharp query, spoken in the Graustark tongue. A little gate beside the big one opened, and the monk, lantern in hand, bade them enter.

"Await me here, captain," commanded the slim, straight soldier, with face turned from the light. A moment later the gate closed and Lorry was behind the walls of St. Valentine's a prisoner again. The monk preceded them across the dark court toward the great black mass, his lantern creating ghastly shadows against the broken mist. His followers dropped some little distance behind, the tall one's arm stealing about the other's waist, his head bending to a level with hers.

"Is it to be good-bye, dearest?" he asked. "Good-bye forever?"

"I cannot say that. It would be like wishing you dead. Yet there is no hope. No, no! We will not say good-bye,—forever," she said, despairingly.

"Won't you bid me hope?"

"Impossible! You will stay here until Quinnox comes to take you away. Then you must not stop until you are in your own land. We may meet again——"

"Yes, by my soul, we shall meet again! I'll do as you bid and all that, but I'll come back when I can stay away no longer. Go to your castle and look forward to the day that will find me at your feet again. It is bound to come. But how are you to return to the castle to-night and enter without creating suspicion? Have you thought of that?"

"Am I a child? Inside of three hours I shall be safely in my bed and but one person in the castle will be the wiser for my absence. Here are the portals." They passed inside the massive doors and halted. "You must remain here until I have seen the prior," she said, laughing nervously and glancing down at the boots which showed beneath the long coat. Then she hastily followed the monk, disappearing down the corridor. In ten minutes— ten hours to Lorry—she returned with her guide.

"He will take you to your room," she said breathlessly, displaying unmistakable signs of embarrassment. "The prior *was* shocked. Good-bye, and God be with you always. Remember, I love you!"

The monk's back was turned, so the new recluse snatched the slight figure to his heart.

"Some day?" he whispered.

She would not speak, but he held her until she nodded her head.

XX

"The American has escaped!" was the cry that spread through Edelweiss the next morning.

It brought undisguised relief to the faces of thousands; there was not one who upbraided Baron Dangloss for his astounding negligence. Never before had a criminal escaped from the Tower. The only excuse, uttered in woe-begone tone, was that the prison had not been constructed or manned for such clever scoundrels as Yankees—good name for audacity. But as nobody criticised, his explanation was taken good-naturedly and there was secret rejoicing in the city. Of course, everybody wondered where the prisoner had gone; most of them feared that he could not escape the officers, while others shrewdly smiled and expressed themselves as confident that so clever a gentleman could not be caught. They marveled at his boldness, his ingenuity, his assurance.

The full story of the daring break for liberty flashed from lip to lip during the day, and it was known all over the water-swept city before noon.

Baron Dangloss, himself, had gone to the prisoner's cell early in the morning, mystified by the continued absence of the guard. The door was locked, but from within came groans and cries. Alarmed at once, the captain procured duplicate keys and entered the cell. There he found the helpless, blood-covered Ogbot, bound hand and foot and almost dead from loss of blood. The clothes of the American were on the floor, while his own were missing, gone with the prisoner. Ogbot, as soon as he was able, related his experience of the night before. It was while making his rounds at midnight that he heard moans from the cell. Animated by a feeling of pity, he opened the slab door and asked if he were ill. The wretched American was lying on the bed, apparently suffering. He said something which the guard could not understand, but which he took to be a plea for assistance. Not suspecting a trick, the kindly guard unlocked the second door and stepped to the bedside, only to have the sick man rise suddenly and deal him a treacherous blow over the head with the heavy stool he had secreted behind him. Ogbot knew nothing of what followed, so effective was the blow. When he regained consciousness he was lying on the bed, just as the captain had found him. The poor fellow, overwhelmed by the enormity of his mistake, begged Dangloss to shoot him at once. But Dangloss had him conveyed to the hospital ward and tenderly cared for.

Three guards in one of the offices saw a man whom they supposed to be Ogbot pass from the prison shortly after twelve, and the mortified chief admitted that some one had gone through his private apartment. As the prisoner had taken Ogbot's keys, he experienced little difficulty in getting outside the gates. But, vowed Dangloss, stormily, he should be recaptured if it required the efforts of all the policemen in Edelweiss. With this very brave declaration in mind, he despatched men to search every street and every alley, every cellar and every attic in the city. Messengers were sent to all towns in the district; armed posses scoured the valley and the surrounding forests, explored the caves and brush heaps for miles around. The chagrin of the grim old captain, who had never lost a prisoner, was pitiful to behold.

The forenoon was half over before Harry Anguish heard of his friend's escape. To say that he was paralyzed would be putting it much too mildly. There is no language that can adequately describe his sensations. Forgetting his bodyguard, he tore down the street toward the prison, wild with anxiety and doubt. He met Baron Dangloss, tired and worn, near the gate, but the old officer could tell him nothing except what he had learned from Ogbot. Of one thing there could be no doubt: Lorry was gone. Not knowing where to turn nor what to do, Anguish raced off to the castle, his bodyguard having located him in the meantime. He was more in need of their protection than ever. At the castle gates he encountered a party of raving Axphainians, crazed with anger over the flight of the man whose life they had thirsted for so ravenously. Had he been unprotected, Anguish would have fared badly at their hands, for they were outspoken in their assertions that he had aided Lorry in the escape. One fiery little fellow cast a glove in the American's face and expected a challenge. Anguish snapped his fingers and sarcastically invited the insulter to meet him next winter in a battle with snowballs, upon which the aggressor blasphemed in three languages and three hundred gestures. Anguish and his men passed inside the gates, which had been barred to the others, and struck out rapidly for the castle doors.

The Princess Yetive was sleeping soundly, peacefully, with a smile on her lips, when her Prime Minister sent an excited attendant to inform her of the prisoner's escape. She sat up in bed, and, with her hands clasped about her knees, sleepily announced that she would receive him after her coffee was served. Then she thought of the wild, sweet ride to the monastery, the dangerous return, her entrance to the castle through the secret subterranean passage and the safe arrival in her own room. All had gone well and he was safe. She smiled quaintly as she glanced at the bundle of clothes on the floor,

blue and black and red. They had been removed
in the underground passage and a loose gown substituted, but she had carried them to her chamber
with the intention of placing them for the time being
in the old mahogany chest that had held so many
of her childhood treasures. Springing out of bed,
she opened the chest, cast them into its depths,
turned and removed the key which had always remained in the lock. Then she summoned her maids.

Her uncle and aunt, the Countess Dagmar (whose
merry brown eyes were so full of pretended dismay
that the Princess could scarcely restrain a smile),
and Gaspon, the Minister of Finance, were awaiting
her appearance. She heard the count's story of the
escape, marveled at the prisoner's audacity, and
firmly announced that everything possible should be
done to apprehend him. With a perplexed frown
on her brow and a dubious twist of her lips, she
said:

"I suppose I must offer a reward?"

"Certainly!" exclaimed her uncle.

"About fifty gavvos, uncle?"

"Fifty!" cried the two men, aghast.

"Isn't that enough?"

"For the murderer of a Prince?" demanded Gaspon. "It would be absurd, Your Highness. He is
a most important person."

"Quite so; he *is* a most important person. I think
I'll offer five thousand gavvos."

"More like it. He is worth that, at least," agreed Uncle Caspar.

"Beyond a doubt," sanctioned Gaspon.

"I am glad you do not consider me extravagant," she said, demurely. "You may have the placards printed at once," she went on, addressing the Treasurer. "Say a reward of five thousand gavvos will be paid to the person who delivers Grenfall Lorry to me."

"Would it not be better to say 'delivers Grenfall Lorry to the Tower'?" submitted Gaspon.

"You may say 'to the undersigned,' and sign my name," she said, reflectively.

"Very well, Your Highness. They shall be struck off this morning."

"In large type, Gaspon. You must catch him if you can," she added. "He is a very dangerous man and royalty needs protection." With this wise bit of caution she dismissed the subject and began to talk of the storm.

As the two young plotters were hastening up the stairs later on, an attendant approached and informed the Princess that Mr. Anguish requested an audience.

"Conduct him to my boudoir," she said, her eyes sparkling with triumph. In the seclusion of the boudoir she and the Countess laughed like children over the reward that had been so solemnly ordered.

"Five thousand gavvos!" cried Dagmar, leaning

back in her chair, to emphasize the delight she felt. "What a joke!"

Tap, tap! came a knock on the door, and in the same instant it flew open, for Mr. Anguish was in a hurry. As he plunged into their presence a pair of heels found the floor spasmodically.

"Oh, I beg pardon!" he gasped, as if about to fly. "May I come in?"

"Not unless you go outside. You are already in, it seems," said the Princess, advancing to meet him. The Countess was very still and sedate. "I am so glad you have come."

"Heard about Lorry? The fool is out and gone," he cried, unable to restrain himself. Without a word, she dragged him to the divan, and, between them, he soon had the whole story poured into his ears, the Princess on one side, the Countess on the other.

"You are a wonder!" he exclaimed, when all the facts were known to him. He executed a little dance of approval, entirely out of place in the boudoir of a Princess, but very much in touch with prevailing sentiment. "But what's to become of me?" he asked, after cooling down. "I have no excuse for remaining in Graustark and I don't like to leave him here, either."

"Oh, I have made plans for you," said she. "You are to be held as hostage."

"What?"

"I thought of your predicament last night, and here is the solution: This very day I shall issue an order forbidding you the right to leave Edelweiss. You will not be in prison, but your every movement is to be watched. A strong guard will have you under surveillance, and any attempt to escape or to communicate with your friend will result in your confinement and his detection. In this way you may stay here until the time comes to fly. The Axphain people must be satisfied, you know. Your freedom will not be disturbed; you may come and go as you like, but you are ostensibly a prisoner. By detaining you forcibly we gain a point, for you are needed here. There is no other way in which you can explain a continued presence in Graustark. Is not my plan a good one?"

He gazed in admiration at her flushed cheeks and glowing eyes.

"It is beyond comparison," he said, rising and bowing low. "So shrewd is this plan that you make me a hostage forever; I shall not mistake its memory if I live to be a thousand."

And so it was settled, in this pretty drama of deception, that Harry Anguish was to be held in Edelweiss as hostage. At parting, she said, seriously:

"A great deal depends on your discretion, Mr. Anguish. My guards will watch your every action, for they are not in the secret—excepting Quinnox,

—and any attempt on your part to communicate with Grenfall Lorry will be fatal."

"Trust me, Your Highness. I have had much instruction in wisdom to-day."

"I hope we shall see you often," she said.

"Daily—as a hostage," he replied, glancing toward the Countess.

"That means until the other man is captured," said that young lady, saucily.

As he left the castle he gazed at the distant building in the sky and wondered how it had ever been approached in a carriage. She had not told him that Allode drove four miles over the winding roads that led to the monastery up a gentler slope from the rear.

The next afternoon Edelweiss thrilled with a new excitement. Prince Bolaroz of Axphain, mad with grief and rage, came thundering into the city with his court at his heels. His wrath had been increased until it resembled a tornado when he read the reward placard in the uplands. Not until then did he know that the murderer had escaped and that vengeance might be denied him.

After viewing the body of Lorenz as it lay in the sarcophagus of the royal palace, where it had been borne at the command of the Princess Yetive, he demanded audience with his son's betrothed, and it was with fear that she prepared for the trying ordeal, an interview with the grief-crazed old man.

The castle was in a furore; its halls soon thronged with diplomatists and there was an ugly sense of trouble in the air, suggestive of the explosion which follows the igniting of a powder magazine.

The slim, pale-faced Princess met the burly old ruler in the grand council chamber. He and his nobles had been kept waiting but a short time. Within a very few minutes after they had been conducted to the chamber by Count Halfont and other dignitaries, the fair ruler came into the room and advanced between the bowing lines of courtiers to the spot where sat the man who held Graustark in his grasp. A slender, graceful figure in black, proud and serious, she walked unhesitatingly to the old man's side. If she feared him, if she was impressed by his power, she did not show it. The little drama had two stars of equal magnitude, neither of whom acknowledged supremacy in the other.

Bolaroz arose as she drew near, his gaunt face black and unfriendly. She extended her hand graciously, and he, a Prince for all his wrath, touched his trembling lips to its white, smooth back.

"I come in grief and sadness to your court, most glorious Yetive. My burden of sorrow is greater than I can bear," he said, hoarsely.

"Would that I could give you consolation," she said, sitting in the chair reserved for her use at council gatherings. "Alas! it grieves me that I can offer nothing more than words."

"You are the one he would have made his wife," said the old Prince, sitting beside her. He looked into her deep blue eyes and tears sprung to his own. His voice failed him, and long moments passed before he could control his emotion. Truly she pitied him in his bereavement.

Then followed a formal discussion of the crime and the arrangement of details in connection with the removal of the dead Prince from Graustark to his own land. These matters settled, Bolaroz said that he had heard of the murderer's escape, and asked what effort was being made to recapture him. Yetive related all that had happened, expressing humiliation over the fact that her officers had been unable to accomplish anything, adding that she did not believe that the fugitive could get away from Graustark safely without her knowledge. The old Prince was working himself back into the violent rage that had been temporarily subdued, and at last broke out in a vicious denunciation of the carelessness that had allowed the man to escape. He first insisted that Dangloss and his incompetent assistants be thrown into prison for life or executed for criminal negligence; then he demanded the life of Harry Anguish as an aider and abettor in the flight of the murderer. In both cases the Princess firmly refused to take the action demanded. She warmly defended Dangloss and his men, and announced in no uncertain tones that she would not order the arrest of the remaining American. Then she acquainted him with her intention to detain Anguish as hostage and to have his every action watched in the hope that a clue to the whereabouts of the fugitive might be discovered, providing, of course, that the friend knew anything at all about the matter. The Duke of Mizrox and others loudly joined in the cry for Anguish's arrest, but she bravely held out against them, and in the end curtly informed them that the American, whom she believed to be innocent of all complicity in the escape, should be subjected to no indignity other than detention in the city under guard, as she had ordered.

"I insist that this man be cast into prison at once," snarled the white-lipped Bolaroz.

Her eyes flashed and her bosom heaved with anger.

"You are not at liberty to command in Graustark, Prince Bolaroz," she said, slowly and distinctly. "I am ruler here."

The heart of every Graustark nobleman leaped with pride at this daring rebuff. Bolaroz gasped and was speechless for some seconds.

"You shall not be ruler long, madam," he said, malevolently, significantly.

"But I am ruler now, and, as such, I ask Your Highness to withdraw from my castle. I did not know that I was to submit to these threats and insults, or I should not have been kind enough to grant you an audience, Prince though you are. When I came to this room it was to give you my deepest sympathy and to receive yours, not to be insulted. You have lost a son, I my betrothed. It ill becomes you, Prince Bolaroz, to vent your vindictiveness upon me. My men are doing all in their power to capture the man who has so unfortunately escaped from our clutches, and I shall not allow you or any one else to dictate the manner in which we are to proceed." She uttered these words cunningly, and, at their conclusion, arose to leave the room.

Bolaroz heard her through in surprise and with conflicting emotions. There was no mistaking her indignation, so he deemed it policy to bottle his wrath, overlook the most offensive rebuke his vanity had ever received, and submit to what was evidently a just decision.

"Stay, Your Highness. I submit to your proposition regarding the other stranger, although I doubt its wisdom. There is but one in whom I am really interested,—the one who killed my son. There is to be no cessation in the effort to find him, I am to understand. I now have a proposition. With me are three hundred of my bravest soldiers. I offer them to you in order that you may better prosecute the search. They will remain here and you may use them in any way you see fit. The Duke of Mizrox will linger in Edelweiss, and with him you and yours may always confer. He, also, is at your com-

mand. This man must be retaken. I swear, by all
that is above and below me, he shall be found, if I
hunt the world over to accomplish that end. He
shall not escape my vengeance! And hark you to
this! On the twentieth of next month I shall demand payment of the debt due Axphain. So deeply
is my heart set on the death of this Grenfall Lorry
that I agree now, before all these friends of ours,
that if he be captured, and executed in my presence,
before the twentieth of November, Graustark shall
be granted the extension of time that would have
obtained in the event of your espousal with the man
he killed. You hear this offer, all? It is bound by
my sacred word of honor. His death before the
twentieth gives Graustark ten years of grace. If
he is still at large, I shall claim my own. This offer,
I believe, most gracious Yetive, will greatly encourage your people in the effort to capture the man we
seek."

The Princess heard the remarkable proposition
with a face deathly pale, heart scarcely beating.
Again was the duty to Graustark thrust cruelly upon
her. She could save the one only by sacrificing the
other.

"We will do all in our power to—to prove ourselves grateful for your magnanimous offer," she
said. As she passed from the room, followed by
her uncle, she heard the increasing buzz of excitement on all sides, the unrestrained expressions of

amazement and relief from her subjects, the patron-
izing comments of the visitors, all conspiring to
sound her doom. Which way was she to turn in
order to escape from herself?

"We must catch this man, Yetive," said Halfont,
on the stairway. "There is no alternative."

"Except our inability to do so," she murmured.
In that moment she determined that Grenfall Lorry
should never be taken if she could prevent it. He
was innocent, and it was Graustark's penalty to
pay.

The next day, amidst pomp and splendor, the
Prince of Axphain started on his journey to the
land of his forefathers, to the tombs of his ancestors, all Edelweiss witnessing the imposing procession that made its way through the north gates of
the town. Far up on the mountain top a man, looking from his little window, saw the black, snakelike
procession wind away across the plain to the north-
ward, losing itself in the distant hills.

XXI

FROM A WINDOW ABOVE

The longest month in Lorry's life was that which followed his romantic flight from the Tower. To his impatient mind, the days were irksome weeks. The cold monastery was worse than a prison. He looked from its windows as a convict looks through his bars, always hoping, always disappointed. With each of the infrequent visits of Captain Quinnox, his heart leaped at the prospect of liberty, only to sink deeper in despair upon the receipt of emphatic, though kindly, assurances that the time had not yet come for him to leave the haven of safety into which he had been thrust by loving hands. From his little window he could see the active city below, with the adored castle; to his nostrils came the breath of summer from the coveted valley, filling him with almost insupportable longing and desire. Cold were the winds that swept about his lofty home; ghastly, grewsome the nights; pallid and desolate the days. Out of the world was he, dreary and heartsick, while at his feet stretched life and joy and love in their rarest habiliments. How he endured the suspense, the torture of uncertainty, the craving for the life that others were enjoying, he could not understand. Big,

310

strong and full of vigor, his inactivity was maddening; this virtual captivity grew more and more
intolerable with each succeeding day. Would they
never take him from the tomb in which he
was existing? A hundred times had he, in his
desperation, concluded to flee from the monastery,
come what might, and to trust himself to the joyous
world below, but the ever-present though waning
spark of wisdom won out against the fierce, aggressive folly that mutinied within his hungry soul. He
knew that she was guarding him with loving, tender
care, and that, when the proper time came, the
shackles of danger would drop and his way would
be cleared.

Still there was the longing, the craving, the loneliness. Day after day, night after night went by
and the end seemed no nearer. Awake or asleep, he
dreamed of her, his heart and mind always full of
that one rich blessing,—her love. At times he was
mad with the desire to know what she was doing,
what she was thinking and what was being done for
her down there in the busy world. Lying on his
pallet, sitting in the narrow window, pacing the halls
or wandering about the cold courtyards, he thought
always of her, hoping and despairing with equal
fervor. The one great question that made his imprisonment, his inactivity so irksome was: Was he
to possess the treasure he longed so much to call
his own? In those tantalizing moments of despair

he felt that if he were free and near her he could win the fight against all odds. As it was, he knew not what mischief was working against his chances in the world from which he was barred.

The prior was kind to him; everything that could be done to provide comfort where comfort was a stranger was employed in his behalf. He lived well —until his appetite deserted him; he had no questions to answer, for no one asked why he was there; he had no danger to fear, for no foe knew where he lived. From the city came the promise of ultimate escape; verbal messages from those who loved him; news of the world,—all at long intervals, however. Quinnox's visits were like sunbeams to him. The dashing captain came only at night and in disguise. He bore verbal messages, a wise precaution against mishap. Not once did he bring a word of love from the Princess, an omission which caused the fugitive deep misery until a ray of intelligence showed him that she could not give to Quinnox the speeches from her heart, proud woman that she was.

Anguish sent words of cheer, with commands to be patient. He never failed to tell him, through Quinnox, that he was doing all in his power to find the real murderer, and that he had the secret coöperation of the old police captain. Of course, the hidden man heard of the reward and the frenzied search prosecuted by both principalities. He laughed

hysterically over the deception that was being practiced by the blue-eyed, slender woman who held the
key to the situation in her keeping.

It was not until the night of the eighteenth of November that Quinnox confirmed his fears by telling
him of the conditions imposed by Prince Bolaroz.
For some reason, the young officer had deceived
Lorry in regard to the all-important matter. The
American repeatedly had begged for information about the fatal twentieth, but on all previous
occasions his visitor doggedly maintained a show of
ignorance, vowing that he knew nothing of the circumstances. Finally Lorry, completely out of patience and determined to know the true state of
affairs, soundly upbraided him and sent word to
the Princess that if she did not acquaint him with
the inside facts he would leave the monastery and
find them out for himself. This authoritative message brought Quinnox back two nights later with
the full story of the exciting conference. She implored him to remain where he was, and asked his
forgiveness for having kept the ugly truth from
him. Quinnox added to his anguish by hastily in-
forming him that there was a possibility of succor
from another principality. Prince Gabriel, he said,
not knowing that he was cutting his listener to the
heart, was daily with the Princess, and it was believed that he was ready to loan Graustark sufficient
money to meet the demand of Bolaroz. The mere

thought that Gabriel was with her aroused the fiercest resentment in Lorry's breast. He writhed beneath the knowledge that she was compelled to endure his advances, his protestations of love, his presence.

As he paced his narrow room distractedly a horrid thought struck him so violently that he cried aloud and staggered against the wall, his eyes fixed on the face of the startled soldier. Perhaps she might submit to Gabriel, for in submitting she could save not only Graustark, but the man she loved. The sacrifice—but no! he would not believe that such affliction could come to her! Marry Gabriel! The man who had planned to seize her and make her his wanton! He ground his teeth and glared at Quinnox as if he were the object of his hatred, his vicious jealousy. The captain stepped backward in sudden alarm.

"Don't be afraid!" Lorry cried savagely. "I'm not crazy. It's your news—your news! Does she expect me to stay up here while that state of affairs exists down there? Let me see: this is the eighteenth, and day after to-morrow is the twentieth. There is no time to be lost, Captain Quinnox. I shall accompany you when you leave St. Valentine's to-night."

"Impossible!" exclaimed Quinnox. "I cannot allow that, sir. My instructions are to——"

"Hang your instructions! All the instructions on

earth can't compel me to sit up here and see this sacrifice made. I am determined to see her and put a stop to the whole affair. It is what I feared would come to pass. She is willing to sacrifice herself or half her kingdom, one or the other, in order that I may escape. It's not right, captain, it's not right, and I'm going to stop it. How soon can we leave this place?" He was pacing the floor, happy in the decision he had reached, notwithstanding the danger it promised.

"You are mad, sir, to talk like this," protested the other, despairingly. "Edelweiss swarms with Axphain soldiers; our own men are on the alert to win the great reward. You cannot go to the city. When a safe time comes, you will be taken from this place, into the mountains instead of through the city, and given escort to Dassas, one hundred miles east. That step will not be taken until the way is perfectly clear. I tell you, sir, you cannot hope to escape if you leave the monastery now. The mountains are full of soldiers every night."

"I didn't say anything about an escape, did I? On the contrary, I want to give myself up to her. Then she can have Gabriel thrown over the castle wall and say to Bolaroz, 'Here is your man; I've gained the ten years of grace.' That's the point, Quinnox; can't you see it? And I want to say to you now, I'm going whether you consent or refuse. I'd just as soon be in jail down there as up here, anyhow. The only favor I have to ask of you is that you do the best you can to get me safely to her. I must talk to her before I go back to the Tower."

"God help me, sir, I cannot take you to her," groaned Quinnox, trying to control his nervous apprehension. "I have sworn to her that I will keep you from all harm, and it would be to break faith with her if I led you into that mob down there."

"I respect your oath, my friend, but I am going, just the same. I'll see her, too, if I have to shoot every man who attempts to prevent me. I'm desperate, man, desperate! She's everything in the world to me, and I'll die before I'll see her suffer."

Quinnox calmly placed his hands on the other's shoulders, and, looking him in the eye, said quietly:

"Her suffering now is as nothing compared to what it will be if you go back to the Tower. You forget how much pain she is enduring to avoid that very suffering. If you care for my mistress, sir, add no weight to the burden she already carries. Remain here, as she desires. You can be of no service down there. I implore you to be considerate."

It was an eloquent appeal, and it struck home. Lorry wavered, but his resolution would not weaken. He argued, first with Quinnox, then with himself, finally returning to the reckless determination to brave all and save her from herself. The soldier begged him to listen to reason, implored him to reconsider, at last turning in anger upon the stubborn American with a torrent of maledictions. Lorry heard him through, and quietly, unswervingly announced that he was ready to leave the monastery at any time his guide cared to depart. Quinnox gave up in despair at this, gazing hopelessly at the man he had sworn to protect, who insisted on placing his head in the lion's jaw. He sat down at the window and murmured dejectedly:

"What will she say to me—what will she say to me?"

"I shall exonerate you, captain. She can have no fault to find with your action after I have told her how loyal you are and how—how—well, how unreasonable I am," said Lorry, kindly.

"You may never live to tell her this, sir. Then what is to become of me? I could not look her in the face again. I could only die!"

"Don't be so faint-hearted, Quinnox!" cried Lorry, stimulated by the desire to be with her, recognizing no obstacle that might thwart him in the effort. "We'll get through, safe and sound, and we'll untangle a few complications before we reach the end of the book. Brace up, for God's sake, for mine, for hers, for your own. I must get to her before everything is lost. My God, the fear that she may marry Gabriel will drive me mad if I am left here another night. Come! Let us prepare to start. We must notify the Abbot that I am to go.

I can be ready in five minutes. Ye Gods, think of
what she may be sacrificing for me!"

The distracted captain gloomily watched the nervous preparations for departure, seeing his own disgrace ahead as plainly as if it had already come
upon him. Lorry soon was attired in the guard's
uniform he had worn from the Tower a month before. His pistol was in his pocket, and the bunch
of violets she had sent to him that very night was
pinned defiantly above his heart. Quinnox smiled
when he observed this bit of sentiment, and grimly
informed him that he was committing an act prohibited in Dangloss's disciplinary rules. Officers on
duty were not to wear nosegays.

"Dangloss will not see my violets. By the way,
the moon shines brightly, doesn't it?"

"It is almost as light as day. Our trip is made
extremely hazardous for that reason. I am sorely
afraid, rash sir, that we cannot reach the castle
unseen."

"We must go about it boldly, that's all."

"Has it occurred to you, sir, that you are placing
me in a terrible position? What excuse can I have,
a captain of the guard, for slinking about at night
with a man whom I am supposed to be tracking to
earth? Discovery will brand me as a traitor. I
cannot deny the charge without exposing Her Royal
Highness."

Lorry turned cold. He had not thought of this

alarming possibility. But his ready wit came again to his relief, and with bright, confident eyes he swept away the obstacle.

"If discovered, you are at once to proclaim me a prisoner, take the credit for having caught me, and claim the reward."

"In that case, you will not go to the castle, but to the Tower."

"Not if you obey orders. The offer of reward says that I must be delivered to the undersigned. You will take me to her and not to the Tower."

Quinnox smiled and threw up his hands, as if unable to combat the quick logic of his companion. Together they made their way to the prior's cell, afterward to the Abbot's apartment. It was barely eleven o'clock and he had not retired. He questioned Quinnox closely, bade Lorry farewell and blessed him, sent his benediction to the Princess and ordered them conducted to the gates.

Ten minutes later they stood outside the wall, the great gates having been closed sharply behind them. Above them hung the silvery moon, full and bright, throwing its refulgent splendor over the mountain top with all the brilliancy of day. Never had Lorry seen the moon so accursedly bright.

" 'Gad, it is like day," he exclaimed.

"As I told you, sir," agreed the other, reproof in his voice.

"We must wait until the moon goes down. It

won't do to risk it now. Can we not go somewhere
to keep warm for an hour or so?"

"There is a cave farther down the mountain. Shall
we take the chance of reaching it?"

"By all means. I can't endure the cold after
being cooped up for so long."

They followed the winding road for some distance down the mountain, coming at last to a point
where a small path branched off. It was the path
leading down the side of the steep overlooking the
city, and upon that side no wagon-road could be
built. Seven thousand feet below stretched the
sleeping, moon-lit city. Standing out on the brow
of the mountain, they seemed to be the only living
objects in the world. There was no sign of life
above, below or beside them.

"How long should we be in making the descent?"
asked Lorry, a sort of terror possessing him as he
looked from the dizzy height into the ghost-like dim-
ness below.

"Three hours, if you are strong."

"And how are we to get into the castle? I hadn't
thought of that."

"There is a secret entrance," said Quinnox, maliciously enjoying the insistent one's acknowledg-
ment of weakness. "If we reach it safely, I can
take you underground to the old dungeons beneath
the castle. It may be some time before you can
enter the halls above, for the secret of that passage

is guarded jealously. There are but five people who know of its existence."

"Great confidence is placed in you, I see, and worthily, I am sure. How is it that you are trusted so implicitly?"

"I inherit the confidence. The captain of the guard is born to his position. My ancestors held the place before me, and not one betrayed the trust. The first-born in the last ten generations has been the captain of the guard in the royal palace, possessing all its secrets. I shall be the first to betray the trust—and for a man who is nothing to me."

"I suppose you consider me selfish and vile for placing you in this position," said Lorry, somewhat contritely.

"No; I have begun the task and I will complete it, come what may," answered the captain, firmly. "You are the only being in the world for whom I would sacrifice my honor voluntarily,—save one."

"I have wondered why you were never tempted to turn traitor to the Princess and claim the fortune that is represented in the reward."

"Not for five million gavvos, sir!"

"By George, you are a faithful lot! Dangloss, Allode and Ogbot and yourself, four honest men to whom she trusts her life, her honor. You belong to a rare species, and I am proud to know you."

The stealthy couple found the cave and spent an hour or more within its walls, sallying forth after the tardy darkness had crept down over the mountain and into the peaceful valley. Then began the tortuous descent. Quinnox in the lead, they walked, crawled and ran down the narrow path, bruised, scratched and aching by the time they reached the topmost of the summer houses along the face of the mountain. After this, walking was easier, but stealthiness made their progress slow. Frequently, as they neared the base, they were obliged to dodge behind houses or to drop into the ditches by the roadside in order to avoid patroling police guards or Axphain sleuth-hounds. Lorry marveled at the vigil the soldiers were keeping, and was somewhat surprised to learn from the young captain that prevailing opinion located him in or near the city. For this reason, while other men were scouring Vienna, Paris and even London, hordes of vengeful men searched day and night for a clue in the city of Edelweiss.

The fugitive began to realize how determined was the effort to capture him and how small the chance of acquittal if he were taken. To his fevered imagination the enmity of the whole world was shaping itself against him. The air was charged with hatred, the ground with vengeance, the trees and rocks with denouncing shadows, while from the darkness behind merciless hands seemed to be stretching forth to clutch him. One simple, loyal love stood alone antagonistic to the universal desire to crush and kill.

A fragile woman was shielding him sturdily, un-
waveringly against all these mighty forces. His
heart thrilled with devotion; his arm tingled with
the joy of clasping her once more to his breast; his
wistful eyes hung upon the flickering light far off
in the west. Quinnox had pointed it out to him, saying that it burned in the bedchamber of the Princess
Yetive. Since the memorable night that took him
to the cell in St. Valentine's, this light had burned
from dusk to daylight. Lovingly, faithfully it had
shone for him through all those dreary nights, a
lonely signal from one heart to another.

At last, stiff and sore, they stole into the narrow
streets of Edelweiss. Lorry glanced back and shivered, although the air was warm and balmy. He
had truly been out of the world. Not until this
instant did he fully appreciate the dread that possesses a man who is being hunted down by tireless
foes; never did man's heart go out in gratitude and
trustfulness as did his toward the strong defender
whose sinewy arm he clasped as if in terror.

"You understand what this means to me," said
Quinnox, gravely, as they paused to rest. "She will
call me your murderer and curse me for my miserable treason. I am the first to dishonor the name of
Quinnox."

XXII

The Princess Yetive had not flinched a hair's breadth from the resolution formed on that stormy night when she sacrificed pride and duty on the altar of love and justice. Prince Bolaroz's ultimatum overwhelmed her, but she arose from the wreckage that was strewn about her conscience and remained loyal, steadfast and true to the man in the monastery. To save his life was all she could hope to accomplish, and that she was bound to do at any cost. She could be nothing to him—not even friend. So long as he lived he would be considered the murderer of Lorenz, and until the end a price would hang over his head. She, Princess of Graustark, had offered a reward for him. For that reason he was always to be a fugitive, and she, least of all, could hope to see him. There had been a brief, happy dream, but it was swept away by the unrelenting rush of reality. The mere fact that she, and she alone, was responsible for his flight placed between them an unsurmountable barrier.

Clinging tenaciously to her purpose, she was still cognizant of the debt she owed the trusting, loving people of Graustark. One word from her could avert the calamity that was to fall with the dawn of the fatal twentieth. All Graustark blindly trusted and adored her; to undeceive them would be to administer a shock from which they could never recover.

Her heart was bursting with love for Lorry; her mind was overflowing with tender thoughts that could not be sent to him, much as she trusted to the honor of Quinnox, her messenger. Hour after hour she sat in her window and marveled at the change that had been wrought in her life by this strong American, her eyes fixed on the faraway monastery, her heart still and cold and fearful. She had no confidant in this miserable affair of her heart. Others, near or dear, had surmised, but no word of hers confirmed. A diffidence, strange and proud, forbade the confession of her frailty, sweet, pure and womanly though it was. She could not forget that she was a Princess.

The Countess Dagmar was piqued by her reticence and sought in manifold ways to draw forth the voluntary avowal, with its divine tears and blushes. Harry Anguish, who spent much of his time at the castle and who invariably deserted his guards at the portals, was as eager as the Countess to have her commit herself irretrievably by word or sign, but he, too, was disappointed. He was, also, considerably puzzled. Her Highness's manner was at all times frank and untroubled. She was apparently light-hearted; her cheeks had lost none of their freshness; her eyes were bright; her smile was quick and merry; her wit unclouded. Receptions, drawing-rooms and State functions found her always vivacious, so much so that her court wondered not a little. Daily reports brought no news of the fugitive, but while others were beginning to acquire a haggard air of worry and uncertainty, she was calmly resigned. The fifteenth, the sixteenth, the seventeenth, the eighteenth and now the nineteenth of November came, and still the Princess revealed no marked sign of distress. Could they have seen her in the privacy of her chamber on those dreary, maddening nights they would not have known their sovereign.

Heavy-hearted and with bowed heads the people of Graustark saw the nineteenth fade in the night, the breaking of which would bring the crush of pride, the end of power. At court there was the silent dread and the dying hope that relief might come at the last hour. Men, with pale faces and tearful eyes, wandered through the ancient castle, speechless, nerveless, miserable. Brave soldiers crept about, shorn of pride and filled with woe. Citizens sat and stared aimlessly for hours, thinking of naught but the disaster so near at hand and so unavoidable. The whole nation surged as if in the last throes of death. To-morrow the potency of

Graustark was to die, its domain was to be cleft in twain,—disgraced before the world.

And, on the throne of this afflicted land sat the girl, proud, tender, courageous Yetive. To all Graustark she was its greatest, its most devoted sufferer; upon her the blow fell heaviest. There she sat, merciful and merciless, her slim white hand ready to sign the shameful deed in transfer, ready to sell her kingdom for her love. Beneath her throne, beneath her feet, cowered six souls, possessors of the secret. Of all the people in the world, they alone knew the heart of the Princess Yetive, they alone felt with her the weight of the sacrifice. With wistful eyes, fainting hearts and voiceless lips, five of them watched the day approach, knowing that she would not speak and that Graustark was doomed. Loyal conspirators against that which they loved better than their lives—their country—were Dangloss, Quinnox, Allode, Ogbot and Dagmar. Tomorrow would see the north torn from the south, the division of families, the rending of homes, the bursting of hearts. She sanctioned all this because she loved him and because he had done no wrong.

Aware of her financial troubles and pursuing the advantage that his rival's death had opened to him, Prince Gabriel, of Dawsbergen, renewed his ardent suit. Scarce had the body of the murdered Prince left the domain before he made his presence marked. She was compelled to receive his visits, distasteful

as they were, but she would not hear his proposi‑
tions. Knowing that he was in truth the mysterious
Michael who had planned her abduction, she feared
and despised him, yet dared make no public denun‑
ciation. As Dawsbergen was too powerful to be an‑
tagonized at this critical time, she was constantly
forced to submit to the most trying and repulsive of
ordeals. Tact and policy were required to control
the violent, hot-blooded young ruler from the South.
At times she despaired and longed for the quiet of
the tomb; at other times she was consumed by the
fires of resentment, rebelling against the ignominy
to which she was subjected. Worse than all to her
were the insolent overtures of Gabriel. How she
endured she could not tell. The tears of humiliation
shed after his departure on the occasion of each
visit revealed the bitterness that was torturing this
proud martyr.

He had come at once to renew his offer of a loan,
knowing her helplessness. Day after day he haunted
the castle, persistent in his efforts to induce her to
accept his proposition. So fierce was his passion,
so implacable his desire, that he went among the
people of Edelweiss, presenting to them his pro‑
posal, hoping thereby to add public feeling to his
claims. He tried to organize a committee of citi‑
zens to go before the Princess with the petition that
his offer be accepted and the country saved. But
Graustark was loyal to its Princess. Not one of her
citizens listened to the wily Prince, and more than

one told him or his emissaries that the loss of the whole kingdom was preferable to the marriage he desired. The city sickened at the thought.

His last and master-stroke in the struggle to persuade came on the afternoon of the nineteenth, at an hour when all Edelweiss was in gloom and when the Princess was taxed to the point where the mask of courage was so frail that she could scarce hide her bleeding soul behind it.

Bolaroz of Axphain, to quote from the news-despatch, was in Edelweiss, a guest, with a few of his lords, in the castle. North of the city were encamped five thousand men. He had come prepared to cancel the little obligation of fifteen years' standing. With the hated creditor in the castle, his influence hovering above the town, the populace, distracted by the thoughts of the day to come, Gabriel played what he considered his best card. He asked for and obtained a final interview with Yetive, not in her boudoir or her reception room, but in the throne room, where she was to meet Bolaroz in the morning.

The Princess, seated on her throne, awaited the approach of the resourceful, tenacious suitor. He came, and behind him strode eight stalwart men, bearing a long, iron-bound chest, the result of his effort with his bankers. Yetive and her nobles looked in surprise on this unusual performance. Dropping to his knee before the throne, Gabriel said, his voice trembling slightly with eagerness and fear,

"Your Highness, to-morrow will see the turning point in the history of two, possibly three nations—Graustark, Axphain and Dawsbergen. I have included my own land because its ruler is most vitally interested. He would serve and save Graustark, as you know, and he would satisfy Axphain. It is in my power to give you aid at this last, trying hour, and I implore you to listen to my words of sincerest friendship—yes, adoration. To-morrow you are to pay to Prince Bolaroz over twenty-five million gavvos or relinquish the entire north half of your domain. I understand the lamentable situation. You can raise no more than fifteen millions, and you are helpless. He will grant no extension of time. You know what I have proffered before. I come to-day to repeat my friendly offer and to give unquestioned bond as to my ability to carry it out. If you agree to accept the loan I extend, ten million gavvos for fifteen years at the usual rate of interest, you can on to-morrow morning place in the hand of Axphain when he makes his formal demand the full amount of your indebtedness in gold. Ricardo, open the chest!"

An attendant threw open the lid of the chest. It was filled with gold coins.

"This box contains one hundred thousand gavvos. There are in your halls nine boxes holding nine times as much as you see here. And there are nine

times as much all told on the way. This is an
evidence of my good faith. Here is the gold. Pay
Bolaroz and owe Gabriel, the greatest happiness that
could come to him."

There was a dead silence after this theatrical
action.

"The interest on this loan is not all you ask, I
understand," said Halfont, slowly, his black eyes
glittering. "You ask something that Graustark cannot and will not barter—the hand of its sovereign.
If you are willing to make this loan, naming a fair
rate of interest, withdrawing your proposal of marriage, we can come to an agreement."

Gabriel's eyes deadened with disappointment, his
breast heaved and his fingers twitched.

"I have the happiness of your sovereign at heart
as much as my own," he said. "She shall never
want for devotion, she shall never know a pain."

"You are determined, then, to adhere to your
original proposition?" demanded the Count.

"She would have married Lorenz to save her land,
to protect her people. Am I not as good as Lorenz?
Why not give——" began Gabriel, viciously, but
Yetive arose, and, with gleaming eyes and flushing
cheeks, interrupted him.

"Go! I will not hear you—not one word!"

He passed from the room without another word.
Her court saw her standing straight and immovable,
her white face transfigured.

XXIII

THE VISITOR AT MIDNIGHT

Below the castle and its distressed occupants, in a dark, damp little room, Grenfall Lorry lived a year in a day. On the night of the eighteenth, or rather near the break of dawn on the nineteenth, Captain Quinnox guided him from the dangerous streets of Edelweiss to the secret passage, and he was safe for the time being. The entrance to the passage was through a skilfully hidden opening in the wall that enclosed the park. A stone doorway, so cleverly constructed that it defied detection, led to a set of steps which, in turn, took one to a long, narrow passage. This ended in a stairway fully a quarter of a mile from its beginning. Ascending this stairway, one came to a secret panel, through which, by pressing a spring, the interior of the castle was reached. The location of the panel was in one of the recesses in the wall of the chapel, near the altar. It was in this chapel that Yetive exchanged her male attire for a loose gown, weeks before, and the servant who saw her come from the door at an unearthly hour in the morning believed she had gone

there to seek surcease from the troubles which op-
pressed her.

Lorry was impatient to rush forth from his place
of hiding and to end all suspense, but Quinnox de-
murred. He begged the eager American to remain
in the passage until the night of the nineteenth,
when, all things going well, he might be so fortunate
as to reach the Princess without being seen. It was
the secret hope of the guilty captain that his charge
could be induced by the Princess to return to the
monastery, to avoid complications. He promised to
inform Her Highness of his presence in the underground room and to arrange for a meeting. The
miserable fellow could not find courage to confess
his disobedience to his trusting mistress. Many
times during the day she had seen him hovering
near, approaching and then retreating, and had wondered not a little at his peculiar manner.

And so it was that Lorry chafed and writhed
through a long day of suspense and agony. Quinnox had brought to the little room some candles,
food and bedding, but he utilized only the former.
The hours went by and no summons called him to
her side. He was dying with the desire to hold her
in his arms and to hear her voice again. Pacing to
and fro like a caged animal, he recalled the ride in
West Virginia, the scene in her bedchamber, the
day in the throne room and, more delicious than all,
the trip to the monastery. In his dreams, waking

or sleeping, he had seen the slim soldier, had heard
the muffled voice, and had felt the womanly caresses.
His brain now was in a whirl, busy with thoughts
of love and fear, distraught with anxiety for her
and for himself, bursting with the awful consequences of the hour that was upon them. What was
to become of him? What was to be the end of this
drama? What would the night, the morrow, bring
about?

He looked back and saw himself as he was a year
ago in Washington, before she came into his life,
and then wondered if it could really be he who was
going through these strange, improbable scenes,
these sensations. It was nine o'clock in the evening
when Quinnox returned to the little room. The
waiting one had looked at his watch a hundred times,
had run insanely up and down the passage in quest
of the secret exit, had shouted aloud in the frenzy
of desperation.

"Have you seen her?" he cried, grasping the newcomer's hand.

"I have, but, before God, I could not tell her
what I had done. Your visit will be a surprise, I
fear a shock."

"Then how am I to see her? Fool! Am I to
wait here forever——"

"Have patience! I will take you to her to-night—
aye, within an hour. To-morrow morning she signs
away the northern provinces, and her instructions

are that she is not to be disturbed to-night. Not even will she see the Countess Dagmar after nine o'clock. It breaks my heart to see the sorrow that abounds in the castle to-night. Her Highness insists on being alone, and Bassot, the new guard, has orders to admit no one to her apartments. He is ill, and I have promised that a substitute shall relieve him at eleven o'clock. You are to be the substitute. Here is a part of an old uniform of mine, and here is a coat that belonged to Dannox, who was about your size. Please exchange the clothes you now have on for these. I apprehend no trouble in reaching her door, for the household is in gloom and the halls seem barren of life."

He threw the bundle on a chair and Lorry at once proceeded to don the contents. In a very short time he wore, instead of the cell keeper's garments, a neat-fitting uniform of the royal guard. He was trembling violently, chilled to the bone with nervousness, as they began the ascent of the stairs leading to the chapel. The crisis in his life, he felt, was near at hand.

Under the stealthy hand of Quinnox the panel opened and they listened intently for some moments. There was no one in the dimly lighted chapel, so they made their way to the door at the opposite end. The great organ looked down upon them and Lorry expected every instant to hear it burst forth in sounds of thunder. It seemed alive and watching

their movements reproachfully. Before unlocking
the door, the captain pointed to a lance which stood
against the wall near by.

"You are to carry that lance," he said, briefly.
Then he cautiously peered forth. A moment later
they were in the broad hall, boldly striding toward
the distant stairway. Lorry had been instructed to
proceed without the least sign of timidity. They
passed several attendants in the hall and heard Count
Halfont's voice in conversation with some one in an
ante-room. As they neared the broad steps, who
should come tripping down but Harry Anguish. He
saluted Quinnox and walked rapidly down the corridor, evidently taking his departure after a call on
the Countess.

"There goes your hostage," said the captain,
grimly. It had required all of Lorry's self-possession to restrain the cry of joyful recognition. Up
the staircase they went, meeting several ladies and
gentlemen coming down, and were soon before the
apartments of the Princess. A tall guard stood in
front of the boudoir door.

"This is your relief, Bassot. You may go," said
Quinnox, and, with a careless glance at the strange
soldier, the sick man trudged off down the hall, glad
to seek his bed.

"Is she there?" whispered Lorry, dizzy and faint
with expectancy.

"Yes. This may mean your death and mine, sir,

but you would do it. Will you explain to her how I came to play her false?"

"She shall know the truth, good friend."

"After I have gone twenty paces down the hall, do you rap on the door. She may not admit you at first, but do not give up. If she bid you enter or asks your mission, enter quickly and close the door. It is unlocked. She may swoon, or scream, and you must prevent either, if possible. In an hour I shall return, and you must go back to the passage."

"Never! I have come to save her and her country, and I intend to do so by surrendering myself this very night."

"I had hoped to dissuade you. But, sir, you cannot do so to-night. You forget that this visit compromises her."

"True. I had forgotten. Well, I'll go back with you, but to-morrow I am your prisoner, not your friend."

"Be careful," cautioned the captain, as he moved away. Lorry feverishly tapped his knuckles on the panel of the door and waited with motionless heart for the response. It came not, and he rapped harder, a strange fear darting into his mind.

"Well?" came from within, the voice he adored.

Impetuous haste marked his next movement. He dashed open the door, sprang inside and closed it quickly. She was sitting before her escritoire, writing, and looked up, surprised and annoyed.

"I was not to be disturbed—oh, God!"

She staggered to her feet and was in his arms before the breath of her exclamation had died away. Had he not supported her she would have dropped to the floor. Her hands, her face were like ice, her breast was pulseless and there was the wildest terror in her eyes.

"My darling—my queen!" he cried, passionately. "At last I am with you. Don't look at me like that! It is really I—I could not stay away—I could not permit this sacrifice of yours. Speak to me! Do not stare like that!"

Her wide blue eyes slowly swept his face, piteous wonder and doubt struggling in their depths.

"Am I awake?" she murmured, touching his face with her bewildered, questioning hands. "Is it truly you?" A smile illumined her face, but her joy was short-lived. An expression of terror came to her eyes and there was agony in the fingers that clasped his arm. "Why do you come here?" she cried. "It is madness! How and why came you to this room?"

He laughed like a delighted boy and hastily narrated the events of the past twenty-four hours, ending with the trick that gave him entrance to her room.

"And all this to see me?" she whispered.

"To see you and to save you. I hear that Gabriel has been annoying you and that you are to give up

half of the kingdom to-morrow. Tell me everything. It is another reason for my coming."

Sitting beside him on the divan, she told of
Gabriel's visit and his dismisal, the outlook for the
next day, and then sought to convince him of the
happiness it afforded her to protect him from an
undeserved death. He obtained for Quinnox the
royal pardon and lauded him to the skies. So rav-
ishing were the moments, so ecstatic the sensations,
that possessed them that neither thought of the consequences if he were to be discovered in her room,
disguised as one of her guardsmen. He forgot the
real import of his reckless visit until she commanded
him to stand erect before her that she might see
what manner of soldier he was. With a laugh he
leaped to his feet and stood before her—attention!
She leaned back among the cushions and surveyed
him through the glowing, impassioned eyes which
slowly closed as if to shut out temptation.

"You are a perfect soldier," she said, her lashes
parting ever so slightly.

"No more perfect than you," he cried. She remembered, with confusion, her own masquerading,
but it was unkind of him to remember it. Her allusion to his uniform turned his thoughts into the
channel through which they had been surging so
turbulently up to the moment that found him tap-
ping at her door. He had not told her of his deter-

mination, and the task grew harder as he saw the sparkle glow brighter and brighter in her eye.

"You are a brave soldier, then," she substituted. "It required courage to come to Edelweiss with hundreds of men ready to seize you at sight,—a pack of bloodhounds."

"I should have been a miserable coward to stay up there while you are so bravely facing disaster alone down here. I came to help you, as I should."

"But you can do nothing, dear, and you only make matters worse by coming to me. I have fought so hard to overcome the desire to be near you; I have struggled against myself for days and days, and I had won the battle when you came to pull my walls of strength down about my ears. Look! On my desk is a letter I was writing to you. No; you shall not read it! No one shall ever know what it contains." She darted to the desk, snatched up the sheets of paper and held them over the waxed taper. He stood in the middle of the room, a feeling of intense desolation settling down upon him. How could he lose this woman?

"To-morrow night Quinnox is to take you from the monastery and conduct you to a distant city. It has been all planned. Your friend, Mr. Anguish, is to meet you in three days, and you are to hurry to America by way of Athens. This was a letter to you. In it I said many things and was trying to write farewell when you came to this room. Do

you wonder that I was overcome with doubt and
amazement—yes, and horror? Ach, what peril you
are in here! Every minute may bring discovery, and
that would mean death to you. You are innocent,
but nothing could save you. The proof is too
strong. Mizrox has found a man who swears he
saw you enter Lorenz's room."

"What a damnable lie!" cried Lorry, lightly. "I
was not near his room!"

"But you can see what means they will adopt to
convict you. You are doomed if caught, by my men
or theirs. I cannot save you again. You know now
that I love you. I would not give away half of the
land that my forefathers ruled were it not true.
Bolaroz would be glad to grant ten years of grace
could he but have you in his clutches. And, to see
me, you would run the risk of undoing all that I
have planned, accomplished and suffered for. Could
you not have been content with that last good-bye at
the monastery? It is cruel to both of us—to me
especially—that we must have the parting again."
She had gone to the divan and now dropped limply
among the cushions, resting her head on her hand.

"I was determined to see you," he said. "They
shall not kill me nor are you to sacrifice your father's
domain. Worse than all, I feared that you might
yield to Gabriel——"

"Ach! You insult me when you say that! I
yielded to Lorenz because I thought it my duty and

because I dared not admit to myself that I loved you. But Gabriel! Ach!" she cried, soulfully. "Grenfall Lorry, I shall marry no man. You I love, but you I cannot marry. It is folly to dream of it, even as a possibility. When you go from Graustark to-morrow night you take my heart, my life, my soul with you. I shall never see you again —God help me to say this—I shall never allow you to see me again. I tell you I could not bear it. The weakest and the strongest of God's creations is woman." She started suddenly, half rising. "Did any one see you come to my room? Was Quinnox sure?"

"We passed people, but no one knew me. I will go if you are distressed over my being here."

"It is not that—not that. Some spy may have seen you. I have a strange fear that they suspect me and that I am being watched. Where is Captain Quinnox?"

"He said he would return for me in an hour. The time is almost gone. How it has flown! Yetive, Yetive, I will not give you up!" he cried, sinking to his knees before her.

"You must—you shall! You must go back to the monastery to-night! Oh, how I pray that you may reach it in safety! And, you must leave this wretched country at once. Will you see if Quinnox is outside the door? Be quick! I am mad with the fear that you may be found here—that you may be taken before you can return to St. Valentine's."

He arose and stood looking down at the intense face, all aquiver with the battle between temptation and solicitude.

"I am not going back to St. Valentine's," he said, slowly.

"But it is all arranged for you to start from there to-morrow. You cannot escape the city guard except through St. Valentine's."

"Yetive, has it not occurred to you that I may not wish to escape the city guard?"

"May not wish to escape the—what do you mean?" she cried, bewildered.

"I am not going to leave Edelweiss, dearest. It is my intention to surrender myself to the authorities."

She gazed at him in horror for a moment and then fell back with a low moan.

"For God's sake, do not say that!" she wailed. "I forbid you to think of it. You cannot do this after all I have done to save you. Ach, you are jesting; I should have known."

He sat down and drew her to his side. Some moments passed before he could speak.

"I cannot and will not permit you to make such a sacrifice for me. The proposition of Bolaroz is known to me. If you produce me for trial you are to have a ten years' extension. My duty is plain.

I am no cowardly criminal, and I am not afraid to face my accusers. At the worst, I can die but once."

"Die but once," she repeated, as if in a dream.

"I came here to tell you of my decision, to ask you to save your lands, protect your people, and to remember that I would die a thousand times to serve you and yours."

"After all I have done—after all I have done," she murmured, piteously. "No, no! You shall not! You are more to me than all my kingdom, than all the people in the world. You have made me love you, you have caused me to detest the throne which separates us, you have made me pray that I might be a pauper, but you shall not force me to destroy the mite of hope that lingers in my heart. You shall not crush the hope that there may be a—a— some day!"

"A some day? Some day when you will be mine?" he cried.

"I will not say that, but, for my sake,—for my sake,—go away from this place. Save yourself! You are all I have to live for." Her arms were about his neck and her imploring words went to his heart like great thrusts of pain.

"You forget the thousands who love and trust you. Do they deserve to be wronged?"

"No, no,—ach, God, how I have suffered because of them! I have betrayed them, have stolen their rights and made them a nation of beggars. But I would not, for all this nation, have an innocent man condemned—nor could my people ask that of me. You cannot dissuade me. It must be as I wish. Oh, why does not Quinnox come for you!" She arose and paced the floor distractedly.

He was revolving a selfish, cowardly capitulation to love and injustice, when a sharp tap was heard at the door. Leaping to his feet, he whispered:

"Quinnox! He has come for me. Now to get out of your room without being seen!"

The Princess Yetive ran to him, and, placing her hands on his shoulders, cried with the fierceness of despair:

"You will go back to the monastery? You will leave Graustark? For my sake—for my sake!"

He hesitated and then surrendered, his honor falling weak and faint by the pathway of passion.

"Yes!" he cried, hoarsely.

Tap! tap! tap! at the door. Lorry took one look at the rapturous face and released her.

"Come!" she called.

The door flew open, an attendant saluted, and in stepped—Gabriel!

XXIV

The tableau lasted but a moment. Gabriel advanced a few steps, his eyes gleaming with jealousy and triumph. Before him stood the petrified lovers, caught red-handed. Through her dazed brain struggled the conviction that he could never escape; through his ran the miserable realization that he had ruined her forever. Gabriel, of all men!

"I arrive inopportunely," he said, harshly, the veins standing out on his neck and temples. "Do I intrude? I was not aware that you expected two, Your Highness!" There was no mistaking his meaning. He viciously sought to convey the impression that he was there by appointment, a clandestine visitor in her apartments at midnight.

"What do you mean by coming to my apartment at this hour?" she stammered, trying to rescue dignity from the chaos of emotions. Lorry was standing slightly to the right and several feet behind her. He understood the Prince, and quickly sought to interpose with the hope that he might shield her from the sting.

"She did not expect me, sir," he said, and a men-

acing gleam came to his eyes. His pistol was in his
hand. Gabriel saw it, but the staring Princess did
not. She could not take her eyes from the face
of the intruder. "Now, may I ask you why you
are here?"

Gabriel's wit saved him from death. He saw
that he could not pursue the course he had begun,
for there was murder in the American's eye. Like
a fox he swerved, and, with a servile promise of submission in his glance, he said:

"I thought you were here, my fine fellow, and I
came to satisfy myself. Now, sir, may I ask why
you are here?" His fingers twitched and his eyes
were glassy with the malevolence he was subduing.

"I am here as a prisoner," said Lorry, boldly.
Gabriel laughed derisively.

"And how often have you come here in this manner as a prisoner? Midnight and alone in the apartments of the Princess! The guard dismissed! A
prisoner, eh? Ha, what a prison!"

"Stop!" cried Lorry, white to the lips.

The Princess was beginning to understand. Her
eyes grew wide with horror, her figure straightened
imperiously and the white in her cheeks gave way to
the red of insulted virtue.

"I see it all! You have not been outside this
castle since you left the prison. A pretty scheme!
You could not marry him, could you, eh? He is not
a Prince! But you could bring him here and hide

him where no one would dare to think of looking for him—in your apartments——"

With a snarl of rage, Lorry sprang upon him, cutting short the sentence that would have gone through her like the keenest knife-blade.

"Liar! Dog! I'll kill you for that!" he cried, but, before he could clutch the Prince's throat, Yetive had frantically seized his arm.

"Not that!" she shrieked. "Do not kill him! There must be no murder here!"

He reluctantly hurled Gabriel from him, the Prince tottering to his knees in the effort to keep from falling. She had saved her maligner's life, but courage deserted her with the act. Helplessly she looked into the blazing eyes of her lover and faltered:

"I—I do not know what to say or do. My brain is bursting!"

"Courage, courage!" he whispered, gently.

"You shall pay for this," shrieked Gabriel. "If you are not a prisoner you shall be. There'll be scandal enough in Graustark to-morrow to start a volcano of wrath from the royal tombs where lie her fathers. I'll see that you *are* a prisoner!" He started for the door, but Lorry's pistol was leveled at his head.

"If you move I'll kill you!"

"The world will understand how and why I fell by your hand in this room. Shoot!" he cried, tri-

"You Dog, I'll Kill You For That!"

umphantly. Lorry's hand trembled and his eyes filled with the tears of impotent rage. The Prince held the higher card.

A face suddenly appeared at the door, which had been stealthily opened from without. Captain Quinnox glided into the room behind the Prince and gently closed the door, unnoticed by the gloater.

"A prisoner?" sneered Gabriel. "Where is your captor, pray?"

"Here!" answered a voice at his back. The Prince wheeled and found himself looking at the stalwart form of the captain of the guard. "I am surely privileged to speak now, Your Highness," he went on, addressing the Princess, significantly.

"How came you here?" gasped Gabriel.

"I brought my prisoner here. Where should I be if not here to guard him?"

"When—when did you enter this room?"

"An hour ago."

"You were not here when I came!"

"I have been standing on this spot for an hour. You have been very much excited, I'll agree, but it is strange you did not see me," lied Quinnox.

Gabriel looked about helplessly, nonplussed.

"You were here when I came in?" he asked, wonderingly.

"Ask Her Royal Highness," commanded the captain, smiling.

"Captain Quinnox brought the prisoner to me an hour ago," she said mechanically.

"It is a lie!" cried Gabriel. "He was not here when I entered!"

The captain of the guard laid a heavy hand on the shoulder of the Prince and said, threateningly:

"I was here and I am here. Have a care how you speak. Were I to do right I should shoot you like a dog. You came like a thief, you insult the ruler of my land. I have borne it all because you are a Prince, but have a care—have a care. I may forget myself and tear out your black heart with these hands. One word from Her Royal Highness will be your death warrant."

He looked inquiringly at the Princess, as if anxious to put the dangerous witness where he could tell no tales. She shook her head, but did not speak. Lorry realized that the time had come for him to assert himself. Assuming a distressed air, he bowed his head and said, dejectedly:

"My pleading has been in vain, then, Your Highness. I have sworn to you that I am innocent of this murder, and you have said I shall have a fair trial. That is all you can offer?"

"That is all," she said, shrilly, her mind gradually grasping his meaning.

"You will not punish the poor people who secreted me in their house for weeks, for they are convinced of my innocence. Your captain here, who found

me in their house to-night, can also speak well of
them. I have only this request to make, in return
for what little service I may have given you: Forgive the old people who befriended me. I am ready
to go to the Tower at once, captain."

Gabriel heard this speech with a skeptical smile on
his face.

"I am no fool," he said, simply. "Captain,"
shrewdly turning to Quinnox, "if he is your prisoner, why do you permit him to retain his revolver?"

The conspirators were taken by surprise, but
Lorry had found his wits.

"It is folly, Your Highness, to allow this gentleman and conquering Prince to cross-examine you.
I am a prisoner, and that is the end of it. What
odds is it to the Prince of Dawsbergen how and
where I was caught or why your officer brought me
to you?"

"You were ordered from my house once to-day,
yet you come again like a conqueror. I should not
spare you. You deserve to lose your life for the
actions of to-night. Captain Quinnox, will you kill
him if I ask you to end his wretched life?" Yetive's
eyes were blazing with wrath, beneath which
gleamed a hope that he could be frightened into
silence.

"Willingly—willingly!" cried Quinnox. "Now,
Your Highness? 'Twere better in the hall!"

"For God's sake, do not murder me! Let me go!" cringed the Prince.

"I do not mean that you should kill him now, Quinnox, but I instruct you to do so if he puts foot inside these walls again. Do you understand?"

"Yes, Your Highness."

"Then you will place this prisoner in the castle dungeon until to-morrow morning, when he is to be taken to the Tower. Prince Gabriel may accompany you to the dungeon cell, if he likes, after which you will escort him to the gates. If he enters them again you are to kill him. Take them both away!"

"Your Highness, I must ask you to write a pardon for the good people in whose house the prisoner was found," suggested Quinnox, shrewdly seeing a chance for communication unsuspected by the Prince.

"A moment, Your Highness," said the Prince, who had recovered himself cleverly. "I appreciate your position. I have made a serious charge, and I now have a fair proposition to suggest to you. If this man is not produced to-morrow morning, I take it for granted that I am at liberty to tell all that has happened in this room to-night. If he is produced, I shall kneel and beg your pardon."

The Princess turned paler than ever, and knew not how she kept from falling to the floor. There was a long silence following Gabriel's unexpected but fair suggestion.

"That is very fair, Your Highness," said Lorry. "There is no reason why I should not be a prisoner to-morrow. I don't see how I can hope to escape the inevitable. Your dungeon is strong and I have given my word of honor to the captain that I shall make no further effort to evade the law."

"I agree," murmured the Princess, ready to faint under the strain.

"I must see him delivered to Prince Bolaroz," added Gabriel, mercilessly.

"To Bolaroz," she repeated.

"Your Highness, the pardon for the poor old people," reminded Quinnox. She glided to the desk, stunned, bewildered. It seemed as though death were upon her. Quinnox followed, and bent near her ear. "Do not be alarmed," he whispered. "No one knows of Mr. Lorry's presence here, save the Prince, and if he dares to accuse you before Bolaroz our people will tear him to pieces. No one will believe him."

"You—you can save him, then?" she gasped, joyously.

"If he will permit me to do so. Write to him what you will, Your Highness, and he shall have the message. Be brave, and all will go well. Write quickly! This is supposed to be the pardon."

She wrote feverishly, a thousand thoughts arising for every one that she was able to transfer to the paper. When she had finished the hope-inspired scrawl she arose and, with a gracious smile, handed to the waiting captain the pardon for those who had secreted the fugitive.

"I grant forgiveness to them gladly," she said.

"I thank you," said Lorry, bowing low.

"Mr. Lorry, I regret the difficulty in which you find yourself. It was on my account, too, I am told. Be you guilty or innocent, you are my friend, my protector. May God be good to you." She gave him her hand calmly, steadily, as if she were bestowing favor upon a subject. He kissed the hand gravely.

"Forgive me for trespassing on your good nature to-night, Your Highness."

"The five thousand gavvos shall be yours to-morrow, Captain Quinnox," she said, graciously. "You have done your duty well." The faithful captain bowed deep and low, and a weight was lifted from his conscience.

"Gentlemen, the door," he said, and, without a word, the trio left the room. She closed the door and stood like a statue until their footsteps died away in the distance. As one in a daze, she sat at the desk till the dawn, Grenfall Lorry's revolver lying before her.

Through the halls, down the stairs and into the clammy dungeon strode the silent trio. But before Lorry stepped inside the cell Gabriel asked a question that had been troubling him for many minutes.

"I am afraid I have—ah—misjudged her——" muttered Gabriel, now convinced that he had committed himself irretrievably.

"You will find she has not misjudged you," said the prisoner, grimly. "Can't I have a candle in here, captain?"

"You may keep this lantern," said Quinnox, stepping inside the narrow cell. As he placed the lantern on the floor, he whispered: "I will return in an hour. Read this!" Lorry's hand closed over the bit of perfumed paper.

The Prince was now inside the cell, peering about curiously, even timorously. "By the way, Your Highness, how would you enjoy living in a hole like this all your life?"

"Horrible!" said Gabriel, shuddering like a leaf.

"Then take my advice: don't commit any murders. Hire some one else."

The two men eyed each other steadily for a moment or two. Then the Prince looked out of the cell, a mad desire to fly from some dreadful, unseen horror coming over him.

Quinnox locked the door, and, striking a match, bade His Highness precede him up the stone steps.

In the cell, the prisoner read and reread the incoherent message from Yetive:

"It is the only way. Quinnox will assist you

to escape to-night. Go, I implore you; as you love me, go. Your life is more than all to me. Gabriel's story will not be entertained and he can have no proof. He will be torn to pieces, Quinnox says. I do not know how I can live until I am certain you are safe. This will be the longest night a woman ever spent. If I could only be sure that you will do as I ask, as I beg and implore! Do not think of me, but save yourself. I would lose everything to save you."

He smiled sadly as he burned the "pardon." The concluding sentences swept away the last thought he might have had of leaving her to bear the consequences. "Do not think of me, but save yourself. I would lose everything to save you." He leaned against the stone wall and shook his head slowly, the smile still on his lips.

XXV

"BECAUSE I LOVE HIM"

The next morning Edelweiss was astir early. Great throngs of people flocked the streets long before the hour set for the signing of the decree that was to divide the north from the south. There were men and women from the mountains, from the southern valleys, from the plains to the north and east. Sullen were the mutterings, threatening the faces, resentful the hearts of those who crowded the shops, the public places and the streets. Before nine o'clock the great concourse of people began to push toward the castle. Castle Avenue was packed with the moving masses. Thousands upon thousands of this humbled race gathered outside the walls, waiting for news from the castle with the spark of hope that does not die until the very end, nursing the possibility that something might intervene at the last moment to save the country from disgrace and ruin.

A strong guard was required to keep the mob back from the gates, and the force of men on the wall had been quadrupled. Business in the city was suspended. The whole nation, it seemed, stood before the walls, awaiting, with bated breath and dismal faces, the announcement that Yetive had deeded to Bolaroz the lands and lives of half of her subjects. The northern plainsmen who were so soon to acknowledge Axphain sovereignty, wept and wailed over their unhappy lot. Brothers and sisters from the south cursed and moaned in sympathy.

Shortly before nine o'clock, Harry Anguish with his guard of six, rode up to the castle. Captain Dangloss was beside him on his gray charger.

They had scarcely passed inside the gates when a cavalcade of mounted men came riding up the avenue from the Hotel Regengetz. Then the howling, the hissing, the hooting began. Maledictions were hurled at the heads of Axphain noblemen as they rode between the maddened lines of people. They smiled sardonically in reply to the impotent signs of hatred, but they were glad when the castle gates closed between them and the vast, despairing crowd, in which the tempest of revolt was brewing with unmistakable energy.

Prince Bolaroz, the Duke of Mizrox and the Ministers were already in the castle, and had been there since the previous afternoon. In the royal palace the excitement was intense, but it was of the subdued kind that strains the nerves to the point where control is martyrdom.

When the attendants went to the bedchamber of the Princess at seven o'clock, as was their wont, they found, to their surprise, no one standing guard.

The Princess was not in her chamber, nor had she been there during the night. The bed was undisturbed. In some alarm, the two women ran to her parlor, then to the boudoir. Here they found her asleep on the divan, attired in the gown she had worn since the evening before, now crumpled and creased, the proof positive of a restless, miserable night.

Her first act, after awakening and untangling the meshes in her throbbing, uncomprehending brain, was to send for Quinnox. She could scarcely wait for his appearance and the assurance that Lorry was safely out of danger. The footman who had been sent to fetch the captain was a long time in returning. She was dressed in her breakfast gown long before he came in with the report that the captain was nowhere to be found. Her heart gave a great throb of joy. She alone could explain his absence. To her it meant but one thing: Lorry's flight from the castle. Where else could Quinnox be except with the fugitive, perhaps once more inside St. Valentine's? With the great load of suspense off her mind, she cared not for the trials that still confronted her on that dreaded morning. She had saved him, and she was willing to pay the price.

Preparations began at once for the eventful transaction in the throne room. The splendor of two courts was to shine in rivalry. Ten o'clock was the hour set for the meeting of the two rulers, the victor and the victim. Her nobles and her ladies, her Ministers, her guards and her lackeys moved about in the halls, dreading the hour, brushing against the hated Axphain guests. In one of the small waiting-rooms sat the Count and Countess Halfont, the latter in tears. The young Countess Dagmar stood at a window with Harry Anguish. The latter was flushed and nervous, and acted like a man who expects that which is unexpected by others. With a strange confidence in his voice, he sought to cheer his depressed friends, but the cheerfulness was not contagious. The sombreness of a burial hung over the castle.

Half an hour before the time set for the meeting in the throne room, Yetive sent for her uncle, her aunt and Dagmar. As Anguish and the latter followed, the girl turned her sad, puzzled eyes up to the face of the tall American, and asked:

"Are you rejoicing over our misfortune? You do not show a particle of regret. Do you forget that we are sacrificing a great deal to save the life of your friend? I do not understand how you can be so heartless."

"If you knew what I know you'd jump so high you could crack those pretty heels of yours together ten times before you touched the floor again," said he, warmly.

"Please tell me," she cried. "I knew there was something."

"But I'm afraid so high a jump would upset you for the day. You must wait awhile, Dagmar." It was the first time he had called her Dagmar, and she looked startled.

"I am not used to waiting," she said confusedly.

"I think I can explain satisfactorily when I have more time," he said, softly, in her ear, and, although she tried, she could find no words to continue. He left her at the head of the stairs, and did not see her again until she passed him in the throne room. Then she was pale, and brave, and trembling.

Prince Bolaroz and his nobles stood to the right of the throne, the Graustark men and women of degree to the left, while near the door, on both sides, were to be seen the leading military men of both principalities. Near the Duke of Mizrox was stationed the figure of Gabriel, Prince of Dawsbergen. He had come, with half a dozen followers, among a crowd of unsuspecting Axphainians, and had taken his position near the throne. Anguish entered with Baron Dangloss, and they stood together near the doorway, the latter whiter than he had ever been in his life.

Then came the hush of expectancy. The doors swung open, the curtains parted and the Princess entered.

She was supported by the arm of her tall uncle, Caspar of Halfont. Pages carried the train of her dress, a jeweled gown of black. As she advanced to the throne, calm and stately, those assembled bent knee to the fairest woman the eye ever had looked upon.

The calm, proud exterior hid the most unhappy of hearts. The resolute courage with which her spirit had been braced for the occasion was remarkable in more ways than one. Among other inspirations behind the valiant show was the bravery of a guilty conscience. Her composure sustained a shock when she passed Allode at the door. That faithful, heart-broken servitor looked at her face with pleading, horror-struck eyes, as much as to say: "Good God, are you going to destroy Graustark for the sake of that murderer? Have pity on us—have pity!"

Before taking her seat on the throne, she swept the thrilled assemblage with her wide blue eyes. There were shadows beneath them and there were wells of tears behind them. As she looked upon the little knot of white-faced northern barons, her knees trembled and her heart gave a great throb of pity. Still the face was resolute. Then she saw Anguish and the suffering Dangloss; then the accusing, merciless eyes of Gabriel. At sight of him she started violently and an icy fear crept into her soul. Instinctively, she searched the gorgeous company for the captain of the guard. Her staunchest ally was not there. Was she to hear the condemning words alone? Would the people do as Quinnox had prophesied, or would they believe Gabriel and curse her?

She sank into the great chair and sat with staring, helpless eyes, deserted and feeble.

At last, the whirling brain ended its flight and settled down to the issue first at hand—the transaction with Bolaroz. Summoning all her self-control, she said:

"You are come, most noble Bolaroz, to draw from us the price of our defeat. We are loyal to our compact, as you are to yours, sire. Yet, in the presence of my people and in the name of mercy and justice, I ask you to grant us respite. You are rich and powerful, we despoiled and struggling beneath a weight we can lift and displace if given a few short years in which to grow and gather strength. At this last hour in the fifteen years of our indebtedness, I sue in supplication for the leniency that you can so well accord. It is on the advice of my counsellors that I put away personal pride and national dignity to make this request, trusting to your goodness of heart. If you will not hearken to our petition for a renewal of negotiations, there is but one course open to Graustark. We can and will pay our debt of honor."

Bolaroz stood before her, dark and uncompromising. She saw the futility of her plea.

"I have not forgotten, most noble petitioner, that you are ruler here, not I. Therefore I am in no way responsible for the conditions which confront you, except that I am an honest creditor, come for his honest dues. This is the twentieth of November. You have had fifteen years to accumulate enough to meet the requirements of this day. Should I suffer for your faults? There is in the treaty a provision which applies to an emergency of this kind. Your inability to liquidate in gold does not prevent the payment of this honest debt in land, as provided for in the sixth clause of the agreement. 'All that part of Graustark north of a line drawn directly from east to west between the provinces of Ganlook and Doswan, a tract comprising Doswan, Shellotz, Varagan, Oeswald, Sesmai and Gattabatton.' You have two alternatives, Your Highness. Produce the gold or sign the decree ceding to Axphain the lands stipulated in the treaty. I can grant no respite."

"You knew when that treaty was framed that we could raise no such funds in fifteen years," said Halfont, forgetting himself in his indignation. Gaspon and other men present approved his hasty declaration.

"Am I dealing with the Princess of Graustark or with you, sir?" asked Bolaroz, roughly.

"You are dealing with the people of Graustark, and among the poorest, I. I will sign the decree. There is nothing to be gained by appealing to you. The papers, Gaspon, quick! I would have this transaction finished speedily," cried the Princess, her cheeks flushing and her eyes glowing from the flames of a burning conscience. The groan that went up from the northern nobles cut her like the slash of a knife.

"There was one other condition," said Bolaroz, hastily, unable to gloat as he had expected. "The recapture of the assassin who slew my son would have meant much to Graustark. It is unfortunate that your police department is so inefficient." Dangloss writhed beneath this thrust. Yetive's eyes went to him, for an instant, sorrowfully. Then they dropped to the fatal document which Gaspon had placed on the table before her. The lines ran together and were the color of blood. Unconsciously she took the pen in her nerveless fingers. A deep sob came from the breast of her gray old uncle, and Gaspon's hand shook like a leaf as he placed the seal of Graustark on the table, ready for use.

"The assassin's life could have saved you," went on Bolaroz, a vengeful glare coming to his eyes.

She looked up and her lips moved as if she would have spoken. No words came, no breath, it seemed to her. Casting a piteous, hunted glance over the faces before her, she bent forward and blindly touched the pen to the paper. The silence was that of death. Before she could make the first stroke, a harsh voice, in which there was combined triumph and amazement, broke the stillness like the clanging of a bell.

"Have you no honor?"

The pen dropped from her fingers as the expected condemnation came. Every eye in the house was turned toward the white, twitching face of Gabriel of Dawsbergen. He stood a little apart from his friends, his finger pointed throneward. The Princess stared at the nemesis-like figure for an instant, as if petrified. Then the pent-up fear crowded everything out of its path. In sheer desperation, her eyes flashing with the intensity of defiant guilt, bitter rage welling up against her persecutor, she half arose and cried:

"Who uttered those words? Speak!"

"I, Gabriel of Dawsbergen! Where is the prisoner, madam?" rang out the voice.

"The man is mad!" cried she, sinking back with a shudder.

"Mad, eh? Because I do as I did promise? Behold the queen of perfidy! Madam, I will be heard. Lorry is in this castle!"

"He is mad!" gasped Bolaroz, the first of the stunned spectators to find his tongue.

There was a commotion near the door. Voices were heard outside.

"You have been duped!" insisted Gabriel, taking several steps toward the throne. "Your idol is a traitress, a deceiver! I say he is here! She has seen him. Let her sign that decree if she dares! I command you, Yetive of Graustark, to produce this criminal!"

The impulse to crush the defiler was checked by the sudden appearance of two men inside the curtains.

"He is here!" cried a strong voice, and Lorry, breathless and haggard, pushed through the astonished crowd, followed by Captain Quinnox, upon whose ghastly face there were bloodstains.

A shout went up from those assembled, a shout of joy. The faces of Dangloss and Allode were pictures of astonishment and—it must be said—relief. Harry Anguish staggered but recovered himself instantly, and turned his eyes toward Gabriel. That worthy's legs trembled and his jaw dropped.

"I have the prisoner, Your Highness," said Quinnox, in hoarse, discordant tones. He stood before the throne with his captive, but dared not look his mistress in the face. As they stood there the story of the night just passed was told by the condition of the two men. There had been a struggle for supremacy in the dungeon and the prisoner had won. The one had tried to hold the other to the dungeon's safety, after his refusal to leave the castle, and the other had fought his way to the halls above. It was then that Quinnox had wit enough to change front and drag his prisoner to the place which, most of all, he had wished to avoid.

"The prisoner!" shouted the northern nobles, and in an instant the solemn throne room was wild with excitement.

"Do not sign that decree!" cried some one from a far corner.

"Here is your man, Prince Bolaroz!" cried a baron.

"Quinnox has saved us!" shouted another.

The Princess, white as death and as motionless, sat bolt upright in her royal seat.

"Oh!" she moaned, piteously, and, clenching her hands, she carried them to her eyes as if to shut out the sight. The Countess Halfont and Dagmar ran to her side, the latter frantic with alarm. She knew more than the others.

"Are you the fugitive?" cried Bolaroz.

"I am Grenfall Lorry. Are you Bolaroz?"

"The father of the man you murdered. Ah, this is rapture!"

"I have only to say to Your Highness, I did not kill your son. I swear it, so help me God!"

"Your Highness," cried Bolaroz, stepping to the throne, "destroy that decree. This brave soldier has saved Graustark. In an hour your ministers and mine will have drawn up a ten years' extension of time, in proper form, to which my signature shall be gladly attached. I have not forgotten my promise."

Yetive straightened suddenly, seized the pen and

fiercely began to sign the decree, in spite of all and
before those about her fairly realized her intention.
Lorry understood, and was the first to snatch the
document from her hands. A half-written Yetive,
a blot and a long, spluttering scratch of the pen told
how near she had come to signing away the lands of
Graustark, forgetful of the fact that it could be of
no benefit to the prisoner she loved.

"Yetive!" gasped her uncle, in horror.

"She would have signed," cried Gaspon, in wonder and alarm.

"Yes, I would have signed!" she exclaimed, starting to her feet, strong and defiant. "I could not have
saved his life, perhaps, but I might have saved him
from the cruel injustice that that man's vengeance
would have invented. He is innocent, and I would
give my kingdom to stay the wrong that will be
done."

"What! You defend the dog!" cried Bolaroz.
"Seize him, men! I will see that justice is done. It
is no girl he has to deal with now."

"Stop!" cried the Princess, the command checking
the men. Quinnox leaped in front of his charge.
"He is my prisoner, and he shall have justice. Keep
back your soldiery, Prince Bolaroz. It is a girl you
have to deal with. I will say to you all, my people
and yours, that I believe him to be innocent and that
I sincerely regret his capture, fortunate as it may be

for us. He shall have a fair and a just trial, and I shall do all in my power, Prince Bolaroz, to secure his acquittal."

"Why do you take this stand, Yetive? Why have you tried to shield him?" cried the heart-broken Halfont.

She drew herself to her full height, and, sweeping the threatening crowd with a challenge in her eyes, cried, the tones ringing strong and clear above the growing tumult:

"Because I love him!"

As if by magic the room became suddenly still.

"Behold an honest man. I would have saved him at the cost of my honor. Scorn me if you will, but, listen to this. The man who stands here accused came voluntarily to this castle, surrendering himself to Captain Quinnox, that he might, though innocent, stand between us and disaster. He was safe from our pursuit, yet returned, perhaps to his death. For me, for you and for Graustark he has done this. Is there a man among you who would have done as much for his own country? Yet he does this for a country to which he is a stranger. I must commit him to prison once more. But," she cried in sudden fierceness, "I promise him now, before the trial, a royal pardon. Do I make my meaning clear to you, Prince Bolaroz?"

The white lips of the old Prince could frame no reply to this daring speech.

"Be careful what you say, Your Highness," cried the prisoner, hastily. "I must refuse to accept a pardon at the cost of your honor. It is because I love you better than my life that I stand here. I cannot allow you and your people to suffer when it is in my power to prevent it. All that I can ask is fairness and justice. I am not guilty, and God will protect me. Prince Bolaroz, I call upon you to keep your promise. I am not the slayer of your son, but I am the man you would send to the block, guilty or innocent."

As he spoke, the Princess dropped back in the chair, her rash courage gone. A stir near the doorway followed his concluding sentence, and the other American stepped forward, his face showing his excitement.

"Your Highness," he said, "I should have spoken sooner. My lips were parted and ready to cry out when Prince Gabriel interposed and prevented the signing of the decree. Grenfall Lorry did not kill the young Prince. I can produce the guilty man!"

XXVI

The startling assertion created a fresh sensation. Sensations had come so thick and so fast, however, that they seemed component parts of one grand bewildering climax. The new actor in the drama held the center of the stage undisputed.

"Harry!" cried Lorry.

"Prince Gabriel, why do you shake like a leaf? Is it because you know what I am going to say?" exclaimed Anguish, pointing his finger accusingly at the astonished Prince of Dawsbergen.

Gabriel's lips parted, but nothing more than a gasp escaped them. Involuntarily his eyes sought the door, then the windows, the peculiar, uncontrollable look of the hunted coming into them. Bolaroz allowed his gaze to leap instantly to that pallid face and every eye in the room followed. Yetive was standing again, her face glowing.

"An accomplice has confessed all. I have the word of the man who saw the crime committed. I charge Prince Gabriel with the murder of His Highness, Prince Lorenz."

With a groan, Gabriel threw his hands to his heart and tottered forward, glaring at the merciless face of the accuser.

"He is My Prisoner! He Dies who Dares to Touch Him!"

"Confessed! Betrayed!" he faltered. Then he whirled like a maniac upon his little coterie of followers. "Vile traitor!" he shrieked, "I will drink your heart's blood!"

With a howl he leaped toward one of the men, a dark-faced nobleman named Berrowag. The latter evaded him and rushed toward the door, crying:

"It is a lie! a lie! He has tricked you! I did not confess!"

The Prince was seized by his friends, struggling and cursing. A peculiar smile lit up the face of Harry Anguish.

"I repeat, he is the assassin!"

Gabriel broke from the detaining hands and drawing a revolver, rushed for the door.

"Out of the way! I will not be taken alive!"

Allode met him at the curtains and grasped him in his powerful arms, Baron Dangloss and others tearing the weapon from his hand. The utmost confusion reigned—women screaming, men shouting—and above all could be heard the howls of the accused Prince.

"Let me go! Curse you! Curse you! I will not surrender! Let me kill that traitor! Let me at him!" Berrowag had been seized by willing hands, and the two men glared at each other, one crazy with rage, the other shrinking with fear.

Dangloss and Allode half carried, half dragged the Prince forward. As he neared Bolaroz and the

Princess he collapsed and became a trembling, moaning suppliant for mercy. Anguish's accusation had struck home.

"Prince Bolaroz, I trust you will not object if the Princess Yetive substitutes the true assassin for the man named in your promise to Graustark," said Anguish, dramatically. Bolaroz, as if coming from a dream, turned and knelt before the throne.

"Most adorable Yetive," he said, "I sue for pardon. I bow low and lay my open heart before the truest woman in the world." He kissed the black lace hem of her gown and arose. "I am your friend and ally; Axphain and Graustark will live no more with hatred in their hearts. From you I have learned a lesson in justice and constancy."

Prince Gabriel was raving like a madman as the officers hurried him and Berrowag from the room. A shout went up from those assembled. Its echo, reaching the halls, then the gardens, was finally taken up by the waiting masses beyond the gates. The news flew like wild-fire. Rejoicing, such as had never been known, shook Edelweiss until the monks on the mountain looked down in wonder.

After the dazed and happy throng about the throne had heaped its expressions of love and devotion upon the radiant Princess a single figure knelt in subjection, just as she was preparing to depart. It was the Duke of Mizrox.

"Your Royal Highness, Mizrox is ready to pay

his forfeit. My life is yours," he said, calmly. She did not comprehend until her uncle reminded her of the oath Mizrox had taken the morning after the murder.

"He swore, on his life, that you killed Lorenz," she said, turning to Lorry.

"I was wrong, but I am willing to pay the penalty. My love for Lorenz was greater than my discretion. That is my only excuse, but it is one you should not accept," said Mizrox, as coolly as if announcing the time of day. Lorry looked first at him and then at the Princess, bewildered and uncertain.

"I have no ill will against you, my Lord Duke. Release him from his bond, Your Highness."

"Gladly, since you refuse to hold him to his oath," she said.

"I am under an eternal obligation to you, sir, for your leniency, and I shall ever revere the Princess who pardons so graciously the gravest error."

Yetive begged Bolaroz to continue to make the Court his home while in Graustark, and the old Prince responded with the declaration that he would remain long enough to sign and approve the new covenant, at least. Before stepping from the throne, Yetive called in low tones to Lorry, a pretty flush mantling her cheek:

"Will you come to me in half an hour?"

"For my reward?" he asked, eagerly.

"Ach!" she cried, softly, reprovingly. Count Halfont's face took on a troubled expression as he caught the swift communication in their eyes. After all, she was a Princess.

She passed from the room beside Halfont, proud and happy in the victory over despair, glorying in the exposure of her heart to the world, her blood tingling and dancing with the joys of anticipation. Lorry and Anguish, the wonder and admiration of all, were given a short but convincing levee in the hallway. Lords and ladies praised and lauded them, overwhelming them with the homage that comes to the brave. But Gaspon uttered one wish that struck Lorry's warm, leaping heart like a piece of ice.

"Would to God that you were a Prince of the realm," said the minister of finance, a look of regret and longing in his eyes. That wish of Gaspon's sent Lorry away with the sharp steel of desolation, torturing intensely as it drove deeper and deeper the reawakened pangs of uncertainty. There still remained the fatal distance between him and the object of his heart's desire.

He accompanied Captain Quinnox to his quarters, where he made himself presentable before starting for the enchanted apartment in the far end of the castle. Eager, burning passion throbbed side by side with the cold pulsings of fear, a trembling race between two unconquerable emotions. Passion longed for the voice, the eyes, the caresses; fear cried aloud in every troubled throb: "You will see her and kiss her and then you will be banished."

The two emotions thus thrown together, clashing fiercely for supremacy, at last wove themselves into a single, solid, uncompromising whole. Out of the two grew an aggressive determination not to be thwarted. Love and fear combined to give him strength; from his eyes fled the hopeless look, from his brain the doubt, from his blood the chill.

"Quinnox, give me your hand—don't mind the blood! You have been my friend, and you have served her almost to the death. I injured and would have killed you in that cell, but it was not in anger. Will you be my friend in all that is to follow?"

"She has said that she loves you," said the captain, returning the hand clasp. "I am at your service as well as hers."

A few moments later Lorry was in her presence. What was said or done during the half hour that passed between his entrance and the moment that brought them side by side from the room need not be told. That the interview had had its serious side was plain. The troubled, anxious eyes of the girl and the rebellious, dogged air of the man told of a conflict now only in abeyance.

"I will never give you up," he said, as they came from the door. A wistful gleam flickered in her eyes, but she did not respond in words.

Near the head of the stairway an animated group of persons lingered. Harry Anguish was in the center and the Countess Dagmar was directly in front of him, looking up with sparkling eyes and parted lips. The Count and Countess Halfont, Gaspon, the Baron Dangloss, the Duke of Mizrox, with other ladies and gentlemen, were being entertained by the gay-spirited stranger.

"Here he comes," cried the latter, as he caught sight of the approaching couple.

"I am delighted to see you, Harry. You were the friend in need, old man," said Lorry, wringing the other's hand. Yetive gave him her hand, her blue eyes overflowing.

"Mr. Anguish had just begun to tell us how he— how he——" began Dagmar, but paused helplessly, looking to him for relief.

"Go ahead, Countess; it isn't very elegant, but it's the way I said it. How I 'got next' to Gabriel is what she wants to say. Perhaps Your Highness would like to know all about the affair that ended so tragically. It's very quickly told," said Anguish.

"I am deeply interested," said the Princess, eagerly.

"Well, in the first place, it was all a bluff," said he, coolly.

"A what!" demanded Dagmar.

"Bluff," responded Harry, briefly; "American patois, dear Countess."

"In what respect," asked Lorry, beginning to understand.

"In all respects. I didn't have the slightest sign of proof against the festive Prince."

"And you—you did all that 'on a bluff'?" gasped the other.

"Do I understand you to say that you have no evidence against Gabriel?" asked Halfont, dumfounded.

"Not a particle."

"But you said his confederate had confessed," protested Dangloss.

"I didn't know that he had a confederate, and I wasn't sure that he was guilty of the crime," boasted Anguish, complacently enjoying the stupefaction.

"Then why did you say so?" demanded Dangloss, excited beyond measure.

"Oh, I just guessed at it!"

"God save us!" gasped Baron Dangloss, Chief of Police.

"Guessed at it?" cried Mizrox.

"That's it. It was a bold stroke, but it won. Now, I'll tell you this much. I was morally certain that Gabriel killed the Prince. There was no way on earth to prove it, however, and I'll admit it was intuition or something of that sort which convinced me. He had tried to abduct the Princess, and he was madly jealous of Lorenz. Although he knew there was to be a duel, he was not certain that Lorenz would lose, so he adopted a clever plan to get rid of two rivals by killing one and casting suspicion on the other. These deductions I made soon after the murder, but, of course, could secure no proof.

Early this morning, at the hotel, I made up my mind to denounce him suddenly if I had the chance, risking failure but hoping for such an exhibition as that which you saw. It was clear to me that he had an accomplice to stand guard while he did the stabbing, but I did not dream it was Berrowag. Lorry's sensational appearance, when I believed him to be far away from here, disturbed me greatly, but it made it all the more necessary that I should take the risk with Gabriel. As I watched him I became absolutely convinced of his guilt. The only way to accuse him was to do it boldly and thoroughly, so I rang in the accomplice and the witness features. You all know how the 'bluff' worked."

"And you had no more proof than this?" asked Dangloss, weakly.

"That's all," laughed the delighted strategist.

Dangloss stared at him for a moment, then threw up his hands and walked away, shaking his head, whether in stupefied admiration or utter disbelief, no one knew. The others covered Anguish with compliments, and he was more than ever the hero of the day. Such confidence paralyzed the people. The only one who was not overcome with astonishment was his countryman.

"You did it well," he said in an undertone to Anguish; "devilish well."

"You might at least say I did it to the queen's taste," growled Anguish, meaningly.

"Well, then, you did," laughed Lorry.

XXVII

Three persons in the royal castle of Graustark, worn by the dread and anxiety of weeks, fatigued by the sleepless nights just past, slumbered through the long afternoon with the motionless, deathlike sleep of the utterly fagged. Yetive, in her darkened bedchamber, dreamed, with smiling lips, of a tall soldier and a throne on which cobwebs multiplied. Grenfall Lorry saw in his dreams a slim soldier with troubled face and averted, timid eyes, standing guard over him with a brave, stiff back and chin painfully uplifted. Captain Quinnox dreamed not, for his mind was tranquil in the assurance that he had been forgiven by the Princess.

While Lorry slept in the room set apart for him, Anguish roamed the park with a happy-faced, slender young lady, into whose ears he poured the history of a certain affection, from the tender beginning to the distracting end. And she smiled and trembled with delight, closing not her ears against the sound of his voice nor her heart to the love that craved admission. They were not dreaming.

After dinner that evening Lorry led the Princess out into the moonlit night. The November breezes were soft and balmy and the shadows deep.

"Let us leave the park to Dagmar and her hero, to the soldiers and the musicians," said Yetive. "There is a broad portico here, with the tenderest of memories. Do you remember a night like this, a month or more ago? the moon, the sentinel and some sorrows? I would again stand where we stood on that night and again look up to the moon and the solemn sentinel, but not as we saw them then, with heartache and evasion."

"The balcony, then, without the old restrictions," Lorry agreed. "I want to see that dark old monastery again, and to tell you how I looked from its lofty windows through the chill of wind and the chill of life into the fairest Eden that was ever denied man."

"In an hour, then, I will meet you there."

"I must correct you. In an hour you will find me there."

She left him, retiring with her aunt and the Countess Dagmar. Lorry remained in the hall with Halfont, Prince Bolaroz, Mizrox and Anguish. The conversation ran once more into the ever-recurring topic of the day, Gabriel's confession. The Prince of Dawsbergen was confined in the Tower with his confederate, Berrowag. Reports from Dangloss late in the afternoon conveyed the intelligence that the prisoner had fallen into melancholia. Berrowag admitted to the police that he had stood guard at the door while Gabriel entered the Prince's room and killed him as he slept. He described the cunning, deliberate effort to turn suspicion to the American by leaving bloodstains. The other Dawsbergen nobles, with the exception of two who had gone to the capital of their country with the news of the catastrophe, remained close to the hotel. One of them confessed that but little sympathy would be felt at home for Gabriel, who was hated by his subjects. Already there was talk among them of Prince Dantan, his younger brother, as his successor to the throne. The young Prince was a favorite with the people.

Bolaroz was pleased with the outcome of the sensational accusation and the consequent removal of complications which had in reality been unpleasant to him.

One feature of the scene in the throne room was not discussed, although it was uppermost in the minds of all. The positive stand taken by the Princess and her open avowal of love for the dashing American were never to be forgotten. The serious wrinkles on the brow of Halfont and the faraway expression that came frequently to his eyes revealed the nature of his thoughts. The greatest problem of them all was still to be solved.

As they left the room he dropped behind and

walked out beside Lorry, rather timidly detaining him until the others were some distance ahead.

"You were closeted with the Princess this morning, Mr. Lorry, and perhaps you can give me the information I desire. She has called a meeting of the ministers and leading men of the country for to-morrow morning. Do you know why she has issued this rather unusual call? She did not offer any explanation to me."

"I am only at liberty to say, your excellency, that it concerns the welfare of Graustark," answered the other, after a moment's thought. They walked on in silence for some distance.

"I am her uncle, sir, but I love her as I would my own child. My life has been given to her from the day that her mother, my sister, died. You will grant me the right to ask you a plain question. Have you told her that you love her?" The Count's face was drawn and white.

"I have, sir. I loved her before I knew she was a Princess. As her protector, it was to you that I would have told the story of my unfortunate love long ago, but my arrest and escape prevented. It was not my desire or intention to say to her what I could not speak about to you. I do not want to be looked upon as a coward who dares not face difficulties. My love has not been willingly clandestine, and it has been in spite of her most righteous objections. We have both seen the futility of love, however strong and pure it may be. I have hoped, your excellency, and always shall."

"She has confessed her love to you privately?" asked Halfont.

"Against her will, against her judgment, sir."

"Then the worst has come to pass," groaned the old Count. Neither spoke for some time. They were near the foot of the staircase when Halfont paused and grasped Lorry's arm. Steadily they looked into each other's eyes.

"I admire you more than any man I have ever known," said the Count, huskily. "You are the soul of honor, of courage, of manliness. But, my God, you cannot become the husband of a Princess of Graustark! I need not tell you that, however. You must surely understand."

"I do understand," said Lorry, dizzily. "I am not a prince, as you are saying over and over again to yourself. Count Halfont, every born American may become ruler of the greatest nation in the world —the United States. His home is his kingdom; his wife, his mother, his sisters are his queens and his princesses; his fellow citizens are his admiring subjects if he is wise and good. In my land you will find the poor man climbing to the highest pinnacle, side by side with the rich man. The woman I love is a Princess. Had she been the lowliest maid in all that great land of ours, still would she have been my queen, I her king. When first I loved the mistress of Graustark she was, you must not forget, Miss Guggenslocker. I have said all this to you, sir, not in egotism nor in bitterness, but to show my right to hope in the face of all obstacles. We recognize little as impossible. Until death destroys this power to love and to hope I must say to you that I shall not consider the Princess Yetive beyond my reach. Frankly, I cannot, sir."

The Count heard him through, unconscious admiration mingling with the sadness in his eyes.

"There are some obstacles that bravery and perseverance cannot overcome, my friend," he said, slowly. "One of them is fate."

"As fate is not governed by law or custom, I have the best reason in the world to hope," said Lorry, yet modestly.

"I would indeed, sir, that you were a Prince of the realm," fervently cried the Count, and Lorry was struck by the fact that he repeated, word for word, the wish Gaspon had uttered some hours before.

By this time they were joined by the others, whereupon Grenfall hurried eagerly to the balcony, conscious of being half an hour early, but glad of the chance afforded for reflection and solitude. Sitting on the broad stone railing he leaned back against a pillar and looked into the night for his thoughts. Once more the moon was gleaming beyond St. Valentine's, throwing against the sky a jagged silhouette of frowning angles, towering gables and monstrous walls, the mountain and the monastery blending into one great misty product of the vision. Voices came up from below, as they did on that night five weeks ago, bringing the laughter and song of happy hearts. Music swelled through the park from the band gallery; from afar off came the sounds of revelry. The people of Edelweiss were rejoicing over the unexpected deliverance from a fate so certain that the escape seemed barely short of miraculous.

Every sound, every rustle of the wind through the plants that were scattered over the balcony caused him to look toward the door through which she must come to him.

At last she appeared, and he hastened to meet her. As he took her hands in his, she said softly, dreamily, looking over his shoulder toward the mountain's crest:

"The same fair moon," and smiled into his eyes.

"The same fair maid and the same man," he added. "I believe the band is playing the same air; upon my soul, I do."

"Yes, the same air, La Paloma. It is my lullaby. Come, let us walk. I cannot sit quietly now. Talk to me. Let me listen and be happy."

Slowly they paced the wide balcony, through the moonlight and the shadows, her hand resting on his arm, his clasping it gently. Love obstructs the flow of speech; the heart-beats choke back the words and

fill the throat. Lorry talked but little, she not at all.
Times there were when they covered the full length
of the balcony without a word. And yet they understood each other. The mystic, the enchanting silence
of love was fraught with a conversation felt, not
heard.

"Why are you so quiet?" he asked, at last, stopping near the rail.

"I cannot tell you why. It seems to me that I
am afraid of you," she answered, a shy quaver in
her voice.

"Afraid of me? I don't understand."

"Nor do I. You are not as you were before this
morning. You are different—yes, you make me
feel that I am weak and helpless and that you can
say to me 'come' and 'go' and I must obey. Isn't it
odd that I, who have never known submissiveness,
should so suddenly find myself tyrannized?" she
asked, smiling faintly.

"Shall I tell you why you are afraid of me?" he
asked.

"You will say it is because I am forgetting to be
a Princess."

"No; it is because you no longer look upon me as
you did in other days. It is because I am a *possibility*, an entity instead of a shadow. Yesterday
you were the Princess and looked down upon the
impossible suitor; to-day you find that you have
given yourself to him and that you do not regard the

barrier as insurmountable. You were not timid until you found your power to resist gone. To-day you admit that I may hope, and in doing so you open a gate through the walls of your pride and prejudice that can never be closed against the love within and the love without. You are afraid of me because I am no longer a dream, but a reality. Am I not right, Yetive?"

She looked out over the hazy, moonlit park.

"Yesterday I might have disputed all you say; to-day I can deny nothing."

Leaning upon the railing, they fell into a silent study of the parade ground and its strollers. Their thoughts were not of the walkers and chatterers, nor of the music, nor of the night. They were of the day to come.

"I shall never forget how you said 'because I love him,' this morning, sweetheart," said Lorry, betraying his reflections. "You defied the whole world in those four words. They were worth dying for."

"How could I help it? You must not forget that you had just leaped into the lion's den defenseless, because you loved me. Could I deny you then? Until that moment I had been the Princess adamant; in a second's time you swept away every safeguard, every battlement, and I surrendered as only a woman can. But it really sounded shocking, didn't it? So theatrical."

"Don't look so distressed about it, dear. You couldn't help it, remember," he said, approvingly.

"Ach, I dread to-morrow's ordeal!" she said, and he felt the arm that touched his own tremble. "What will they say? What will they do?"

"To-morrow will tell. It means a great deal to both of us. If they will not submit—what then?"

"What then—what then?" she murmured, faintly.

Across the parade, coming from the direction of the fountain, Harry Anguish and Dagmar were slowly walking. They were very close together, and his head was bent until it almost touched hers. As they drew nearer, the dreamy watchers on the balcony recognized them.

"They are very happy," said Lorry, knowing that she was also watching the strollers.

"They are so sure of each other," she replied, sadly.

When almost directly beneath the rail, the Countess glanced upward, impelled by the strange instinct of an easily startled love, confident that prying eyes were upon her. She saw the dark forms leaning over the rail and rather jerkily brought her companion to a standstill and to a realization of his position. Anguish turned his eyes aloft.

"Can you, fair maid, tell me the names of those beautiful stars I see in the dark dome above?" he asked, in a loud, happy voice. "Oh, can they be eyes?"

"Eyes, most noble sir," replied his companion. "There are no stars so bright."

"Methought they were diamonds in the sky at first. Eyes like those must belong to some fair divinity."

"They do, fair student, and to a divinity well worth worshiping. I have heard it said that men offer themselves as sacrifices upon her altars."

"Unless my telescope deceives me, I discern a very handsome sacrifice up there, so I suppose the altar must be somewhere in the neighborhood."

"Not a hand's breadth beneath her eyes," laughed the Countess, as she fled precipitately up the steps, followed by the jesting student."

"Beware of a divinity in wrath," came a sweet, clear voice from the balcony, and Anguish called out from his safe retreat, like the boy he was:

"Ah, who's afraid!"

The Princess was laughing softly, her eyes radiant as they met those of her companion, amused yet grave.

"Does he have a care?" she asked.

"I fear not. He loves a Countess."

"He has not to pay the price of ambition, then?" said she, softly.

"Ambition is the cheapest article in the world," he said. "It concerns only a man's self."

XXVIII

THE MAID OF GRAUSTARK

Expectancy, concern, the dread of uncertainty marked the countenances of Graustark's ministers and her chief men as they sat in the council chamber on the day following, awaiting the appearance of their Princess, at whose call they were unexpectedly assembled. More than two score eyes glanced nervously toward the door from time to time.

All realized an emergency. No sooner were they out of one dilemma than another cast its prospects across their path, creating the fear that rejoicing would be short. While none knew the nature of the business that called them together, each had a stubborn suspicion that it related to the stirring declarations of the day before. Not one in that assembly but had heard the vivid, soulful sentence from the throne. Not one but wished in secret as Gaspon and Halfont had wished in open speech.

When the Princess entered with the prime minister they narrowly scanned the face so dear to them. Determination and cowardice were blended in the deep blue eyes, pride and dejection in the firm step, strength and weakness in the loving smile she bestowed upon the faithful counsellors. After the greetings she requested them to draw chairs about the great table. Seating herself in her accustomed

seat, she gazed over the circle of anxious faces and
realized, more than at any time in her young life,
that she was frail and weak beyond all comparison.
How small she was to rule over those strong, wise
men of hers; how feeble the hand that held the
sceptre.

"My lords," she said, summoning all her strength
of mind and heart, "I am gratified to find you so
ready to respond to the call of your whimsical sovereign. Yesterday you came with hearts bowed down
and in deepest woe. To-day I assemble you here
that I may ask your advice concerning the events of
that strange day. Bolaroz will do as he has promised. We are to have the extension papers this
afternoon, and Graustark may breathe again the
strong, deep breath of hope. You well remember
my attitude on yesterday. You were shocked, horrified, amazed by my seemingly ignoble efforts to preserve my preserver's life. We will pass over that,
however. It is to discuss my position that I have
called you here. To begin, I would have sacrificed
my kingdom, as you know, to save him. He was innocent and I loved him. If, on yesterday, I would
not let my kingdom stand between me and my love,
I cannot do so to-day. I have called you here to
tell you, my lords, that I have promised to become
the wife of the man who would have given his life
for you and for me—that I love as a woman, not as
a Princess."

The silence of death stole into the room. Every

man's eyes were glued upon the white face of the Princess and none could break the spell. They had expected it, yet the shock was overwhelming; they had feared it, yet the announcement stupefied them. She looked straight before her, afraid to meet the eyes of her subjects, knowing that sickening disapproval dwelt in them. Not a word was uttered for many seconds. Then old Caspar's tense muscles relaxed and his arms dropped limply from their crossed position on his breast.

"My child, my child!" he cried, lifelessly. "You cannot do this thing!"

"But the people?" cried Gaspon, his eyes gleaming. "You cannot act against the will of the people. Our laws, natural and otherwise, proscribe the very act you have in mind. The American cannot go upon our throne; no man, unless he be of royal blood, can share it with you. If you marry him the laws of our land—you know them well—will prohibit us from recognizing the marriage."

"Knowing that, my lords, I have come to ask you to revise our laws. My throne will not be disgraced by the man I would have share it with me." She spoke as calmly as if she were making the most trivial request instead of asking her ministers to overthrow and undo the laws and customs of ages and of dynasties.

"The law of nature cannot be changed," muttered Caspar, as if to himself.

"In the event that the custom cannot be changed,

I shall be compelled to relinquish my right to occupy the throne and to depart from among you. It
would break my heart, my lords, to resort to this
monstrous sacrifice, but I love one man first, my
crown and my people after him."

"You would not leave us—you would not throw
aside as despised the crown your ancestors wore for
centuries?" cried Gaspon. "Is Your Royal Highness mad?"

The others were staring with open mouths and icy
hearts.

"Yes, as much as it would grieve me, I would do
all this," she answered, firmly, not daring to look
at her uncle. She knew his eyes were upon her and
that condemnation lurked in their depths. Her heart
ached to turn to him with a prayer for forgiveness,
but there could be no faltering now.

"I ask you, my lords, to acknowledge the marriage of your ruler to Grenfall Lorry. I am to be
his wife; but I entreat you to grant me happiness
without making me endure the misery that will come
to me if I desert my father's throne and the people
who have worshipped me and to whom I am bound
by a tie that cannot be broken. I do not plead so
much for the right to rule as I do for the one who
may rule after I am gone. I want my own to follow
me on the throne of Graustark."

Then followed a long, animated discussion, growing brighter and more hopeful as the speakers' willing hearts warmed to the proposition. Lorry was

a favorite, but he could not be their prince. Heredi-' tary law prohibited. Still his children, if God gave him children, might be declared rightful heirs to the throne of their mother, the Princess. The more they talked, the more the problem seemed to solve itself. Many times the Princess and her wise men met and overcame obstacles, huge at first, minimized in the end, all because they loved her and she loved them. The departure from traditional custom, as suggested by the Princess,—coupled with the threat to abdicate,—was the weightiest, yet the most delicate question that had ever come before the chief men of Graustark. It meant the beginning of a new line of princes, new life, new blood, a complete transformation of order as it had come down through the reigns of many Ganlooks. For the first time in the history of the country a woman was sovereign; for the first time there had been no direct male heir to the throne. With the death of old Prince Ganlook the masculine side of the illustrious family ended. No matter whom his daughter took for a husband, the line was broken. Why not the bold, progressive, rich American? argued some. Others fell in with the views of the few who first surrendered to the will of Yetive, until at last but one remained in opposition. Count Caspar held out until all were against him, giving way finally in a burst of oratory which ended in tears and sobs, and which made the sense of the gathering unanimous.

The Princess Yetive won the day, so far as her

own position was concerned. But, there was Lorry
to be considered.

"Mr. Lorry knows that I called you together in
consultation, but he does not know that I would
have given up my crown for him. I dared not tell
him that. He knows only that I was to ask your
advice on the question of marriage, and that alone.
Last night he told me he was confident you would
agree to the union. He is an American, and does
not appreciate the difficulties attending such an espousal. Over there distinction exists only in wealth
and intelligence—position, I believe they call it, but
not such as ours. He is a strange man, and we have
yet to consult him as to the arrangement," she said
to her lords, pursing her lips. "I fear he will object
to the plan we have agreed upon," she went on. "He
is sensitive, and it is possible he will not like the
idea of putting our marriage to the popular vote of
the people."

"I insist, however, that the people be considered
in the matter," said Gaspon. "In three months'
time the whole nation can say whether it sanctions
the revision of our laws of heredity. It would not
be right or just for us to say who shall be their future rulers, for all time to come, without consulting
them."

"I have no hesitancy in saying that Graustark already idolizes this brave American," said Halfont,
warmly. "He has won her affection. If the question is placed before the people to-morrow in proper

form, I will vouch for it that the whole nation will rise and cry: 'Long live the Princess! Long live the Prince Consort!' "

.   .   .   .

"Going back, I see," said Sitzky, the guard, some months later, addressing a very busy young man, who was hurrying down the platform of the Edelweiss railway station toward the special train which was puffing impatiently.

"Hello, Sitzky! Is it you? I'm glad to see you again. Yes, we are going back to the land of the Stars and Stripes." The speaker was Mr. Anguish.

"You'll have fine company's fer as Vienna, too. D' you ever see such celebration's dey're havin' here to-day? You'd t'ink d' whole world was interested in d' little visit Her Royal Highness is goin' to pay to Vienna. Dummed if d' whole city, soldiers an' all, ain't down here to see 'er off. Look at d' crowd! By glory, I don't b'lieve we c'n pull d' train out of d' station. 'Quainted wid any of d' royal crowd?"

"Slightly," answered Anguish, smiling. He was watching a trim figure in a tailor-made gown as it approached, drawing apart from the throng. It was Mrs. Harry Van Brugh Anguish.

"Say, you must cut some ice wid dese people. But dat's jest like an American, dough," the little guard went on. "De Princess married an American an' dey say he's goin' to put d' crown away where d' moths won't git at it an' take her over to live in Washington fer six months. Is it a sure t'ing?"

"That's right, Sitzky. She's going back with us and then we're coming back with her."

"Why don't he keep 'er over dere when he gits her dere? What's d' use—what's d' use?"

"Well, she's still the Princess of Graustark, you know, Sitzky. She can't live always in America."

"Got to be here to hold her job, eh?"

"Inelegant, but correct. Now, look sharp! Where do we find our—Ah!" His wife was with him and he forgot Sitzky.

The guard turned to watch the procession—a file of soldiers, a cavalry troop, carriages and then—*the* carriage with spirited horses and gay accoutrements. It stopped with a jangle and a man and woman descended.

"The Princess!" cried Sitzky.

"Long live the Princess!" cried the crowd. "God save our Yetive!"

Sitzky started as if shot, staring at the tall man who approached with the smiling Sovereign of Graustark. "Well," he gasped, "what d' you t'ink o' dat!"

The train that was to carry them out of the East into the West puffed and snorted, the bell clanged, the people cheered, and they were off. Hours later, as the car whirled through the Hungarian plain, Yetive, looking from her window, said in that exquisite English which was her very own:

"Ah, the world, the dear world! I am so sorry for queens!"

www.ingramcontent.com/pod-product-compliance
Lightning Source LLC
Chambersburg PA
CBHW020252030726
47499CB00001B/162